A family

THE ASHTONS:
COLE, ABIGAIL
& MEGAN

Three of your favourite authors bring you
three sexy and seductive romances following
the scandalous Ashton dynasty

We're proud to present

MILLS & BOON
SPOTLIGHT™

*A chance to buy collections of bestselling
novels by favourite authors every month –
they're back by popular demand!*

March 2010

The Ashtons: Cole, Abigail & Megan

Featuring

Entangled by Eileen Wilks
A Rare Sensation by Kathie DeNosky
Society-Page Seduction by Maureen Child

Their Child?

Featuring

Lori's Little Secret by Christine Rimmer
Which Child Is Mine? by Karen Rose Smith
Having The Best Man's Baby
by Shawna Delacorte

THE ASHTONS: COLE, ABIGAIL & MEGAN

EILEEN WILKS

KATHIE DeNOSKY

MAUREEN CHILD

⊚™ MILLS & BOON®

All the characters in this book have no existence outside the imagination of
the author, and have no relation whatsoever to anyone bearing the same name
or names. They are not even distantly inspired by any individual known or
unknown to the author, and all the incidents are pure invention.

THE ASHTONS: COLE, ABIGAIL & MEGAN
© Harlequin Books S.A. 2010.

First published in Great Britain 2010
Harlequin Mills & Boon Limited,
Eton House, 18-24 Paradise Road, Richmond, Surrey TW9 1SR

The publisher acknowledges the copyright holders of the individual works, which
have already been published in the UK in single, separate volumes, as follows:

Entangled © Harlequin Books S.A. 2005
A Rare Sensation © Harlequin Books S.A. 2005
Society-Page Seduction © Harlequin Books S.A. 2005

Special thanks and acknowledgement are given to Eileen Wilks, Kathie
DeNosky and Maureen Child for their contributions to the
DYNASTIES: THE ASHTONS series.

ISBN: 978 0 263 88032 8

64-0310

Printed and bound in Spain
by Litografia Rosés S.A., Barcelona

ENTANGLED

BY
EILEEN WILKS

THE ASHTONS

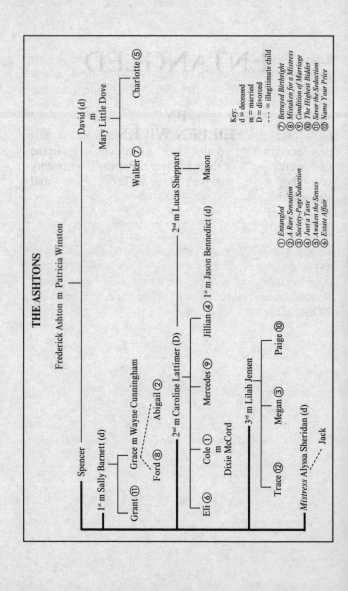

Frederick Ashton m Patricia Winston

David (d)
m
Mary Little Dove

Walker ⑦   Charlotte ⑤

Spencer

1st m Sally Barnett (d)

Grant ⑪

Ford ⑧

Grace m Wayne Cunningham

Abigail ②

2nd m Caroline Lattimer (D)   2nd m Lucas Sheppard

Mason

Eli ⑥

Cole ①
m
Dixie McCord

Mercedes ⑨   Jillian ④ 1st m Jason Bennedict (d)

3rd m Lilah Jensen

Trace ⑫   Megan ③   Paige ⑩

Mistress Alyssa Sheridan (d)

Jack

Key:
d = deceased
m = married
D = divorced
- - - = illegitimate child

① Entangled
② A Rare Sensation
③ Society-Page Seduction
④ Just a Taste
⑤ Awaken the Senses
⑥ Estate Affair

⑦ Betrayed Birthright
⑧ Mistaken for a Mistress
⑨ Condition of Marriage
⑩ The Highest Bidder
⑪ Savor the Seduction
⑫ Name Your Price

Eileen Wilks is a fifth-generation Texan. Her great-great-grandmother came to Texas in a covered wagon shortly after the end of the Civil War – excuse us, the War between the States. But she's not a full-blooded Texan. Right after another war, her Texan father fell for a Yankee woman. This obviously mismatched pair proceeded to travel to nine cities in three countries in the first twenty years of their marriage. For the next twenty years they stayed put, back home in Texas again – and still together.

Eileen figures her professional career matches her nomadic upbringing, since she's tried everything – raising two children and any number of cats and dogs along the way. Not until she started writing did she "stay put," because that's when she knew she'd come home. Readers can write to her at PO Box 4612, Midland, TX 79704-4612, USA.

This book is dedicated to my fellow Desire™ authors –
those on the loop and especially those who
participated in this continuity series.

You've been a delight to work with. Desire authors are
a great bunch, giving and supportive and maybe a
little crazy. I'm glad to be one of you.

Prologue

Nobody expected the church to be full. At eleven-thirty on a rainy Wednesday morning in Crawley, Nebraska, most folks were at work. But the postmistress was there, and the druggist and his wife, and the banker with his wife sat in their usual pew. Many of the county's farming families were represented, for the families of the bride and the groom were farmers.

And, of course, the Mortimer twins sat in their usual spots—sixth from the front on the center aisle. Flora and Dora hadn't missed a wedding in this church for fifty-five years. A little rain couldn't dampen their enthusiasm.

"Doesn't young Spencer look handsome," Flora whispered.

Her sister snorted. "Handsome is as handsome does. You can't tell me that hellion would be up there waiting for his bride if—"

The postmistress turned around and gave them an admonishing look.

"Don't you look at me that way, Emmaline Bradley," Dora said. "Francis is still on 'Rock of Ages.' No reason we can't talk when she's still on 'Rock of Ages.'"

Flora tugged on her arm. "Look. They're seating Spencer's father," she whispered. "He doesn't look very happy about the wedding, does he?"

Dora sniffed. "Frederick Ashton hasn't been happy since he was weaned. Got two moods, that man—mad and madder. What Pastor Brown was thinking of to make him a deacon…well, that's beside the point."

Lucy Johnson, on the other side of Flora, leaned closer. "At least Frederick made sure his son did right by poor Sally."

Flora bobbed her head in agreement like a chicken pecking at the dirt. "Poor Sally. I can see why she fell into temptation. That Ashton boy is so…so…"

"Handsome," Dora finished dryly. "I'm not so sure Frederick did Sally any favors."

"Oh, Spencer's just young," Lucy said. "A touch on the wild side, maybe, but so was my Charlie before we married. And we've been together forty-two years now."

Emmaline Bradley turned around again. "Shh!"

Flora flushed, Lucy's lips thinned and Dora didn't notice. She was frowning at the back of Frederick Ashton's head three rows up. There had been rumors that the man used a heavy hand with his sons. He was big, burly and domineering—the kind who liked to say, "Spare the rod, spoil the child." Dora was sure neither Spencer nor his brother, David, had been in danger of being spoiled.

Francis struck the opening chord of Wagner's "Bridal Chorus." *Here comes the bride...*

At the back of the church, Sally Barnett pressed a hand to her unhappy stomach. The satin wedding gown felt cold and slippery.

"Butterflies, sweetheart?" her father said.

More like nausea. But Daddy looked so anxious...surely Mama was right. Spencer would settle down once the babies came. She summoned a smile. "I'm nervous," she whispered.

He patted her hand. "You're supposed to be. This is our cue, honey."

Together they stepped out in the stately slow march that would carry them up the aisle to where Spencer waited. Sally's skirts swished over the carpet and her heart pounded and pounded. She clutched her bouquet so tightly it was a wonder she didn't squeeze it right in two.

Spencer looked so wonderful in his tux. So what if they'd had to rent it? She'd told him over and over that didn't matter...except that it did. To him. He was hungry for things, for the trappings of success. But she understood why. He'd grown up hearing his mother whine about how little they had, how much better things would have been if his father had sold the farm years ago. He'd come to believe that happiness came from things, not people.

She'd show him differently, she promised herself as her father released her and stepped back. She'd be such a good wife to him that he'd never regret this day.

Her heart turned over when Spencer took her hand, just as it always had for him. He didn't love her. Not in the deep, aching way she loved him. But she'd be patient. She'd teach him how to love.

Nausea forgotten, Sally's face shone as she listened to the preacher repeat the familiar words. Her young groom stood tall and straight beside her.

Spencer glanced at Sally. *Look at the stupid bitch smile,* he thought. *Thinks she has me trapped, doesn't she?* The selfish cow had gone crying to her daddy when she found out she was pregnant, and he'd tattled to the old man…. A trickle of cold sweat ran down Spencer's spine.

"Do you, Spencer Winston Ashton, take this woman to be your lawful wedded wife?" the preacher said. "To have and to hold…"

Frederick Ashton was the one person in the world Spencer feared. And however much lip service Frederick paid to the Bible, his real god was his standing in the community. He'd made it clear that Spencer wouldn't be allowed to tarnish that.

"…for richer, for poorer…"

Maybe Sally had won for now, but not for long,

he promised himself. He was destined for great things. He'd always known that.

"…and in health, until death do you part?"

"I do," Spencer said solemnly. Someway, somehow, he'd find a way out of this dead-end town, out into the wide world waiting for him.

One

Napa Valley, California. Forty-three years later.

Dixie turned off the highway with "Cowboys from Hell" blasting away on the stereo—her notion of motivational music. Who could succumb to nerves with Pantera singing about cowboys from *way* down under coming to take the town?

Her palms were damp on the steering wheel.

She'd missed the light the most, she thought as she pointed the nose of her Toyota down the little county road. Seasons took sharp turns in New York. She'd enjoyed that, jazzed by the way winter hit with a howl and a slap, knocking autumn flat on its face. California's seasons jostled for position more politely, one blending into the next in a watercolor wash rather than the charcoal ultimatums of the North.

But the light… January light in the Valley didn't bounce around with the flat, frenetic energy of summer, but smoothed itself around tree trunks and buildings, settling on roads and earth with a visual hum.

She was looking forward to painting that light. And that's why she was here, she reminded herself as she slowed. She had a job to do. If she could settle a few ghosts while she was at it, well and good. The silly things had started tugging on her sleeve after she returned to California. It was time to look them in their pale, wispy little faces and get on with her life.

The arch over the entry was tall and wide, a graceful cast-iron curve with replicas of the property's namesake vines twining up its sides.

She was here. Dixie took a deep breath and turned onto the driveway leading up to The Vines.

The house lay directly ahead. She took the curve to the left, heading for the winery, offices and tasting room, housed together in a large, two-story building with a roof that made her think of a Chinese peasant's peaked hat. She pulled into the parking lot in a car crowded with ghosts, shut off the ignition and sat there a moment, absorbing the changes…and the things that had remained the same.

Then she retrieved her hat and her purse, checked on Hulk and opened the car door.

The air smelled of earth and grapes. The scents slithered past her conscious mind and plopped into the swampy goo of the unconscious, splattering her with memories.

Not sad memories, though. Loud, laughing, sometimes angry, but not sad. That's what made this so hard. She took a deep breath and let the ghosts slide through her, then stepped forward.

"Dixie!" A slim young woman in a cream-colored suit stepped out on the porch. Her hair had undoubtedly started the day in a sleek knot at her nape. The sleek was long gone, but most of the knot remained. She hurried down the steps. "You're late. Was the traffic bad? What did you forget? Where's your cat?"

Laughing, Dixie caught her friend up in a hug. "Traffic sucked, I won't know what I forgot until I can't find it and Hulk is asleep in his carrier. God, you look great!" She stepped back, looking Mercedes over. "Skinny as ever—they'd adore you in New York—and I love the wispies." She flicked one of the curls frantically escaping bondage. "But that is one boring outfit."

"We can't all dress like *artistes*." Mercedes' mouth tucked down and she shook her head. "Not that I could pull off an outfit like that, anyway."

"You like it? I call it my Beach Blanket Bimbo look." Dixie had changed her mind and her outfit five times this morning, finally deciding on a what-the-hell combination of yellow vintage capris and matching halter top with a Hawaiian shirt in lieu of a jacket. The oversize sunglasses and straw hat were more sixties than fifties, but Dixie wasn't a purist.

Mercedes laughed and started for the building. "But that's just it. You look very retro chic, not like a bimbo at all."

"Well, this is the wrong era for you," Dixie said, falling into step beside Mercedes. "I'm the one with a body straight out of the forties or fifties. You'd look great in flapper clothes—long, lean and sophisticated."

"I am so not the flapper type."

"You're wearing a button-down oxford shirt with that suit, Merry. You need help."

Mercedes held a hand up, half laughing, half alarmed. "Oh, no, you don't. Do not help me. I'm not up to it right now."

"Hmm." Dixie stepped up on the porch and looked around. Eleven years ago this had been a smaller, less stylish building. "Someone does good work. The expansion is invisible—it looks like it was always this way. Now show me your lair."

"If you mean the tasting room, it's through here. We're talking about a possible remodel—Jillian's idea."

Dixie tipped her head to one side as she stepped inside. Mercedes was tense, which was weird. *She* was the one whose stomach had every right to be doing the bubble-bubble-toil-and-trouble bit. "Hey, this is nice." She took her hat off and pushed her sunglasses on top of her head, looking around.

Lots of exposed wood, subdued lighting, great views…nice room, yes, but it suffered from split personality. It couldn't make up its mind whether it was rustic or modern. "What did you have in mind for the remodel?"

"Nothing's decided yet, but we want to unify the look, tie it to the theme of the promotional campaign." The tense set to Mercedes' shoulder didn't ease. "The offices are upstairs. Eli's out in the vineyard, so I'll take you to Cole." She headed for a door at the back of the room at a good clip.

Dixie didn't move.

"Dixie?" Mercedes paused with the door open, looking over her shoulder with a frown. "Are you coming?"

"Not until you tell me what has you wound tighter than a cheap watch. And don't pull that princess face on me," she warned. "It won't work."

"I don't know what you're talking about."

"You've turned polite," Dixie observed. "Always a bad sign. What is it? Is Cole upset that you hired me for the illustrations?" The flash of guilt on Mercedes' face made her exclaim, "He does know, right? Mercedes?"

"Not…exactly."

Dixie closed her eyes and put a hand on her stomach. Yep, things were churning around nicely in there. "Am I going to be fired before I start?"

"He can't do that," Mercedes assured her. "We've got a contract, and he and Eli gave me full authority to hire you. That is, they didn't know it was *you*, but I told them all the places your work has appeared, and they were eager to sign you on."

"And here I was afraid you'd grown risk averse," Dixie muttered, opening her eyes. "What were you thinking?"

"That Louret Winery needs you for our new ad campaign. You're the best."

"I won't argue with that," Dixie said, not being one to underestimate her talent. "But it doesn't explain your vow of silence."

"Do you have any idea what it's like to have your two big brothers for bosses?" Mercedes demanded. "I did not want to waste time arguing with Cole. Come on, Dixie. I know this is a little awkward, but it's not like you're really shook. You?" She grinned. "A tornado wouldn't rattle you."

Shook, no. Pit-of-the-stomach scared…yeah, that was about right. "Cole's face ought to be an interesting sight when I walk in."

Mercedes laughed, relieved. "I'm looking forward to it. And then I'm ducking."

"Thanks. You've made me feel so much better."

Behind the tasting room was a short hall with doors leading into the winery proper and stairs to the office area. Not luxurious, Dixie thought as she started up the stairs after Mercedes, but several notches above utilitarian. It looked as if the winery was prospering.

Eleven years was a long time. What was she afraid of, anyway?

That he hated her.

She put a hand on her stomach again. It had been a long time, yes, but Cole was not a tepid man. He ran hot or cold without lingering much in the temperate zone…though most people didn't see that, fooled by the glossy surface.

Cole did have shine, she admitted. But so does a new calculator.

At least he used to. Maybe he'd gotten fat. Mercedes hadn't mentioned it, but Dixie hadn't exactly encouraged her to talk about her brother. "Hey, Merry," she said as she reached the top of the stairs, "has Cole been putting weight on?"

Mercedes gave her a puzzled look. "I don't think so. Why?"

"Ah, well. Can't win them all." However this turned out, she could take comfort in one thing. Cole wouldn't have forgotten her. "Here," she said, digging into her pocket. "After you cut and run, you can go get Hulk out of the suvvy and put him in my room."

Mercedes accepted the keys. "Um…suvvy?"

"SUV sounds ugly. Suvvy sounds cute."

"Suvvy. Right." Mercedes shook her head, smiling—and impulsively reached out and hugged Dixie with one arm. "I'm so glad you moved back. Sorry for the reason, of course, but glad to have you close again."

"Me, too," Dixie said quietly. "On both counts. Well." She ran a hand through her hair, straightened her shoulders, and said, "How does that poem go? 'Forward, the Light Brigade! Charge for the guns! …Into the Valley of Death…' I can't remember the rest."

Mercedes grinned. "Something about 'cannons to the left of them, cannons to the right.' I'm pretty sure Cole doesn't have any cannons in his office." She turned and rapped smartly on the door on her right.

"I notice you're not disputing the Valley of Death part."

Mercedes ignored that and opened the door. "Cole, our artist is here. Shannon's sick, so I've got to man the tasting room in twenty minutes. I thought you might show her around."

"I'd be happy to," said a smooth, almost forgotten baritone. "As soon as I…" His voice trailed away as Dixie stepped in behind Mercedes.

He hasn't changed. That was her first thought—and it was quite wrong.

Cole was still lean as a whip with mink-brown hair cut short in an effort to tame the curl. He had neat, small ears set flat to the head, a strong nose and straight slashes of eyebrows. But the face that had been almost too good-looking eleven years ago had acquired character lines that rubbed off a bit of the gloss.

Then there was the way his mouth was hanging open. That was definitely different. She liked it.

Dixie smiled slowly, hardly noticing when the door closed behind Mercedes. "Hello, Cole."

Cole's face smoothed into a professional smile. "Welcome to The Vines. As I was saying, I'd be glad to show you around…as soon as I've killed my little sister."

Dixie burst out laughing. "And here I'd been thinking you'd be all cold and businesslike."

"And I know how you feel about businesslike. I'll try to avoid it." He gave her a thorough, up-and-down appraisal that stopped an inch short of insult. "You've always tended to run late, but eleven years is excessive, even for you."

She shook her head. "You aren't going to fluster me that way."

"I can try."

Time to switch topics, she decided, and glanced around the office, which was ruthlessly neat everywhere except for the big, dark-wood desk. A spotted canine head poked around the corner of that desk, brown eyes looking at her hopefully. "Oh!" She bent, smiling. "Who's this?"

"Tilly. She won't let you pet her."

"No?" Challenged, she held out her hand for the dog to sniff—and the animal cringed back out of sight behind the desk. "She is timid, isn't she?"

"That, yes. Also neurotic and not too bright," he said, reaching down to fondle the animal Dixie couldn't see. "Tilly's scared of storms, other dogs, birds, new people, loud noises—you name it, she's afraid of it."

Dixie moved around to the side of the desk so she could see the dog. "She's some kind of Dalmatian mix?"

"That and greyhound, the vet thinks, with maybe some plain old mutt mixed in. I found her on the side of the highway about a year ago."

"How in the world did you get her to go with you if she's scared of everyone?"

He glanced down at Tilly, his smile amused—and slightly baffled. "She seemed to think she'd been waiting for me. I stopped, opened my door, and she jumped in."

Dixie shook her head. "She *is* female."

"But not my usual type." His crooked smile hadn't changed—a downtuck on one side, uptilt on the other, as if he were wryly hedging his bets. "All right, Tilly, that's all. Lie down." Amazingly, she did. He looked back at Dixie. "Are you waiting to be invited to sit down? By all means, have a seat."

Dixie thought that the dog seemed just Cole's type—obedient. Consciously virtuous, she forbore to mention that as she sat in the chair in front of the cluttered desk.

So far so good. The tug in the pit of her stomach was mostly memory, she told herself, a response to remembered passion. It had nothing to do with the man in front of her now. "You've done wonders with Louret Wines."

"Eli is the wonder worker. I'm just the bottom-line man. How's life been treating you? You're looking good."

"My life's been full of the usual ups and downs, thank you. How's yours?"

"Busy. You've made a name for yourself. Congratulations."

A laugh sputtered out. "This will teach me to make a big deal out of things. You wouldn't believe how I'd built up this meeting in my mind. Now, after only a couple of quick jabs, we're exchanging polite compliments."

He quirked an eyebrow. "You're disappointed."

"No. Well, maybe a little." She rolled her eyes. "It's not as if I wanted to be treated to that frigid way you have with people you don't like. You can do cold better than the North wind's granny."

Something flashed in his eyes, but his smile was easy. "I'm a warm, lovable guy these days. Mellow."

That made her grin. "I'll believe that when I see it."

"You'll be here a few days, I understand."

"Poking my nose into everything. That's how I work."

"Hmm." He leaned back in his chair. "You've been compared to Maxwell and Rockwell—not in terms of style, but recognition. I'm wondering how we can afford you."

Dixie let herself look amazed, which wasn't hard. She'd had no idea he'd paid attention to her career. "Didn't you read the contract?"

"For some reason Mercedes wanted to handle everything herself," he said dryly.

"Well, you're buying reproduction rights to my paintings, not the paintings themselves. They'd cost you a good deal more." She planned to give one to Mercedes, but that was friendship, not business.

"So you're not doing this as a favor to Mercedes?"

She shrugged. "That's part of it."

At last he stood. "Would you like that tour now?"

"Let's go."

* * *

Cole waved for Dixie to go down the stairs first, which left him looking at the top of her head. It shouldn't have been an enticing view, but her hair had always fascinated him. Dirty blond, she'd called it. Sand colored, he'd thought. A dozen shades of shifting sand falling fine and straight, like sand poured from an open hand.

"Mercedes will have told you in general what we're looking for," he said as they reached the short hall at the bottom of the stairs. "We're planning a series of ads in some of the upscale magazines and want a painterly look for them, nothing high-tech or mass-produced. We want them to convey the hands-on, personal quality of our wines."

"She did." Dixie had a slow smile, as if she liked to take her time and enjoy the process. "She also said you gave her a hard time about some aspects of the concept."

"You can see who won. You're here, even though it's winter—not the best time for pictures of the vineyard."

"But I'm not painting the vineyard. I'm painting the people."

"She said something about that, but I don't see how a picture of Eli fondling the grapes will sell wine."

"She also said you don't listen to her." Dixie shook her head. Her hair swayed gently with the motion. "There are thousands of good wines out there. Yours may be the best, but how do you show that in an image?"

"Wine, grapes, the vines themselves—they're strong images. A good artist could make them memorable."

Her eyebrows lifted. "I could paint you a picture of grapes that would make teetotalers weep for what they're missing. But everyone's seen beautiful pictures of grapes. One more, no matter how well done, won't identify what's unique about Louret. Your ads shouldn't sell wine. They should sell Louret."

"I'm familiar with the idea of branding," he said dryly. "But why pictures of people?" He'd heard Mercedes' reasons—and they were good, or he wouldn't have signed off on the idea. He wanted to hear Dixie's take on it.

"Because with a boutique winery, it's all about the people. You've established yourself with your pinot noir and merlot. Your cabernet sauvignon wins awards routinely. But the reds come from *your* grapes, your soil, unlike the new chardonnay. You want people to understand that they aren't just buying great grapes when they buy a bottle of Louret wine. They're buying Eli's nose and a sip of your mother's heritage."

His eyebrows lifted. This didn't sound like the passionately impractical rebel he'd once known. "Either you've gotten into wine or you've done some research."

"Wine does come up when Mercedes and I talk, but yes, I've done research. I paint quickly, but I spend a good deal of time researching my subject before I start."

"What happened to your art?" he asked, suddenly curious. "The noncommercial stuff, I mean."

She shrugged. "The art world is intensely parochial. If you aren't playing in whatever stream is fashionable, you aren't doing 'significant work'—which means being part of the dialogue between artists, other artists and art critics."

"You used to like the avant-garde stuff."

"I still do. I just don't want to play in that stream myself. I want to do representational art—which is only slightly less damning than doing commercial art. Which I also do, obviously." She chuckled. "An instructor once told me that I have the soul of an illustrator. He did not mean it as a compliment."

"Some bastards shouldn't be allowed to teach."

"No, he was right. Of course, I think of Rembrandt as a superb illustrator, too." She grinned. "I've never been accused of false modesty."

Or any other kind, he thought, amused. Pity he found that so attractive. "You don't find it, ah, stifling to your creativity to work on the commercial end of the spectrum?"

"I'm in a position to pick and choose my jobs these days. I have a good deal of artistic control, and I don't take work that doesn't excite me."

Yet she'd accepted this job…and for less money, he suspected, than she usually charged. A favor for a friend? "You're excited about wine?"

She leveled a long, thoughtful look at him. "Are you going to give me that tour, or not?"

"By all means." He pushed open the nearest door.

"This is the bottling room. Randy handles things here."

Dixie hadn't changed much. She still had a body that could make a man beg, and a smile that suggested she'd like it if he did. And she still drew people to her, male and female alike. For the next hour, Cole watched her charm everyone she met.

Randy fell easily, but he was young and born to flirt. Russ, who was foreman at the vineyards, wasn't much more of a test—he was older, but he was still male. The real challenge came when she met Mrs. McKillup. The crotchety old bookkeeper actually smiled. Cole didn't think he'd seen her do that over anything less important than a new spreadsheet program.

And none of it bothered him. That realization gusted in while he was watching her twist Russ around her little finger. Jealousy wasn't even a smudge on the horizon. It wasn't there at all.

The lightness around his heart grew with each introduction. He hadn't needed proof that he was over her. Once he knew she'd really left him he'd set out to forget her, and had done a damn fine job of it. Some men enjoyed sighing over a lost love. Not him.

But he hadn't known for sure he was past the jealousy, not until today. He could stand back and watch her flirt, appreciate her body and her easy laugh, without sinking into that old swamp.

Maybe he wouldn't kill his sister.

"You let me have a look at your laptop," Mrs.

McKillup was saying as they prepared to leave her to her numbers. "I suspect you just need more memory. Very easy to install, if so."

"Thanks." Dixie smiled ruefully. "I'd really appreciate help from someone with a functioning left brain. I think mine gave up on me years ago in disgust."

"Not much doubt about the health of Mrs. McKillup's left brain," Cole said when they were on the stairs, headed down. "You could cut yourself on it."

"What an image." She grinned as they reached the bottom floor. "She reminds me of my third-grade teacher. The woman terrified me."

"You weren't showing any signs of fear."

"Oh, I decided a long time ago that it's easier to like people, and you know how I hate to waste energy. It's also much more interesting."

And that, he understood, was the root of her charm. It wasn't about getting people to like her. It was about liking them. Which might be what had gone wrong with them—there'd been too much she hadn't really liked about him.

The flash of anger surprised him. He squelched it. Old news. "Some people aren't easy to like."

"True. And a few aren't worth the effort, but you can't know that until you've tried." She opened the door to the tasting room. "I'd better get the rest of my stuff unloaded. I'm not sure where to put it, though."

"Mother has you in the carriage house. You'll remember it."

She stopped with the door open and aimed a glance over her shoulder at him, her face quite blank. "Yes," she said after a moment. "Yes, I do."

The carriage house was set away from the main house—not far, but enough to offer some privacy. On that long-ago summer, he'd been living in the big house still; Dixie had moved in with her mother after graduating while she looked for work. She'd come to visit Mercedes one day.

By that night, she and Cole had been lovers. They'd met at the carriage house often. Made love there.

She gave a little shake of her head, half of a smile settling on her mouth without touching her eyes. He couldn't decipher the emotion there. "You going to give me a hand with my things, or do you need to get back to work? I warn you—I don't travel light."

"No problem. I love to flex my muscles for the girls."

Her gaze wandered over him, head to toe, a spark of mischief replacing the unknown emotion. "Got a tank top? It would be so much more fun to watch you flex in one of those."

The rolling rise of heat didn't surprise him. She was a woman who'd always provoke a response in a man, and when she looked at him like that he'd have to be dead not to respond. But the strength of it was unwelcome. "Still playing with matches, Dixie?" he asked softly.

"I run with scissors sometimes, too."

She was far too amused. For now, he'd let her get

away with that. Later, though... Dixie wasn't a woman for the long haul. He knew that, and he knew why. But she was hell on wheels for the short term.

"Let's go exercise my muscles," he said lightly, leaving it up to her to decide what kind of exercise he had in mind.

PRETENSES

away with them, alone, though ... Dixie would not
bother to explain, but she knew him, and she knew
away the last of the objects left here when the studio rental property had come on the market, the remaining items the buyer had rejected. Or those she'd
overlooked and needed to get. Granted, there weren't
that ... managed. He would be prompting ...

"Ah ..." ...

Two

"**Y**ou're driving an SUV."

"I prefer to call it a suvvy." Dixie did not care for
the look of unholy delight on Cole's face. She
opened the door on the driver's side. "Were you
going to ride to the carriage house with me, or would
you prefer to tote and flex over there on foot?"

He climbed in, looking around. "I could have pictured you in a Ferrari. Or something tiny and fuel efficient with a bumper sticker asking if I've hugged
a tree today. But an SUV?" He shook his head, grinning. "It's so soccer mom."

"Nothing wrong with soccer moms." She hit
the accelerator a little too hard. "I do a fair amount
of work on location. I needed to be able to haul

around my equipment, not to mention the Hulk, and this *is* the most fuel efficient suvvy on the market." And why was she so defensive, anyway? "So what are you driving these days? A shiny new Beamer or a Benz?"

"A five-year-old Jeep Grand Cherokee, eight cylinders, standard," he answered promptly.

"An SUV."

"Yep."

She glanced at him—and they both burst out laughing. "Were we really that shallow before?" she asked. "Arguing about cars as if it mattered." She shook her head, remembering.

"Speak for yourself. I wasn't shallow. Just stupid."

Not stupid, she thought. Obsessed, maybe. Ambitious, certainly. Grimly determined to outdo the father who'd walked out on him, to prove that he and his family didn't need Spencer Ashton in any way— definitely. Dixie had understood that. She just hadn't been able to live with it.

The carriage house was located just behind and to the east of the main house, but to get there by car they had to drive well past the house and circle back, passing through a portion of the vineyards and a small grove of olive trees. Even in January, the trees were picturesque with their knotty limbs and gray-green foliage, and the hummingbird sage and licorice plants beneath them were green.

The grove was even prettier in the summer, surrounded by rows and rows of lush vines, Dixie remembered wistfully. But perhaps it was just as well she was here in January.

"So why a suvvy?" she asked lightly as she came to a stop in front of the small stucco building. "You can't need to haul things around that often."

"Not as much these days, no. But for a while I was. I bought a small cabin a few years ago and have been working on it ever since."

"A fixer-upper?" she asked, surprised. The Cole she'd known had wanted the newest and best of everything.

"You could call it that, if you're feeling generous." He opened the door.

She got out. "What would you call it?"

"Pretty decent now. Uninhabitable when I bought it. I wanted the land, the view, and planned to tear down the cabin and put up something new and shiny. Somewhere along the line, though, I got hooked on power tools. The cabin's been my excuse to use them. Do you need *all* of that carried in?" He gestured at the piles in the back.

She grinned. "I warned you."

"So you did."

Dixie carried the smaller suitcase and the tote with her paints. Cole grabbed the other suitcase and the huge roll of untreated canvas. This diminished but didn't empty the pile in her suvvy.

The door to the carriage house was unlocked. Dixie pushed it open and stopped a foot inside.

Nothing had changed. From the pine paneling to

the white curtains to the simple furniture, everything looked just as it had eleven years ago.

Cole nudged her. "Sightsee later. This is heavy. Are you sure you don't have a body rolled up inside?"

"Of course not. The blood would make a mess of my canvas."

"Your weights, then? Move, Dixie."

She moved, stopping beside the battered leather couch. The last time she'd seen that couch, she'd been naked. "Isn't this the same Navajo blanket on the back of the couch?" A bit worn now, but the colors were as beautiful faded as they had been new. Bemused, she ran a hand over it.

"I remember how it looked wrapped around you."

Her hand remained on the blanket. Her gaze flew to Cole's—and the past crashed into the present, smashing itself all over her, making a mess of her mind and her heartbeat.

At that moment she wanted him. Wanted him badly.

Twenty-two fuzzy pounds thumped against her leg, nearly knocking her over and making a noise like a chain saw.

Cole's eyes widened. "What in the world—?"

"Meet Hulk." *Thank you, Hulk,* she told him silently, bending to pick him up. He sprawled, limp with pleasure, over her shoulder while she ran a hand over cowlicky gray fur. Hulk loved attention.

"As in The Incredible?" Cole looked dubious. "He *is* a cat, right?"

"That's the rumor."

"I'd better let my mother know about him."

"She's not allergic or something, is she? Mercedes said it was okay to bring him." She rubbed him under the chin the way he liked, and his motor revved loudly. "He always travels with me."

"I'm sure it will be fine. I don't think she was prepared, though. She hasn't stocked the grounds with antelope or gazelle for him to feed on." He eyed the cat. "Good thing there aren't any small children in the neighborhood."

"Very funny. Hulk's big, but he's a sweetie. He loves everyone, children included."

"For dessert?"

She huffed out a breath. "What do you have against my cat?"

"Tilly."

"There shouldn't be a problem. If he has to, Hulk will take to a tree, but he isn't easily intimidated."

"Tilly is. Though terrified describes her better."

Oh. She grimaced. "I'll try to keep him in." She detached Hulk and poured him onto the couch. He gave her a reproachful look and jumped down. Cat honor demanded that he not stay where he'd been put, even if he wanted to.

It took three more trips to finish unloading her suvvy. Dixie managed not to slide back into memory land, but she was very ready for Cole to leave by the time they brought in the last few items. Her emotions were a jumble. She needed a sit.

With typical contrariness, once he'd deposited

her bag of books Cole seemed ready to stay and chat. "Weird pillow," he said, nodding at the zafu she'd placed on the floor by an empty wall. "Gives me all kinds of kinky thoughts."

"It's for my sits." When he looked blank she added, "Meditation, Cole. You have heard of meditation?"

"Ah." He nodded. "Does that mean you aren't practicing witchcraft anymore?"

"It wasn't my path." She huffed out an impatient breath. "Look, do you still run all the time?"

"Two or three times a week."

"That's your mental-health break. I sit."

He burst out laughing. "No, no—" he said, holding up a hand. "Don't blow up at me. I just thought that I should have known you'd prefer sitting to running."

She couldn't help grinning. It *was* appropriate. "I can't see the appeal in sweating." Though it was hard to argue with the results. Cole was as lean and sculpted at thirty-five as he'd been at twenty-four.

At least, he seemed to be. A dress shirt and slacks don't make everything clear... *Don't go there,* she told her imagination.

He leaned against the wall, crossing his arms over his chest. "Going to offer me a cold drink now that I've flexed my muscles for you?"

"You didn't put on the tank shirt," she pointed out, setting her laptop on the table. "Besides, I haven't been to the store yet."

"Mother will have seen that the refrigerator and pantry are stocked with the basics." He cocked his head. "Nervous, Dixie?"

"Of course not." Oh, God would get her for that lie. "But I do need to get settled in. Shouldn't you be working?"

"I've been known to go for whole minutes at a time without my calculator these days. So why are you here?"

She blinked. "You're having a little trouble with your memory?"

"You're in a position to pick and choose your jobs. You picked Louret. I want to know why."

She made her shrug as casual as she could, considering the irritating way her heartbeat was behaving. "First, you're paying me a good deal of money. Second, Mercedes asked me to do it. Third…while ignoring your existence has been a pleasant habit, it's getting in the way of my friendship with your sister now that I'm back in California."

"So you're here because of me." He started toward her.

"Your ego is showing."

"Call it unfinished business, then."

He was standing too close, but damned if she was going to retreat. "That's part of it. A small part."

"Good." He leaned in even closer and kissed her.

Shock held her still for the first instant, long enough for the liquid roll of desire to hit. Instinct had her reacting in the next.

She shoved him. Hard.

He staggered back a step, tripped over Hulk and fell flat on his butt.

Dixie burst out laughing.

To her surprise, he chuckled, too. "The idea was for me to sweep you off your feet, not to get knocked off mine. Your demon cat—"

"You'd better not have hurt him." She looked around and saw Hulk sitting by the couch, busily smoothing his ruffled fur with his tongue. No damage there, obviously.

"That's right. Worry about your cat, not me."

"You're bigger than he is."

"Not by much." But he was grinning as he got to his feet.

She raised her eyebrows. "You have changed."

"I'm not twenty-four anymore." The smile lingered on his mouth, but his eyes held a different message. One that hit her harder than that so-brief kiss. "Understand this—what we had eleven years ago is a closed account. That doesn't keep us from opening a new one."

"I'm not interested." Her body might be, but her body wasn't in charge.

"I am. Tell me—do you still have that tattoo?"

"Go away, Cole."

"I'll be out of town for a couple days, but when I come back, I plan to find out about that tattoo." With that he turned and left, pulling the door closed behind him.

All sorts of emotions jostled around inside Dixie. She bit her lip. For a second she tasted him again, salt and coffee and the subtle blend that was pure Cole. Oddly, though, her ghosts were silent.

Maybe memories are like the moon, she thought. Reflected light is never as bright and strong as what you get direct from the source…and the source of her ghosts had just kissed her for the first time since she left him eleven years ago.

Shouldn't she be cautioning herself about all sorts of things?

But the interior tumult gradually settled into a smile, and it was filled with speculation, not nostalgia. She'd agreed to the job as a favor to Mercedes and because she did need to deal with some ghosts. But curiosity had played a part, too.

It looked as if the next two weeks would be anything but boring.

Early in the morning the following Monday, Dixie went strolling along the curving driveway that circled the front of the property, looking for a gray blob. Hulk had gotten out. He'd managed to do that at least once a day since she arrived.

Not that it mattered. Cole had left on a business trip the day after Dixie got here. He'd taken Tilly with him.

"Hey, Hulk," she called. Dawn had arrived, but the bank of storm clouds nearly hid the fact. The wind was blustery, promising rain, and the temperature was a cool forty-five degrees. "You know how you hate to get wet. Time to come in." No sign of him.

It was probably just as well Cole had taken off. The reminder of his priorities could only be good for her, even if, like a lot of things that are good for you, it tasted nasty going down. But dammit, when a man announces his intention of inspecting a woman's tattoo, he ought to stay around long enough for her to turn him down.

Funny how alike she and Cole were in some ways, she thought, crossing to the next row. Most people don't take their pets with them on business trips. Yet in other ways, they stood on opposite sides of a chasm.

Of course, it wouldn't be odd for Tilly to go with him if it wasn't really business that had taken him away.

No. She shook her head. Cole had faults—huge, heaping bunches of them. But unless he'd changed beyond all recognition, he played fair. No lies, no tricks. Besides, she couldn't picture his mother fibbing for him.

Dixie smiled. She liked Caroline Ashton Sheppard, even if the woman was the source of some of Cole's more irritating assumptions about the female half of the gender divide. Had Caroline been born a couple thousand miles to the east, she would have made a great Southern belle—gentle, soft-spoken, with an innate sense of style and a will of iron.

She liked Cole's stepfather, too. Lucas Sheppard was one of those salt-of-the-earth types who serve as a reminder to cynics like her that not all men are cads, little boys or idiots.

Another thing she and Cole had in common, she thought wryly. They both had father issues.

Of course, his went a lot deeper. Dixie's father hadn't meant to die and leave her, while Cole's father had abandoned him intentionally. Not that Cole had told Dixie about it, not Mr. I-Don't-Talk-About-Personal-Stuff. But Mercedes had. When Cole was eight, Spencer Ashton had walked out on his family to marry his secretary, somehow swindling his wife out of most of her inheritance. He'd never looked back.

There was no sign of Hulk. Dixie called again, but she didn't expect him to answer. Hulk would show up when he darned well pleased.

Ah, well. She'd felt duty bound to try. Shaking her head, she turned and headed back. Even in winter the vineyards were a pleasant place to stroll, with the aisles between the rows of vines green with a cover crop of legumes and barley. Russ had told her the plants would be tilled under in the spring, adding nitrogen to the soil.

Sure didn't seem like winter, though. The grass was green, for one thing. Most people grew cool-season grasses here, and that's what she'd grown up with…but she'd been away a long time. Long enough for it to seem both strange and strangely familiar to wander around outside in January without bundling up.

Which led to the subject of clothes. She had a winter wardrobe she'd not be able to…

Who was that? Dixie stopped, frowning. There

was a man standing in front of The Vines. Not one of the vineyard workers, she thought, though he was dressed casually, in jeans and a plain shirt. But she'd met all of the workers now, hadn't she?

Maybe not. She'd have remembered this one—a tall, rugged sort, he looked as if he'd just ridden in off the range. Though there was something vaguely familiar about him…intrigued, she headed his way.

"Hello," she said as she drew near. "You looking for someone?"

He turned. There was gray in his dark hair and interesting crinkles around his eyes—from squinting as he rode off into the sunset, she decided, amused by herself. "Not really. Just curious."

"The winery loves curious tourists," she assured him, "but not until ten o'clock, when the tasting room opens. This area is private property." She cocked her head. "You look familiar."

"I don't think we've met," he said politely. "Are you one of the owners? The, ah, Ashtons?"

"No, just a temporary employee and a friend. It's the head shape," she said, pleased to have figured it out. "And something about the set of the eyes. If I could line your skull up next to Cole's and Eli's, I'll bet the occipital surfaces and zygomatic arches would be identical."

He looked faintly alarmed. "I hope you don't plan to make the attempt. You're a doctor? Or an anthropologist?"

She laughed. "None of the above. An artist. You

wouldn't be some long-lost Ashton cousin, would you?"

He shook his head and studied her a moment longer, a faint smile on his mouth, something unreadable in his eyes. "I'd better be going, since this is private property. Nice speaking with you."

Cole had spent four frustrating days in Sacramento. Some of the frustration had been professional, but a fair portion arose from his inability to keep his mind where it belonged.

Dixie had left The Vines on Friday afternoon, planning to be gone all weekend. Which she was entitled to do, of course. But Cole kept wondering who she was spending the weekend with. A woman like Dixie was only alone if she wanted to be.

At two o'clock that morning, alone in his hotel room, he'd been fighting with memories and questioning his sanity. Why in the world would he consider getting involved with her again?

He was attracted, yes. What man wouldn't be, especially if he knew just how hot it could be between them? But he was old enough to know that fire burns, and long past the point where he could be led around by his gonads.

He didn't need the heartache or the hassle, he'd finally decided, and had at last dropped off to sleep.

So it was annoying to learn, as he pulled into the parking lot at the winery, that he was looking forward to seeing her again. He grabbed his briefcase, opened the Jeep's door and slid out.

Eli was waiting for him. "How'd it go?"

"Lots of talk, not much action." He opened the back door and Tilly jumped down, politely sniffed Eli's hand, then wandered away to check out the shrubbery in front of the tasting room.

"Everyone agrees that we need better coordination between the various growers' associations," Cole said, opening his briefcase and removing a stack of papers. "Especially when it comes to lobbying in Sacramento. No one wants to actually do the work of setting up a coordinating group."

"I thought Joe Bradley was keen on running things."

"I'm not letting Joe turn this into one of his dog-and-pony shows. He starts out big, loses interest and then things fizzle."

Eli sighed. "I suppose that means you agreed to run things."

"Nope." Cole was still mildly astonished at himself. Somewhere along the line, though, doing it all—and proving he could do it better—had stopped being fun. "I've got enough on my plate already."

"I know that. I didn't think you did."

"Here," Cole said, handing Eli the papers. "A copy of the minutes. There are a few things of interest in there."

Eli scowled. "Summarize it for me."

Cole grinned. Eli's hatred of paperwork was a chain he loved to yank. "Can't. I've got enough on my plate."

"I'm going to break that damn plate over your

head," Eli informed him without heat. "This new leaf of yours doesn't have anything to do with that old girlfriend of yours who's following me around, does it?"

"Dixie is following you around?" He made that sound so casual he almost believed himself.

"Everywhere I turn, there she is with that blasted camera. Says she wants lots of candid shots before she starts painting." Eli grimaced. "Why the hell didn't you and Mercedes tell me this promotional campaign was going to use my face?"

"It's more fun to surprise you." Cole started for the door.

"Well, I don't like it." Eli fell into step beside him. "Not that I have any problem with Dixie's company."

"Who would?" She'd undoubtedly been flirting with Eli, Cole thought. For Dixie, flirting came as naturally as breathing.

"She's fun to have around, not to mention being eye candy from top to toe. I just wish she'd ditch the camera." Eli stopped, facing Cole so that he had to stop, too. "So…you have any claim there?"

Cole's eyebrows snapped down. "With Dixie?"

"I think that's who we're talking about, yeah. I know the two of you had something going years ago, but you don't seem to be picking up where you left off."

"I've been in Sacramento," Cole snapped. Just because he'd decided to step back didn't mean he wanted to watch his brother move in.

"And I've been here, and I've been looking. Thought I'd better let you know before I made a move."

"You can't find a woman of your own?" Cole demanded, furious. "You want my hand-me-downs?"

Eli infuriated him by chuckling. "I'd like to be there when Dixie hears you refer to her as hand-me-downs."

He wasn't entirely crazy. "Bad choice of words," he admitted. "But you'd still better keep your greedy hands to yourself."

"We'll see. If you don't—"

Tilly rounded the corner of the building at a dead run, hotly pursued by a huge gray cat. The dog skidded to a halt behind Cole's legs, trembling. And Dixie rounded the corner at a run—face flushed, long hair flying, long legs bare beneath ragged cut-offs.

She jerked to a stop several feet away. So did Hulk, but Cole wasn't looking at the cat.

He was older and wiser now…but flexibility was an aspect of maturity, right? He could change his mind.

Three

Cole's mouth kicked up in a grin. "I don't think I've ever seen you move that fast before."

"I was trying to rescue your stupid dog." She was out of breath and disheveled, her chest heaving beneath a skimpy T-shirt that read, Well-Behaved Women Seldom Make History.

Tilly was calmer now that she'd found backup, though she still huddled behind Cole. He ran a hand over the top of her head soothingly and tried to sound severe. "You're supposed to keep your demon cat inside."

"Guess what? He got out."

"Wouldn't matter," Eli said, "if Cole's dog weren't so pathetic." He looked at Tilly, crouched behind Cole. "I know the cat is big, but you still out-weigh him by fifty pounds."

"Like that matters." Cole shook his head. "As far as Tilly's concerned, everything in the world is bigger and meaner than she is."

Dixie sauntered closer, as casually graceful as her cat and a lot more interesting to watch. "She may be right about meaner. I've seen earthworms with more backbone."

"Earthworms are invertebrates."

"You get my point."

Eli had been noticing Dixie's legs. In all conscience, Cole couldn't blame him. "Aren't you cold?" Eli asked, concerned. "This isn't exactly shorts weather."

Cole could have warned him not to suggest that Dixie didn't know what she was doing at all times. He wouldn't have, of course, but he could have.

Dixie eyebrows flew up. "It's shorts weather to me. I've gotten used to a more rugged climate."

"Rugged." Cole nodded. "Yeah, that's the first word I think of when I think of you. I like the T-shirt."

"I noticed that you'd become a slow reader."

Since the letters were stretched across a pair of lovely breasts, he just grinned.

While they were talking, Hulk was infiltrating. Nonchalant as only a cat can be, he'd wandered closer. Tilly kept retreating until she was behind Eli. Hulk, triumphant, stropped himself against Cole's leg, purring.

"Yeah, I can see how innocent you are," Cole said, bending to pick the cat up. He promptly went limp, purring manically. Automatically Cole stroked him.

Dixie smirked. "He likes to be rubbed behind the ears."

"That's a dog thing."

"Tell him, not me."

"Okay, I get it." Eli nodded. "See you two later."

Cole glanced at him. "What are you talking about?"

"Going back to work. You remember about work? It's something some of us like to do at this hour on a weekday."

"Good idea." Cole looked back at Dixie. "Take Tilly with you."

"Forget it. You deserve a few handicaps. Nice to see you without that camera, Dixie," he said, then headed off.

Dixie watched Eli leave, looking vexed. "I like your brother."

"So do I, at times." Especially when Eli had the good sense to go away. "Why does that bug you?"

She huffed out a breath. "I wasn't paying attention, I guess. Of course, he's very closed up, even worse than you. Hard to read. But I was *not* trying to play the two of you off each other."

"I didn't think you were. You can't help flirting— that's like breathing for you. A process I enjoyed watching, by the way, while reading your T-shirt, but never mind that for now. You don't play men off each other. That would be calculated, and there's nothing calculating about you."

"That came perilously close to a compliment on something other than my breasts. Backhanded, but averaging more positive than negative."

"Don't let it go to your head. Here." He held out twenty pounds of limp feline. "Take your monster. Tilly's having a breakdown trying to figure out how to hide behind me when I'm holding her enemy."

She draped the beast over her shoulder and started at an easy pace for the carriage house. Cole fell into step beside her.

Dixie slid him a sideways glance. "You think Tilly has some kind of canine PTSD?"

"I'm putting it down to poor parenting. Her former owner must have mistreated her."

"She was previously owned by a cat?"

His lips twitched. "I'd say her fears generalized."

She smiled, but fleetingly, and didn't respond. For a few minutes they walked together in silence, with Tilly on Cole's other side.

Funny, he thought. He'd once found it irksome to walk with Dixie. They'd matched up great in bed, but he hadn't liked matching his steps to hers. She strolled. He wanted to get where he was going as efficiently as possible.

She'd said she didn't see the appeal in sweating. He didn't see the point in taking twenty minutes to get somewhere if you could do it in ten. But it was okay to slow down occasionally, he decided. It gave him a chance to notice the subtle scent she wore…slightly spicy, more herbal than floral, hard to pin down.

Like her. "What did you think of New York?"

"I loved it," she said promptly. "Even during my homesick period, when I was in this horrible little apartment and didn't know anyone, I loved it. There's so much to see and do, and the energy is incredible."

"You liked that? I never could picture you there, part of that lickety-split New York energy."

"You always saw me as a lazy flake," she said philosophically.

"No, I didn't." When she looked at him, all skepticism, he conceded, "An artistic flake, maybe. Not the same thing. You saw me as a dull business grunt."

"Never dull," she murmured. "Driven."

"A word that conjures the echoes of a few of our better arguments."

"Your definition for better being…?" She shook her head. "Never mind. You never wanted to move away, try a new place, did you?"

"My goals, my family, my life—they were all here. They still are. Why did you leave?" As soon as the words were out, Cole wanted to call them back. They'd come out too abruptly, sounding too much like *why did you leave me?*

He knew why. Eventually he'd understood and even agreed with her. Understanding wasn't the same as forgiving.

Either she didn't hear the unspoken question or she didn't want to go there, either. "Itchy feet," she said lightly. "You know what they say about New York—'if you can make it there, you'll make it anywhere.' I wanted to see if I could make it."

"You succeeded." They'd reached the carriage house. He opened the door and held it.

"Women and monsters first."

"Just the monster. I've got to get back to work. What?" she demanded. "What's so funny?"

"You're in a hurry to get back to work and I'm not."

"Okay, that is weird. Be ready to close the door fast." She dumped Hulk onto the floor, stepped back and Cole closed the door—fast, as ordered, with Hulk on the other side and complaining about it. "The deadline for the first painting is pretty tight, and I haven't got it settled yet in my mind. Eli's the subject, but I don't have the right angle on him."

"You pay attention to deadlines?" he asked politely.

"Very funny. I'm not that bad."

"If you tell me you're always on time now, I'll have to ask for ID. Or maybe consult an exorcist."

She grinned. "At least you admit it's demonic to be compulsively punctual."

Her grin was too familiar. It tugged at places inside him that he preferred to keep private. Cole put a hand on the door, keeping her where she was, and leaned in closer. "These are new," he observed, touching his thumb to the corner of one eye, where a faint smile line showed.

She jerked her head away. "You used to be better with compliments. Back off, Cole."

"I'm not going to kiss you. Not right this minute, anyway." He'd forgotten the flecks of gold in her eyes, and how they turned plain brown to a rich caramel.

Her eyebrows lifted in haughty offense over those caramel eyes—but her tongue darted out to moisten her lip. "I see. You suddenly felt weak and couldn't stand up on your own."

"You're nervous. I like that."

"You're obnoxious. I don't like that."

He chuckled and straightened. "How long will you be here at The Vines, Dixie?"

She regarded him suspiciously. "Why?"

"I need to know what my deadline is."

"If I ask why again, and you tell me, am I going to be mad?"

"Probably. No, almost certainly."

"Then we'll skip the questions and go straight to the answers. I'll be here for about two weeks, and I'm not going to bed with you. And now I really need to get back to work." She started back toward the winery.

She was moving faster than usual, he noted. "You're passing up the chance to throw a great temper fit."

"I don't throw fits. Or anything else."

"Lost that artistic temperament, have you? I seem to recall a plate that came sailing my way once. I could have sworn you were mad."

Her lips thinned—but it looked more like an effort to hold back a smile than real temper. "Tell me, Cole. Is this your version of dipping my pigtails in the ink to get my attention? Or are you really spoiling for a fight?"

"Want to watch me turn somersaults? Or I could do chin-ups. They're more macho."

The smile won. She paused. "Push-ups. There's something so manly about push-ups."

He promptly dropped to the ground and began doing push-ups.

She laughed in delight and sat smack-dab on the cold ground to watch, propping her chin on her hand. "Ooh, look at those muscles. You're so strong."

"Don't forget—" he managed one more "—manly. Strong and manly." He stopped before he could embarrass himself, rolling onto his back and sitting up. Maybe he needed to add more upper-body training to his routine. His arms felt rubbery. "That was harder than it looked," he assured her.

"I can't believe you did it—and in dress slacks, yet."

He was surprised, too. "It worked. You quit running away."

"I wasn't running." She drew up her legs and hugged her knees.

"Okay, walking away." He wished she'd stretch her legs out again. Dixie had great legs—firm calves, narrow ankles. He wanted to run a hand up one of them.

"Quit staring at my legs."

"I'm checking for goose bumps. What did you

do—get up and say, 'I'm in California, therefore I must wear shorts?'"

Her mouth twitched reluctantly. "Something like that. It's *almost* warm enough for them."

He leaned back on one hand. "Why the evasive tactics, Dixie? Do you really want me to go away?"

She shrugged, not looking at him. "When I decided to take this job, I wasn't expecting you to put on a full-court press. I tried not to have any expectations at all, but in the back of my mind I guess I thought you'd be in your chill zone with me."

Cole didn't want to hear about how cold she thought he was. "I keep telling you I'm not twenty-four anymore."

"It's damned disconcerting, too." She plucked a blade of grass and ran it up her bare leg. "Like going home after years away and seeing old buildings gone, new ones put up. You turn a corner expecting to see the Wilson's frame house, but they're long gone and the new people have stuccoed the exterior and cut down the big oak tree. So much is the same, but I keep tripping over the differences."

"You've been home for visits, though, haven't you?"

She slid him an amused look. "I was speaking metaphorically."

"I got that. I just wondered if you'd avoided California altogether." And why she'd returned.

"I come back once or twice a year to see Mom and Aunt Jody." She pulled up some more grass and let it sift through her fingers. "Mom's getting married again."

"Yeah?" He tried to sound as if this was a good idea. Her wry look told him he hadn't pulled it off. "This time it might work. Mike's a good guy."

Cole could barely call up an image of Helen McCord Lynchfield. He'd only met Dixie's mother once…and that seemed odd, now that he thought about it.

Of course, their affair had only lasted a little over three months, though they'd known each other off and on ever since Mercedes went off to college. Merry and Dixie had been roommates, and Dixie had come home with her several times during breaks. There'd been trouble at home. The man who'd been her stepfather at the time had been a grade-A bastard.

Dixie's mother had finally left the bastard a month before Dixie graduated. And a month after that, the Valley had sweated under a record-setting heat wave. Cole and Dixie had claimed responsibility for that.

"I imagine your mom is glad to have you nearby. And your aunt, too. She's still in L.A.?" In some ways, Dixie was closer to her mother's sister, an award-winning reporter, than to her mother. While Cole could understand why, it had always made him wary. Jody Belleview was a funny, fiercely independent woman with a finely developed scorn for marriage.

"Aunt Jody's not in L.A. anymore."

Something in Dixie's voice caught his attention.

She was looking down at a small patch of ground she'd absentmindedly denuded of grass. "What is it, Dix?"

"She's the reason I moved back here. Mom couldn't take care of her by herself anymore."

A quick squeeze of hurt for her had him covering her hand with his. "That sounds bad."

"Pretty bad, yeah. She has Alzheimer's."

Stunned, Cole just sat there. He'd met Dixie's aunt just once, at the same time he met her mother. But Jody Belleview was the kind of woman who left an impression. He remembered her laugh and her quick, restless intelligence. "I can't imagine…isn't she younger than your mother? Only fifty or so?"

"Fifty-four. I'm still in denial. Which is not as easy to do on this coast as it was while I was across the country." She gave him a brittle smile, then gathered herself and rose to her feet.

He stood, too. "Dixie—"

She shook her head. "I'm sorry. I can't talk about it."

When she walked away she was moving fast, not strolling, her back straight and stiff. And Cole just stood there and let her go, feeling as if the earth had shifted under him.

She couldn't talk about it? That didn't sound like Dixie. Maybe she meant she couldn't talk about it with him…but that wasn't what she'd said. It wasn't what he'd felt radiating from her with the kind of buried intensity he knew only too well.

He was the one who stuffed things into compartments, banged the lid shut and sat on it to keep them there. Dixie had always possessed a terrifying honesty, with herself as well as others. She lifted lids and peeked inside. She didn't turn away from painful truths.

At least, that's how he remembered her.

Cole stood there a few moments longer, frowning at the path she'd vanished down. Then he went looking for his sister.

Four

At ten o'clock that night, Dixie stood on a drop cloth in the center of her temporary living room, slashing color across a canvas. The light was lousy for painting, but it didn't matter. She wasn't really painting. She was venting. No one but her would ever see this.

Red roiled with brown in a muddy whirlpool at the lower right, while a mountain of black and gray reared over a pale green center like a granite wave about to crash. It was lousy art, she thought, stepping back to look it over. But damn satisfying.

The knock on her door brought a frown to her face. On the couch, Hulk lifted his head, lazily contemplating the possibility of company. To Hulk, company meant someone who could be cozened into rubbing his jaw or chin. To Dixie, it meant conversation.

She didn't want to talk. She considered not answering, but it probably wouldn't work. Scowling, she snapped, "Just a minute," then poked her brush into the wire loop that held it in the cleaner. She grabbed a rag and wiped some of the paint from her fingers as she headed to the door.

Cole stood on her stoop with a frown to match her own—and a small leather tote in one hand, like an overnight case.

She eyed that tote, eyebrows raised. "Not exactly subtle, Cole."

"It doesn't hold my shaving gear. No full-court press tonight. No moves, no passes, no fouls. May I come in?"

She studied his face. It didn't tell her much. "Why not?" she said at last, and stepped back.

"I did some research," he said as he entered. "Nothing you haven't already read, probably, but…" Words and feet both drifted to a stop as he saw her easel in the center of the room. And what sat on the easel.

In spite of her mood, his expression tickled her.

"Interesting," he said after a moment in a careful voice. "I thought you didn't do that kind of abstract art."

She chuckled. "That isn't art, it's therapy. My version of smashing crockery."

"That would be why it looks like crap, then."

"Probably. I'll scrape the canvas and reprime it

later." She cocked her head to one side. "You aren't here to inspect my visual therapy."

"No, I…" Hulk had abandoned the couch and was rubbing against Cole's leg, making like a chain saw. Cole bent and rubbed behind his ears. "Hello, monster."

Dixie ambled over to retrieve her brush, which needed to be washed. She'd made the canvas about as ugly as it needed to be. Might as well shut down for the night and find out what Cole was up to.

In the tiny kitchen, she turned on the tap and worked soap into the soft bristles. "Hulk appreciates company, no matter what the hour. I'm not in the mood."

"Tough." He'd set the mysterious tote on the coffee table. "You probably know all this," he said gruffly, taking out a fat folder, "but I wasn't sure how far your denial extended, so I thought I'd pass it on."

She put down her brush and returned to the living area, curious. He handed her the folder. Inside, she found pages and pages of information—about Alzheimer's. Organized into sections, with neatly printed tab tops dividing them: Stages…Treatments…Theories…Caretaker Support…

"That's all from reputable sites," he told her. "There's a lot of information out there, but not all of it is reliable."

"This must have taken hours," she murmured, paging through the printouts.

"I wanted to know about your aunt's condition, and you weren't talking. Which brings us to another question."

She looked up. "Us?"

"All right, me. It brings me to another question."
He moved restlessly, paused to frown at her visual
therapy, then looked back at her. "Why aren't you
talking about it?" he demanded.

"Just because I didn't talk to you—"

"You haven't unloaded on Mercedes, either."

"I told her about Aunt Jody," she protested.

"Yeah, and that's all. You haven't…you know."
He waved vaguely. "Talked about your feelings."

"Ah…" Deep inside, a laugh was trying to climb
out. "Let me get this straight. *You* are nagging *me* to
talk about my feelings?"

"Bottling everything up—that's my deal. I'm
used to that. Comfortable with it. You aren't." He sat
on her couch without waiting for an invitation and
began pulling more things out of his tote and putting
them on the pine coffee table.

A bottle of wine. Two glasses. A box of chocolates. Nail polish. Peppermint-scented foot lotion.
Cotton balls. Polish remover.

She sank down on the other end of the couch. The
laugh was getting closer to the top. She waved
weakly at the objects on the coffee table. "Cole?
You want to clue me in here?"

"Just call me Sheila. I'm a stand-in."

"For?" A smile started.

"This is one of those female parties. The kind
where you women get together to do each other's
hair or nails and end up telling each other the
damnedest things." He shook his head, marveling.

Oh. *Oh.* He was giving her every signal he could, even playing surrogate female, to tell her he was here as a friend, and nothing more. Because he was worried about her. Dixie's eye's filled. She stood, took two quick steps, bent and kissed him on the cheek. "This is about the sweetest thing...thank you."

"You're not going to cry, are you?"

She laughed. And if it came out a bit watery, tough. "I'm not making any promises. Are you going to paint your nails or mine?"

"I'm going to drink the wine." He inserted the bottle opener and twisted. He had strong hands, and they made quick work of the cork. "But you're welcome to join me."

"Does cabernet sauvignon go with chocolate?" She sat down and opened the box of candy. "Mmm. Dark chocolate at that."

"Mercedes seemed to think chocolate was essential."

She slid him a look. "You talked about this with Merry?"

"Yeah." He poured wine into one of the glasses, and its heady perfume drifted her way. "For some reason she thinks you're fine."

"Maybe because I am." She selected one she thought might have caramel. She loved caramel.

"Glad to hear it. So what do you talk about at these female shindigs?"

"Pretty much anything—men, work, hair, men, family, movies, men, books, politics...did I mention men?"

"The rat bastards," he said promptly, handing her a glass of wine. Hulk jumped up beside him and pointed out that no one was petting him by bumping his head against Cole's arm. Wine sloshed in the glass without spilling. Absently he began scratching the side of Hulk's face. "They never call."

Dixie shook her head sadly. "Or remember your birthday."

"And if they do, they forget the card. Would it kill them to spend some time picking out a card?"

"So true. And they only want one thing."

"Damn straight. Uh-oh. Sorry—I slid out of character there for a moment."

"Watch it." She took a sip, trying to keep a straight face. "Hey, this is good."

"Ninety-eight was one of our better years." He swirled the wine in his glass to release the scent, held it up and inhaled, his eyes half-closed. For a moment she glimpsed the closet sybarite in the pure, sensual pleasure on his face. Cole was a deeply sensual man. He mostly didn't let it show. "It's aging well," he observed, and took a sip.

"So what were you doing in ninety-eight?" She leaned back and nibbled at her chocolate. She liked to eat them slowly, let the taste melt into her tongue. "Note that I don't ask *who* you were doing."

"I'd get in trouble if I put it that way." He continued to send Hulk into a stupor of delight with those elegant fingers.

Quit staring at his hands, she told herself.

"Women can say things to each other that men can't get away with."

"So you talk about sex at these things?"

"Sure. It's a subheading under men. For most of us," she added. "I had a couple of lesbian friends in New York—my downstairs neighbors. We mostly did not talk about sex, out of consideration for my comfort level."

He chuckled. "My comfort level, on the other hand—"

"Don't go there, Sheila." She reconsidered. "On the other hand, I've always wondered why men get excited by—"

"You were right the first time," he said. There was a spark of amusement—and something else, something warmer—in his eyes as he took another sip of wine. "We'd better skip the sex talk."

She met his eyes as she took another sip, letting the wine sit on her tongue for a moment to develop the secondary flavors the way he'd taught her.

Not a good idea, enjoying her own sensual side while looking at Cole. "A hint of blackberry," she said hastily, looking away. "See how well I know the lingo? Should be nice with chocolate." She took another nibble of that. "Want to argue about politics?"

"Not the effect I'm going for tonight."

"You probably voted for the governor," she said darkly. "All right, all right—I won't get into that. So we're left discussing work or hair. I vote for hair." She tilted her head. "Who does yours?"

"Carmen at The Mane Place. She has magic fingers. I like your hair." The warmth in his voice did not belong to anyone named Sheila, unless Sheila had been of the same persuasion as Dixie's New York neighbors. "You left out a couple choices. Movies, books...family."

She took a healthy swallow of wine. "Read any good books lately?"

"No. How's your mom?"

She huffed out an impatient sigh. "Your male side is showing, Sheila."

So he asked again, but in an absurd falsetto, "How's your mom?"

Dixie nearly choked, trying not to laugh, and gave up. "The same as ever, pretty much. Only happier."

"Because of this man she's going to marry?"

Dixie nodded, sipped, and a smile slipped out. "She always used to try so hard with whatever man she thought was going to fix everything for her. With Mike, she's relaxed. She isn't desperate to make him happy, or trying too hard to be happy herself. She just feels good with him, and it shows. Not that she doesn't hurt because of what's happening to Jody, but she's... I don't know. Somehow she's okay about it."

"You aren't okay about it."

She frowned, not answering. He didn't say anything, either. Just sat there and sipped and petted Hulk, watching her.

"All right." She set her glass down with a snap. "All right! You want to hear about my feelings? I'm mad. Pissed as hell."

"You would be, of course."

She shoved to her feet and started to pace. "It's so horrible and so unfair. She still knows who we are. She isn't so far gone that she's lost that, but she will. She's already lost so many pieces of herself, and it hurts me. This shouldn't be about me, but every time I see her…the bewildered look on her face… My mother's dealing with this so much better than I am."

"She's been here, watching it happen. She's had time to adjust."

"And I've been on the other side of the continent, letting her deal with everything. You know what makes me crazy?" She stopped, shook her head. "Never mind. It's stupid."

"I have no problem with you being stupid."

"You're in danger of slipping out of supportive-friend mode," she warned him.

"Afraid you'll shock me?"

"No." She took two steps, stopped and threaded the fingers of both hands through her hair. "It's all this praise I keep getting. It makes me nuts."

"Yeah, I hate it when people praise me."

"Very funny. You know how often I hear some version of how strong I am?" she demanded. "Or that I'm such a great daughter and niece for moving back here. God. Aunt Jody was diagnosed two years ago. Two years. And I'm just now showing up."

"I guess you haven't done anything to help these past two years."

"I sent money. Big deal. I gave up a couple of vacations, flew out for more of the holidays. Then I'd go home and throw myself into work so I wouldn't have to think about Jody."

He shook his head. "Now that I can't understand. Throwing yourself into work to avoid dealing with something? You mystify me."

A reluctant smile touched her mouth. "You hinting that you have some experience in those lines?"

"I might." He stood, ignoring Hulk's protest at being disarranged. Crossing to her, he rested his hands on her shoulders. "What is it you think you should be doing differently, Dixie? Hurting less? Fixing things so your aunt doesn't hurt?"

"Don't forget the part about keeping my mother from hurting, too." The shape of his hands woke a visceral memory, a wordless surge of feeling that tangled past and present. She swallowed. "I said it was stupid."

"According to you, feelings are never stupid. They just are. It's what we do about them that matters."

"I could have sworn you never listened to my preaching."

Cole smiled that half up, half down smile without answering.

Dixie felt the impact low in her belly. Her heartbeat picked up as the present turned compelling, wiping out the whispers from the past. Desire bit, sharp and sweet. Her lips parted.

His gaze dipped there, lingered. His hands tightened on her shoulders, and the look on his face was unmistakable. He was going to kiss her…and she wanted that, wanted the taste and heat of him.

He dropped his hands and stepped back, his smile lost.

The disappointment was as disorienting as his sudden retreat. She put a hand on her stomach as if she could ease the sense of loss that way and tried to sound amused. "What was that? An attack of nobility, or common sense?"

He snorted. "You think I know?" He turned away, heading for the door. "This was a dumb idea. Enjoy the wine and chocolate and carry on with the nail painting. I'm leaving before I forget Sheila entirely."

"Cole."

He paused but didn't look at her.

"I was the one who switched the dial to another channel, not you. You…what you did helped."

He glanced back at her, conflicted emotions chasing over his face before he got it smoothed out. "Does this mean I'm invited to your next sleepover?"

"Not likely," she said dryly.

"Good. Because the next time I visit you at night, I won't be planning to sleep."

After the door closed behind him, Hulk came over, voicing his protest at being abandoned. "Don't come complaining to me," Dixie muttered, contradicting her words by picking him up and rubbing behind his ears. "At least you got stroked for a while. I didn't."

Which she ought to feel a lot better about, dammit.

Five

Louret's cellars had been a disappointment to Dixie when Cole first showed them to her. She'd hoped for earthen-floored caves or something appropriately dungeonlike. Instead, the barrels and bottles were aged in perfectly ordinary underground rooms with high-tech climate control and lousy lighting.

Lousy from her perspective, that is. To a winemaker, the dim lighting was necessary, as was strict control of temperature and humidity. But her imaginings would have made such a cool setting for Eli's painting…*well,* she thought, studying the barrels from her vantage point on the cement floor, *you work with what you've got.*

The barrels themselves were interesting. She'd

use lots of browns in the painting, she decided. Earth tones would suit Eli and suggest Louret's old-fashioned, hands-on approach while evoking the earth the grapes sprang from.

And gold for Caroline's painting, she decided, staring dreamily into space. Hints of brown to tie it to the earth and Eli's painting, touches of blue for the sky, and lots of gold—pale, glowing gold, like the sunlight that joins earth and sky.

Oh, yes. She'd use Eli and the barrels for the earth the vines were grown in, Caroline for the golden sunshine that made the grapes rich. For the end product, the wine itself…maybe a group picture? The family gathered around the dinner table, talking and interacting, their wineglasses catching the glow of sunset.

Set it outside then? And what about—

"Sorry I'm late," Eli's deep voice said from behind her.

"That's okay," she said, picking up her sketch pad and rising. "I don't think I'll draw you here, after all."

Uncertainty, she'd noticed, looked a lot like a scowl when it settled on Eli's face. "You aren't going to paint me with the barrels?"

"No, I'm definitely putting you against the barrels. But I've got photos for that. Today I need to draw you. Outside, I think. I need a peek at your bones. Strong light and shadows will help me get that." She gave him a smile as she passed, heading for the stairs.

After a moment she heard him following her up.

"You want to draw me outside, but you're not painting me outside."

"I use the photos for technical accuracy. Drawing helps me learn you. I don't know a subject until I've sketched him or her."

Eli looked pained. "I don't see why you need to use my face at all, but you don't have to, uh, know me to paint it."

She glanced over her shoulder as she reached the top of the stairs, mischief in her voice. "Oh, but I want more than your face for the painting. I want a bit of your soul."

He muttered something it was probably just as well she didn't catch. She was grinning as they stepped out the side door. "This will do." The light was good, strong and slanting. She got a charcoal pencil from her fanny pack and opened her sketch pad.

Eli squinted at the sunshine, looking profoundly uncomfortable. Better get him talking so he'd forget what she was up to. "Tell me about oaking," she said, her charcoal flying over the page. "I gather it's somewhat controversial?"

"More a matter of taste. Most people like some degree of oak. Heavy oaking can mask the subtleties of a really good red, but that's poor winemaking."

"What about whites? You're aging your new char-donnay in oak barrels." Needs to be heavier around the jaw, she decided, and darkened that line. "Is that standard?"

He shrugged. "Some use steel vats. We won't."

She had the definite impression he didn't think much of the winemakers who used steel. "Was that your decision or your mother's? With the new wine being named for her, I'd guess she had some input."

"Mostly mine. Mom likes the vanilla notes from oaking, though, so it was fine with her."

She flipped to a new page, shifted to get a different angle, and started another sketch. "And whose idea was the new chardonnay?"

"Cole's." He looked directly at her. "I thought you knew that."

"Okay, so I'm fishing." She frowned at the sketch. Something was off. The zygomatic arches? No, something about the way they related to his forehead. Dixie studied his brow line intently. "You missed your cue. You're supposed to discreetly fill me in on him without my having to ask."

He chuckled. It was an unexpected sound, coming from a man who tended toward angry or dour. "It's damned disconcerting to have you stare at me that way when you're talking about my brother. What did you want to know?"

She looked at him reproachfully and repeated, "*Without* my having to ask."

"Well, he's not seeing anyone right now, and he thinks you're hot."

"Mmm." Damn. It was his left eye—she'd set it too close to the bridge of the nose. Try again. She flipped to a new page. "I'm trying to come up with a modest way of saying, 'I know.'"

Again the low chuckle. "I think so, too. When I asked him if he'd staked a claim already—"

"You didn't."

"Of course I did. You two were involved before. I needed to know if he was interested. Funny thing is, he didn't seem to know, himself. I guess he's made up his mind now."

"I guess so." He seemed pretty sure that he wanted to get her into bed, anyway. "He claims he's mellowed."

"Mellow? Cole?" There was a note of humor in his voice, but it was fleeting. "Not the word I'd choose. He's got more control than I do, but there's a lot of intensity beneath that control."

"Good way to put it. He's still pretty wrapped up in the business, I guess." Her hand and eyes were working automatically now, which was just as well. Her mind wasn't on the sketch.

"He doesn't put in the sixty and eighty hour weeks he used to. That's why you left him, isn't it?"

Surprised, she looked at him—at Eli, that is, not at Eli's bones. Their eyes met. "That was a big part of it."

"Louret is always going to be important to him, and he's always going to like winning. You won't get a lap cat with Cole."

Annoyed, she sketched two tiny horns at the top of Eli's head. "I don't want a lap cat. I don't want to come last, either. There's bound to be something in between."

"It messed him up when you left."

"From my perspective, he was already messed up. So was I," she said, closing the sketch pad. "That was the problem."

Eli nodded. "That's valid. But this time…just be careful with him, okay? Don't promise more than you mean to follow through on."

"Are you asking my intentions?"

"I guess I am."

She smiled suddenly, took two quick steps and went up on tiptoes to kiss his cheek. "That's sweet. I don't have any idea what my intentions are yet, and when I do I'll let Cole know, not you. But it's sweet that you wanted to ask."

His ears turned red. "If you're finished with me, I've got stuff to do."

"I'm sure you do," she said, enjoying his embarrassment more than she should have. "I hope I'll be able to bring out your inner softie in the painting."

Now he was positively alarmed. "My what?"

She laughed and patted his arm. "Don't worry. Your portrait will be very manly."

Once Eli made his escape, though, her amusement evaporated. She was frowning as she headed for the carriage house so she could work on the composition for Eli's portrait.

It was only natural for Cole's brother to worry about him, she supposed. Only natural that he'd see her as the one at fault for having left Cole eleven years ago. But it left her feeling flat and a little lonely. There was no one worrying about her that way, no one warning her of potential heartbreak if she got involved with a man who'd hurt her before.

Not that she'd listen, she supposed wryly as she opened the door to her temporary home. But it might be nice to have someone worry, just this once.

"You used charcoal when you sketched Eli," Caroline observed.

"Mmm-hmm." Dixie's gaze flew back and forth between the woman in front of her and her sketch pad. Her pencil moved swiftly. They were in what Dixie thought of as the covered porch, though the family called it the lanai. It was open on the north side, which made the light good.

"I wondered why you're doing my sketch in pencil."

"I don't know." There was something about the flesh over the right cheek that wasn't right...Dixie smudged the shadow beneath the cheek with her finger to soften it, looked at Caroline again, then used the side of her pencil to pull the shadow back toward the ear.

Better. "I'll use the photos I took for technical precision," she explained. "The sketches are to learn you. When I get your shapes down with my hands, I know them, see? I wanted charcoal to learn Eli. I wanted pencil for you."

Caroline smiled. "My shape's rounder than it used to be. I suppose you have to show my double chin?"

"You don't have a double chin." Dixie spoke absently as she adjusted the brow line, which defined the eyes. "The jaw has softened with age, but... whoops. Forgot tact."

The older woman laughed. "Tell me something. Since you won't cater to my vanity in one way... you're sure it's okay if I talk?"

"Absolutely." Dixie turned to a new page, moved slightly to the left and began a gesture drawing from the new angle in a series of quick sweeps of her pencil.

"I've sometimes wondered if anything of me showed up in my boys. The girls, yes. I see something of myself in them. But Cole and Eli..."

Dixie heard another question in the way Caroline's voice trailed into silence. How much did her sons resemble the man who'd fathered and deserted them?

"The girls do take after you more than Eli and Cole do," she said casually, as if she hadn't noticed the unspoken part of the question. In Jillian's case the resemblance was more a matter of manner than genetics, but Dixie could be tactful when it mattered. "But Eli has your nose and your ears."

"And Cole?"

Cole...whom Mercedes said most resembled their father. "He has your hands. Great hands," she added, crouching for another angle. "I plan to use them."

When Caroline chuckled it took Dixie a moment to realize why. Then she flushed. "Ah...in the painting. I'm going to use your hands in the painting. Not

Cole's hands. I'm not planning to use them for, ah..."

Caroline smiled. "How delightful. I didn't think anything flustered you. You're a rather formidable young woman."

"Me?" Dixie was astonished. Caroline was the one with the inbred class and composure, the soft voice and gentle ways Cole had once thrown up at Dixie as the feminine ideal.

"But of course. Look at all you've accomplished at such a young age. Though I suppose you don't think of yourself as terribly youthful." Her smile turned amused. "The young never do. I hope I didn't insult you, dear. It's just that you're so very competent and confident. I wasn't, not at your age."

And yet what Dixie's pencil had captured was a calm, determined woman. She turned back to the finished sketch, then reversed her pad to show Caroline. "Here's what I see—strength, kindness, grace."

"Oh, my," Caroline said softly, taking the pad. "You've made it difficult for me to pry the way I'd intended. May I have this?"

"Of course." Dixie accepted the return of her sketch pad with a silent, fervent wish that Caroline would continue to find it difficult to pry.

"I don't know what you charge, but—"

"You'll insult me if you offer to pay. The paintings are business. This isn't."

"Then I'll just thank you. I'd like to frame it and give it to Lucas for our anniversary." Her cheeks were a little pinker than usual. "Perhaps it's vain, giving him a likeness of myself, but I think he'd like it."

Dixie smiled. "You'll be giving him a picture of someone at the center of his life. Of course he'll like it." She closed the pad. "I'll need to hang on to it until I've finished the painting, though."

"Our anniversary isn't for another two months. No rush." Caroline stood. "I take it you're through with me?"

"For now," Dixie said cheerfully. "I'll be starting the paintings soon, and I may need to stare at you some more then. Or not. First I'm going to pester your vineyard foreman for a day or two."

"I suspect Russ won't mind," Caroline said dryly. "Dixie?"

She slid her pad into her tote. "Yes?"

"My son was deeply hurt when you left him. I'm concerned about your reappearance in his life."

Dixie froze. *Déjà vu, all over again,* she thought. First Eli, now Caroline.

And what could she say? That Cole was the one doing the pursuing? It was true, but if she was honest, she'd have to admit she enjoyed the game they were playing. "I don't know what to tell you. He isn't serious."

"Isn't he?" Caroline let that question dangle a moment, then smiled. "You probably want to suggest I mind my own business. I understand. We'll change the subject. I'm having a small dinner party Friday, mostly family. I'd like it if you could join us."

"Thank you," Dixie said, wary.

Caroline shook her head ruefully. "I'm not usually so maladroit. The dinner invitation has nothing to do with the question I didn't quite ask you. Truly, I would like to have you join us."

"And I'm not usually so prickly." Dixie's smile warmed. "I'd love to come."

"Head over any time after six, then. Casual dress. We'll eat around seven-thirty."

Dixie was frowning as she headed for the carriage house. She didn't resent Caroline's delicate prying. Mothers were allowed to worry—it was in the contract. They were also entitled to think the best of their offspring. Dixie couldn't very well tell Cole's mother that all he was after was a quick roll in the hay.

Well...maybe not quick. Her lips curved. That had never been one of Cole's faults.

Her smile didn't last. She suspected his pursuit rose, in part, from the desire to prove that he was over her. If that thought pinched a bit, she could understand it. Because Caroline had been right about the other. Dixie was sure she'd hurt Cole.

He'd hurt her, too. But his had been sins of omission, not commission. He hadn't lied or cheated. He just hadn't *been* there enough. Business had come first, second and sometimes third with Cole. All too often, Dixie had been an afterthought.

She'd been so desperately in love. And he...he'd been halfway in love. In the end, she hadn't been able to handle that.

Dixie rounded the corner of the house—and almost walked right into Cole. And her cat, who was purring madly in Cole's arms.

"Good grief." She shook her head, disgusted. "He got out again?"

"I was working on a budget projection and turned away to get a file. When I turned back, there he was, sitting on top of a stack of quarterly reports, cleaning his face and looking smug. Tilly's still hiding under my desk. Hey." He touched her arm lightly with his free hand. "Is something wrong?"

"Just thinking deep, philosophical thoughts. It interferes with my digestion." She started walking again. He fell into step beside her. "Is Tilly okay?"

"She's fine, now that I removed her tormenter." He smiled. "That's three, Dixie. And still two days to go."

"I know, I know." She and Cole had a bet on. Cole had bet that Hulk would escape at least half a dozen times before Friday.

It should have been an easy win for her. Not because she fooled herself that she controlled Hulk, but she did know his ways. She'd figured her cat would escape once a day, no matter what she did—but if she let him stay out long enough to get his outside fix, he'd be content to stay in the rest of the time.

She hadn't counted on his obsession with Cole's dog. "I think you're sneaking him out," she said darkly.

"Would I do that? He may be teleporting. Here." Cole dumped the cat into her arms. "Where did you find Cattila the Hun, anyway?"

Had Cole always had this deliciously wry sense of humor, and she'd forgotten? "He just showed up one day, sitting outside my apartment as if he'd been waiting for me. I opened the door and he strolled in, demanded dinner, then curled up in my lap and informed me it was time to pet him."

Cole nodded. "I can see where you wouldn't want to argue with him."

"He was half-starved."

"He's made up for it." There was a hint of the devil in his sidelong glance. "Maybe I should borrow his technique. As I recall, you're a great cook. If I show up demanding dinner—"

She laughed. "You won't get in the door. I suspect your priorities are different from Hulk's."

"You're right." His voice dropped as he stroked her arm. "I'd want to go straight to the petting."

Just that light touch, and her system hummed happily. She wanted more, and there was no one around but herself to warn her of the dangers. "Hands off. I can't defend myself with my arms full of Hulk."

"I know. I like you helpless."

"You've never seen me helpless," she retorted. They'd reached the carriage house. "Open the door, will you, so I can put my monster back where he belongs."

Instead he leaned against the door, smiling. "Bribe me."

"Oh, come on, Cole—"

"Just a kiss. I'll even promise to keep my hands

to myself." But he wasn't. He'd reached for a strand of her hair and was tickling her with it—under her chin, along her throat. "One kiss…or don't you dare?"

She raised an eyebrow even as a shiver touched her spine. "You think I'm juvenile enough to jump at that bait?"

"I can hope." He moved even closer, stopping with scant inches between them. The heat of his body seemed to set the air between them ashimmer with possibilities. "Why not, Dixie? It's not as if you don't want to kiss me."

Her heart was pounding. "Your neck ever get tired from holding up that swollen head of yours?"

He just smiled. "It's only a kiss. What could it hurt?"

*All kinds of things—me, you…*but apparently she wasn't very good at listening to herself, because she went up on tiptoe, pausing with her lips a breath away from his. "No hands," she murmured. And she kissed him. Slowly. Just a skimming of lips at first…

"Uh-uh," she said when he tried to take over. "This one's mine."

Hulk was between them, so their bodies didn't touch. Just their mouths. The scent of him was a heady intimacy as she tickled his bottom lip with her tongue, then touched it to each corner of his mouth, and arousal was pure pleasure. The ache grew, gradually focusing like a perspective drawing, when all lines lead to a single point.

Dixie opened her mouth over his and took his breath inside her—which was just as well, for she didn't seem to have enough of her own. For a moment they met fully, lips, tongues, breath.

Then she eased back, smiling. And was pleased by the stunned look on his face.

He reached for her. She stepped back, shaking her head. "No hands, remember? Open the door, Cole."

"The door." He blinked. "Right. Anything you say. Sure you wouldn't like all my worldly goods instead?"

"Not just now, thanks." She sauntered inside, still holding her cat…with her heart pounding and pounding, and a little voice inside asking if she'd lost her mind.

This had to be about the stupidest thing he'd ever done, Grant thought as he gunned his pickup in order to keep up with the shiny blue Mercedes half a block ahead on the busy highway. He was acting like some two-bit private eye, for crying out loud.

But Grant didn't give up easily. Some called him pigheaded. He preferred to think of himself as determined. And so far, Spencer Ashton had refused to see him, leaving Grant only two options: give up and go home, or somehow force the bastard to talk to him.

The bastard who'd fathered him. His father. Grant forced himself to use the word, though it went down about as well as ground glass.

Looked as if they were heading out of the city. Spencer owned a big, fancy mansion near Napa. If that's where he was going, Grant was out of luck. He'd already been turned away from that door. From the high-rise office building here in San Francisco where Spencer went most mornings, too.

Which is why Grant was playing P.I. Sooner or later the man would go someplace where none of his servants or employees manned the gates.

Sooner or later his *father* would have to speak to him.

Grant scowled. More than once he'd wished he'd never seen that damn TV show. He'd come in from working on the older of his two tractors, showered and settled down with a cold beer. The game hadn't started yet, so he'd been thinking about the weather while some documentary about winemaking finished up. A perky young reporter had been interviewing Spencer Ashton of Ashton-Lattimer, a corporation that owned vineyards and a large commercial winery.

Ashton Estate Winery. The name had snagged Grant's attention, naturally, since it matched his own surname. But it was the face that had riveted him.

Spencer Ashton's face looked like the one he saw in the mirror every day. Not in any one feature, maybe, but something about the way they were grouped. That had been spooky, but it hadn't occurred to Grant the man might be his father. Even though the names were the same, he'd known it was impossible. His father had died when he was barely a year old.

Then the interviewer had mentioned Spencer's

Nebraska upbringing. They'd flashed a picture of him as a young man—and the man in that photo had been identical to the one standing beside Grant's mother in the yellowed wedding photo she'd kept by her bed until the day she died.

Two weeks later, Grant had climbed in his pickup and started for San Francisco, leaving Ford in charge at the farm.

Ford had asked what he expected to accomplish. Grant had told his nephew he wanted to meet the half brothers and half sisters he'd never known existed. That was true, if only a partial truth.

So far he hadn't mustered the nerve. He'd driven out to The Vines one morning, but hadn't been able to bring himself to ring the doorbell. It was weird to walk up to a bunch of strangers and say, "Hi, I'm your brother." Their money complicated matters. They were likely to think he wanted something from them.

He did, but it had nothing to do with money. Family mattered. These strangers were family. He needed to know what they were like.

What he hadn't told Ford was that he also needed to look the man who'd fathered him in the eye and say, "You can't pretend I don't exist. I do."

What good that would do, he couldn't say. But he was going to do it. Maybe today, maybe later, but he wasn't leaving California until he did.

On Friday, Cole took Dixie to Charley's restaurant in Yountville for lunch.

"I can't believe I let you finagle me into this," Dixie said, sliding out of Cole's suvvy.

"You lost the bet." Cole was entirely too pleased with himself.

"That part I understand. How I let you talk me into making such a dumb bet, I don't."

"Maybe you didn't really want to win." He held the door for her.

"I knew you were going to say that. The fact is, Hulk's gone over to the Dark Side. He conspired with you."

"You're talking about a cat, Dixie."

"I'm talking about Hulk."

"I get your point. Table for two," he told the hostess. "I have a reservation."

"Of course, Mr. Ashton. This way."

Dixie raised her eyebrows. "They know you here."

"We sell them wine."

She nodded. "And just when did you make that reservation?"

"The same day we made the bet, of course."

Dixie wouldn't have admitted it for anything, but she was glad she'd lost the bet. Charley's had been around awhile, but she couldn't afford the place back when she lived here before and somehow she'd never made it here on her visits home.

The restaurant was set on twelve acres of olive groves, vineyards and gardens brimming with seasonal flowers, herbs and vegetables. Most of the herbs and produce used in their dishes came out of the ground the same day it was cooked. Plus they had an exhibition kitchen.

Dixie considered cooking every bit as much of an art as painting. She was looking forward to watching the pros at work.

"I've been thinking," Cole said after the manager stopped by to welcome them. "If I'd lost the bet, I would have had to donate money to a charity of your choice. Having won the bet, I'm still spending money. What's wrong with this picture?"

She chuckled. "You set the terms, not me."

He shook his head. "What was I thinking?"

As they debated their selections, Dixie admitted to herself that she wasn't just enjoying the place. She was enjoying the man. Had she had this much pure fun with Cole before?

All week, the present had been poking holes in the preconceptions of the past. Dixie remembered an ambitious, rather grim young man who'd had little time to spare for anything except business. This Cole was intense, yes, but he possessed a keen sense of the ridiculous. Even his pursuit of her had been flavored with humor.

And that, she told herself as she placed her order, was more dangerous than a sexual buzz, however potent. She had to be on her guard…because she was beginning to hope. She was trying not to define that hope, but it fizzed around inside, a giddy effervescence that bubbled up into smiles and easy laughter.

Cole selected the wine—one from another vine-

yard, so he could see what the competition was up
to, he said. She picked the entrées. They argued
about home schooling, sushi and a recent action
movie, and found themselves agreeing about reality
TV, garlic and childproof safety caps.

Dixie had a wonderful time until the waiter took
their desert orders and left. All at once, Cole's face
froze.

"What is it?" she asked.

"Nothing." He was staring over her shoulder in a
way that should have turned whoever he was looking at into a Popsicle.

She craned her head around. A small knot of people blocked the entrance. Her eyebrows rose. She
recognized one of them—the Western-looking man
who'd been wandering around the vineyard earlier
that week. The manager seemed upset with him.

The other two she'd never seen before, yet she recognized one. Not the curvy blonde in the red power
suit. The older man resting a possessive hand on her
back.

He had silver hair and an impeccably tailored suit
over a lean body. His eyebrows were straight, his
nose strong, his small, neat ears set flat to his head.
His features were symmetrical, possessing the kind
of balance people call handsome in a man, beauty
in a woman.

He looked exactly like Cole would in another
thirty years.

"Dammit, Dixie, don't stare." Cole's voice was
low and angry. "He doesn't matter."

That was blatantly false, so she ignored it. "That's your father, isn't it?"

"My real dad is married to my mother. That man is nothing. Nothing at all."

The problem, whatever it was, appeared to be resolved. The manager was escorting Western Man out of the restaurant—and one of the waiters was leading Cole's father and the woman with him their way.

The woman's hair woke envy in Dixie's heart. It was long, pale blond with a hint of curl. Her situation didn't. She looked as if she didn't appreciate the hand resting on her back. And the man escorting her didn't seem to know his son existed.

The waiter stopped at their table, looking flustered. "My apologies, sir. There's been some mistake. This table is reserved."

"I know," Cole said in his refrigerator voice. "I reserved it."

"But…I'm terribly sorry, sir, but this is Mr. Ashton's table."

"Good. I'm glad we agree."

The poor waiter didn't know what to say. Nothing Man was too bored and important to wrangle in public, and besides was busy pretending he didn't see his son sitting there. The woman with him looked too uncomfortable to do anything to defuse the situation. She even took a small step away, maybe distancing herself from the looming scene, maybe ditching that possessive hand. And Cole wasn't about to make anything easier for anyone, including himself.

So Dixie took over. She smiled at the waiter. "There's a misunderstanding, but it's easily cleared up. There are two Mr. Ashtons present. That, I believe, is Mr. Spencer Ashton." She nodded at Cole's father, eyebrows raised. "Aren't you?"

He was faintly surprised, as if a chair had addressed him. "Yes, I am. And this is my assistant, Kerry Roarke. You are—?"

"Dixie McCord." She turned her smile up a notch. "And this is your son, Cole Ashton."

Cole choked and began coughing.

The manager came rushing up. "Idiot. Idiot." That seemed to be addressed to the waiter. "Go away. I'll handle this. I am so terribly sorry," he said, spreading his hands to include both Mr. Ashtons in the apology. "We have your table, of course, Mr. Ashton." A small nod indicated the older man. "It's right over here. If you'll follow me—?"

As soon as they were out of earshot Cole said, "If you think I'm going to thank you for that bit of interference—"

"I'm not that naive. I suppose you want to leave now that you've defended your territory."

He stood and tossed his napkin on the table.

Dixie ached for him. Not one word had his father spoken to him. There hadn't been even a glance—no curiosity, nothing. *Nothing Man is a good name for him,* she thought as Cole scattered a few bills on the table.

She knew better than to let Cole see how she hurt for him. Hold out a hand in sympathy right now and he'd snap it off. The walls he'd pulled behind were steep and silent—but then, he had a lot of anger for them to hold back.

It began spilling out when they got in his suvvy. "Did you see that bimbo with him? His *assistant*." He made the word sound obscene. "Doesn't look like he's changed his habits."

"I don't think she's a bimbo." Dixie fastened her seat belt. It looked as if they were in for a rough ride.

"Bimbo, mistress, what's the difference?" He backed out, slammed the car into Drive and stepped on the gas. "I wonder if Bimbo Number One knows about Bimbo Number Two."

Bimbo Number One, she assumed, would be his stepmother, the woman Spencer Ashton had had an affair with. The one he'd married as soon as the divorce from Cole's mother was final. The woman he'd raised a second family with—a family he hadn't deserted. "There may be nothing to know. I don't think that woman is his mistress," Dixie repeated patiently. "The body language was wrong."

"Oh, he's staked a claim there, all right." Cole swung out onto the street with barely a pause. "Trust me on that."

"He may be staking a claim, but she hasn't accepted it."

"Don't be naive. She was uncomfortable at being spotted with him by his son. Probably didn't realize I'm from his *other* family—the one he doesn't see, speak to or give two cents about."

Dixie decided they had better things to fight about

than a woman they'd never see again. "You are not like him, Cole."

"Where did that come from?" He was cutting through traffic as if he needed to be somewhere, anywhere, other than where he was right now. "You don't know what the hell you're talking about."

"You look like him. That doesn't mean you're *like* him."

"I don't want to talk about it."

"Okay. We'll save it for when you aren't driving."

"There's nothing wrong with my driving."

She rolled her eyes. "If you want to argue, fine. But you don't get to pick the subject."

"And you do, I suppose?"

"Yes, because you'd have us fighting about all the wrong things. What you really need to fight about—"

"I told you I don't want to talk about him."

At least Cole had moved close enough to the real subject to say "him" instead of "it." Dixie decided to let him hole up inside his turbulence until he wasn't behind the wheel, so she said nothing.

Neither did he. The silence held until she noticed which way they were heading. "This is not the way to The Vines."

"I need to drive for a while. It clears my head."

"You have a destination in mind, or are we just going to dodge traffic?"

"My cabin."

Six

Cole spent the drive to his cabin caught up in a whirlwind of thoughts and feelings. When would he be old enough for it to stop mattering? So what if his father was a sorry sonofabitch? Millions of people had lousy fathers. He ought to be able to shrug off the bastard's indifference by now.

Most of the time he could. He did. Today, though…there was just something about seeing Spencer with his newest side piece, pulling the same shit that had wrecked Cole's life all those years ago. It rubbed him raw, too, that Dixie had been there. He didn't know why. It just did.

If he hadn't looked up to the man so much when he was a kid, tried so hard to win his approval…

The past was a closed book, he reminded himself, pulling to a stop in front of his cabin. Put it back on the shelf and leave it alone. "Go on inside," he told Dixie, climbing out. "I'm going to chop some wood."

"Oh, good idea," she said, getting out and shutting her door. "Go play with an ax while you're too mad too see straight. I'll get the bandages and tourniquet ready."

He flicked one glance at her then walked away, heading for the edge.

The cabin was surrounded on three sides by oak, pine and brush, but the strip along the front was clear all the way to the drop-off. There, the land fell away in dizzying folds. The view always opened him up, made him breathe easier.

It didn't do a damn thing for him today. He stopped a pace back from the rocky edge and shoved his hands in his pockets.

Dixie had followed him, of course. "This would be easier if you really were Sheila. I can't help you vent in the traditional male way, by getting into a fistfight."

"I should have known all that silence was too good to last."

"If you wanted silence, you should have come here alone."

Why hadn't he? He was in no mood for company, yet it hadn't occurred to him to take her back to The Vines before heading here. "If you wanted me to drop you off, you should have said something."

"I'm just putting you on notice. You brought me along. Now you have to put up with me."

"I want to show you the cabin." There. He knew he'd had a reason for bringing her. "But I need a minute to myself first."

"You need to do something with all the stuff churning around inside you, all right. Try talking."

"I'm not in the mood for amateur therapy."

"You know, people were talking—sometimes even listening—for a few thousand years before Freud called it therapy."

He gave her an ugly look. "You won't let it be, will you? You have to poke and prod and try to fix me."

"I used to do that. It was a mistake."

His eyebrows went up. "You're admitting it?"

"Astonishing, isn't it? But I wasn't the only one. We both tried to fix each other. Your technique was a little different, that's all." She shrugged. "Young and stupid sums it up, I guess. We fell hard and immediately started trying to change each other into people it would be safer to love."

Love. The word scraped across places already raw. "You found plenty that needed fixing, didn't you? There wasn't that much that you liked about me back then."

She winced. "I can see where you got that impression, but it isn't true. There was plenty I liked. And," she admitted, "one or two things I couldn't live with."

She'd made that plain. Restless, he started walking. "Why did you come back, Dixie?"

She fell into step with him. "You keep asking me that."

He didn't know what kind of answer he was looking for. Just that he hadn't gotten it yet.

What was wrong with him, anyway? He'd planned to bring Dixie to his cabin after lunch—but he'd been hoping for a little afternoon delight, not a session mucking around in his least pleasant memories. Not to mention his least pleasant self. "I'm acting like an idiot, aren't I? Sorry." He made himself smile.

She stopped. "Don't do that."

"Don't do what? Be pleasant? Polite?"

"Don't put on a happy face for me."

"What if it isn't for you?" he snapped. "Maybe I need to remind myself I can be civilized."

She stood there, shoulders straight, eyes narrowed as she studied him. God, he used to love the way she faced off with him, not backing down an inch… Cole took a deep breath. Some things it was best not to remember too clearly. "Walk with me a bit, okay?"

"Okay." And that was all she said.

Cole headed for one of his favorite paths, a deer trail that led to a small meadow that was green and pretty now. It would be spectacular in the spring, he thought. Dixie would love it when the wildflowers burst into bloom.

But she wouldn't be here in the spring, would she?

Carpe the damn *diem*, then. If all he had was another week or so, he'd better make the most of them. "What did you think of my cabin? I realize you haven't seen much of it yet."

"I love it. But it wasn't what I'd been expecting."

"What were you expecting?"

The path was too narrow for them to walk abreast, so she was following him. He couldn't see her teasing smile, but he heard it in her voice. "Something more rustic. A *lot* more rustic. You did say you'd done a lot of the work yourself."

"You lack confidence in my carpentry."

"I didn't think you knew one end of a saw from the other."

"I didn't, to start out with," he admitted. "After the wall fell down, I took a couple courses."

She laughed. "It really fell down? Which one?"

As he told her the story of his early, botched attempt at fixing up his place, a wave of relief swept through him. They'd be okay. As long as they kept it light, didn't let things get intense, they'd be fine.

At the end of the tree-shrouded path lay his meadow. His heart lifted as he stepped from shade to sun. There was nothing vast or magnificent about this spot. The beauties here were small and common, but something about the shape of the pocket-size meadow seemed to cup the sunshine, to gather and soften it. He could have sworn the grass grew a little greener here, waving gently in a breeze the trees had blocked. Off to the west a towhee called its name—*to-whee, to-whee.*

"Oh…" Dixie stopped several paces behind him

and turned in a slow circle. "A little piece of perfection, isn't it?"

Her response pleased him. "This is the other reason I bought the place."

"It's lovely." She stood motionless and smiling, glossed by sunshine. The breeze teased her hair and pressed her thin blue dress against a shape that was pure female.

Longing hit, a sweep of emotion that made him feel larger, lighter, full of air and dreams…then receded, leaving him mute and unsteady.

"Cole?" She tilted her head. "Is something wrong?"

"Probably." He'd been wrong. Terribly wrong. He didn't want a few days of friendly, keep-it-light sex from her. He wanted more. Much more.

He walked slowly up to her.

Nerves flickered in her eyes. She knew what was on his mind, oh yes. She didn't back up—but she wanted to, he could see that. Instead she tilted her head back, frowning. "What flipped your switch?"

"You." He put his hands on her arms and ran them up to her shoulders, letting the warmth of her seep into his palms. "You always have."

"I don't think this—"

"Good. Don't think." He crushed his mouth down on hers.

She jolted. He knew that, but only dimly—the ripe taste of her flooded him, a wine more heady than sweet. He pulled her tight against him, running his hands over her, feeding on the feel of her, the scent and taste and heat that was Dixie.

It wasn't enough. He needed more—needed enough of her that she wouldn't leave, couldn't leave him again. His arms tightened around her.

And, dammit to hell, as soon as he did that, she started struggling. Pushing him away.

Cole had to drop his arms and let her go. Again. And it hurt, again.

Her mouth was wet, her hair wildly mussed and her eyes snapping with anger. "I won't be forced."

It was guilt that made him snap back. "Forced? It was a kiss!"

"You were going too fast. Pushing too hard."

His mouth twisted. So did something inside, something that spilled out ugliness. "You've given me every reason to think you'd like to be kissed. Or was that all part of the game? Do you get a charge out of teasing men?"

"Where did that come from?" she snapped.

"You like men, don't you? Eli, Russ, me—you flirt with us all. Am I just one of your men, Dixie?"

She spun around and started back toward the path.

"That's right. Walk away. That's your answer to everything."

She paused. Slowly she turned. "People who leave aren't exactly high on your list, are they, Cole? Or maybe they make the wrong list. Eleven years ago, I was the one to leave. We haven't talked about that."

"That's right, I forgot. Talking is your other answer."

She scowled. "I like yelling, too, sometimes."

"I remember." God, he did remember. Not the exact words of that last fight, but the feelings. She'd been furious, hurt—and the more angry she'd gotten, the colder he'd turned, until he'd thought he might never be warm again. "You yelled plenty when I forgot your birthday. Then you left me."

She stared. "Tell me that isn't the way you remember it."

"It's what happened! I messed up with the dates—"

"You refused to change a dinner with a client to another day!" She advanced, fists clenched at her sides. "We had a date, you and I, but you forgot and booked a dinner with a client for that night. I was hurt, yes, because you'd forgotten, but that wasn't why I left!"

"Then why?" he demanded. "Tell me why, because I remember you screaming at me that if I wouldn't take you out instead of my client, you were leaving—and you did!"

"You could have switched your client to another night instead of putting me off! I came last, like usual. Over and over you showed me where I stood—business came first, your family second, and I finished a poor third. Yet in spite of that, you couldn't stand it if I so much as smiled at another man!"

His lip curled. "Half the time, you smiled at everyone but me. Is it any wonder I wasn't sure of you?"

"You weren't there for me to smile at! God, I'd

be waiting for a phone call, then when it came you'd tell me you had to cancel lunch. Or dinner. By the last month we were together," she finished bitterly, "you'd canceled pretty much everything except sex. That, you had time for."

Her words struck him mute, inside and out. In the flash of mental silence that followed he heard his own words, past and present, echoing in his mind. After a moment he asked quietly, "Did you really think that? That all I wanted from you was sex?"

She gave her head a little shake, as if she were emerging from the fog, too. When she spoke there was a thread of humor in her voice. "Surely I must have screamed something along those lines."

"By then we were accusing each other of everything short of abetting the Holocaust. I didn't think you meant it."

"I, on the other hand, believed you meant every word. You weren't screaming, like me. You were deep in your chill zone, still speaking in complete, grammatically correct sentences…everything you said came out cold and deliberate."

"I have no idea what I said. I was terrified."

Her eyebrows shot up. "You?"

"Oh, yeah. I was losing you and I knew it." He'd never really believed he'd be able to hold on to her, so he'd held on too tightly, letting jealousy twist its knife in him. "I'd bought a ring."

The words just slipped out. Dammit, he'd never wanted her to know that, never wanted anyone to realize how deep and complete a fool he'd been.

Her eyes went huge. "A ring?" she whispered.

"I was going to ask you to wear it on your birthday. Or," he added wryly, "on whatever night I managed to make time to celebrate your birthday."

Her eyes closed. She rubbed her chest as if it hurt. "Give me a minute. You… That's a real leveler." She paced away a few steps, then just stood there, her hand on her chest, looking away…pretty far away, he suspected. About eleven years. "If I'd known…"

"You might not have left. And that," he added with painful honesty, "would probably have been a mistake. I wanted to keep you, but I had no intention of changing. I didn't know how, back then. We'd have made each other miserable."

She looked back at him. "I was sure you'd call. I waited for weeks for you to call and say you'd been wrong and wanted me back."

"I was waiting for you to call and apologize. I gave you a month, being big on tests back then. You mentioned that." He remembered only too well what she'd said. "Or shouted it. You were sick of the way I kept testing you, but as usual I didn't listen. At the end of the month I decided you'd failed the test. I pitched the ring into the deepest canyon I could find. It was all very dramatic."

She shook her head, a sad smile touching her mouth. "God have mercy on the young."

"Young and stupid," he agreed. "Both of us."

Suddenly she laughed. "Pigheaded fits, too. Both of us waiting for the other one to call—"

"Confess their sins—"

"And come crawling back." She grinned. "Admit it. The crawling part figured in your fantasies, too."

"Absolutely." Right up until he threw away the ring that had meant so much…and so little. After that, he'd made up his mind to forget her.

He'd failed.

For a moment they just looked at each other, letting the past settle back into place. Cole found that the shapes it fell into weren't quite the ones it had held before. "I was out of line earlier," he admitted. "Way out. I shouldn't have accused you of being a tease, or…" He swallowed. "Or forced a kiss you didn't want."

"I wanted it," she said, low voiced. "Then I got scared."

"God, I never meant—"

"Of course not," she said quickly. "If I'd let you know…but I don't like to admit it when I'm frightened."

But he knew of another time she'd been frightened, one she'd told him about. That knowledge hung between them.

She'd been eight when her father died, fifteen when her mother became engaged again. Helen McCord had believed she'd found the man who would take care of her and her daughter forever. Dixie hadn't liked him, but she'd kept quiet about it for her mother's sake. They'd just moved in together when Helen's heart condition had grown suddenly worse. She'd gone in for surgery, comforted by the knowledge that the man she loved would be there to take care of her daughter.

The day after her surgery, that man had cornered Dixie in her bedroom. She'd gotten away. She'd even left her mark—the bastard probably bore a scar on his forehead to this day. And she hadn't told her mother about it until Helen was home from rehab.

It was typical of Dixie. Admirable. And it provided a stark exclamation point to all the reasons he'd had for doubting she could ever commit completely to one man. Life had taught her not to trust men. To rely only on herself.

"It wasn't you I was afraid of," Dixie said at last. "Not you. That doesn't mean you're off the hook for your comments," she added with attempted lightness. "Some women may find jealousy attractive. I don't."

"Noted." He nodded, grimly accepting that he'd given her a flashback moment. One more in a long series of mistakes he'd made with her. "You've seen my temper, my favorite spot and my least favorite side of myself. Can I show you my cabin now?"

She shook her head. "I do want to see it, but not today. Things are pretty charged between us right now. I don't want to fall into your bed by accident."

His pulse leaped. *Down, boy,* he told his most optimistic body part, and held out a hand. "Walk back with me?"

She smiled, came to him and took his hand. The connection felt good. After a moment he said, "I guess this means I'll have to postpone my plans for an afternoon of hot sex."

Her laugh was shaky. "Good guess."

Postponed, he thought. What a wonderful word. For a few minutes it had looked as if he was going to lose her all over again. They walked back in a silence every bit as complete as when they'd walked out to the meadow…and wholly different.

Seven

It was surprisingly easy to keep the conversation light on the way back to The Vines. Maybe, Dixie thought, because of that stubborn rascal, hope. It was back, messing with her mind, making her think dangerous thoughts.

She reminded herself that they hadn't really settled anything. Certainly nothing inside her felt settled. Cole had toppled several of her fixed ideas about the past, turning the present into unfamiliar territory.

He'd bought her a ring. He'd been planning to ask her to wear it.

Never, not once, had she dreamed that Cole had given any thought to marriage. He'd wanted more than one summer, yes. He'd urged her to take a job in San Francisco so they could continue their affair. She probably would have, too, even though the New York job she'd been offered was better for her professionally. If not for their last big fight she probably would have stayed in California to be close to him.

What if Cole had taken her out, as planned, on her birthday? What if he'd presented her with that ring? Would she have said yes?

She didn't know. That unsettled Dixie more deeply than anything else she'd learned today. For years she'd thought of herself as the one deeply in love, the one most hurt when they couldn't make their relationship work…now she learned that Cole had been ready to commit to her for life. And she wasn't sure if she would have said yes.

Shouldn't she *know?* If she'd been so deeply in love, why hadn't she thought about marriage?

Dixie couldn't find answers for those questions. Maybe it was impossible to see the past clearly through the lens of the present. After all, the woman who'd loved Cole for that short, mad summer was gone.

But the woman who remembered that summer was sitting beside a man who tempted her in ways the younger Cole hadn't. Hope and humor were beguilements she didn't know how to defend against.

Maybe she didn't want to.

By the time they reached The Vines, the sky was grumbling to itself through stacked-up clouds dark with rain. Dixie was congratulating herself on arriving ahead of the storm when she noticed the two unfamiliar cars in front of the big house.

She groaned. "I forgot about the dinner tonight. Should I change? Cancel that," she said with a glance at her watch. "There isn't time." She started digging in her purse, hoping she'd remembered her lipstick.

Cole grinned. "If I say you look fine, am I being supportive or insensitive?"

"Honest, I hope." No lipstick. She grimaced and took out the little brush. At least she could get rid of the tangles.

He got out, came around to her side and opened her door. She finished with her hair, stashed the brush, stepped out—and he took her hands, both of them, carried them to his mouth and pressed a kiss to the back of each, in turn. "Fine doesn't begin to cover it," he said softly. "I'm not sure how to tell you how good you look."

Her cheeks warmed with pleasure. "Try."

He cocked one wicked eyebrow. "I could say you look like a wet dream."

She laughed and pulled her hands back. "Not when I'm going to dinner with your folks, you can't." She slanted him a mischievous look. "But it's okay if you think it."

"I'm thinking," he assured her as they headed for the door.

The living room lay past the foyer and the gallery with its curving staircase, and opened onto the covered lanai where Dixie had sketched Caroline. It was a cheerful blend of antiques and French country accents, with fabrics ranging from the drapes striped in poppy, grass and sunflower to the chairs covered in poppy-and-black toiles.

At the moment, it was full of tense people. One of them was the man Dixie had seen twice now. The Western Man.

She stopped three paces in, astonished and wary. Whatever he was doing here, no one looked very happy about it.

Mercedes stood near the sofa with her boyfriend *du jour*, Craig Bradford—who must have some virtues Dixie had failed to discover, since he'd lasted longer than most. Good looks alone weren't enough to account for that, given her friend's theories about relationships.

Merry looked stunned. Her sister, Jillian, sat on the couch, staring at the stranger and shaking her head slowly, as if she were denying some monstrous question. Across from them, standing nearest their visitor, was Eli.

Eli was furious.

It wasn't obvious, but Dixie had studied that face. She saw the rigid control in the muscles along his jaw and the emotion seething in eyes that burned like green fire.

They all had green eyes, all of Spencer Ashton's children, didn't they?

Dixie's mouth fell open at a sudden, impossible thought. Her gaze swung to the stranger.

"What's going on?" Cole asked, his voice sharp.

Eli's gaze swung to him. "Let me introduce you. This is Grant *Ashton*. Your oldest brother."

"So he says." Merry's voice was flat.

Oh, yes, Dixie thought. Yes, the head shape was the same. The eyes. She'd seen the resemblance the morning she ran into him, but it hadn't occurred to her…

"What the hell—?" Cole's words were more question than curse. He looked from one to the other of them.

"I know this must be a shock. I'm sorry for that." That was the stranger, Western Man…Grant Ashton.

Cole took a step forward, his face hard. "You'd better have some sort of proof."

"He does." Caroline Ashton stood in the doorway to the kitchen, her face pale but composed. "He showed me his parents' marriage license."

"You spoke to him?" Eli asked, scowling.

She nodded. "I'm sorry. I should have been here when he told you. I…he arrived half an hour ago. After I spoke with him, I went to call Lucas. He's on his way back from the city and would have been here soon anyway, but I…I just wanted to talk to him. I should have been here," she repeated. "I'm sorry."

"Never mind that." Jillian hurried to her mother's side. "Are you all right?"

Caroline smiled. "Of course."

"I wasn't going to tell them until you returned," Grant said. "But your daughter found me waiting for you in the lanai and insisted I join the family in here. She was trying to be hospitable to a guest, I suppose," he said wryly. "Then your son asked my name. I wasn't going to make one up."

"No, of course not. And once you told them you were an Ashton, you had to tell them the rest."

"What's the rest?" Cole demanded.

Grant met his eyes levelly. "My parents married young—a shotgun wedding, you might say. People still do that where I come from, or did, back when my mother found out she was pregnant. Until a couple weeks ago, I thought my father died when I was a year old. Turns out he just took off, leaving my mother to raise me and my sister." He paused. "My father's name is Spencer Ashton."

No one moved. No one spoke. Then Cole's sharp bark of laughter broke the silence. "The bastard started young, didn't he?"

Caroline insisted that Grant join them for dinner. It was an awkward meal.

Merry was withdrawn, mostly silent. Jillian was tense. Dixie had noticed that she was sensitive to others' moods, and the overall mood at the table that night was not jolly. Eli barely spoke—and Cole spoke too much, considering that he substituted grilling their guest for polite conversation.

They learned that Grant was from Crawley, Nebraska; that he had a farm there, which his nephew was running while he was gone; that he'd never married, but had raised his niece and nephew; and that he'd tried repeatedly to speak to Spencer, but the man brushed him off.

"I saw you at Charley's," Cole said. "You were trying to talk to him then?"

Grant nodded and buttered a roll.

"I can see why you'd think he owes you something, and he has plenty of money. Are you hoping to—"

"Cole!" Caroline said sharply. "That is quite enough."

"For the record," Grant said levelly, "I do fine, financially. I don't want anything from him. Or you."

Dixie gave him an approving smile. "For the record, Cole isn't always such an ass. It sneaks up on him occasionally."

Mercedes stifled a giggle. Cole turned to Dixie. "Thank you," he said, dry enough to suck the juice from a mummy, "for your unquestioning support."

"Friends don't let friends talk junk. Especially at their mother's table. Why don't we discuss something innocuous for a while, like religion or politics?"

Surprisingly, it was Craig who came to her rescue. "How about sports? I missed the game last Monday and have been hearing about the Patriots' fumble all week."

Lucas picked up that ball and ran with it, and they managed to stagger on through dessert. Dixie saw that Craig had at least one undeniable virtue—he was socially adroit. He helped her keep the conversation going more than once during the interminable meal. So that was why Merry kept him around—he made the perfect fashion accessory.

Pretty to look at, great at small talk, no obvious vices.

Dixie promised herself to find time soon to have a little talk with Merry. But not tonight. They still had to navigate the postdinner shoals.

She was worried about Cole. He'd made an effort to be civil for the rest of the meal, but the anger simmering in him demanded some kind of outlet. There wasn't much she could do about it right now, though.

When they adjourned to the living room, the atmosphere wasn't as tense as it had been immediately following the big revelation. Caroline and Lucas had cornered Cole and were forcing him to discuss some business involving the new chardonnay. Eli was talking to Grant about farming with Mercedes listening in, and Jillian had stepped out of the room for the moment.

That left Dixie with Craig. Unfortunately, he chose that time to demonstrate why he was Mr. Right Now instead of Mr. Right.

They chatted lightly for a few minutes about generalities. Feeling the need to give credit where credit was due, she thanked him for helping out during dinner.

"Glad I could do it." He moved closer and spoke low, as if confiding in her. "Mercedes has some issues about her father. I admired the way you smoothed things over."

"Mmm." The jerk was trying to look down her dress. She frowned and shifted away slightly. "All of them have issues about Spencer, and with reason."

He nodded solemnly. "Learning that he had yet another family that he abandoned was bound to upset them."

"It wasn't Grant's fault, of course, but it's hard not to associate the messenger with the message."

"I'm fortunate," he said. "My father and I get along great. Are you planning to stay in California, Dixie? I hope so."

Uh-oh. "Probably. Is your family from around here?"

"They're in Frisco. But enough about families. I've been wanting to tell you how much I like your work." His voice turned caressing. "Being an unimaginative business grunt, I admire artists. They're so…unconventional. I'd like to get to know you better."

Hints weren't going to work. "Don't you think it's tacky to come on to me with Mercedes in the room?"

He just smiled and reached up to toy with her hair. "Mercedes and I have an understanding. She likes you. I like you. Where's the harm?"

Dixie sighed. "Coming at you from three o'-clock."

He blinked, confused. "What?"

Cole plucked Craig's wineglass from his hand. "Sorry you have to leave so early, Bradford." The glitter in his eyes did not resemble regret.

"I don't have to—"

"Yes, you do." Cole gripped Craig's elbow with one hand and passed the glass to Dixie. "I'll walk you to the door."

March him to the door was more like it. Craig might not have been the brightest bulb on the tree, but he wasn't stupid enough to protest or try to shrug off the hand propelling him to the front door.

Dixie caught Mercedes' eye across the room. Merry shrugged apologetically, which annoyed Dixie no end. Her friend shouldn't be apologizing for the jerk. She should be dumping him.

Definitely they needed to talk.

Cole came back alone. He didn't look satisfied—more like a volcano ready to erupt. His eyes were hot when he snapped at her, "You ought to know better than to flirt with that idiot."

"Hold on," Eli said. "Dixie didn't do anything."

Cole swung around. "You stay out of this."

"Okay," Dixie said, taking Cole's arm. "That's enough. You tried. You made a valiant effort, but it isn't working." She sent a smile around the room. "Sorry to eat and run, but Cole and I need to go jog or chop wood or something."

"It's pouring down rain!" Lucas protested.

"So we'll swim laps. Come on," she said, pulling on Cole's arm. "Your mother does not want you punching your brother in her living room. Either of your brothers. Or anyone else, for that matter."

Cole stared at her a moment, eyes narrowed. Then he nodded curtly, shook off her hand and headed for the door.

He opened it and looked over his shoulder. "Are you coming or not?"

"Coats," she said, delving into the closet. She

didn't have one with her, so she borrowed a raincoat of Merry's. She tossed Cole his windbreaker.

He shrugged into it impatiently. Then they stepped out into the rain.

Eight

Somewhere to the west, unseen in the murk, the sun was setting. There was no wind; the rain fell straight and cold. Dixie buttoned her borrowed raincoat and resigned herself to wet hair and ruined shoes. Cole was headed for the vineyards.

They tramped along the strip of barley planted between the vines, not touching. Halfway to the grove of olive trees he spoke abruptly. "I'm sorry. You weren't flirting."

"No, I wasn't. It isn't me you're mad at."

"I don't know what's wrong with me." He stopped, jammed his hands in his pockets and tilted his face up, letting the rain wash it. Then he shook his head like a dog, scattering more drops, and started walking again. "I've been flying off the handle all day, and for no good reason."

"You hate your father, and his existence has been shoved in your face today."

"He's old news."

"He abandoned you."

"I put all that out of my mind years ago. Lucas has been a father to me, and a good one."

"The problem with stuffing everything into a compartment labeled 'the past' is that the lid can get jarred off."

He gave a single harsh bark of a laugh. "True. Then the ugly spills out. And there's a lot of ugly."

"Whose ugliness are you talking about? Yours? Or your father's?"

"There's plenty to go around, but we'll stick with his for now." The rain had sleeked all the curl from Cole's hair, laying it flat against his skull. He tilted his face up slightly and let the rain wash over it. "He stole my mother's birthright."

A theft that had made Spencer a rich man. Caroline's father had been of the old school, unable to believe that a woman could run a major business. He'd left his shares of the Lattimer Corporation to his son-in-law, not his daughter. Less than a year later, Spencer had left Caroline. "I didn't think you wanted any part of Lattimer Corporation."

"Not now. Not when it's been his so long. I don't want a damned thing that's his."

Yet hate was just a deep, hard form of wanting. Cole wanted fiercely for his father to have been a different sort of person, or at least for Spencer to suffer as he'd caused others to suffer.

"It was during the divorce that he really put the screws to her," Cole went on bitterly.

"What happened then?"

"He grabbed what was left. Money, properties—everything except The Vines."

"But how? What judge would let him do that?"

"How else? Lies, threats and trickery. He told Mom he'd take us away from her if she fought him. He had people ready to testify that she used drugs."

"God," she murmured, rubbing her middle. "He does turn the stomach, doesn't he?"

He didn't say anything for several minutes, then burst out, "How does he do it? Are people like clothes to him? If you get tired of a shirt you throw it away. He gets tired of a family and he throws them away. They don't exist for him after that."

Dixie thought Spencer Ashton sounded like a classic narcissist. Other people weren't real for him, except as echoes or reflections of his own ego. "What was he like when you were little?"

"I thought he liked me." Cole snorted. "I was stupid, obviously, but...sometimes he was great. He used to ruffle my hair when I brought home a good report card and say, 'Way to go, kid.' But it was winning he liked, not me."

"Was he hard to please?"

"More like hard to predict. If things were going badly for him, we all stayed away. He'd take it out on us. But sometimes he'd make a big deal about us.

Birthdays, for example. He liked throwing parties. When I turned six he threw this big bash—clowns, balloons, pony rides for the kids, a catered picnic for their parents."

The faint, wistful tone in his voice tugged at her. She swallowed. "Do you think parties were another way to enhance his own image?"

He shrugged. "They were more about him than me, but I didn't see that as a kid. He didn't come to school stuff, either, but back then I thought important people like him were always busy."

He fell silent. Dixie walked with him, trying not to slide around too much in her slick-soled shoes. Her hair hung in wet rattails down her neck, dripping water beneath the collar of her raincoat. She tugged it to one side.

They reached the little grove of olive trees. It was darker here, but the trees offered some shelter. She stopped. "What about when he left? Kids often blame themselves when their parents break up."

"I don't remember blaming myself exactly, but…" He didn't look at her. "You had it right when you said I hated him. But until he left, I'd tried to be like him."

"You were a kid. You wanted to please your father, and the only thing that pleases a narcissist is his own reflection."

"And I made myself into a damn good reflection, didn't I?"

"No!" She seized his arm, making him turn and look at her. "Where did you get the idea you're like him?"

"Aside from looking in the mirror, you mean?" Rain ran down the taut lines of his face as if the sky were weeping for him. "Come on, Dixie. You're not dense. I've spent years building Louret up so I could prove to the bastard that we didn't need him. That I'm better than he is in the one way that means anything to him—making money."

"You're ambitious, yes. But you don't use people. You'd never discard someone the way he has."

"You left me because I was like him."

Dixie's breath caught, hard and painful, in her chest. Was that what he'd thought? All these years had he believed, deep down, that her leaving proved he was like his father?

"Cole." She reached up with both hands and cupped his hard, wet face between her hands, blinking back tears. "You idiot."

He searched her face. He couldn't have seen much in the dimness, but apparently he saw enough. He had no trouble finding her mouth with his.

His kiss was soft and slow and unbearably moving. He drifted his mouth over her cheek. "You're cold."

"No kidding." But it wasn't cold that made her shiver. It was his fingers playing along her throat.

He wrapped his arms around her and held on tight. "Warmer?" he murmured next to her ear, then kissed it.

She was cold, wet, muddy, and her heart was knocking against the wall of her chest so hard it was a wonder he couldn't hear it. From fear? Arousal? Sheer exhilaration?

Did it matter? She put her hands on his chest. "Not yet," she whispered, the words barely audible over the *shush-shush* of the rain. "Try harder."

This time his mouth meant business. He kissed, licked and sucked, keeping his arms wrapped tightly around her. Her hands were trapped against his chest. She couldn't move—could only tip her head back and meet his tongue with hers. His breath was warm. His body was warm and hard, and she ached.

She wiggled her arms loose, needing to feel the planes and angles and muscle of him. Sliding her hands under his jacket, she found dry cloth heated by warm skin. She couldn't get close enough, touch enough of him.

Cole must have felt the same. He fumbled with the buttons of her coat, making a low sound of frustration when they wouldn't part fast enough to suit him. Using both hands he ripped it open, popping buttons off into the mud. Then his hands were all over her, too—stomach, waist, breasts.

It was a rough wooing. It made her wild.

He ran his hands up her back, then down to her butt, cupping her and pulling her up against him. But he was too tall. He rubbed against her stomach through their clothes—then, when she went up on tiptoe, rubbed lower.

But not low enough. Not quite.

When he pulled her down, she sank with him to the ground, shielded by trees and rain and the gathering darkness. If the earth below her was cold, the rain had made it giving, and the air was sweet with the scents of sage and rain and wet earth.

He held himself up on his hands, his legs tangled with hers and his pelvis pressing against hers. She moaned, the sound lost in the rush of the rain. He brought his face close to hers—then, instead of kissing her, he rubbed his cheek against hers, a sandpaper tenderness that made her breath hitch.

"Dixie," he breathed against her cheek. Just that. Just her name. For a moment they lay tight and close in the damp and the darkness, unmoving. Holding on to each other.

But her body's urgency wouldn't be denied. Her hips lifted, rolled against him. He responded by raising up to gather the skirt of her dress with one hand, then slid his hand between her legs. She jolted at the first touch.

"Now?" he asked. "Now, Dixie?"

"Yes." She pushed up with her feet, lifting her hips, and he yanked down her panties and tossed them away. When she reached for the zipper on his slacks, his hand was already there. Together they freed him. Then he was cupping her bottom with his hands and pushing inside.

The heat and length of him were perfect. But it had been a long time for her, long enough for the muscles to be tight, resistant. She moaned with frustration, in no mood for slow and easy, and thrust up hard. And he filled her.

He gasped out something, but the words were lost in the storms, inner and outer. Slowly he withdrew, and just as slowly returned. Her world narrowed to *now*—to this moment when the ground was soft and chill against her back, and the rain fell in a liquid rush on leaves, on earth and puddles, as Cole slid slowly back inside her.

She gripped his hips and held him there, held him tight against her, wanting to hold on to the moment. To somehow stop time and stay here, like this, with him.

But time and their bodies defeated her. The moment slipped away in a flood of urgency as he began to move—faster, harder, smacking himself into her with thrusts that shoved her into the ground, winding her tighter and tighter until she cried out, her nails digging into arms rigid with tension, her body bucking. She heard him call out as her mind spiraled off into a place where *now* was white and endless.

Slowly her thoughts reassembled. There was a stone digging into her left buttock. Cole lay on top of her, his chest heaving. He was heavy. Her skirt was up around her waist. She was wet, muddy and cold.

And smiling. A few seconds later, she was giggling.

He groaned and propped himself up on his elbows, frowning down at her. "What?"

In answer, she dug her fingers into a particularly squelchy spot of mud on her right side and painted a big stripe down his nose.

He didn't move, didn't speak. Then he snorted— and then he rolled off her onto the cold, wet ground, laughing. "I can't believe I…we…"

"In the mud!" Giggles wound up into laughter. "Both of us, in the mud!"

"Oh, yeah." He was laughing hard now, holding his stomach. "Such romance, such… I swept you off your feet, didn't I?"

"Right off them, and plopped me down in the mud." She began to sing "Some Enchanted Evening" seriously off-key, the words interrupted by giggles.

Cole hummed along, propped up on one elbow, then bent over and kissed her. "I guess this proves I can get down and dirty."

That sent her off into renewed laughter, more than the small joke warranted. But she felt so *good*.

"Come on, my muddy partner in lust." He rolled to his feet, zipped his pants and held out a hand. "Let's get you inside and warmed up."

"My panties," she said, taking his hand and letting him pull her up. "And my shoe," she added when she noticed she was lopsided.

Fortunately, the shoe wasn't far. Cole presented it to her with a bow. But it was almost completely dark now, though the rain had slowed to a drizzle. "I'm afraid the panties are lost in action," he said.

"We have to find them," she insisted, slipping the wet shoe back on. Yuck. It was cold. "Or someone else will."

"No one will know who they belonged to."

"Oh, now I feel better." But when she looked around she knew he was right. She'd never find them in the dark. She slid an arm around his waist, he put his arm around her shoulders, and they started back. "I'm going to have to buy Merry a new raincoat. This one's ruined."

"You're wearing my sister's coat?" he asked, appalled. "I made love to you on my sister's coat?"

She started giggling again.

They made it to the carriage house unobserved—or so she hoped. Surely no one else was idiotic enough to be out at night in this weather. There they left a trail of clothes on their way to the bathroom, where a warm shower chased away the goose bumps.

Steam, proximity and soap-slick skin had an inevitable effect. But this time they could linger over kisses, touch lightly here, tease a little there. She rediscovered the sensitive spot on his throat, and he remembered the place at the end of her spine where a light stroking made her crazy.

Not that he would indulge her, not until they were both dry and horizontal on a clean, warm bed. She had to admit he had a point—but she also had to pay him back for making her wait.

She knew just how to do that. With hands and lips and tongue she explained payback to him, and she showed no mercy.

Neither did he.

Dixie's bedroom was in the loft, and she'd left the curtains open. By the time she lay lax and limp with sweat cooling on her skin, the sky had cleared. The room was awash in moonlight. The only sound was the quiet *tick-tick-tick* of her windup travel clock...and, from downstairs, a faint crunching as Hulk helped himself to a late-night snack.

Hulk...deserted by someone, claimed by her. Just as Cole had rescued an abandoned Tilly.

We're so alike in some ways, so different in others, she thought, snuggling her head a little more cozily into his shoulder. His eyes were closed, but the half smile on his lips said he wasn't sleeping. Just drifting.

She ran her fingers over his chest, loving his skin, his ribs, the small patch of hair right over his heart. Marveling at the fact that she was lying in Cole's arms once more...and in love once more.

Or still? *Who could say?* she thought drowsily, her eyelids heavy. Life sure was strange.

Maybe there had been a little seed, deep in her heart, left behind by the time when she'd loved him before. A seed that had sprouted the day she saw him again, and flourished...nourished in part, she admitted, by lust. Not much doubt that the seed had burst into full, unmistakable bloom when they rolled around in the mud together.

Partners in lust, she thought, and smiled. She and Cole hadn't truly been friends before. They'd been too young—afraid of being hurt, maybe, but also afraid of being fools. Afraid to trust. They'd loved, but with one foot out the door, ready for the moment when the other failed them.

The passion was still there, but this time there was also friendship. A surprising and very dear friendship. This time, they had a chance...if they were patient with each other, willing to be foolish....

Cole's hand, stroking her hair, brought her back from a doze. Her eyelids lifted partway. "Mmm," she said, to encourage him.

"You still with me?"

"Let's see." She wiggled a foot, fluttered the fingers of one hand. "All the parts seem to be in place, but I've misplaced my bones. Think overcooked spaghetti. Melted butter. Jell-O."

"You sound hungry." He was amused, but there was an ounce of hesitation in his next words. "But happy."

"I am." Her eyes were drifting shut again. "Very happy. I'm going to marry you."

Her eyes popped open. She couldn't believe she'd said that.

Neither could Cole, judging by the way he jolted. "What the...you're joking, right?"

She'd never been more serious in her life. But if she said that, Cole would be back in his clothes and out the door in under two minutes. So she mustered a decent chuckle. "How about another bet? If I get you to propose, you have to be my sex slave for a month."

He relaxed and tugged at a strand of her hair. "And if I don't, you're my sex slave? That's an offer I can't refuse. Be prepared to pay up."

His obvious relief hurt. But she had an uphill road to climb, and she knew it. She'd left Cole once. That was the one unforgivable sin in his book. He had a tendency to shove people who left him into a mental box and leave them there, where they couldn't hurt him again.

But as she'd told him, the problem with boxes was that their lids could pop off. Dixie meant to do anything and everything she could to break out of whatever mental compartment Cole had shoved her in. So she teased him, keeping things light, until he dozed off.

Then she plotted.

Words weren't going to win Cole. Eleven years ago she'd told him she loved him, and she'd left him anyway. If you want to convince a man of something, she decided, you needed to use man-language. And man-language means actions, not words.

How would a man go about convincing a woman he was serious?

Dixie smiled, snuggled close to the man sleeping beside her, and laid her plans.

Nine

The sun was shining brightly through Cole's office window three days later as he punched in a number he'd gotten from a friend. He glanced at his watch as a phone rang on the other end. He needed to get this taken care of before Dixie showed up. She was taking him to lunch today, and he didn't want her to know about…

"Hampstead Investigations," a female voice said in his ear.

"My name is Cole Ashton. I'd like to speak with Mr. Hampstead about an investigation."

"I'd be happy to make an appointment for you, sir."

"I prefer to speak with Mr. Hampstead first."

"Very well. He's on another line. Can you hold for a moment?"

Cole agreed, tapping his fingers on the desk. He caught sight of the orchid sitting on the corner of his desk and his lips curved unwillingly. It looked right there somehow.

Dixie had had it delivered the day after they made love. The next day she'd given him a box of chocolate-covered pecans, and yesterday she'd brought him a small, exquisitely wrapped box. That turned out to be cuff links—handmade, with turquoise set in heavy silver. They'd looked alarmingly expensive, but when he'd protested she'd laughed and said a friend of hers made them.

It was almost as if she was courting him.

Get real, he told himself, glancing at his watch again. This was Dixie. She was playing at role reversal and enjoying the game, that was all.

A pleasant tenor came on the line. "This is Frank Hampstead, Mr. Ashton. How may I help you?"

"I've a confidential family matter I need investigated. I prefer not to drive down to the city right now to see you in person." Cole felt foolish enough about consulting a private investigator. He didn't want to feel foolish in person. "I'm hoping we can arrange things over the phone."

"I generally insist on meeting my clients, sir. You'd be amazed at what some people will do— using a fake name, for example, which complicates the billing process considerably."

"Abe said you'd feel that way." The friend Cole

named was an attorney with a great many connections in this part of the state.

A spark of interest entered the other man's voice. "Abe Rosenberg?"

"Yes, I got your name from him. He suggested you could call him to establish my bona fides."

Hampstead put Cole on hold again while he called Abe. Cole drummed his fingers and looked at the orchid sitting there so bright and exotic.

He wasn't going to take her seriously. That's where he'd gone wrong before, thinking Dixie meant the love words she'd spoken. He supposed she had, at the time. But for Dixie, *I love you* didn't mean *I want to be with you forever.*

He'd enjoy her, enjoy their affair and keep his heart out of it. When it ended, he'd wish her well…and maybe they could remain friends. He found that he really wanted that. If ending their affair meant losing her altogether again…

"Sorry to keep you waiting, Mr. Ashton," Hampstead said. "Tell me about this family matter you need information about. Confidentiality," he added, "is a given."

"It's complicated." Cole paused. He hated discussing his father, but this was necessary. Briefly he explained about the recent advent of Grant "Ashton" into their lives. "I've no real reason to doubt him," Cole finished. "But no reason to believe him, either, and I need to know the truth. The marriage license he showed us doesn't prove anything. I don't know how one goes about obtaining a fraudulent marriage license, but it must be possible."

"And there is potentially a great deal of money involved," Hampstead agreed. "You're wise to be cautious."

As far as Cole was concerned, if Grant wanted to try to swindle Spencer Ashton out of some part of his fortune, more power to him. Cole wouldn't allow his family to be hurt by the man, however. "I don't want anyone to know I'm having him investigated. My family has accepted Grant. They'd be upset if they knew I'd sicced a private eye on him."

"No problem. I only report to my client, and there should be no need to ask questions of any of your family members."

"So is this marriage something you can prove or disprove definitely?"

"Certainly. I'll need a few more specifics from you, then we'll go over my fees."

They wrapped up the conversation and were going over the detective's rates and expenses when something tapped on Cole's window. He looked that way, puzzled.

The sky was completely clear, and he was on the second floor. He must have imagined it. "That's acceptable," he told Hampstead. "You have my number. When can I expect to hear from you?"

"Perhaps in a few days, but all sorts of things can complicate this sort of investigation. Many older records are not in computer databases. If I have to check courthouse records in person, for example, it will take longer."

Plink. Plink-plink.

"And cost more, obviously," Cole said, pushing his chair back. "Fine. Let me know when you learn something." They exchanged obligatory goodbyes, and Cole disconnected. Frowning, he got up and went to the window.

Another pebble hit it as he arrived. And below, ready to toss more missiles his way, was Dixie…on the back of his mother's horse, with his horse in tow. She wore jeans, a denim jacket with a hot pink T-shirt and a battered black cowboy hat.

Cole shook his head, grinning. God only knew where she'd gotten the hat. He opened the window and leaned out. "You don't know how to ride."

"And yet here I am, on a horse. I must have learned at some point." Her face was tilted up to him, her grin as wide-open as the day. "Come along quietly now, and no one will get hurt. You're being kidnapped."

Dixie might be all play, but she was incredibly fun to play with. He shook his head. "Uh-uh. I want to be the bad guy. You can be the marshal and arrest me."

"This is an abduction," she told him severely. "Marshals do not abduct people. Besides, I've got the black hat. I get to be the outlaw."

Cole was grinning as he took the stairs two at a time. He could faintly hear one of the girls in the tasting room giving her spiel, so he took the rear exit.

They had a bad habit of introducing him to the tourists if he walked through at the wrong time, and he didn't feel like making nice to the customers right now. He wanted to see Dixie.

"You look great," he said as he came up to her, laying a hand on her knee. "Almost as if you knew what you were doing."

"Of course I do. Riding's easy. There's no clutch to worry about."

"Thank God." Cole had vivid memories of trying to teach Dixie how to drive a standard transmission. He ran a hand over the girth. "Seems tight, but Trouble has a bad habit of holding his breath." He went to his horse, who was trying to snatch a bite of grass.

"Don't you trust me to get it right?" she demanded.

"Did you saddle them?" The girth was fine.

She flashed a dimple at him. "No."

He laughed. "I didn't think so."

"So I'm not a cowgirl. I did make the picnic food. We've got a beef and sausage tart, marinated baby veggies and—hey!"

Tilly rounded the front corner of the building at a dead run. Trouble sidestepped, throwing his head back. Cole grabbed for the reins. "Damn that cat of yours! Let go before he pulls you off!"

But it wasn't Dixie's cat in pursuit this time. It was a Doberman.

Tilly made for Cole, who was trying to keep Trouble from trampling both of them. Cole hollered at the

Doberman, hoping to scare him off—which scared Tilly, who yelped and retreated.

The Doberman slowed but was growling, hackles raised, looking as if he meant to rip out Tilly's throat. Caroline's mare was normally a placid creature, but this was too much for her. She reared. Dixie slid off just as the Doberman hurled himself at Tilly.

And Hulk launched himself at the Doberman.

The cat seemed to have come out of nowhere. He landed on the dog's shoulders and rode him like a bronc buster—only with claws instead of a saddle for purchase. They served him well. The Doberman yelped and yelped again as he began running in circles.

Trouble was panicked, trying to get away. Cole didn't dare let go, but he wanted desperately to check on Dixie, who was sitting up, cradling her arm. "Are you all right?" he called.

A man came around the corner—large, red faced and yelling. "Dammit, Mustard, I said—hey! Get your cat off my dog!"

Cole swung toward him. "You're the owner of this animal?"

"Damn right I am, and if he's hurt, you'll be hearing from me!"

Hulk made his own dismount, a graceful leap to the ground followed by a bounce up to a high windowsill. Which was probably where he'd come from in the first place. The Doberman beat a quick retreat to his owner, tail between his legs.

Cole, still gripping Trouble's reins, advanced on the red-faced man, who was checking his trembling dog for wounds. "That dog," he said softly, "very nearly caused a disaster. What is your name, sir?"

"Ralph Endicott. But you can't go blaming it all on my poor Mustard. He's bleeding, dammit!"

Cole glanced down. The wounds weren't serious, but puncture wounds did need to be treated properly. "Then you'll take him to a vet."

"Which *you* are going to pay for! That stupid mutt running around loose caused all this. Mustard wouldn't have gotten away from me if—"

"My name," Cole interrupted, his voice very soft and very cold, "is Cole Ashton. My dog is allowed to roam the grounds of my winery and vineyard. Yours is not. I require the name of your insurance company. And your lawyer, if you have one."

The color drained from the man's face. "Insurance? Lawyer? Now, see here, there's no need for all that."

"There damn sure is!" Dixie marched up, face glowing with wrath. "Your failure to control your animal is negligent, possibly criminal! I've sprained my wrist! I can't paint with a sprained wrist. Do you know how much this delay is going to cost Louret? My time alone is worth several thousand, and if this messes up their ad schedule, the television time already purchased will run to—hey, come back here!"

But the man was in full flight, one hand gripping

his dog's collar as he hurried back around the building, heading for the parking lot, and escape.

"You'd better take care of your dog!" Dixie hollered after him.

That night, Cole and Dixie lay in a sweaty heap in the bed at the carriage house, talking about Tilly's adventure. Dixie's sprained wrist had forced them to be inventive in their lovemaking. The results had been memorable.

"I *ought* to have sued that man," she grumbled. "This wrist is going to put me behind."

Cole was just glad a sprained wrist was all the hurt she'd taken. When he'd seen her go sailing off the mare's back... "You frightened him badly enough already," he said soothingly.

"I was just following your lead. Did you see the way the blood drained from his face when you mentioned lawyers?"

"Some people only pay attention when money's involved." Like his father. Cole turned the subject. "Tilly's change of heart is downright spooky."

Dixie chuckled. "You think *you're* spooked. Hulk really doesn't know how to act."

Ever since Hulk rescued Tilly from the Doberman, the dog had been following the cat with big, liquid, adoring eyes.

Cole shook his head. "I never saw a cat take on a big dog that way. Pretty smart, getting on his back where the dog couldn't get to him."

"That part's instinct. Usually they only do it if

they're cornered, though. I guess Hulk didn't want anyone else messing with his dog."

Cole snorted. "He thought the Doberman was coming after him."

"Cynic." She yawned and snuggled closer.

He ran his hand down her hair. He loved having her close enough to pet this way. "There's an art deco exhibition in Frisco this weekend. I hoped you could go with me."

"Wish I could," she said sleepily. "Weekends I stay with Aunt Jody."

For some reason that surprised Cole. She'd moved back to help take care of her aunt, so of course she'd spend time there. Yet somehow he hadn't thought of her giving up every weekend…that's where she'd been last weekend, he realized. When he'd thought she was out playing with her current boyfriend.

He grimaced. His assumptions obviously needed adjusting. "Um…she needs round-the-clock care?"

"She can't be left alone. Mom stays with her on weekdays—she's retired now, and living with her fiancé, so she can do that. We've got a home health aide who stays with her at night during the week."

That would add up fast. As delicately as possible he asked, "Is money an issue?"

"Right now we're managing okay. Aunt Jody had accumulated a pretty good nest egg for retirement, and her insurance covers most of the medical stuff. Not long-term care, though."

"I'll go with you this weekend and help." The offer slipped out unplanned, which made him uneasy. He wasn't used to making impulsive decisions. But it was the right thing to do…wasn't it?

Dixie lifted her head, then propped herself up with one arm to study his face. "Are you sure? It's a lot like taking care of a child. A large, sometimes angry child."

"I'm sure." Of course it was the right thing to do. It was the sort of thing you did for a friend, after all. He wasn't making any kind of commitment, just giving up a weekend. Big deal.

Her slow smile dawned. "Thanks, then," she said, and kissed him lightly on the lips.

Usually Aunt Jody went to bed early, in part because of her medication, but she'd been delighted to have a man around. By the time Dixie washed up in the upstairs bathroom and headed down the hall to the guest room where she and Cole were sleeping, she was exhausted.

Cole had been wonderful with Aunt Jody. When she'd come downstairs for dinner with lipstick smeared in fat circles on her cheeks in honor of his visit, he'd flirted with her gently.

Dixie had had to leave the room to cry. Jody had always been immaculate about her appearance. Elegant.

"Sorry I ducked out on you earlier," she said as she padded up to the bed.

"I tagged along to help, not to issue demerits. You're doing enough of that yourself." He held the covers up invitingly, and she climbed in beside him.

"You think you aren't supposed to have feelings about what's happening to your aunt?"

"Mama would have just smiled. It doesn't get to her like it does me." Dixie sighed and nestled close. "It's not that she doesn't care. She does, deeply. She just handles it better."

Dixie had always loved her mother…but, she admitted, she hadn't always respected her. Helen had depended on men for so much, and they'd let her down, over and over. Even Dixie's father had let her down by dying.

Years ago, Dixie had decided she wanted to be like her aunt, bold and independent, not like her mother. She was being forced to see them both in a new light. And herself.

"Your mom handles it differently than you," Cole said. "Different isn't better. Maybe it doesn't hurt her as much to see Jody being childish because she remembers her being a child. You don't. The only Jody you knew was the adult."

"Why does she have to lose that?" Dixie burst out. "She built the person she was, year by year, and now it's all being taken away!"

"I don't know, sugar." He stroked her hair. "I don't know."

Dixie was silent a few moments. "I get scared. It could happen to me."

"To any of us. And it is scary."

Cole continued stroking, and it helped. He'd helped all weekend, just by being there. He'd offered to come here with her, and that meant so much…too much? The quick spurt of fear made her bite her lip. She was relying on him too much, wanting him to be there for her, like this, from now on. That wasn't healthy…

No, she told herself. Hadn't she learned anything? She was afraid of relying on others, yes. And maybe she had reason. But pure independence didn't exist. People had to help others sometimes, but being willing to help wasn't enough. Sometimes you had to be willing to accept help, and that was a lot harder.

For her, anyway. But watching her aunt had shown her that pure self-sufficiency was an illusion.

Her eyes began to drift shut. "Sorry," she murmured. "I'm really tired."

"Then sleep. You're not my personal houri," he said, an edge to his voice. "I'll survive not having sex for one night."

That stung, mostly because there was some truth in his assumption that she felt obliged to offer sex. She didn't like seeing that about herself.

Eleven years ago, she'd believed he was mainly interested in her because of the sex, yet he'd been ready to propose. And she hadn't had a clue…his fault, in part. He'd pulled back emotionally. But she'd screwed up, too. She'd begun to depend on him, and that had scared her even more than losing him. Leaving him had been incredibly painful, yet easier than staying and facing her fears.

Not this time, she promised herself as her eyes closed. She wouldn't run away again.

Cole watched the woman sleeping in his arms. In the moon-washed darkness he could see the way sleep erased the troubles from her face. He thought he could even make out a few of the pale freckles on her nose.

Why was she so hard on herself? All weekend he'd seen a woman who found the strength to laugh with Cole at some of her aunt's absurdities, such as her conviction that they had a king, not a governor, who lived in a castle in Hollywood. Dixie had been endlessly patient, letting the older woman tell the same story again and again, acting just as interested the fifth time as the first.

At one point Jody had grown angry because Dixie wouldn't let her slice the tomatoes. She'd kicked her niece. Dixie had told her firmly that kicking wasn't allowed and gone on fixing supper.

Cole had distracted Jody at that point, but how many times had Dixie had to deal with that sort of thing when no one was around to help? And all Dixie could think about was how much better she ought to be handling things.

Had she been like this before, and he'd failed to notice? Because this wasn't the flighty, inconstant woman he'd remembered…that he'd been determined to remember, he thought with a strange ache beneath his breastbone. This was a woman who would stick by a man…if she truly loved him.

Apparently she hadn't loved Cole enough.

That was past, he told himself fiercely. They were

lovers again, but this time they weren't in love. At least, she wasn't.

Cole swallowed. He'd come close, painfully close, to falling for her all over again. He had to pull back. He didn't want this affair to end with her out of his life completely—because it would end. She'd left him before, and she would leave him again.

Not because she was lacking. Because he was.

But she wanted him. He knew that very surely. And he would use it.

Ten

Cole was pulling back. Just as he had before.

"I'm still not sure about leaving those two alone together," he said darkly as he signaled for the turn.

"Relax. Hulk has decided he likes having a groupie."

"More like an acolyte. Your cat has stolen my dog."

Dixie chuckled. "He's never had a dog of his own before. I didn't know he wanted one."

She was imagining things, she told herself. Cole liked to keep things light and friendly, yes, but that was no change. Just because he hadn't spent every one of the past five nights with her didn't mean he'd lost interest. They were on the way to his cabin now, weren't they? And he certainly hadn't looked disinterested when he invited her. He'd promised her a tour, dinner and a fire in the fireplace, and had asked her to wear her blue sundress, the one with the full skirt and buttons all the way down. He had designs on her buttons, he'd said.

She had to be patient. Just because he wasn't tumbling back into love as fast as she had didn't mean he wouldn't fall eventually. It would take time, that's all. Trust wouldn't come easily for him.

"You had your suitcase out when I picked you up," Cole said casually. "You aren't leaving yet, are you?"

"Hmm?" Dixie dragged her attention back. "No, not for another week or so. My wrist has delayed things. Didn't your mom tell you?"

"Tell me what?"

"She asked Grant to stay awhile. He's going to move into the carriage house, so I'm moving to your old room in the big house. We'd have to make other arrangements soon anyway, wouldn't we?" she added when he didn't respond. "I'll be through with all the preliminary work soon."

"And then?" he asked in an even voice.

"I'll do the paintings at my studio." Trying not to sound insecure she added, "I'm assuming you're interested in more than a couple of weeks together."

He hesitated a moment. "I'm up for a longer run if you are."

It wasn't the kind of response designed to lift her heart. Anxiety twisted in her gut, but she kept her voice dry. "Try not to overdo the hearts and flowers. You'll embarrass me."

In answer he reached out and took her hand. It helped...some.

They reached the cabin at dusk. Dixie was thinking of the other time she'd been here, without going inside. Maybe Cole was, too. He didn't say much, just opened the door, turned on the light and gestured for her to go inside.

It was not what she'd expected. "But this is fabulous!" she said, turning in a slow circle.

"Thought I'd screwed it up when I said I did the work myself, didn't you?"

"Partly." She slanted him a mischievous glance. "And partly I thought you'd go for something safer, more traditional. This looks as if an upscale designer planned it."

"Don't insult me." But he looked pleased. "I didn't do it all myself—I needed the experts to replace a load-bearing wall with those wooden pillars, and remove part of the top floor over the living area."

The entire downstairs, save for the bathroom in one corner, was one big room, with half of it two stories high. The stone fireplace was original, he said, but he'd put in the plank floors himself. He'd also replaced the Sheetrock and applied the Venetian plaster. It was a warm terra-cotta with golden undertones. "I'm impressed. I think you've invented a new style—European rustic."

"I haven't done much to the kitchen, I'm afraid."

"I'd sort of guessed that," she said dryly, looking at an avocado-green stove, a refrigerator that belonged in a museum and the single counter covered in worn Formica. "Did you ever learn how to cook?"

"Sure. I can scramble eggs with the best of them."

"If I didn't know we'd brought dinner with us, I'd be worried."

They ate on a thick, faded Oriental carpet in front of the fire—enchiladas from one of Napa's best Mexican restaurants, followed by strawberries dipped in chocolate.

And wine, of course. A rich merlot from Louret's vineyards with dinner, and French champagne with dessert. "This did not come from your winery," she pointed out.

"Nope. But I've a fondness for bubbles." He topped off her glass—again.

"Are you trying to get me drunk?" Dixie asked, amused. She sipped. "You must be hoping to have your way with me."

"You know, I believe I am."

None of the lights were on. There was just the fire to warm his skin with its orange glow, and in the dimness, Cole's eyes looked very dark, his smile secretive. "You've been having fun with your courting games. My turn now." He reached forward and gently removed the glass he'd just filled. "I think we'll get started. We're doing things my way tonight, Dixie."

Something in his voice tugged at her belly. "I can handle that."

"Can you?" He leaned in and kissed her softly, lingering over it. "You like games," he murmured against her lips.

"Mmm-hmm." She drew a line along his bottom lip with her tongue.

"And you like being in charge." He pulled back slightly, smiling. "In control."

"Sometimes." She threaded a hand into his hair to bring his mouth back.

"Uh-uh." He shook his head, still smiling...not letting her have the kiss she wanted. "We're playing a different game tonight. And you aren't in charge."

Her heartbeat kicked up. She raised one eyebrow. "No?"

"No." He reached into the basket that had held their dinner and pulled out a long red scarf. He played with it, pulling it through his hands like a silky snake. "You trust me, don't you?"

"Of course." But her mouth was dry.

"Good. Hold out your hands."

She hesitated, eyeing that scarf. "What kind of game did you have in mind?"

He just smiled. And waited.

After a moment she shrugged. "In for a penny," she said, and held out her hands.

He looped the scarf around them and tied it. The silk was cool against her skin...which was probably two degrees hotter than it had been a minute ago. "Bondage. I've never..." Her laugh came out nervous. "What do I do now?"

"Nothing." He leaned in again and kissed her

lightly, brushing his fingertips along her throat, light as a butterfly kiss. "I do it all. You aren't in control tonight, Dixie."

"I don't think I'm good at that."

"This isn't about being good. Or being good at something." He reached for her buttons. "I do like this dress," he murmured, and slid the first button loose. Then the next.

He worked slowly, button by button, all the way down. She sat there with her hands bound in silk and watched him looking at what he revealed. His heavy eyelids lifted slightly to pass her a smile when he finished. Then he parted the dress.

She wasn't wearing a bra. The way her hands were tied snugged her arms into her breasts, squeezing them together. Her breath was coming faster. "You like?" she asked, her voice husky.

"Oh, yeah." This time when he leaned close, he bent. He laved one areola slowly with his tongue, then flicked it over the nipple. She squirmed. "Hold still," he told her, and put his mouth on her other nipple, sucking lightly. "There." He sat back. "I like the way they look, wet and shiny from my mouth."

She liked the look on his face. But he was going too slowly, and she wanted to touch him. "I'm getting a little overheated."

He cocked an eyebrow at her. "The fire too hot?"

"Something is."

"Maybe you're overdressed for the occasion."

"We could take off the scarf."

He shook his head. "My game," he said softly, and

drifted his fingertips down the slopes of both breasts to their tips. He took them between his fingers and squeezed rhythmically. "But we can make you a little more comfortable. Why don't you lie down?"

He was playing with her mind as well as her breasts. And winning. The ache between her legs pulsed along with his fingers. "I…" *Am finding it hard to breathe.* "You'll have to let go first. And my hands…lying down is awkward without hands."

"Oh," he said, as if surprised. "Of course. I'll help you." And at last he looked at her face again—and in his eyes was pure heat. When he leaned close and took her mouth this time, he wasn't slow and careful.

She kissed him back, half-frantic with the need to touch, yet it was incredibly erotic to be able to touch him only with her lips, her tongue. She felt his hands at her shoulders, lowering her to the floor.

But he didn't follow her down and cover her with his body the way she craved. When he pulled away, she cried out in frustration.

"Easy," he said soothingly, stroking her legs, pushing the dress completely apart so that it puddled on the floor on either side of her. "Easy," he told her again, and put his mouth on her, right through her panties.

She jolted, so aroused that the damp warmth almost immediately brought her to the edge.

Then he stopped.

"I'm going to…" she sputtered, but couldn't think of the right threat. Maybe because she couldn't think, period. "Dammit, Cole!"

"You're not used to this. You aren't in control at all. I am." He tugged on her panties, pulling them down an inch at a time.

She narrowed her eyes. "You're enjoying this too much."

Briefly his grin flashed. "Define 'too much.' I am for damn sure enjoying myself."

That glimpse of his grin relaxed her, reminding her that this was a game. But she was finding it harder and harder to play. "I'm not sure I like feeling this vulnerable."

He tossed her panties aside. "How does this feel? Is it exciting?"

He put one finger inside her—and yes, it was exciting. Beyond exciting. She couldn't keep from moving. Two fingers… "Cole."

"Soon, sweetheart," he crooned. "Let me play a little more." Three fingers, in and out, the rhythm driving her crazy. Then his thumb pressed lightly on her, and she exploded.

Aftershocks pinged through her. She lay motionless, her eyes closed, trying to catch her breath, her muscles wasted…and she ached. Ached fiercely. After a moment she felt him, smooth and blunt, probing at her entrance, and lifted heavy eyelids. He'd scrambled out of his clothes while her eyes were closed, and at last was as naked as she.

"The scarf," she whispered, holding up her bound hands. "Take it off." She needed to be able to touch as well as be touched. Needed more than pleasure.

He paused. The arms he propped himself up with

were so rigid they shook. There was no play left in his eyes, only hunger and something akin to desperation.

He shoved inside. His face spasmed, and he groaned. And then, with shaky hands, he untied the scarf.

She gasped with relief and reached for him, and they made the last part of the journey together. It was a quick, rough climb, and if her second climax didn't hit with the force of the first, this one satisfied.

And afterward, with his weight heavy and limp on top of her, she lay there for a long while in the dying firelight, stroking him. Feeling the need to soothe him. As if he were the one who'd been pushed to the limit and beyond.

And she didn't know why. She didn't understand at all.

Eleven

Sweat rolled down Cole's forehead, stinging his eyes, as his feet thudded on the path near his cabin. He'd forgotten the sweatband—had pulled on his shorts and a T-shirt, shoved his feet into his running shoes and taken off.

The morning was barely broken, the sun a sliver at the horizon. The air was chilly—or had been, before he started running.

Too late echoed in his head with every footfall. He pushed himself a little faster.

It was amazing what a fool he'd been, thinking he could just enjoy Dixie. Thinking love was a decision, or something he could avoid, like stepping out of the way of a speeding car. Nope, no thanks, don't want to get hit today.

Too late.

Or that love could be made into play. That's all he'd meant by that game with the scarf—some sexy game. With, maybe, a whiff of the need to keep her interested, make her want to continue the affair.

Somewhere along the line it had taken a serious turn. He'd wanted her tied and bound to him. Forever.

Too late.

This morning he'd woken up reaching for her. She hadn't been there, of course. He'd taken her back to The Vines last night—a move born of panic, he admitted. She'd be sleeping now, sleeping in the room he'd moved out of years ago.

Too late, he thought, his feet dragging to a stop. He stood with his head down, his hands on his thighs, dragging in air. Maybe it had been too late from the moment she walked into his office again after an eleven-year absence.

He was in love with Dixie. Desperately in love. He was running because that's what he wanted to do—run away from the feeling. From her. It was impossible, of course. He couldn't escape what he felt. Not the love. Not the fear, either.

Or maybe he could—the fear, anyway. If he left her.

Cole had been terrified of going to the dentist as a child. When he was ten, he'd realized that the fear was as bad as the event, maybe worse. He hadn't conquered it, but he had stopped putting it off. It would happen whether he delayed or not, so why wait, dragging out the fear?

But dental visits truly couldn't be avoided. Was losing Dixie just as inevitable?

He'd been telling himself he knew she would leave. Maybe not for months, but eventually she would go. But now, faced with the prospect of living with the fear of losing her or walking away himself, he discovered a stubborn core of hope.

There were the gifts she'd given him, the orchid and chocolates, the cufflinks. Just yesterday she'd given him a goofy card, telling him sternly, "Take note. Women *love* to get cards. You get extra points for a blank card that you write in yourself."

He'd told himself they were part of the game for her, but they'd gotten to him underneath, where words don't reach.

There was the way they laughed together, too, and the sheer comfort he felt with her sometimes. And sometimes, when she was looking at him, her face seemed to glow—not with the blazing heat of desire, but a gentler warmth, like a welcoming candle. Was that just friendship? And when she'd reached for him last night as he entered her...that had felt very like love.

If only he could know, one way or the other!

Cole ran his forearm over his forehead, wiping off the sweat that was chilling him as it dried. He'd better keep moving. He'd stiffen up if he just stood here.

Slowly he started back to the cabin. He could ask her what she felt for him. That was as logical as it was terrifying. But what would it prove? Even if she said she was passionately in love, could he believe her? She'd spoken of love before. It hadn't kept her from leaving.

He had to be sure of her. One way or the other, he had to know.

Moving faster now, he laid his plans.

"Look, I'm sorry," Cole said, rubbing the back of his neck with the hand that wasn't holding the phone. "This came up unexpectedly, and I can't get out of it."

Silence.

This wasn't part of his plan. He'd put off seeing her for two days, citing work—he'd been spending a lot of time with her, he'd said, and had to catch up. It was halfway true, but the real reason was that he needed to see if she'd take off.

Having a genuine business emergency hadn't been part of his plan. "I'll make it up to you for canceling tonight. We'll go out Friday. Maybe to that new club—"

"I'll be at my aunt's on Friday night."

Right. "Okay, Thursday. We'll do whatever you want."

More silence, then: "Are you getting that déjà vu feeling? I used to hear that a lot. Or maybe you aren't feeling anything at all. That would be safer, wouldn't it?"

"Dammit, Dixie, I didn't conjure this guy out of thin air. He's the rep for a major distributor, and if he wants to talk about carrying our new chardonnay, I'm for damn sure going to talk to him. He's only in town for this one day."

"And no one else can handle this?"

"Lucas is down with a stomach bug. Mercedes and Jillian don't know enough about the production end, or where else we're committed. And Eli wouldn't know what kind of volume discount to agree to. Besides, he's lousy at this sort of thing."

"You're doing it again. Hiding behind work, finding excuses to pull back."

"Don't be childish," he snapped. "I can't dance attendance on you every minute."

The sudden dial tone in his ear made him wince. *Way to go, Ashton.* But it was the thickness he'd heard in her voice that haunted him as he got ready for his meeting. It had sounded a lot like tears.

"Dixie?" Mercedes paused in the doorway. "What's wrong?"

"Nothing." Furious at being caught crying, she wiped away the evidence.

"Right," Merry said dryly, coming into Dixie's room—the one that used to be Cole's. "I know. You're feeling sentimental because it's National Oatmeal Month."

"Always gets to me." Dixie sniffed. "National Opposites Day is coming up, too."

"And Ben Franklin's birthday. Another big occasion."

This was a game they'd played back in college, when any excuse to shop, eat chocolate or sleep in late was a good excuse. Congress was always making special days that no one paid any attention to,

Dixie had told Merry. It was their solemn duty to see that no occasion went unobserved.

"Is it National Hugging Day yet?" Dixie's smile was a tad watery, but she did feel better.

"Close enough." Merry honored the almost-occasion by giving Dixie a hug. "So what's up? Your work going okay?"

Dixie flopped her hand in a so-so gesture. In fact, work was going fine—so well that she was dragging out the last sketches so she'd have an excuse to stay at The Vines a little longer.

Merry sat on the bed beside her. "Your aunt?"

"Not this time. Your brother."

"Uh-oh. I thought things were going great with you two. Tell me what's wrong. As long as it doesn't involve sex," she added hastily. "I do not want to hear about your sex life when it's my brother you're having sex with."

"Oh, no. The sexual part of our relationship makes me scream with joy, not cry."

Merry looked pained.

Dixie's grin hardly wobbled at all. "Okay, okay. No sex talk. The thing is…oh, I don't know what the thing is."

She shoved to her feet and started pacing. "He's giving me these mixed signals. I'm trying not to mention sex, but that is part of it. When we're together that way, it feels important. Like I truly matter to him. But if I so much as mention the future, he turns vague. Casual."

I'm up for a longer run if you are. She sniffed

again, but more in scorn than sorrow this time. Even if they'd been having a purely casual affair, that comment lacked grace.

"Lots of men have trouble committing," Merry offered. "It takes them longer to admit what they're feeling. You two haven't been back together very long, Dixie."

"I know, but…oh, everything I could mention sounds trivial. I haven't seen him for two days, and he just canceled our dinner tonight. That shouldn't be a big deal, and yet…it's not what he does, but the way he does it. I feel like it's happening all over again," she finished sadly. "Just like eleven years ago. I can feel his walls going up."

And she wasn't sure she could handle it. All the pep talks in the world didn't stop the hurt. Or the doubts. How could she make herself believe she could count on Cole when, for no reason she could see, he suddenly started tacking up Keep Out signs?

Merry didn't say anything for several moments. "Cole's got walls," she admitted. "Big, high, scary ones. Half the time you seem to slip in under them easier than anyone. The other half, you trigger them."

"Yeah." Dixie plopped down on the bed again. "I'm scared."

"Goes with the territory, unless you're sensible enough to be like me and just date losers. No gain, no pain, I always say."

"I've been meaning to talk to you about Craig," Dixie began.

"Uh-uh. No. Not today. You can give me advice after you get your love life straightened out."

"When I'm seventy, you mean?"

"If you're lucky."

Dixie sighed. Cole had promised they'd get together tomorrow night. Maybe she should press him for some frank talk. Or would that be pushing for too much, too soon?

Never mind. She'd think of something. "How about a girls' night out tonight?"

"Sorry." Merry carefully removed a piece of fuzz from her slacks. "Wednesdays I have supper with Jared. Used to be the three of us, but..." She shrugged. "We've kept it up since Chloe died. It seemed to help him, especially at first, to have someone to talk with about her. We've become good friends."

Dixie slid her a curious glance. Chloe had been a friend of theirs in college. She and Merry had stayed close afterward, since they lived nearby. But a standing dinner date with Chloe's widower six years after Chloe's death? That sounded like more than friendship...but then, who was she to say?

Merry was right. Dixie needed to get her own life figured out before she tried to straighten out anyone else's.

"I need to paint," she said suddenly. "Or go mess with paint, anyway."

An art therapy session might tell her what she needed to know—even if she wasn't sure she wanted to learn it.

* * *

Thursday afternoon Cole stared at the faxed report in his hand. His brain felt numb. Fuzzy. Rain beat against the office window. The only light came from his desk lamp. All else had faded into gloom with the arrival of the storm.

He shook his head. This couldn't be right. There had to be some mistake. He reached for the phone and punched in the number of the detective who'd investigated Grant Ashton.

Fifteen minutes later the numbness was gone. Rage gathered in its place, questions ping-ponged around in his head—and beneath all lay a vast bewilderment.

The detective would bill him. How was he supposed to sign the check? *Cole Ashton*...that's who he was, who he had been all his life.

He could have become Cole Sheppard when he was ten. Lucas had wanted to adopt them, but Spencer had refused to relinquish his rights. He hadn't wanted his children, but he hadn't wanted anyone else to claim them, either.

And now he'd made Cole's entire life into a lie.

Cole slammed his fist down on the desk. "Damn him!" He jerked to his feet, grabbed his jacket and headed for the door. And didn't notice that his jacket had brushed against the delicate orchid sitting on one corner of his desk, sending it crashing to the floor.

Twelve

Cole drove for hours. Drove through the rage and into bitterness. Passed from that to bewilderment and questions, many of which couldn't be answered from behind the wheel of his Suburban. But they could be listed mentally, ordered, given consideration and assigned priorities. He drove until, finally, he had to pull over at a motel and sleep before he killed himself and maybe others.

Hours later, he woke to the sound of traffic. Light streamed through the cracks between the wall and the fiberglass drapes. He was fully dressed, the bed beneath him was hard, and there was a water stain on the ceiling.

For a moment he had no idea where he was or

how he'd gotten there. Slowly memory seeped back.
With it came another fact.

Today was Friday. The day that regularly arrived
right after Thursday—which was when he'd promised to take Dixie out.

He groaned. Could his timing have possibly
been worse?

She'd understand, he told himself as he rushed
through a shower. There wasn't much hot water, but
he didn't see anything with too many legs crawling
around, which was a relief, given the condition of his
accommodations.

Which were where, exactly? He wasn't even sure
what part of the state he was in. No, wait—he dimly
remembered crossing the state line shortly before he
decided to pull over. He was in Nevada. Somewhere
in Nevada. They'd know at the front desk.

As he scrambled into yesterday's clothes, he assured himself that once he told Dixie what he'd
learned, she'd understand why everything else had
been blasted clean out of his mind.

Dressed, somewhat damp and more than a little
desperate, he tried to call her. But the phone by the
bed didn't work, and he'd forgotten his cell phone.
He'd rushed out the door without anything but his
jacket and what he'd had in his pockets.

He'd run off without calling Dixie.

She was going to ask why. She probably would
understand that he'd been badly shaken. She was a
compassionate person. But she'd wonder why it had
never once occurred to him to turn to her.

So did he.

* * *

Cole gassed up, grabbed a breakfast burrito and a large coffee, and left the tiny town of Basalt, Nevada, behind. He didn't stop again until he pulled up in front of his parents' house five endless hours later.

He'd driven longer last night, but last night he'd lacked any kind of destination. Time hadn't mattered. It did now.

Tilly rushed up to greet him as soon as he stepped out, and he was smitten by guilt. Someone would have fed her when it was obvious he'd taken off, but he must have worried everyone. Including his dog.

He took a moment to pet and reassure Tilly, then headed into the house. It was two in the afternoon, so Dixie would be working—which meant she might be anywhere. But she'd set her easel up in the lanai, so he checked there first.

No sign of her. Or anyone else, for that matter. No one seemed to be home at all.

He'd check her room anyway, just to make sure. He took the stairs two at a time.

She wasn't there, but Mercedes was. She was packing Dixie's things.

Cole stood in the doorway, frozen. Faint and faraway, he heard the echo that had haunted him on his morning run three days ago: *too late, too late, too late…*

Mercedes finished folding a pair of slacks, laid them carefully in Dixie's suitcase and straightened, scowling at him. "It's about time you showed up! Where in the world have you been?"

"I'll tell you later." He would have to. They'd all have to know. But right now his lips were numb and there wasn't enough air. He could barely get the next words out. "Where is she?"

"Gone, obviously," Mercedes snapped.

"Mercy." The childhood nickname slipped out as he crossed to her and put his hands on her shoulders. "I have to find her. I *have* to. Where did she go?"

Mercedes searched his face. Her expression softened into worry. "She didn't leave because you're a jerk. You are, but that isn't why she left."

The quick stab of anxiety made him tense. "Then why?"

"Her mother had a heart attack yesterday."

"Oh, no." Cole closed his eyes for a second. "Is she—?"

"It was a mild one, apparently. She's in the hospital now, but they say she'll be okay. But that isn't all. She called the ambulance herself when she realized what was happening. Only..." She swallowed. "She was taking care of Jody at the time. And in all the confusion, Jody wandered off."

"Oh, God." Cole thought about the storm last night. "Tell me she isn't still missing."

"I can't. She's been gone almost a full day now."

Dixie sat at the table in her aunt's kitchen with her head in her hands. The table was covered by maps— a large topographic map, a city map, a county map.

She couldn't think of anything else to do, anywhere to look that they hadn't already checked. How far could a confused sixty-year-old woman go?

The phone rang. She'd been carrying it from room to room with her, so she grabbed it immediately. "Yes?"

It was Jillian, checking in. Everyone had been so good. They'd practically shut Louret down for the day in order to look for Jody. The authorities were looking, too, of course. It just wasn't doing much good.

Everyone was looking...except Cole. Who had vanished as completely as her aunt.

His mother had told her not to worry too much about him. "He does this sometimes," she'd said gently. "When Cole has a personal snarl he needs to work through, he drives."

Dixie knew what snarl he was working on. Her. Apparently she was a huge snarl, too, since he'd not only stood her up, but had stayed gone all night. Somewhere around midnight, up at the hospital, she'd decided she'd take care of that tangle for him. If it was that hard to decide whether he even wanted to go out to dinner with her...

When the back door opened she looked up dully, expecting one of the searchers.

It was Cole.

She went hot, then cold, the fluctuation hitting as abruptly as if a switch had been thrown. For a second she wondered if she might faint, which would be too mortifying to bear. She looked away.

"No word?" he asked softly.

She shook her head and looked at the table. She'd had too little sleep, that was all. A couple hours snatched on a hard couch in the waiting room at the hospital. She didn't *need* Cole, not after he'd shown her how true all her doubts had been.

But her aunt might. There were colored buttons on the topo map, each representing a searcher or group of searchers. She cleared her throat. "If you're here to help look for Aunt Jody, fine. I'll assign you an area. If you're here for anything else, go away."

"I'll search. But I want to know how you're holding up."

"I'm fine." Her stupid, traitorous eyes chose that moment to water. "I'll be fine. This area, here, by Waters Street." She tapped the city map. "It's been searched already, but they might have missed her. Or she could have wandered back after they looked. There's a coffee shop there. It's…it was…one of her favorite…" Her voice broke as her eyes filled, and she finished in a whisper. "She might find her way there."

"Ah, hell, sweetheart." He crossed to her quickly, pulled her out of the chair and folded his arms around her.

She hit him in the chest with both fists. "Don't you call me sweetheart! Damn you, where did you— where—" But the tears were winning, her words broken apart by sobs. "I wanted you last night! I needed you, and you pulled a vanishing act!"

"I know, honey. I'm sorry. So sorry. Cry it out. You can hit me later. Hate me later."

At first she tried to break loose, but he held her too closely. Or maybe she just gave up. It felt too good to have his arms around her, his strength to lean on. So she cried.

It didn't last long. Dixie didn't understand how some people could cry for hours—when tears hit her, they hit hard and fast. And left just as fast, like a storm in the desert.

Once she was through crying, she pulled away. She didn't want to, which infuriated her. She wiped her face, sniffed, and looked around for the tissues. Crying always made her nose run.

Cole handed her the box.

"Thanks," she said, making it as cold as she could. She blew her nose.

"Have you had any sleep?"

"A little. And before you ask, I'm not going to go lie down. Later I'll have to. I don't have to yet."

He studied her face a moment. "All right. I'll tell you what happened last night, but later. How's your mom? I could take over here for a bit so you could go see her."

"She'd just send me back here. Or tell me to sleep—as if I could." Dixie sniffed one last time and tossed the tissue in the trash. "It's ridiculous! She blames herself, as if she could have timed her heart attack better!"

He nodded. "I should've known you came by that tendency honestly."

She scowled. "What are you talking about?"

"Tell me you aren't convinced you should have somehow kept this from happening. Maybe you think you should have stayed with Jody last night. You had no idea you would be needed, but you ought to have guessed. Or maybe you should have intuitively known that your mother's heart was going to act up. Or—"

"I get the point." She even felt the ghost of a smile touch her lips. "It's not my fault. I know that, and yet..." She rubbed her forehead wearily. "It's just so awful to think of Jody out there somewhere. She must be so frightened. Maybe she's hurt, or...."

"And hard to stop thinking about it. Come on," he said, taking her arm. "Sit down. Have you eaten?"

She let him steer her to a chair. "Your mother force-fed me a sandwich a couple hours ago." There. That was a real smile this time. "I don't know how she can speak so softly, be so gentle and polite and be utterly immovable at the same time."

"That's my mom." He was rummaging in the cabinets. "How about some coffee? It won't make you feel better, but you can worry more alertly."

Coffee actually sounded good. "Okay." She wasn't forgiving him. She just didn't have the energy to hate him right now. "It's in the cabinet by the sink. Make plenty," she added. "People come and go a lot."

Neither of them spoke as he prepared the pot. When it was ready, he sat down with her and his own cup and had her tell him who was searching, where they all were, what areas had already been searched.

It steadied her, reminding her that they were doing all they could.

Over the next hour one of the police officers stopped by and had a cup of coffee. He briefed them on what the official searchers were doing. The phone rang a couple of times—Mercedes called to say she was on her way back, then a telemarketer gave Dixie a chance to snarl at someone.

Cole didn't seem to be going anywhere. He seemed to have an instinct for when to speak and distract her, when to remain silent. She was pacing again when she decided she couldn't let him hang around and coddle her. "The cops took another look on Waters Street, but you could check out that gully by the supermarket."

"I'll do that." He took another sip of coffee. "Just as soon as Mercedes gets here."

She wanted him to stay. The longing was as stupid as it was selfish, when she ought to be pushing him out the door—for her own sake as well as Aunt Jody's. "I don't need to be baby-sat."

"You don't need to be alone right now, either."

She was mustering up the anger to snap at him when the phone rang again. She glanced at it and grimaced. "If that's another telemarketer—"

"I'll get it." He snaked out an arm and snagged it before she could. "Hello?"

His face told the story before he spoke. "That's wonderful. Yes…of course. We'll be right there." He put the phone down and stood, his smile wide. "She's at the newspaper office in Napa. God only knows how she got there, but she's okay. They're feeding her doughnuts. She's tired and grouchy and she doesn't want to leave," he added wryly. "She thinks she works there."

Dixie's eyes closed. Her knees all but buckled beneath the wave of relief. "She did," she managed to say. "Thirty years ago."

Thirteen

Cole drove Dixie to the newspaper offices. On the way she placed a dozen phone calls, notifying everyone who was searching that Jody had been found.

Jody had marched into the newspaper offices as if she belonged, moving so assuredly that, despite her bedraggled appearance, the receptionist hadn't stopped her. She'd stopped in the middle of the bullpen and demanded to know what they'd done with her desk. One of the reporters had realized she was the missing woman they'd been notified about. She'd settled Jody at an old typewriter so she could "get to work," and called the police.

Cole helped coax Jody into leaving work early, then soothed, flirted with and cajoled her out of a temper fit when she learned she had to stay in the hospital overnight for observation.

Jody did not like hospitals. She was somewhat mollified when she found out her sister was there, though, and fell asleep right after supper. She'd had a rough twenty-four hours. She probably would have died from exposure if she hadn't found an unlocked car last night. She'd curled up in the back seat and slept.

Her version of things, of course, was a little different. For once, the mists of Alzheimer's had some benefit—she didn't remember being lost and terrified. She believed she'd been driving to work when the rain hit, and had pulled over and gone to sleep. "Then the stupid car wouldn't start," she'd grumbled, "so I got out and walked."

God only knew how far she'd walked before she saw something that looked familiar to her shrouded mind—the newspaper office—and went inside. It was strange, Dixie thought, but some things about her aunt hadn't changed. Like her indomitable spirit. She might not have known where she was, how she got there or how to get home, but she hadn't given up.

It had been weird, going back and forth between the two hospital rooms. Dixie and her mother laughed about it, agreeing that the hospital really ought to put the sisters on the same floor to make things easier for their visitors.

Little aftershocks of fear kept pinging through Dixie when she thought about what might have happened. She wished she could find the owners of that car and thank them for not locking it. She wished…a huge yawn shut down her fuzzy thoughts.

"We're there," Cole said, pulling up in the driveway of Jody's home.

So they were. It was ten o'clock at night after an extraordinarily long day with almost no sleep the night before. She was brain-dead with fatigue, but she did notice it when Cole got out, too.

Dixie stopped with one foot on the porch, staring at him through narrowed eyes. She ought to shake his hand, thank him and send him on his way. That would be the smart thing to do…only she was so tired. And it felt so right for him to be here.

His wry smile suggested he'd guessed some of her thoughts. "C'mon, warrior," he said, draping an arm around her shoulders and nudging her toward the door. "You can be tough tomorrow. Tonight you're staggering like a drunk woman. You need sleep."

She let him steer her into the house, then pulled free. "You're not sleeping with me," she informed him as she headed upstairs, but her voice may have lacked conviction. The yawns were hitting with every other word now.

He didn't follow her up the stairs, though, so it seemed he'd accepted the boundaries she'd set. Good, she told herself. But she felt weepy with frustration when she couldn't find her suitcase. Where had Merry put the stupid thing?

Never mind. She stripped and climbed into bed,

and that was all she knew for several hours…except for a few moments when she rose partway from the depths and noticed Cole's arm around her waist, his breathing steady and quiet in the darkness.

That was all right, then. She went back to sleep.

She woke at nine-ten the next day—rested, alone and confused.

For several minutes she lay quietly in bed, remembering the day before. And the night, when nothing had happened…except that it had, somehow. While she was sleeping, something had changed.

When she pushed back the covers and sat up, she smelled bacon and saw her suitcase. Had it been by the foot of the bed all along, or had Cole brought it up?

A frown pleating her forehead, she gathered some clothes and headed down the hall to the bathroom for a shower. Thirty minutes later, she went downstairs.

She wasn't surprised to find Cole still there, reading the paper. "Your mom and your aunt both spent a good night. We can pick Jody up around noon."

We? She nodded cautiously, heading for the coffeepot. "Thanks for checking on them."

"I wanted to know, too. Coffee's reasonably fresh," he added, looking back at his paper, "but the bacon's cold. Do you want some eggs?"

Her mouth twitched. His one culinary achievement. "I'm okay with bacon and toast." She padded to the pantry and took out the bread.

Neither of them spoke as Dixie put together a simple breakfast. Cole seemed entirely comfortable with both the silence and the company. Or else he was just absorbed in his newspaper.

Dixie, on the other hand, felt uncharacteristically awkward, off balance. Naturally this made his ease irritating. "Anything interesting in the news?" she asked as she brought her toast, bacon and coffee to the table.

He looked up with a slight smile. "You interested in the Dow Jones?"

"No."

"Then probably not." He went back to his paper.

She resisted the urge to snatch it out of his hands, congratulated herself on her maturity and applied herself to her meal.

He'd left the back door open. The air was fresh and surprisingly warm, the sky clear and sunny. She could hear birds talking to each other, the hum of tires on the street out front and giggles mixed with bouncing noises from next door. The kids there had a trampoline.

Cole had never liked having the TV or radio on first thing in the morning. Neither did she.

When she finished eating she carried the plate to the dishwasher, loaded it and brought the coffeepot back with her. She poured herself a second cup, then topped off Cole's. And spoke. "Put the paper down."

He looked up. After a moment he nodded, un-smiling this time, and folded the paper. "Do I get a trial, or are we going straight to the sentencing?"

"We're still in the investigation stage." She sat across from him, sipping coffee and studying him over the rim of the mug. "Why?" she asked softly. "Why did you run?"

For a long moment he looked at her, not speaking. He drummed his fingers once, then nodded. "I'll tell you what happened—now, if you like—but it had nothing to do with you. I'm hoping you'll be willing to reach a verdict without knowing more."

She shook her head, confused. "Why not just tell me?"

For a moment she glimpsed emotion, stark and ragged, in his eyes. Then he looked away. "This isn't easy for me to say, but you were right. I've been holding back from you emotionally. Making excuses to stay away. I did it on purpose. I was testing you."

Feelings rippled through her, strong and complex. "I guess I failed, then, if you had to run off."

"No." His head swung back. "I told you, that had nothing to do with you. I found out something about my father. Something…" He shook his head. "I should have come to you. It didn't occur to me, which doesn't say much for the way I handle things, but…all I can say in my defense is that I've always kept stuff about him to myself. I reacted the way I'm used to reacting. I went off to deal with it alone."

She hurt for him. "What did you learn?"

"It's big, it's important, but not as important as this." He reached across the table and took her hands in his. "Not as important as what I finally realized. I wanted you to love me, you see."

She swallowed. "Cole—"

"Let me finish." His grip tightened. "I didn't just want you to love me—I wanted you to prove it. I thought I couldn't live with the uncertainty. Then, when I came back from my driveabout, I thought you'd left me." His voice turned bleak. "That cleared things up wonderfully for me. I'd driven you away."

He was talking faster now, the words tumbling out. "All I could think was that I wanted you back. No tests, no guarantees—none of that mattered. I wanted you back. Period." He met her eyes, then one corner of his mouth kicked up. "And then, of course, I found out that your leaving didn't have a thing to do with me."

She blinked several times. She'd cried too much in the past two days. "No, it didn't. But why don't you want to tell me why you left?"

"Because," he said softly, "I wonder if you're doing the same thing I was. Testing me. Waiting for me to fail. If you need reasons to trust me, Dixie, I'll give them to you. This is not a test. But I'm hoping…" He had to stop and swallow. "I'm hoping you'll take me on faith. Because that's how I'm taking you from now on. I love you, and love means trust, not tests."

Just like that, the thing that had changed while she slept fell into clear, shining focus. Somewhere along the line she'd stopped seeing Cole. All she'd been able to see were her fears. But those fears had been phantoms, and they'd faded when real tragedy loomed…then evaporated once he was there with her.

As if she'd swallowed a year's worth of sunshine and it was rising, irresistibly making its way into every cell of her body and every corner of her mind, Dixie smiled, slow and certain. "Good. Because I'm crazy in love with you."

He let out one clear, loud crow of laughter. "Then come here, woman! What are you doing so far away?"

She was laughing, too, as he caught her up in his arms. Oh, she was caught, all right—caught for good, hopelessly entangled, tied up in knots…and set free in Cole's arms.

Epilogue

"Do you think your mother is ever going to forgive me?" Dixie asked, leaning forward to check her lipstick in the mirror on the back of the visor. It was nearly eight at night. They were running a little late—but it had been a busy day.

"No need," Cole said wryly. "She blames me entirely for our decision to run off to Vegas. You're in the clear."

"Well, my mother blames me for depriving her of a wedding, and thinks you hung the moon. So we're even." She flipped the visor up, smiled at the ring on her finger and glanced in the back of the suvvy.

Tilly was curled up on the back seat, sleeping. Hulk was back there, too, in his carrier—but with the carrier door open. The cat had decided that if Tilly didn't have to ride in a box, he shouldn't, either, but he wasn't ready to abandon the safety of his walls. The open carrier was a compromise.

Life was full of those. Dixie faced front again and reached for Cole's hand as they turned into the drive leading to The Vines. The big house was lit and welcoming. "You okay?" she asked softly.

He nodded without speaking. His hand was tense as he gripped hers.

So far, only his mother and stepfather knew about the detective Cole had hired, and what he'd learned. Cole had told them that afternoon, within hours of returning from Vegas. They'd agreed that the best way to present the news was in one big dose, and had arranged for everyone to be there tonight.

What Cole had to tell them would shake their worlds. No one should have to hear that kind of news secondhand.

"Everyone" included Grant now. Cole had accepted the relationship intellectually, though he had a baffled look in his eyes when he spoke of Grant. Dixie suspected he was trying too hard to feel brotherly toward a man who was still mostly a stranger.

Don't sweat it, she'd told him. It can take time for feelings to catch up. All in all, she thought he was dealing with everything remarkably well. She was proud of him.

Caroline met them at the door with a kiss and a hug for them both. Tilly and Hulk followed them in. Hulk was loudly requesting refreshments.

Caroline laughed. If there was a certain strain around her eyes, her smile was as warm as ever. "I see you brought the rest of the family with you. Everyone else is in the living room. And Hulk, if you're good I'll slip you some of the canapés. We have caviar."

"Oh, don't teach him to like that!" Dixie exclaimed. She and Caroline kept up a flow of light chatter on the way to the living room.

Cole was quiet, but no one noticed that at first. They had to hug and exclaim and chide him and Dixie for running off instead of having a proper ceremony. Dixie exchanged glances with Cole.

They'd tied the knot fast because they were sure it was right, they didn't want to wait—Cole said he was taking no chances on either of them screwing things up again—and because the family was about to be plunged into turmoil. It was not going to be a great time for an elaborate wedding.

After the first round of congratulations had run their course, Cole shifted to the center of the room. "I think Mom told you all that I had some news," he began.

"We've sort of figured it out!" Jillian said, grinning. "A sudden marriage, news to share—when am I going to be an aunt?"

Several of them laughed. Amazingly, Cole's ears turned pink. But his expression as he shook his head stilled the laughter. "Not that kind of news, I'm afraid," he said gently. "This will be upsetting. I have to start with an admission that some of you won't like. I hired a private detective to look into Grant's claims."

No, they didn't like that. It was Grant who quieted them, though. He nodded and spoke over the others. "Don't give him a hard time. It was the reasonable thing to do. Expensive," he added dryly, "but sensible."

"Thanks," Cole said, surprised. "You'll not be surprised to learn the P.I. confirmed everything you've told us."

"Then why the big meeting?" Mercedes asked.

"I'm getting there. I've brought copies of the report, if anyone wants to see it. Basically it says that Spencer Ashton married Sally Barnett in Crawley, Nebraska, just as Grant said. She had twins a few months later, and he left her when the babies were a year old. Sally died when the children were twelve. Her parents raised them after that."

"And your point is?" Eli demanded. "None of this is news. Except maybe about Grant's mother dying when he was so young." He turned to Grant. "I'm sorry to hear that. I knew she was gone, but not that you were so young when it happened."

Grant nodded, a slight frown on his face as he watched Cole.

"There's something Grant left out, probably because he doesn't know it, either." Cole paused. "Spencer left Grant's mother forty-two years ago. He married our mother thirty-seven years ago. But he neglected to do one thing. He never got a divorce from his first wife."

In the sudden silence, Cole looked around the room at their faces—blank, shocked, disbelieving. "The detective checked very thoroughly. There is no record of a divorce."

"But—but this means…" Merry's voice trailed off.

"It means that our father's marriage to our mother was invalid. I have no idea where that leaves us in terms of the divorce settlement that gave him everything. Or," he added bleakly, "whether the surname listed on our birth certificates is correct. I don't know if we're Ashtons or not."

* * * * *

A RARE SENSATION

BY
KATHIE DeNOSKY

Kathie DeNosky lives in her native southern Illinois with her husband and one very spoiled Jack Russell terrier. She writes highly sensual stories with a generous amount of humour. Kathie's books have appeared on the Waldenbooks bestseller list and received the Write Touch Readers' Award from WisRWA and the National Readers' Choice Award. She enjoys going to rodeos, travelling to research settings for her books and listening to country music. Readers may contact Kathie at: PO Box 2064, Herrin, Illinois 62948-5264, USA or e-mail her at kathie@kathiedenosky.com.

Look for a new trilogy from Kathie DeNosky starting in July 2010 with *Bossman Billionaire*, a Mills & Boon® Desire™.

Prologue

1963

Spencer Ashton glanced over at his wife, Sally, and the two squalling babies on her lap as he drove away from the Crawley cemetery. Damn, but he looked forward to not having to suffer any more of Sally's pathetic adoration, or listen to the twins' constant howling. Grant wasn't so bad. At least the boy shut up once in a while. But Grace's nonstop screeching made life a living hell. And one that Spencer had every intention of escaping.

He glanced in the truck's rearview mirror at the cemetery workers filling in the new grave. Now that his controlling old man was dead of a heart attack, Spencer was free. Free to be rid of Sally and the twins. Free to shake the dust off his heels and pursue his own dreams. Free to leave Crawley, Nebraska, as far behind as his old Ford and the hundred bucks in his pocket would take him.

"Can't you shut that kid up?" he growled when the baby girl's screaming reached a crescendo.

"She's teething," Sally said, in that singsong voice that made his skin crawl. She kissed the top of the kid's little, bald head. "There, there, Gracie. Daddy doesn't like it when he knows you're hurting."

Spencer fought the bile that rose in his throat every time Sally referred to him as "Daddy." He might have spawned the two sniveling brats on her lap, but he never had been, nor would he ever be, their daddy.

Steering his truck onto the dirt-packed road leading to the Barnett farm, he was glad that Sally's folks had decided to drive on into Crawley after his old man's funeral. It would make leaving a whole lot easier. At least he wouldn't have her sad-eyed parents staring at him, much the way they'd done since the day he'd been forced to marry their daughter and move in with them.

When he parked the truck, he got out and, with a purposeful stride, walked toward the two-story house that he'd come to think of as his prison. He didn't stop to help Sally with the twins, nor did he look back to see if she followed him as he climbed the porch steps and opened the front door. Taking the stairs two at a time, he went straight to the bedroom he and Sally had shared since their wedding night and pulled a worn leather duffel bag from the top shelf of the closet.

"Spencer, what are you doing?" Sally asked, sounding out of breath. He supposed she was winded from carrying two babies up a flight of stairs without assistance.

He mentally shrugged as he stuffed clothes into the bag. It was one of many things she'd have to get used to doing without help.

"I'm leaving."

Just putting his intentions into words made him feel almost giddy from the relief coursing through him. He'd been waiting for this day from the moment his old man had forced him to marry Sally after learning Spencer had gotten her pregnant.

"Where are you going?" The sound of her quivering voice sent a chill up his spine much the way fingernails scraping a blackboard did.

"As far away from you and your whelps as I can get."

He knew his words cut her more deeply than any knife ever could. But he didn't care. She and her brats were the reason his plans for a better life had been put on hold for the past fifteen months.

Her broken sobs grated on his nerves and had him zipping the bag shut. To hell with the rest of his things.

He'd be buying new ones once he reached California, anyway.

Anxious to escape Sally and the wailing twins, he grabbed the bag and walked out of the room. He heard her footsteps behind him, but he didn't bother to look back. He never intended to look back.

He would try to stay in touch with his younger brother, though. Spencer was kind of fond of the kid.

But David had always been a bit of a sentimental fool about things. Even with the Ashton farm in foreclosure, and their old man dead from a heart attack because of it, the dumb kid had turned down Spencer's offer at the cemetery to go with him. David had said he couldn't imagine living anywhere but Nebraska and intended to make a fresh start in a new town—another godforsaken place just like Crawley.

When Spencer reached the door, Sally's words broke through his introspection, causing him to pause. "But these…are your children…Spencer. Don't they mean… anything to you?"

Turning, he gave her a disdainful smile as he watched her grip the newel post as if it might be the only thing keeping her on her feet. "Not a damn thing. As far as I'm concerned, you and your two squalling brats never existed."

Spencer watched her crumple into a pathetic, sobbing heap at the bottom of the stairs. Disgusted, he shook his head, then walked out the door and slammed it behind him.

He whistled a tune as he walked to his truck, threw the duffel bag on the seat, then slid behind the wheel. He was a free man now, and nothing was going to stop him from living the life he not only wanted but, without question, deserved.

One

February 2005

Abigail Ashton stepped out of the carriage house, tilted her head back and enjoyed the morning sun bathing her face with its warm rays. California in February was light-years away from the weather she'd left behind in western Nebraska. When she'd flown out of the town of Scottsbluff yesterday morning, the temperature had been in the midteens and there was almost a foot of snow covering the ground. But here in Napa Valley, the temperature was a good forty degrees warmer and felt almost balmy in comparison.

No wonder her uncle had extended his stay in California. Even if his quest to meet with his father had thus far been futile, the weather was enough to tempt anyone.

Looking around at the neatly kept grounds of Lucas and Caroline Sheppard's estate, The Vines, Abby smiled. It had been extremely generous of Caroline to invite her and her Uncle Grant to stay with them for as long as they wanted to visit the Napa Valley area. All things considered, the woman had no reason to be kind to, or even like, them. After all, they had to be a painful reminder of Caroline's first marriage—to Abby's grandfather, Spencer Ashton. She shook her head in disgust. When he married Caroline, he'd conveniently failed to mention that he had a family he'd left behind in Nebraska, or that he hadn't bothered to divorce his first wife, Sally.

As Abby blindly stared across the dormant vineyard stretching out for acres behind the estate, her heart went out to Caroline. The woman hadn't so much as a clue that her marriage to Spencer had been illegal, until Uncle Grant showed up last month in hopes of meeting with his father for the first time in over forty years.

But even though she'd been shocked by the news, Caroline had been the epitome of class and graciousness. Once she'd learned that Uncle Grant was Spencer's son, she'd insisted that family was family and he needed to get acquainted with her children—his half siblings.

Abby bit her lower lip to keep it from trembling. She worried about Uncle Grant. He so wanted to confront his father and learn the reasons behind the abandonment of his first family. But the man simply refused to give Uncle Grant the time of day. For that matter, he refused to meet with Caroline's children, either.

Starting to walk toward the small lake behind the carriage house, Abby decided that she didn't care if she ever met her duplicitous grandfather. Anyone who could leave his young wife and eight-month-old twins in Nebraska, marry another woman in California without obtaining a divorce, then abandon that woman to marry his secretary and have yet another family wasn't worth knowing. Nor was he worth wasting time thinking about.

Besides, she would much rather concentrate on the fact that she was finally free. After working her tail off in school, she'd earned her degree, and she fully intended to enjoy every minute of the first vacation she'd had in years. Then, when she returned to Crawley, she'd be relaxed and ready to jump into her career with both feet.

A mixture of satisfaction and excitement coursed through her. By the end of spring, she'd realize the dream she'd had since she was twelve years old—she'd be practicing veterinary medicine in her own large-animal clinic.

Strolling down a path leading away from the carriage house, her mouth turned up in a smile when she spotted the stables not far from the small lake. Without missing a step, she headed straight for them. Painted white, with hunter green shutters, the building looked like a horse lover's paradise, and she couldn't wait to go inside.

The double doors on either end of the structure were open, allowing fresh air to flow through, and Abby didn't think twice about entering the shadowy interior. It took a moment for her eyes to adjust to the lower light, but when they did, her breath caught. The stable was everything she'd thought it would be. And more.

The bottom halves of the stalls were constructed of tongue-and-groove spruce boards, while the top halves had black grille front bars for maximum ventilation. Wide, split doors gave easy access to the enclosures and allowed the horses inside to appease their curiosity by hanging their heads over them when the top halves were swung back.

A beautiful blue roan gelding poked its head over the stall door as Abby walked by, and she stopped to rub the gentle animal's soft muzzle. As she scratched his broad forehead, she noticed that the inside walls of the stall were covered with a metal that resembled stainless steel and could easily be hosed down and disinfected. As a veterinarian and horse enthusiast, she was very impressed, and she highly approved of the Sheppards' choices for the welfare of their animals.

But as she stood there wishing she had the same setup at the farm in Nebraska, sudden movement at the far end of the stable caught her attention. As she watched, a man, wearing a wide-brimmed cowboy hat, chambray shirt and jeans, opened one of the stall doors to go inside. She couldn't help but think that he'd look more at home in a barn in Nebraska than in a stable in California wine country.

But her smile quickly faded and she forgot all about how out of place he looked when he led a beautiful dapple gray mare from the stall. The horse was limping badly, and it was obvious she had something wrong with her left hind leg.

"What seems to be the problem?" Abby asked, hurrying toward them.

Without looking her way, the man bent over to examine the mare. "I don't know how she did it, but Marsanne has managed to cut her fetlock."

"I'll take a look. I might be able to do something for her."

Shaking his head, he straightened to his full height. "I think we'd better leave it alone and let the vet take care of this one."

Abby caught her breath and her pulse skipped several beats when he turned to face her. The man standing on the other side of the mare wasn't just good-looking, he was heart-hammering gorgeous. With straight, dark-blond hair slipping from beneath his black Resistol to hang low on his forehead, a fashionable beard stubble covering his lean cheeks and startling blue eyes, he was without a doubt the best-looking cowboy she'd ever laid eyes on. Bar none.

When she realized that she must be staring at him like a schoolgirl with her first crush, she shook off her uncharacteristic reaction and walked around the horse to take a look at the injury. "Get the first-aid kit." Bending down beside the horse's hindquarters, she quickly assessed the wound. "The cut isn't as deep as it looks. It hasn't severed any of the ligaments or tendons, and won't need suturing." When she straightened, she glanced around the floor. There was a good drainage system, and it wouldn't be necessary to walk the horse outside to treat her. "Could you bring the hose over here? We'll need to cold rinse the wound to reduce the swelling before I apply a dressing."

"Now hold it right there, lady. You're not doing anything to this horse." Clearly annoyed, he walked around the mare to place his hands on Abby's shoulders, and, backing her away from the horse, he shook his head. "I'm going to call the vet and you're going to go back to the house, or wherever it is you came from."

His large hands on her shoulders sent a shiver of excitement up her spine, and she had to concentrate hard in order to ignore it. Luckily, it wasn't too difficult to do. He might be the best-looking guy she'd seen in all of her twenty-four years, but she wasn't the type to give in to anything as silly as attraction. Nor did she intend to be dismissed like so much fluff.

"I'm sorry, I didn't get your name," she said, careful to hide her irritation.

He dropped his hands to his sides. "Russ Gannon."

When he started to turn away, Abby placed her hand on his arm to stop him. Her breath lodged in her lungs at the feel of his hard muscles flexing beneath the blue fabric of his sleeve. She forced herself to ignore it and concentrate on the mare in need of treatment.

"It's nice to meet you, Russ. My name is Abigail Ashton. *Dr.* Abigail Ashton, DVM. But please call me Abby."

"You're a vet?" His skeptical expression told her that he still had his doubts about her treating one of the Sheppards' horses.

"More precisely, a large-animal veterinarian," she said, nodding. "Now, get the first-aid kit and a hose. I have a horse to treat."

Russ stared at the auburn-haired beauty barking orders at him like a drill sergeant. She sure didn't look like any of the veterinarians he'd ever met. Most of the ones he knew were men, and didn't have eyes the color of new spring grass or soft, feminine features that could easily grace the cover of a fashion magazine.

When she bent to look at the wound on Marsanne's

fetlock, the sight of her cute little upturned rear just about caused him to have a coronary. None of the vets he'd met had a figure that could stop traffic or remind him of just how long it had been since he'd been with a woman, either.

"Don't just stand there," she said impatiently. "This mare's fetlock needs treatment. And when you get the hose, bring some petroleum jelly and grease down her heel to keep it from getting sore."

Turning to get the hose and first-aid kit, he couldn't believe he was allowing this woman to order him around. He was used to giving orders, not taking them.

It had to be a case of shock. That's all he could think of that might explain his letting her order him around.

Where the hell had she come from, anyway? he wondered. He knew all of the Ashtons here at The Vines, and had heard about most of their relatives, but he couldn't recall them mentioning this one's name.

He shook his head as he gathered what she wanted. One thing was certain—if he'd ever met her, he damned sure would have remembered it. He had a weakness for redheads. And Dr. Abigail Ashton not only had hair the color of cinnamon and a killer body, she was an absolute knockout.

"What took you so long?" she asked when he returned with the requested items.

"Did anyone ever tell you you're a bossy little number?" he grumbled, handing them to her.

"My brother, Ford, tells me that all the time." Removing her jean jacket, she pushed the sleeves of her blue sweater up to her elbows, then tucked behind her ear a strand of hair that had escaped her ponytail. "Did anyone ever tell you that you're slower than molasses in January?"

Russ stared at her for a moment before he burst out laughing. It appeared that Abby Ashton could hold her own with the best of them.

"Now, what do you say we call a truce until after we get this mare on the road to recovery?" she asked, grinning.

His heart stalled and he had to take a deep breath to get it going again. When Abigail Ashton was issuing orders, she was awesome. But when she smiled, she was absolutely beautiful.

"What's the matter?" Her easy expression turned to one of concern. "You look like you were just treated to the business end of a cattle prod."

Damn! Was he that transparent? Apparently, he needed to make a trip into Napa and see if he could find a willing little filly to help him scratch the itch that he suddenly seemed to have developed.

"I'm fine," he lied.

"Good." She handed him the jar of petroleum jelly.

"Now, spread this over the mare's heel, then start running cold water on her leg so that it trickles down over the wound." She looked thoughtful for a moment. "Do you keep Epsom salts here in the stable?"

"Of course," he said, bending to coat the mare's heel with a good amount of the lubricant. "Do you intend to soak it or apply a hot compress after running cold water over the area?"

"I'm going to apply a hot compress in order to draw out bacteria." She paused. "By the way, do you have hot water out here, as well?"

Nodding, he stood up and handed her the jar of petroleum jelly. "I'll get it while you cold hose the mare's leg."

"That's not necessary," she said, smiling. "Just tell me where to find—"

"I'll take care of it," Russ said firmly.

He might not be as educated or refined as the Ashtons, but he did have manners. He wasn't about to stand by and watch a woman struggle with a heavy bucket of water.

Besides, he needed to put a little distance between them. Every time she turned her killer smile his way, certain parts of his body twitched and his heart felt like it was going to beat a hole in his rib cage.

He took a deep breath and did his best to regain his perspective. If he didn't get a hold on the situation, he just might have to use the cold water hose on himself.

* * *

An hour later, Russ watched Abby finish applying a poultice to the mare's fetlock, then wrap a bandage around it to hold it in place. Fortunately, Marsanne was a very well-mannered horse and tolerated the treatment without further injury to herself, Abby or him.

"I'll check on her again tomorrow morning and apply a fresh dressing, but I think she'll be fine," Abby said, standing up.

When she ran her hand along the horse's hindquarters, Russ swallowed hard. How would her delicate hands feel on his skin?

His heart slammed against his ribs. What the hell was wrong with him? He'd met her a little over an hour ago and he was fantasizing about her touching him?

Oh, brother, did he ever need that trip into town for a cold beer and a willing woman—and not necessarily in that order.

When she'd pulled the sleeves of her sweater back down to her wrists and shrugged into her blue jean jacket, she turned and stuck out her hand. "It was nice meeting you, Russ."

He automatically took her hand in his, but the moment their palms touched, he knew he'd made a serious error in judgment. An electric charge zinged up his arm, through his upper body, then traveled down to the region south of his belt buckle.

"I'll see you around," he managed, although he wasn't sure how the words made it through the cotton coating his throat.

"Are you feeling all right?" she asked, dropping his hand faster than he could blink. Her breathless tone and the pretty shade of pink coloring her creamy cheeks indicated that she'd felt it, too.

Good. At least he wasn't the only one suffering the unsettling sensation.

"Yeah, I'm fine," he said, fighting to keep from grinning. "How about you?"

She lifted her little chin and squared her slender shoulders as she started around him and the mare. "I couldn't be better."

Russ bit back a groan as he watched Abby walk the distance to the stable doors. The woman had legs that would tempt a eunuch. And his body was reminding him that was one thing he definitely was not.

Disgusted with himself and his own foolishness, he led Marsanne back into her stall, then headed toward the end of the stable where he kept his own horses, Blue and Dancer. Even if the woman was willing to indulge in a little vacation fun, he wasn't.

Number one, she was an Ashton, and his sense of loyalty and obligation just wouldn't allow him to disappoint Caroline or Lucas in any way. He snorted. And number two, what the hell could a book-smart beauty like Abby find appealing about a simple man with nothing more going for him than a knack for growing grapes and the ability to make the eight-second whistle when he rode bulls?

Two

"Thank you for the tour, Mercedes," Abby said, as she and Caroline's oldest daughter entered the Louret Vineyards tasting room.

Director of Marketing and Public Relations for the Sheppards' boutique winery, Mercedes Ashton smiled. "Oh, it's not over yet. The best is yet to come." She pointed to a small table by a floor-to-ceiling window. "Have a seat and I'll be right back."

Seating herself at the table Mercedes had indicated, Abby couldn't help but marvel at the ambience of the tasting room. The use of rich woods and muted lighting was extremely romantic, but the view of the vineyards from the narrow window was breathtaking. She could easily imagine herself staring out at the countryside somewhere in the south of France.

When Mercedes returned carrying a silver tray with cheese and samplings from the Louret award-winning reserve cellar, she grinned. "The best part of touring a winery is tasting the fruits of its labor."

After her new friend spent several minutes schooling her in the use of her senses to appreciate the clarity, bouquet and body of the wine, Abby shook her head as she reached for a piece of cheese. "I didn't realize there was such an art to tasting wine or that so much work went into the making of it."

Mercedes laughed. "It's more than just picking a few grapes and squeezing out the juice, that's for sure." She swirled the chardonnay in her glass. "Things are fairly quiet around here in winter. The wine is aging and there really isn't much going on beyond pruning the vines, maintenance on equipment and assessing which vines need to be replaced in the spring. Our busiest time of year is late summer and early fall, when the crush begins."

"Crush?" Abby was quickly learning that winemakers had their own language.

"The crush is what we call the harvest," Mercedes explained. "It starts when the grapes are picked and goes all the way through the process of making the wine. That's when Eli and Russ really get a workout."

"Russ Gannon?" Abby asked before she could stop herself.

Nodding, Mercedes gave her a curious glance. "You've met him?"

"Briefly." Abby shrugged and tried not to sound too interested. "He was in the stable this morning and I thought that's where he worked."

"It's a safe bet that's where you'll find him when he's not in the vineyards or off competing in a rodeo somewhere," Mercedes said, nodding. "But his official title is Vineyard Foreman. Russ is an absolute genius when it comes to growing things, and Eli relies on him for almost everything to do with the vines and during the crush."

"What's his event in rodeo?" Abby loved the sport and had even competed as a barrel racer a few times when she was in high school.

Mercedes looked thoughtful. "Russ doesn't talk about it, but I think Eli said he rides bulls." She paused. "But that's Russ. He doesn't talk about much of anything he does."

Abby grinned. "The mysterious type."

"Not really." Mercedes sighed. "Poor Russ. Life hasn't exactly been easy for him. His parents were killed in a car accident when he was only fifteen."

"Oh, how terrible," Abby gasped.

Although their circumstances were somewhat different, she knew what it was like to grow up without parents. Even before she'd abandoned her children, Grace Ashton had never been a mother to them, had never nurtured and cared for them the way a mother was supposed to. And, although her uncle Grant had loved her and her brother, and raised them as his own, it wasn't the same as having a mother and father.

"I feel so bad for him," she said, meaning it.

Mercedes nodded. "That's when he came to live with us. Lucas and Mr. Gannon had been best friends since grade school, and when Lucas found out that Russ had no family to turn to, he and Mother took Russ in."

"That was very kind of them." The more she learned about Caroline and Lucas Sheppard, the more she came to realize just how very special they were. "But that must have been devastating for him to lose both parents at the same time, and so tragically."

"I'm sure it was," Mercedes agreed, standing up to place their empty glasses on the tray. "Being older, I didn't become as close to him as my youngest brother, Mason. He's only a year younger than Russ and they became best friends."

"I don't think I've met Mason," Abby said, rising to help clear the table.

"He's in France studying new wine-making techniques," Mercedes said, laughing.

Abby waited for her to carry the serving tray over to

one of the uniformed attendants that Mercedes had referred to at the beginning of the tour as "wine educators." When she returned, they walked out a side door and onto a path that led back to the mansion.

"Did I miss something?" Abby asked. "I don't understand what's so funny about Mason studying in France."

Mercedes's lips turned up slightly at the corners. "You've always heard the old saying about someone trying to build a better mousetrap?"

"Let me guess," Abby laughed. "He's going to try to make a better wine?"

"So he says." Mercedes smiled fondly and Abby could tell that she adored her youngest brother. "But I think it's just an excuse to backpack through France before he settles into a position here at Louret with Eli and Russ."

"I'm sure that will make it easier for Russ to go to a few more rodeos," Abby said before she could stop herself. Why did she keep mentioning him?

"Russ seems to have made a big impression on you." Mercedes gave her a questioning look. "You wouldn't happen to be interested, would you?"

"Good Lord, no!" Abby shook her head. "I don't have time for him or any other man in my life."

"Really? He's a great guy and extremely good-looking. And, just for the record, available." From the twinkle in her eyes and the teasing tone of her voice, Abby could tell that Mercedes wasn't the least bit convinced of her disinterest.

"I've worked too long and hard at getting my degree to become distracted now." As they walked onto the covered lanai at the back of the estate, she added, "Besides not having the time to become involved, Russ lives a thousand miles away. I'll be way too busy with my practice for a long-distance boyfriend."

"If you say so," Mercedes said, once again treating Abby to a knowing grin.

Realizing that she'd protested a little too much, it suddenly became clear that she wasn't trying to convince Mercedes as much as she was trying to convince herself. "I'm pretty tired," Abby said, suddenly needing time alone. "I think I'll take a nap before dinner." She hugged her new friend. "Thank you for the tour and wine tasting. I really enjoyed it."

"I'm glad." Mercedes hugged her back. "I probably won't see you at dinner this evening. I'm going out with a friend."

"Have a good time."

Turning to walk the short distance to the carriage house where she and her uncle were staying, Abby wondered what had gotten into her. Talking about Russ had been more unsettling than she could have ever imagined, and she needed time to get herself back on track.

All of her life she'd focused on her goal of becoming a large-animal vet, studied her tail off in school and made it happen. And along the way, she'd purposely avoided becoming involved with anyone. It was a distraction she didn't need and a chance she couldn't afford to take. Her biggest fear had been, and probably always would be, that she'd turn out to be just like her mother—a man-crazed tramp who cared very little for anyone or anything beyond her own selfish pursuits of pleasure.

But the most disconcerting realization of all was that when she and Mercedes had talked about Russ Gannon, she couldn't seem to keep her pulse from skipping beats or a funny, fluttery feeling from settling deep in the pit of her stomach. When she'd found herself attracted to boys in high school or college, she'd never experienced anything even remotely close to what she felt when she thought about Russ. And that bothered her. A lot.

Sighing, she entered the carriage house and climbed the stairs. "You have serious issues, Abigail Ashton," she muttered. "And at the moment, the biggest one is a wine-making rodeo cowboy named Russ Gannon."

When Russ arrived at dawn a few days later to feed the horses and muck out the stalls, he wasn't the least bit surprised to see Abby already in the stable with her sleeves rolled up, changing Marsanne's bandages. Three out of the last four mornings, she'd arrived before him.

And whether he liked it or not, he'd started looking forward to their morning encounters.

"You're up even earlier than usual," he said, strolling over to where she bent down to change the dressing on the mare's fetlock.

Straightening, she gave him a smile that caused his pulse to take off like a racehorse out of the starting gate. He swallowed hard. She not only had auburn hair, she had his second biggest weakness—dimples. Why hadn't he noticed that before?

"When I'm at home, I'm used to getting up a lot earlier than this."

She brushed her hands off on the seat of her jeans and he almost groaned aloud. He'd love to run his hands over her sweet little rear.

Oblivious to his discomfort, she laughed and continued talking. "There's only two reasons a person sleeps late when they live on a farm—they're either too sick to get out of bed or it's snowing so hard they can't find the barn. And most of the time *that* doesn't even stop us."

"How often do you have blizzards?" he asked when he found his voice.

He didn't like the idea of her facing such harsh weather. But he was damned if he could figure out why it bothered him so much. She wasn't his to worry about, nor would she ever be.

"A blizzard moves through maybe once or twice a

year," she said, shrugging. "The rest of the time I'm up well before sunrise tending to my horses, then helping Uncle Grant, Ford and our hired hand, Buck, with the rest of the livestock."

"Cattle?"

She nodded as she bent to wrap a fresh bandage around the mare's lower leg. "We have a herd of about two hundred Black Angus."

"That sounds more like a ranch."

"Ranch or farm, whatever you want to call it." She finished securing the dressing, then stood up to face him. "When my great-grandparents owned it, they only had a few hundred acres. But when Uncle Grant took over, he bought up a couple of farms that were going under and now it's several thousand acres. We plant the majority in corn every year, as well as a couple thousand more that Uncle Grant leases. Then there's more than five hundred for pasturing the horses and cattle."

Russ couldn't help but be envious. He loved working the land and would give almost anything to have a place of his own to do just that.

Untying Marsanne to lead her out to the corral, he asked, "How many horses do you have?"

"Eight." She unrolled the sleeves of her jean jacket. "But only three of them are mine. The rest belong to Uncle Grant and Ford."

While Abby put the first-aid kit back together, he led

the gray mare out to the corral in order to muck out her stall. But when he returned, he found Abby already working at the task.

"Hey, you don't have to do that," he said, reaching for the pitchfork she held.

She shook her head and kept on forking the dirty straw into a wheelbarrow. "I don't mind. I'd rather be busy, anyway." Giving him a grin that made him weak in the knees, she added, "This vacation stuff is all right, but after a while it gets kind of boring."

Russ could understand her need to stay active. He'd never been able to stand being idle any longer than it took him to find something to do. "Well, if you're sure."

"I am." There was no hesitation, and Russ was certain that Abby meant what she said.

"Okay, while you finish up here, I'll turn the other horses and the pony out into the pasture, then bring back fresh straw."

By the time he returned, he found that Abby had mucked out three of the stalls and was ready to start on another one. "You work fast," he said, taking the pitchfork from her, "but it's my turn. Why don't you take it easy for a while?"

"But I don't mind," she argued.

He liked ambition in a woman, but he wasn't about to stand around while she did all the work. "I'll make you a deal. You go up to The Vines and have breakfast.

Then, after you eat, come back out here and we'll take my horses for a ride."

Her pretty, emerald eyes lit up, and she gave him a grin that made his heart thump his rib cage. "You've got yourself a deal, cowboy. What time?"

"Time?" How was he supposed to think when she was looking at him that way? Hell, he was lucky to remember his own name.

"When do you want me to come back out here?" she asked patiently.

"Whenever you get finished with breakfast will be fine." He was definitely going to have to stay focused when Abby was around. Otherwise, she was going to think he was a complete fool.

"I'll be back in a flash," she said, hurrying down the wide aisle.

As he watched her pretty little backside disappear through the open doors at the far end of the stable, Russ let out the breath he was pretty sure he'd been holding since he'd walked in and found her working on the mare. Damn, but the woman could send his blood pressure into stroke range with nothing more than a smile. And that's what made her dangerous.

Stabbing the pitchfork into the straw, he gazed off into space. He wasn't looking for a relationship. Especially not with a woman who lived a thousand miles away. His life was here, working for Lucas and Caroline Sheppard. And even though they'd never asked him for anything, and had always tried to make him feel a part of their family, he felt an obligation to them for taking him in after his folks died.

He took hold of the pitchfork and began forking dirty straw into the wheelbarrow.

Besides, Abby would be returning to Nebraska in another week or so to start her veterinary practice and resume her life on the family farm. And that was the way it was supposed to be.

But it didn't mean they couldn't have a good time and enjoy each other's company for as long as she visited Napa Valley, did it? He could show her around and she could tell him more about her life in Nebraska and all that land he'd love to work.

Satisfied that he'd come up with a solution they could both live with, he whistled a tune as he finished mucking out the stalls. There was no chance of either of them being hurt as long as there was no emotional investment.

A smile tugged at the corners of his mouth. As long as he kept that in mind, they'd both be just fine.

Russ's lower body tightened when he watched Abby put her foot in the stirrup and swing up into the saddle on Dancer's back. The sight of her jeans pulled tightly over her sweet little rump, and her long slender legs straddling the gelding, had him wondering why he'd thought taking her for a ride was such a good idea. All he could think about was how her legs would feel wrapped around him as he sank himself deep—

"How old are your horses?" she asked, breaking into his erotic thoughts.

"Dancer is five," Russ said, mounting the blue roan. He shifted in the saddle to keep from emasculating himself. "I sometimes use him to haze steers for a couple of friends who compete in steer wrestling." He patted the roan's neck. "And Blue is six. I used to do a little team roping on him."

She smiled as they rode away from the stables. "Mercedes said you rode bulls, but she failed to mention that you rope, too. How often do you compete?"

Abby had been asking some of the Ashtons about him? The thought pleased him more than he could have imagined.

"I try to make as many rodeos as work around the vineyard permits." He chuckled. "The rest of the time, I have to be content with riding Blue and Dancer around here."

"Are they both registered with the Quarter Horse Association?"

"Yep." He wasn't surprised that Abby knew what breed they were. Considering her background with animals, she'd naturally recognize the classic traits of the breed. "Dancer's full name is Stormy Jack Dancer, and Blue's is Diablo's Blue Lightning."

"Beautiful names for beautiful animals," she murmured.

They rode in silence for several minutes and Russ found himself admiring the easy way Abby sat a horse. Relaxed and confident, he could tell she'd spent many hours in the saddle.

"What about your horses? What breed are they?" he asked.

"Mostly mixed. Magic is a quarter-horse-and-Arabian mix gelding. He's the one I ride the most. Then there's my mare, Angel. She's mostly quarter horse, but we're not sure about the rest of her bloodlines." Abby laughed. "She's the product of Uncle Grant's mare giving a come-hither look over the fence to our nearest neighbor's stallion."

An electric charge zinged up his spine at the sound of her soft voice and delightful laughter. He had to clear the rust out of his throat before he could speak. "I thought you said you had three horses."

She nodded. "The third one is a mustang I adopted from the BLM a few years ago. His name is Crazy Horse."

"I've heard about the Bureau of Land Management's Adopt-A-Horse program. Did you name him after the Native American chief?"

"No. He's a crazy horse." Laughing, she shook her head. "Ford named him because Crazy gives a whole new meaning to the word *wild*. Like all mustangs, he's rebellious and distrustful, and I'm the only one he's ever let get near him. But I love him even though I know he'll never be tame enough to ride."

"It sounds like you really enjoy living on the farm," Russ said, reining Blue in.

"I do." She brought Dancer to a halt beside him. "Living out on the prairie has its downside when the temperatures drop and the windchill feels like you've been transported to the Arctic, or it gets so hot and humid in the summer that you feel like you're in a sauna. But I really couldn't imagine living anywhere else."

They'd ridden around the entire vineyard and back to the small lake a hundred or so yards behind the stables. "Do you want to sit and talk for a while?" he asked.

"Sure."

When they'd dismounted, they ground tied the two horses and walked over to sit beneath a grove of oak trees at the water's edge.

"What about you, Russ? Have you always lived in Napa Valley?"

He lowered himself to sit beside her on the carpet of grass. "No. Until I was fifteen, I lived about a hundred and fifty miles north of here, on a ranch outside of Red Bluff."

"I'm so sorry about your parents," she said, placing her hand on his arm. "Mercedes said that you lost them in a car accident."

The warmth of her hand through his shirtsleeve, and the sincere tone of her voice, caused a tightness in his chest. "That was eleven years ago," he said, nodding. "Lucas brought me here right after Mom and Dad's funeral, and I've lived here ever since." They sat in silence for some time before he asked, "What about your parents, Abby? I've heard you talk about your brother and uncle, but I've never heard you mention your mom and dad."

"That's because there isn't a whole lot to talk about." He could tell it wasn't a pleasant subject for her.

"I'm sorry," he said, wishing he'd kept his mouth shut. "I didn't mean to pry."

He watched her pluck a blade of grass and shred it into strings, then toss it aside and pluck another. "I don't mind talking about it, exactly," she finally said. "It's just that it's rather embarrassing to have to tell someone that your mother was the town tramp and you have no clue who your father is."

Russ wasn't sure what he'd expected her to say, but it certainly hadn't been that. "That's a pretty harsh thing to say about the woman who gave you life, honey."

"But it's the truth." She didn't look at him when she continued, but he could tell she was embarrassed by the heightened color on her cheeks. "Grace was sixteen when she got pregnant with my brother, and eighteen when she had me. But she never would tell our great-grandparents or Uncle Grant who our father—or fathers—were." She sighed. "That in itself is no big deal. But Grace made sure we knew that she didn't want us. She always told us that if our great-grandparents hadn't insisted that she stay and take responsibility for us, she'd have left Crawley as soon as she found a way out."

"Your mother and uncle were raised by their grandparents?" Russ had never known anything but love from his parents, and it was hard for him to grasp that a woman had been so callous toward her own children.

"My great-grandparents finished raising Grace and Uncle Grant after their mother, Sally, died of cancer," Abby said, nodding. "They were twelve."

"I know from experience that losing a parent isn't easy," Russ said gently. "It can bring out a rebellious streak in some people."

"That might have been the case if Grace had been someone else, but I can never remember a time when she acted as though we actually meant anything to her." She shrugged one slender shoulder. "Uncle Grant told us that she was just like their father, Spencer. He's narcissism personified, and so was his daughter."

"You talk about her like she isn't around anymore," Russ said, reaching out to take Abby's hand in his.

"She isn't." She stared off across the lake. "Grace abandoned me and Ford when I was six and he was eight. But we were lucky—Uncle Grant loved us and finished raising us as his own." Her fond smile was evidence of how much she loved the man. "He's always been more of a father to us than an uncle."

The more Russ heard about Grace Ashton, the more he understood why Abby didn't like talking about her. "Where did your mother go?"

Abby's laughter held little humor. "Who knows? She went to the store one day and just didn't bother coming home. We're almost certain that she ran off with a sales representative who made frequent visits to the Crawley General Store."

"Do you know his name? Maybe if you find out where he is, you'd be able to track her down."

"His name is Wayne Cunningham, but that's about all we know." Brushing a strand of hair from her porcelain cheek, she turned her gaze back to him. "Uncle Grant checked with the company Wayne worked for, but that was a dead end. They were looking for him, too. It turns out that he disappeared at the same time as Grace, and without bothering to turn in the money from his latest sales."

"Real nice guy," Russ said, unable to hold back his sarcasm. He'd tried all of his life not to be judgmental, but this was one time he couldn't help himself. "It sounds to me like your mom got hold of a real loser when she hooked up with this Wayne character."

Abby nodded. "Uncle Grant doesn't have much to say about it, but Ford and I think they probably deserve each other."

"I'm sorry for the way it all turned out, honey," Russ said, pulling her into his arms.

He'd only meant the gesture to be comforting, but the feel of Abby's soft, feminine body pressed to his chest sent a shock wave straight through him, and his good intentions took a hike. He could no more stop himself from kissing her than he could stop the sun from setting in the west.

Three

Gazing into Abby's pretty, emerald eyes, Russ slowly lowered his mouth to hers. The feel of her soft lips had his heart thumping inside his chest like a sultry jungle drum. But when she tentatively moved to bring her arms up to circle his neck, then tangled her fingers in the hair at his nape, his pulse took off at a gallop.

He lightly traced the seam of her mouth with his tongue, and when she parted for him on a soft sigh, Russ slipped inside. As he stroked her inner recesses, her sweet taste and shy response sent his blood pressure soaring and brought his neglected hormones to full alert.

Without breaking the kiss, he lowered her to the soft grass and partially covered her body with his. She felt so damned good beneath him. In twenty-six years of life, he'd never wanted a woman as quickly or as fiercely as he wanted Abby at that very moment.

Parting her legs with one of his, he pressed his thigh against her feminine warmth as he eased his hand inside her jean jacket to cup her breast. Rewarded by her soft moan of pleasure, he chafed the peak with his thumb through the layers of her clothing.

His body hardened predictably, and he allowed her to feel what she was putting him through, how she made him want her. But a split second later, he felt her go perfectly still, then push against his chest.

"Please stop," she said, her tone clearly bordering on panic.

Russ immediately removed his hand and untangled their legs to help her sit up. "What's wrong?" He didn't think he'd gotten so carried away that he'd hurt her. And he was sure she'd enjoyed what he'd been doing.

"I…have to go." She scrambled to her feet, and before he could stop her, she ran over to where Dancer grazed a few feet away.

Bewildered, Russ watched her quickly mount the gelding, then rein the horse toward the stable. Jumping to his feet, he caught Blue's reins and swung up into the saddle to follow her. But Abby had nudged Dancer into a gallop and was already disappearing around the side of the building.

When he reached the double doors, Russ dismounted and led Blue inside. He wasn't sure what the problem was, but he damned sure intended to find out.

"Abby, what happened out there?"

"Please, not now." She didn't look at him as she continued to remove Dancer's saddle.

He noticed that her hand shook slightly when she picked up the brush to groom the bay, and, reaching out, he started to take it from her. "I'll see to the horses," he said gently. When she flinched and pulled back, he let his hand drop to his side. "Abby, honey, talk to me. What's wrong?"

"I rode him. I'll take care of brushing him down," she said, ignoring his question and turning back to Dancer.

For the next several minutes, they worked in uneasy silence as they groomed the horses. Russ suspected Abby's sudden panic might have something to do with what she'd told him about her mother. But if she wouldn't talk to him, he had no way of finding out if that was what bothered her, or if it was something else.

When she finished brushing Dancer, she led him to his stall, then started toward the open doors at the end of the stable. "Thank you for letting me ride your horse," she said as she walked past him.

"Abby, we need to talk." He placed his hand on her shoulder.

She didn't look at him, but he felt her body stiffen a moment before she sidestepped his touch and continued walking. "There's nothing to say."

Russ waited until she'd disappeared through the double doors before he cut loose with a string of cuss words that could have blistered paint. Abby might think there was nothing to discuss, but he sure as hell did. And when she arrived tomorrow morning to take care of the dressing on Marsanne's fetlock, he had every intention of being here, waiting for her.

Just as she'd done for the past three mornings, Abby waited until she was sure Russ had finished tending the horses and gone to the winery to work with Eli before she walked down to the stables to check on the gray mare. She knew it was the coward's way of dealing with how she'd acted the day he'd kissed her, but she really didn't know any other way to handle the situation.

She didn't want to have to explain to Russ why she'd panicked. It was too embarrassing to admit that her mother's reputation around Crawley had forced her to prove, time and again, that she wasn't cut from the same cloth. Nor was she eager to tell him that she'd had intimacy issues since almost losing her virginity when she was fifteen, simply because her date for the homecoming dance didn't believe that Grace Ashton's daughter meant what she said when she'd told him "no."

Kicking a pebble, Abby watched it skitter to the edge of the path. Whether it was fair or not, she'd been having to live down the sins of her mother from the time she was old enough for boys to notice her. That's why she'd finally just given up dating and concentrated on finishing school early.

But when Russ had kissed her, she'd encountered a problem she'd never had to deal with before—she hadn't wanted him to stop. And that's what bothered her. She'd wanted him to hold her close, to touch her in ways she'd never been touched. That had been the sole reason for her uncharacteristic panic attack.

What made being with Russ different? Could she really be like Grace after all?

As she entered the stable and walked down the aisle toward the tack room, Abby decided there were no easy answers. She had a feeling that, unlike Grace, not just any man could make her feel the way Russ did. Unfortunately, she couldn't risk finding out why his kiss made her burn in ways that she'd never even imagined. If she did take the chance, she might learn things about herself that she'd rather not know.

"I was wondering when you were going to show up."

Lost in her disturbing thoughts, Abby jumped. "What

are you doing here? Aren't you supposed to be working in the winery?"

Russ was sitting on a bench in the tack room, close
to the cabinet where the medical supplies were stored,
his legs stretched out in front of him with his boots
crossed at the ankles. He looked relaxed, confident and
sexier than any man had a right to look.

Smiling, he used his thumb to push up the wide brim
of his Resistol, then shook his head. "I decided to take
the day off."

"Why?" She didn't mean to sound so blunt, but she
found it extremely disconcerting to have the object of
her thoughts appear seemingly out of nowhere.

He shrugged. "I have some unfinished business to
take care of."

She stepped over his legs to get to the storage cabinet. "Then why aren't you off somewhere taking care
of it?"

His smile caused her knees to feel as if the tendons
had been replaced with rubber bands. "Now that you're
here, I can."

"I can't imagine why my being here makes any difference," she lied as she reached inside the cabinet.

"You're my unfinished business, honey."

She laughed nervously. "I have no idea why on earth
you'd think we have business to settle."

Her breath caught when he rose to his feet, placed

both hands on her shoulders and turned her to face him. "Don't play dumb with me, Abby. We both know you're too smart for that."

With Russ standing only inches away, she found it extremely hard to catch her breath. "I don't think this is a good idea."

"I do." His easy expression had been replaced with one of unwavering determination. "I want to know why you ran when I kissed you."

She stared into his deep blue gaze for several seconds before she shrugged out of his grasp to turn back to the cabinet. "You wouldn't understand." Finding the supplies she needed, she brushed past him to walk out into the wide stable aisle.

Before she could take more than a couple of steps, he caught her by the arm. "I understand a whole lot more than you think I do." Cupping her cheek with his palm, he tilted her head, forcing her to look at him. The tenderness she saw in his eyes caused her chest to tighten. "Do you want to know why I think you got so upset, Abby?"

"No."

"You're afraid," he said as if she hadn't spoken.

Shaking her head, she laughed, but the sound was hollow even to her own ears. "That's where you're wrong, cowboy."

"Really?" The look on his face warned her that he intended to prove her a liar. "Then let me kiss you, Abby."

A mixture of excitement and panic coursed through her. "This is ridiculous."

"You're not your mother," he said, gently pulling her into his arms.

Suddenly feeling defeated, she didn't have the strength to resist. God help her, she didn't even want to. She wanted Russ to hold her close, wanted him to kiss her again. "But what if you're wrong?"

"Believe me, I'm not." His reassuring smile as he lowered his mouth to hers sent a shiver up her spine. "Not about this."

When his firm lips covered hers, Abby tried to remain impassive, to prove to herself as much as to Russ that she was unaffected. But the tender way he traced her lower lip with his tongue, and the masculine taste of him when he coaxed her to open for him, quickly had her forgetting her resolve not to let it happen again.

Dropping the bandaging supplies, she curled her fingers in the fabric of his shirt and held on for dear life. The feel of his hard muscles beneath the chambray, and the steady beat of his heart, caused tingles of excitement to race up her spine and her knees to give way. When he slipped his tongue inside to explore and tease, a sweet warmth began to flow through her veins and a delicious fluttery feeling settled deep in the pit of her stomach.

She'd been kissed before, but never like this. Never with such mind-shattering tenderness or such mastery.

Abby couldn't stop a tiny moan of pleasure from escaping when Russ tightened his arms around her and aligned her body to his. The feel of his hard male frame against her softer feminine one sent a streak of longing throughout her entire body, and without a thought, she melted against him.

But when she became aware of his insistent arousal pressed to her lower belly, the heat coursing through her began to form a tight coil of need deep in the very core of her. And it scared her as little else could.

Pulling back, she shook her head. "R-Russ...I can't—"

"It's all right, honey." He allowed her to put space between them, but continued to hold her in the circle of his arms. "I'm not going to lie to you, Abby. I want you. But it's never been my style to force myself on a woman. And I'm not about to start now."

The sincerity in his brilliant blue eyes took her breath. She had no doubt he meant what he said. But what she was feeling at the moment wasn't his problem. It was hers.

"I know that. You're name isn't Harold." She hadn't intended to say the name of the boy who'd taken her to homecoming her sophomore year. Hoping Russ hadn't noticed, she hurried to add, "I'm the one I'm worried will do something stupid."

"Whoa. Back up just a minute. Who's Harold?"

Abby closed her eyes and took a deep breath. She should have known Russ would pick up on her blunder. "He was my date for a dance in high school. But that's not important."

"I disagree." His brow furrowed into a deep frown. "Did he try to—"

"Yes, but he decided differently."

Russ's frown deepened. "What changed his mind?"

The man was as tenacious as a bulldog going after a juicy bone. "Are you always this nosy?"

"Are you always this evasive?" His expression softened. "Tell me what happened, honey."

She sighed. It was clear Russ wasn't going to give up. "When I told him 'no,' Harold tried to force the issue. But my knee to his groin convinced him otherwise." She shook her head. "When I walked away, he was writhing on the ground, moaning and looking like he was going to throw up."

Russ winced as if he knew what Harold must have been feeling. "I can't say that he didn't get what he deserved. But damn, I'll bet that hurt like hell."

"I'm sure it did." Abby wasn't happy or proud of what she'd had to do. She didn't like hurting anything or anyone. But she wasn't going to be a victim if it was within her power to prevent it. "I'm sorry I had to hurt him, but it must have taught him a lesson. He never bothered me again."

Russ laughed. "I can't say I blame him."

She bit her lip in an effort to keep from smiling. "In fact, he refused to be anywhere near me unless there was a group of people around."

Russ's expression turned serious. "Abby, I give you my word that you'll never have to worry about something like that happening with me. I promise not to touch you unless you tell me to."

Staring into his steady blue gaze, she saw nothing but sincerity and she knew she could trust him to maintain his control no matter how heated the moment became. "Like I said before, it's not you I'm worried about."

He shook his head. "I don't think you have to be concerned about you, either. From what you've told me about your mother, and what I know about you, you're nothing like her."

"I hope not."

Releasing her, he bent to pick up the dressings for the gray mare. When he straightened and handed them to her, he smiled. "Have dinner with me tonight, Abby."

"I don't know—"

"I promise it will be just a couple of friends getting together for the evening. Nothing more."

"I don't even know where you live." Was she actually considering his offer?

"I live in the guest cottage on the other side of the lake." He opened the stall's half door and led the mare out into the wide aisle. "And I make great spaghetti and meatballs."

Abby weighed her options as she bent to assess the wound on the horse's fetlock. Uncle Grant had plans for the evening and Mercedes had another date with her boyfriend, Craig. Did she really want to spend the evening alone in the carriage house watching television?

Straightening, Abby shook her head. "I don't think we'll have to continue dressing it. The wound is almost completely healed."

"That's great." He led the mare back into her stall, then, securing the door, turned to face Abby. "Now, what about dinner? I could come by for you around seven."

She took a deep breath and made her decision. "Don't bother. I'll walk."

When he heard the knock on the front door, Russ wiped his hands on a towel and walked over to open it. The sight of Abby standing on the small porch, her dark auburn hair down around her shoulders, robbed him of breath. She was one of the most beautiful women he'd ever had the privilege to meet, and unless he missed his guess, she didn't even know it.

"You're just in time to help with the salad while I drain the spaghetti." He could tell she was nervous, and wanting to put her at ease, he grinned. "If I try to toss the damned stuff, we'll be sweeping it off the floor."

"What makes you think I can do any better?" she asked, laughing.

The delightful sound caused a warm feeling to spread throughout his chest. "You're a wo—"

"Watch it, buster." Her dimples appeared when she smiled. "You're about to get in over your head."

His heart stalled and he wasn't sure it would ever beat again. She had his two biggest weaknesses—red hair and dimples—and the evening was going to be a true test of his control.

Clearing the rust from his throat, he tried to remember what they'd been talking about. "I was just going to tell you that you're a woman…who should sit down and rest while I toss the salad."

"Good save, cowboy." She laughed as she walked into his tiny kitchen, picked up the two oversize wooden forks and began tossing the salad. "Not that I believe for a minute that's what you intended to say."

They worked side by side in companionable silence for several minutes—he putting the finishing touches on the spaghetti and she filling salad plates and setting the table.

"Would you like some wine?" he asked, holding the chair for her at the small, wooden kitchen table.

She shook her head. "I have to confess that I'm not much of a wine connoisseur. I normally drink water or iced tea with my meals."

"Don't feel bad, honey." He laughed. "I never touch the stuff, either."

Her expressive eyes widened. "But you make wine for a living."

Reaching into the refrigerator, he brought out a pitcher of tea, poured them each a glass, then sat down opposite her. "When I drink, which isn't all that often, I prefer beer."

She lifted her glass. "Here's to wine-making, beer-drinking, rodeo cowboys."

Grinning, he touched his glass to hers. "And to beautiful, large-animal vets with attitude."

They talked over dinner and Russ learned about Abby's brother, Ford, developing a highly successful cattle feed while he was still in college. He'd leased the patented formula to several major feed companies and now the product was distributed not only in the States, but in several foreign countries, as well.

"Is he still in development?" Russ asked.

"No. Ford's an independent consultant to large cattle breeders, now." She grinned. "And when he's not in some other part of the country tromping through somebody's feedlot, he's out in our fields working on his tan."

The reappearance of Abby's dimples caused the air to lodge in Russ's lungs, and he had to concentrate hard on what she'd said. "There's nothing wrong with that. In July and August, when the temperature hits the upper nineties around here, I've been known to take my shirt off while I work in the vineyards."

"I thought the weather in Napa Valley was mild all the time," she said, placing her fork on the edge of her plate.

"It is." As if to contradict him, lightning flashed outside, followed by the rumble of thunder.

They both laughed.

"Well, most of the time the weather's nice," he said, rising to take their plates to the sink. "I baked an apple pie for dessert. Would you like some now or do you want to wait and have it with coffee later?"

"You made a pie? I'm impressed."

Turning to face her, he gave her a sheepish grin. "I didn't say I made it. Just baked it."

"Oh, I see." Her smile sent his blood pressure soaring and had him wondering if he'd be able to keep the promise he'd made her earlier in the afternoon. "I think having pie with coffee later would be nice."

He nodded. "Sounds good to me. I'll start the coffeemaker." A sudden flash of lightning illuminated the room a split second before thunder rattled the plates in the sink and everything went completely dark. "Or not."

She laughed, and the sound sent a shaft of longing straight up his spine and had him deciding that he'd been a complete fool for promising to keep his hands to himself. "I think we'll be eating that pie by candlelight," she said.

"Looks like it," he agreed, cursing himself for not thinking of using candles during dinner. It appeared he needed to brush up on his dating techniques, he decided as he opened the drawer where he kept a flashlight, candles and an odd assortment of small tools.

But as he pulled two fat, red candles from the drawer and set them on saucers to light the wicks, he wondered who the hell he was kidding. How often did he entertain a woman at the cottage? And especially one like Abby? Hell, he could count on one hand the number of times he'd even been out with a woman who had a college education, let alone one with a doctorate.

"Let's sit in the living room," he said, leading the way into the small sitting area. "The power will probably be back on in a few minutes."

At least, he hoped it would. Sitting on the couch with a beautiful woman in the romantic glow from the candles was not going to be easy on his libido.

"I'm used to the electricity going off," Abby said, sitting beside him. "In winter, our power lines snap from the cold, and in spring and summer, winds from thunderstorms tear them down."

"We don't have outages that often," he said, wondering what on earth he'd been thinking when he'd asked her to dinner. In about two seconds they were going to exhaust talking about the weather. Then what? He had a few ideas, but all of them involved her in his arms.

Damn! He should have known that promise not to touch her until she told him to was going to come back and bite him in the butt.

"When are you competing again?" she asked, breaking into his morose thoughts.

"This weekend, down in Wild Horse Flats." He shrugged. "It's a small rodeo about three hundred and fifty miles south of here, but I always do well there."

She gave him a smile that made his heart pound. "Sometimes the smaller rodeos are the most fun."

"You like watching rodeo?"

She nodded. "When we were in high school, I used to do a little barrel racing and Ford competed as a calf roper at some of the ones around Crawley."

He lifted his arm to put it on the back of the couch behind her shoulders, then dropped it back onto his thigh—she might think he was going back on that damned promise.

"Why did you stop competing?"

"I had to make a choice between taking summer classes to finish school early or doing something fun. I chose school." She gave him an odd look. "Were you going to put your arm around me?"

He cleared his throat. "Actually, I was going to rest it along the back of the couch, but—"

Her eyes widened. "Don't you think you're taking what you said this afternoon to the extreme?"

"Not really."

He'd keep his word, even if it killed him. And with her sitting so close, it just might.

"Well, I do." She shifted on the couch to face him. "You mean you aren't even going to try to kiss me?"

He shook his head. "I gave you my word. The only way I'll touch you is if you tell me to."

Abby stared at Russ for several long seconds, her heart hammering against her ribs for all it was worth. Could she really be that forward? Did she have the nerve to tell him that she wanted him to modify his promise?

After walking back to the carriage house, she'd spent the rest of the afternoon thinking about what he'd told her. And he was right—she wasn't her mother, nor was she anything like her.

Grace Ashton was weak-willed, hedonistic and self-ish. But her daughter was a strong, capable woman who was just coming into her own. A woman who was learning to trust her instincts and determine exactly what she wanted. And heaven help her, at the moment she wanted Russ to hold her, wanted him to kiss her like she'd never been kissed before.

But he'd made that dumb promise and she was going to have to do something she wasn't exactly comfortable with. She was either going to have to ask him to kiss her, or she was going to have to kiss him.

Deciding that action spoke louder than words, her heart skipped a beat when she leaned forward and pressed her lips to his. She'd never in all of her twenty-four years done anything like this, but as she nibbled at his firm, warm mouth, she found the experience extremely exciting and, to a degree, liberating.

When he groaned and shifted toward her, she expected him to put his arms around her and take over. But other than kissing her back, he just sat there. Apparently, Russ was waiting for her to verbalize what she wanted.

She leaned back and noticed that both of his hands were balled into tight fists at his sides. He wanted to hold her as badly as she wanted to be held. But he wasn't going to make a move until she let him know that she was ready for him to take an active role.

"Russ?"

"What, Abby?" His eyes were still closed and he sounded as if he was having trouble breathing.

"Will you please touch me?"

Four

Abby watched Russ's eyes fly open a moment before he groaned and reached out to pull her into his arms. "Good Lord, woman, I thought you'd never ask."

"I have something else I want you to do." A shiver raced up her spine at the feel of his hard body pressed to hers.

"What's that, honey?" he asked, nuzzling the side of her neck.

"I want you to forget about that promise."

She felt him go perfectly still a moment before he drew back to look at her. His expression was a mixture of relief and confusion.

"Are you sure?"

Taking a deep breath, she nodded. "I'll let you know if something makes me nervous or uncomfortable."

"That works for me." He lightly kissed her cheek. "But do me a favor."

Her skin tingled where his lips had been. "And that would be?"

"Just keep in mind that I'm not Harold." Giving her a grin that made her stomach flutter, he added, "All you have to do is tell me no. It doesn't take a knee to the groin to get my attention."

"I'll remember that," she said, putting her arms around his wide shoulders. "Now, kiss me like you mean it, cowboy."

His wicked grin caused her insides to quiver. "I aim to please, ma'am."

Abby's heart raced and her stomach felt as if it did a backflip when he slowly lowered his mouth to cover hers. Circling his neck with her arms, she savored the feel of his firm lips teasing hers, reveled in the contrast of their bodies. Honed by years of physical labor, Russ had muscles strong enough to crush her, yet he held her to him as gently as if he held a small child.

But when he slipped his tongue inside to stroke hers with infinite care, she ceased to think and tentatively met him halfway. As she tasted and explored him as he did her, she was rewarded with his groan of pleasure, and a feminine power that she'd never experienced before began to fill her. For the first time in her life, she was exploring her own sexuality, beginning to understand what it meant to be a woman. And she loved it.

A tremor passed through his big body a moment before he broke the kiss and lifted her to sit on his lap. "Honey…we'd better stop…before this goes any…further," he said, sounding completely out of breath.

His hard arousal pressing against her backside caused an answering tightness to form deep in her belly and a spark of need to skip along every nerve ending in her body. Scooting off his lap to sit beside him, she decided that she'd tested her newfound freedom as far as she was comfortable with for one night.

"Thank you for dinner, but it's getting late and I should probably go." She listened to the gently falling rain outside. "Do you think you could drive me back to the carriage house?"

"Sure," he said, nodding. "But we'll have to wait a minute or two."

"Why?"

His deep chuckle sent a wave of goose bumps shimmering over her skin. "At the moment, I don't think I have enough blood north of my belt buckle to keep from passing out when I stand up."

Her cheeks heated, and for the first time in her life, she couldn't think of a thing to say.

Reaching out, his smile faded as he threaded his fingers through her hair, then cupped the back of her head and pulled her forward for a quick kiss. "Go to the rodeo down in Wild Horse Flats with me this weekend, Abby."

She stared at him for endless seconds. "Russ, I'm not sure that would be a good idea."

Why was she hesitating? Why wasn't she telling him "no" outright?

He shook his head and placed his index finger to her lips. "We'll leave here on Friday and be back Monday. And in case you're wondering about the sleeping arrangements, my horse trailer has living quarters with two beds." Kissing her again, he rose to his feet and held his hand out to help her from the couch. "Just think about it. You can let me know your answer later in the week."

"Uncle Grant, I haven't heard you mention much about the Spencer situation in the past few days," Abby said over breakfast the next morning. "How are things going with that?"

Looking over the rim of his coffee cup, her uncle shrugged. "About the same. He refuses to meet with me or any of the other Ashtons from here at The Vines."

His obsession with meeting his father was beginning to concern her. "What are you going to do?"

"Wait him out." He gave her a fatherly smile. "I have a meeting this morning with Cole and Eli to discuss our options. If we're lucky, we'll come up with something to prompt Spencer to meet with us. They'd like their questions answered, too. One of the ideas we've come up with is having me go to the media with the story."

"Do you think that will work?" she asked, clearing their empty plates to put them in the sink.

For the past few mornings, she'd prepared breakfast for the two of them in the carriage house. It was really the only time they'd found to talk.

Her uncle nodded. "I hope so. I doubt that he'd want his business associates to know that he was guilty of bigamy, or that he gained control of the Lattimer Corporation by means of fraud." He smiled. "But I don't want you worrying about it, Abby. Things will work out for the best."

"I hope so," she said, praying he was right. Uncle Grant deserved answers from the man who'd deserted him all those years ago.

"But enough about me." He motioned for her to sit down and finish her coffee. "I have a few minutes before I'm supposed to meet with Cole and Eli. Tell me what you've been up to, Sprite."

His use of the nickname he'd given her when she was small caused her heart to swell with love for the man who had sacrificed so much at such an early age for her and her brother. Her uncle had only been twenty-four when his sister walked out and left him to raise her two children. But Abby could never remember a single time that she'd heard him complain or express any regrets for the way his life had turned out. He'd never married and, although he hadn't said as much, she suspected that he'd given her and Ford his undivided attention in an attempt to make up for the lack of love from Grace.

"There's really not much to tell," she said. "Mercedes gave me a tour of the winery the other day and tried to educate me in the fine art of wine tasting." Grinning, she added, "And I've come to a conclusion about that."

"Really?"

She nodded. "I've decided that wine must be an acquired taste."

He laughed. "That's true. Anything else going on?"

"Other than treating one of the horses down at the stable for a lacerated fetlock, I really haven't been doing a lot," she said, trying to decide if she should bring up Russ asking her to go to the rodeo in Wild Horse Flats with him.

Normally, she discussed everything with her uncle, listened to his opinion, then made her decisions. But going away for the weekend with a man was a lot more personal than making up her mind whether to become a large-animal veterinarian or which college to attend.

Deciding that she'd have to explain her absence if she did accept Russ's invitation, she took a deep breath. "Uncle Grant, have you met Russ Gannon, the vineyard foreman?"

"No, but I've heard a lot of good things about him."
He took a sip of his coffee. "Cole speaks very highly of
him. And Eli thinks if Gannon set his mind to it, he
could grow grapes on the moon."

"I don't know much about his ability to manage a
vineyard, but he is nice," she murmured, wondering
how to proceed. This was one of the rare times Abby
missed not having a mother or older sister to talk to.

Uncle Grant's green eyes twinkled mischievously. "It
sounds to me like he's made quite an impression on you,
Sprite."

That's an understatement, she thought, rising to refill
their coffee mugs. "Russ took me horseback riding a few
days ago and we had dinner at his place last night." When
she returned to the table, she met her uncle's curious gaze
head on. "And he's asked me to go with him to a rodeo
he's competing in down in Wild Horse Flats this weekend."

"Are you going?" Uncle Grant asked, raising one
dark eyebrow as he lifted his cup to take a sip.

Abby shrugged. "I'm not sure."

Slowly setting the mug back on the table, he reached
across to cover her hand with his. "Are you asking me
what I think you should do?"

She frowned. Was she asking for his opinion?

"Not really," she said, thinking aloud. "I just wanted
to let you know so that you don't worry if I'm not
around this weekend."

"So you're considering it?"

"Yes."

"And you're leaning in that direction?"

When she nodded, he stared at her for several long moments before he finally spoke. "You might not have asked for my opinion, but I'm going to give it to you anyway."

Abby had expected no less of him. "I'm listening."

"You've always been more like a daughter to me than a niece," he said, his voice slightly rough. "And the father in me says hell, no, there isn't a man alive that's good enough for you." He paused to clear his throat. "But you're old enough to know what you want. And you've always had a good head on your shoulders." He gave her hand a gentle squeeze. "I trust your judgment, Abby." He stood up to leave for his meeting. "No matter what choice you make, I know it will be the right one for you."

Rising to her feet, she hugged him. "Thank you, Uncle Grant."

"You're welcome, Sprite." He chuckled as he wrapped her in a bear hug. "Even if I'm not sure what for."

Abby kissed his lean cheek. "For always knowing exactly what to say."

On Thursday afternoon, Russ had just finished grooming Dancer and started brushing down Blue when Abby walked into the stable. He hadn't seen her since driving her back to the carriage house the night he'd had her over for dinner. And, truth to tell, he wasn't the least bit surprised that she'd been avoiding him.

In the past three days, he'd decided that she probably thought he had mush for brains. And he couldn't say he blamed her. They barely knew each other, had been on one date—if that's what dinner at his place could be called—and he'd asked her to go away for the weekend. He knew how much she worried about turning out like her mother. What the hell had he been thinking?

"Hi," she said, walking up to stand on the other side of Blue.

Her soft voice sent a shock wave straight through him, and he gripped the brush he held so tightly, he'd probably end up leaving his fingerprints in the wood.

Damn, but she looked good. Her cinnamon-colored hair was pulled back in a loose ponytail, exposing her slender neck and the satiny skin that he'd love to kiss. His body tightened predictably.

"Hi, yourself," he finally managed to get out around the cotton coating his throat. "I haven't seen you for a while."

"Mercedes asked me to go with her to San Francisco for a couple of days of shopping." She smiled. "I don't think I could have gotten a better workout on a StairMaster."

Laughing, he nodded. "Some of those hills are pretty steep."

They both fell silent, and he knew his invitation was the reason neither of them had much to say. Continuing to brush the gelding, he tried to think of a way to gracefully retract his request before she had the uncomfortable task of turning him down.

When he finally decided to just tell her straight out that he understood why she wouldn't be going with him to Wild Horse Flats, they both spoke at once.

"Abby, I think—"

"Russ, I've decided—"

Stopping, they both laughed nervously.

"Ladies first."

Her gaze dropped to her boot tops and he figured he knew what was coming. But when she raised her gaze to meet his, she smiled. "I've given it a lot of thought and if you still want me to attend the rodeo with you this weekend, I'd like to go."

His heart thumped double-time and he suddenly found it extremely hard to breathe. He'd mentioned the living quarters in the horse trailer having two beds, and he fully intended for her to sleep in one and him in the other. But considering they couldn't keep their hands off each other, she had to know there was a strong possibility they'd end up making love.

The thought had him harder than hell in less than two seconds flat. Resting his forearms on Blue's back, he was glad the gelding stood between them. At least she couldn't see how her accepting his offer affected him, beyond his grinning like a damned fool.

"That's great. Do you think you could be ready to leave by noon tomorrow?" he asked.

She nodded. "When is your first event?"

"Not until Saturday morning. But it's a seven hour drive and I'd like to get there in time to get a good night's sleep."

"I can understand that," she said, running her hand along Blue's back. The horse's hide quivered with pleasure at her touch, and Russ couldn't help but wish it was his skin she was stroking. "Do you want me to come down here early enough to help load the horses?"

"Thanks, but Dancer is the only one I'm taking," he said, laying aside the brush he'd been using on Blue. "A couple of friends called this week and asked me to haze for them during the steer wrestling."

"Okay." She turned to leave. "I guess I'll see you at noon tomorrow."

"Where do you think you're going?" he asked, walking around the roan.

Stopping, she looked uncertain. "I thought I'd go back to the carriage house to start packing."

He shook his head and reached for her. "Don't think you're getting away that easy." Pulling her to him, Russ smiled. "I missed you, Abby."

"I missed you, too."

Her smile sent his blood pressure soaring and, even if his life depended on it, there was no way he could stop himself from covering her mouth with his. The moment he touched her perfect lips, they parted on a soft sigh, and he didn't think twice about slipping his tongue inside.

In the past three days, he'd craved the taste of her, the feel of her body pressed to his. As short a time as they'd known each other, it was completely insane, but he was quickly becoming addicted to her sweetness.

When she responded to his kiss by touching her tongue to his, fire streaked through his veins, and his knees threatened to buckle. He wanted her with a fierceness that robbed him of all reason and, needing to touch her, he slid his palm up along her side to the swell of her breast. He heard her soft intake of breath when he cupped the soft mound with his palm, but to his satisfaction, she didn't pull away. Instead, he felt her arms tighten around him and her fingers grip the back of his shirt for support.

Encouraged by her acceptance of his exploration, he used the pad of his thumb to chafe the hardened tip through the layers of her T-shirt and bra. Her moan of pleasure sent a jolt of desire straight up his spine and caused an answering groan to rumble up from deep in his chest.

Realizing that he was close to losing the tight grip he held on his control, Russ slowly moved his hand down to her waist as he broke the kiss. "Honey, I'd like nothing better than to stay here like this for the rest of the day, but it could prove dangerous."

"Why…do you…say that?" she asked, sounding as out of breath as he felt.

His chest tightened when he leaned back to look down at her. Her porcelain cheeks wore the rosy blush of desire, and her lips were slightly swollen from his kiss. She was absolutely beautiful, and his body throbbed with the need to claim her as his.

He laughed, dispelling some—but not nearly enough—of his pent-up tension. "If this goes on much longer, I'm afraid I might end up suffering the same fate as poor old Harold."

To his surprise, instead of laughing, she shook her head. "You don't need to worry about that ever happening," she said softly. Then, leaning forward, she pressed a kiss to the skin exposed at the open collar of his shirt. "I'll see you tomorrow, Russ."

Feeling as if his heart was about to pound a hole right through his rib cage, he watched Abby walk to the end of the stable and disappear through the wide double doors. He had to concentrate on taking first one deep breath, then another.

He'd bet everything he owned that one of two things was going to happen this weekend. They were either going to make love, or he was going to go stark raving mad.

Five

While Russ parked the gooseneck trailer at the campground next to the rodeo grounds, Abby led Dancer over to the small barn not far from their campsite. When they'd first arrived, Russ had explained that, because of the many small rodeos and horse shows the arena hosted, the campground owners provided stalls for horses as a courtesy to visiting contestants.

After she got the gelding settled into one of the large stalls, she returned to the trailer to find Russ unlocking the door to the living quarters. Grinning, he stepped back and swept off his Resistol in a gallant gesture. "Your home away from home awaits."

Laughing, she stepped up into the camper area of the trailer and looked around. There was a tiny bathroom with a shower, a galley kitchenette and a bench-type sofa that could be converted into a bed. In the elevated gooseneck section, a large, comfortable-looking bed spanned the entire width of the trailer.

"This is really nice, Russ."

He shrugged, but she could tell by the look on his face that her comment pleased him. "It's not The Vines, but it makes traveling a lot easier." He opened the small refrigerator. "Would you like something to drink before we turn in?"

His mention of them going to bed caused her stomach to flutter. They wouldn't be sleeping in the same bed, but there would only be a few feet and a flimsy privacy curtain separating them. Why hadn't she thought of how intimate sharing such a small space was going to be?

Taking a deep breath, she decided it was better not to think of that now. "Thank you, but I think I'll pass on the soda." They'd stopped a couple of hours ago to unload Dancer in order for him to stretch his legs, and, before getting back on the interstate, they'd gotten a burger and French fries at a fast-food restaurant. "I'm still stuffed from dinner."

"I don't see how," he said, frowning. "You ended up giving me most of your fries and part of your sandwich."

"I wasn't very hungry." Abby wasn't about to tell

Russ that her lack of appetite had been due to the butterflies in her stomach that seemed to multiply the closer
they got to the campground.

Switching on the built-in television, he smiled and
reached for the doorknob. "Why don't you kick off your
boots and get comfortable while I feed Dancer and see
that he has plenty of water for the night. When I get
back, it'll just about be time to go to bed."

Every time he made a reference to *night, turning in*
or *bed,* her spine tingled and her stomach did a backflip.
"When does the first event start tomorrow morning?"

"Not until ten, but registration starts at seven," he
said, opening the door. "Besides, we'll need to eat
breakfast. And by that time, I'm betting you'll be pretty
hungry."

"Maybe." She doubted she'd be able to eat much of
anything all weekend.

"Make yourself at home while I'm gone." He stepped
down, out of the trailer. "I'll be back in a few minutes."

Abby waited until he'd closed the door before she released the breath she'd been holding. What on earth
had she been thinking when she'd made the decision to
come to the rodeo with him? The living quarters were
miniscule. And hadn't it been proven, time and again,
that they couldn't be close without falling into each
other's arms?

But even as she questioned her reasoning, she knew

the answer. She simply didn't want to be away from him. And that made no sense at all.

They'd only known each other a little less than two weeks. But when she'd gone on the shopping trip with Mercedes, all she'd been able to think about was getting back to The Vines, and Russ.

Removing her boots, she curled up on the couch and blindly stared at the small television. Could she be falling for him? Was it possible to care for someone that much in such a short amount of time?

When she was with him, she had a sense of belonging, of being where she was supposed to be. And when they were apart, all she could think about was how much she missed his deep laughter, his warm embrace and the kisses that threatened to turn her into a cinder.

Uncle Grant had always said that when she saw something she wanted, she knew it right away and wasn't afraid to go after it. But he'd been talking about her education and career, not affairs of the heart.

Was it time to release the tight grip she'd always kept on herself? Did she dare let herself go, and take the chance that she might fall in love with Russ?

Before she could reach any conclusions about herself and her feelings for Russ, the door opened and he entered the trailer.

"How would you like to go to a dance tomorrow night, honey?"

"Is that part of the rodeo festivities?"

"Not usually." He grinned as he sat beside her on the couch to pull off his boots. "I was talking to a friend of mine down at the barn and he said some of the guys' wives and girlfriends have been complaining about it being Valentine's weekend and them being stuck here at the rodeo."

She laughed. "In other words, the men are trying to make amends by throwing an impromptu dance."

"Something like that. A couple of guys heard their names used in conjunction with 'insensitive' and 'un-romantic.' But when some of the women threatened to make them sleep in the barn with the horses, they fig-ured the situation was getting serious." Grinning, he stood to remove his keys and change from his jeans pocket. "So, would you like to go?"

"Sure." She laughed. "It sounds like a lot of fun. But I think I'd better warn you—I haven't gone dancing in ages. I might step on your toes a lot."

His deep laughter sent a tiny electric charge skipping over every nerve in her body. "It won't be a problem. I only dance the slow ones, and mainly just stand in one spot, hold my partner close and sway in time to the music."

The thought of having Russ hold her close made her feel warm all over. Deciding to put a little distance be-tween them, she rose to her feet and looked around for the small overnight bag that she'd given Russ to load into the camper before they'd left The Vines.

"If you could tell me where you put—"

Before she could ask where he'd stored the bag, he reached into the tiny closet and removed some bedding and her overnight case. "Here you go," he said, handing it to her. "The bathroom is pretty small, but I think there's room in there to change."

Stepping into the cramped little room, Abby quickly stripped out of her clothes and put on her nightshirt. But as she started to open the door, she realized that she'd forgotten to pack her robe.

"Now what are you going to do?" she muttered, thoroughly disgusted with herself.

"Did you say something?" Russ called.

"No, just talking to myself."

Glancing down at the thin cotton shirt that ended well above her knees, she decided she had two choices. She could either change back into her clothes and go to bed fully dressed, which wasn't at all appealing. Or, she could hold her head up and act as if nothing was out of the ordinary, walk the few feet to the couch and dive under the covers Russ had taken from the closet.

She really didn't see that she had a choice and before she could chicken out, she opened the door and walked out of the bathroom.

"I could have made my own bed," she said, when she

found him tucking the sheet and blanket under the end of the couch cushion.

"You take the bed. I'll sleep here."

His back was to her, but when he turned around, it was all Russ could do to keep his mouth from dropping wide open. In his entire life he'd never seen a sexier sight than Abby standing there in that light turquoise, oversize T-shirt. It wasn't, by any stretch of the imagination, supposed to be provocative. But he'd never seen her look so hot.

The soft fabric loosely draped her breasts, but did little to hide their hardened peaks, leaving no doubt that she'd removed her bra. When he noticed that the hem of the damned thing barely reached midthigh, it was all he could do to keep from groaning aloud. She had the longest, shapeliest legs he'd ever seen. His overactive imagination—not to mention his hormones—were off and running. When he thought of how it would feel to have her wrapped around him as they made love, his body came to full erection, and he clenched his back teeth together so hard, it would probably take a crowbar to pry them apart.

As he continued to stare, he noticed that Abby's cheeks had turned a pretty pink and he could tell she was embarrassed. But she held her head high and her gaze never faltered.

"I forgot to bring my robe."

Without thinking twice, he stepped forward and pulled her to him. "Don't get me wrong, honey. I'm not complaining about what you're wearing." He drew some much-needed air into his lungs. "Actually, make that what you're *not* wearing. But you're about to give me a heart attack, and it's getting damned near impossible for me to keep my hands to myself."

Her soft body pressed to his was heaven and hell rolled into one, and he'd have liked nothing more than to strip them both, climb into bed and spend the rest of the night loving her. But she trusted him not to push for more than she was ready to give. And he'd walk through hell before he let her down. The only trouble was, he was damned close to reaching his limit, and he was man enough to admit it.

Knowing that he'd be lost if he so much as kissed her, he nuzzled the satiny skin along the column of her neck. "I'm giving this chivalry thing my best shot, honey. But I'm fighting a losing battle. That's why I think it's time for you to go to bed."

When he released her and stepped back to pull on his boots, she looked confused. "Where are you going?"

Reaching for the door, he stopped long enough to give her a quick kiss. "I'm going to run a few laps around the campground, then I'll find a couple of horses to bench-press. After that, I may wrestle a bull or two."

Russ stepped out of the trailer, closed the door behind him and walked away before he could change his mind, go back inside and make love to her until they both passed out from exhaustion.

As he walked down the path to the barn, he released a frustrated breath and willed himself to relax. He was in a place he'd never been before and he had no idea how he was going to handle it, or even if it could be handled. Something told him that it was beyond his control, and that's what had him tied in knots.

There was no doubt that Abby aroused him physically. Hell, he'd been hard almost from the minute he'd laid eyes on her. But the fact that she turned him on emotionally was what had him waging an internal battle with himself.

He'd thought they could have a good time while she was visiting California and, when the time came for her to go back to her farm in Nebraska, there would be no feelings involved and no regrets. But somehow she'd managed to get under his skin as no other woman ever had, and if they made love, he had a feeling he'd never be the same again.

Shaking his head, he sat on a bale of straw outside of Dancer's stall. Something else that had to be considered was the fact that he was almost positive she was still a virgin. And that put a whole different spin on the situation.

He was old-fashioned enough to believe that when

a man took a woman's virginity it meant something more than just a roll in the hay for physical relief. A woman's first time making love should be special, and with a man she cared for deeply and who cared for her in return.

There was no doubt in his mind that they both had that going for them. But the logistics were all wrong for them to build any kind of lasting relationship. Her home was a thousand miles away, and he had nothing to offer her if she stayed here.

Rising to his feet, he slowly started back toward the trailer. If they made love, could they both come away from their time together without suffering some kind of emotional pain? Or when the time came for her to return to Nebraska, would he be able to watch her go without his heart going with her?

The following afternoon, Abby watched Russ back the bay gelding into the hazer's box for the fourth time as he prepared to help another one of his friends compete in the steer wrestling event. He and Dancer were apparently in high demand for the job of keeping the animal on a straight course while the competing cowboy slid from his mount to wrestle the steer to the ground. And Abby knew why. Moving as one, Russ and Dancer made the task look effortless and the cowboys they hazed for did well in the timed event.

"And just where have you been hiding all my life, sugar?" a male voice whispered close to her ear.

Glancing up, Abby found a handsome cowboy with a leering grin preparing to sit down beside her. She scooted over to put as much space between them as possible.

"You sure are a pretty little gal," he said, sitting a bit closer than she was comfortable with.

She'd encountered his type before and giving him a quelling look, she turned her attention back to the action in the arena without comment.

"What's the matter, sugar? Cat got your tongue?" he asked, putting his arm around her.

Without a word, Abby slapped his arm from her shoulders and stood up to find another seat.

"Now that's no way to be," he said, rising to his feet. "I'm just trying to be friendly."

"Number one, I don't want to be your friend," she said, spotting an empty seat several rows down the bleachers. "And number two, my name *isn't* sugar."

He caught her by the arm. "How can we get to know each other if—"

She glared at him as she pulled from his grasp. "If you don't want your hand broken, you'd better keep it to yourself."

Noticing that the steer wrestling event had concluded, she descended the steps and started walking toward the bucking chutes. She spotted Dancer standing docilely just outside the arena gate. But when she looked for Russ, he was nowhere in sight.

"You sure are a feisty little thing," the irritating cowboy said, trotting to keep up with her.

She kept on walking as flashes of the past and a persistent boy named Harold crept into her mind. She tried to quell the sudden twinge of panic that began clawing at her insides. She was longer a teenager and they were far from being alone in a crowd of fifteen hundred people.

"What do you say we find a nice quiet place where we can get to know each other better?" The man slipped his arm around her waist and turned her to face him. "I'd make sure you enjoyed—"

Before she could raise her knee and stop the harassment once and for all, Russ seemed to come out of nowhere to spin the guy around. "Touch her one more time, you son of a bitch, and you'll be picking your teeth out of the dirt."

The man looked as if he wanted to argue the point.

"Go ahead, give me a reason." It was clear that Russ was furious and meant every word he said.

"You're welcome to her, buddy," the cowboy said sullenly as he backed away. "She's not worth that much trouble."

Once the man disappeared in the crowd, Russ turned back to her. "Are you all right?"

She nodded. "I could have handled the situation."

"Not as long as I'm around you won't," he said, taking her into his arms. "You have my word that I'll move heaven and earth to keep creeps like that away from you, Abby."

"I was just about to give him the same lesson in manners that I gave Harold," she said, snuggling into his embrace.

Russ's arms tightened around her. "When I looked up into the stands and saw that bastard's filthy hands on you, I couldn't get off Dancer fast enough."

"Nothing happened." His protectiveness caused a warm feeling to fill every fiber of her being and for the first time in her life, she felt as safe as if she'd been with her uncle, brother, or their hired hand, Buck.

"Honey, I could stay here with you in my arms for the rest of the day, but the bull riding is about to start," Russ said when the next event was announced over the loud speaker. He kissed he temple. "Will you be all right for a few minutes while I go kick some bovine butt?"

Abby raised up on tiptoe to place a kiss on his lean cheek. "I'll be fine, but I want you to promise me something."

"What's that?"

"Be careful."

"You bet." His tender smile sent shivers racing straight through her. "I have a date tonight that I don't intend to miss."

* * *

Two hours later, Abby led the bay gelding back to the barn at the campground and couldn't help but wonder what was going on. Russ had been acting strangely since the conclusion of the bullriding event and immediately afterward, he'd told her he had something he needed to take care of and asked if she minded getting Dancer settled into his stall for the night. Then, handing her his keys to the trailer, he'd given her a quick kiss, got into a truck with another cowboy and left the rodeo grounds in a cloud of dust.

"Your owner is up to something," she told the gelding as she brushed him down. "He has a great ride on an ornery bull, makes the eight-second whistle, then takes off for parts unknown, leaving me and you to fend for ourselves."

Dancer snorted and stomped his foot.

"I couldn't agree more," she said, laughing as she patted his dark brown neck.

Making sure the horse had a fresh bucket of water and a scoop of oats, Abby walked up the path to the trailer. She'd just started to unlock the door to the living quarters when the truck Russ had left in came to a sliding halt a few feet away.

When he got out, he waited until the truck drove on down to a horse trailer several yards away. Then, holding his arm behind him, he walked toward her.

"Did you take care of whatever you needed to do?" she asked.

"Sure did." His smile made her insides quiver when he brought his arm from behind his back and handed her a single red rose in a cut-crystal vase. "Happy Valentine's Day, honey."

Touched by his thoughtfulness, her eyes filled with tears and her hand shook when she took the rose from him. "Oh, Russ! It's beautiful!"

Putting his arms around her, he held her close. "I didn't mean to make you cry."

"I can't help it." She rested her cheek against his wide chest. "This is one of the nicest things anyone has ever done for me. Thank you."

"These are happy tears. Right?"

She nodded. "Oh, yes."

His chest expanded and she knew he was breathing a sigh of relief. "I wanted to buy a dozen, but the florist was closing for the day when J.B. and I got there. We bought the last two roses she had left."

"This is perfect," she said, meaning it.

"I'm glad you like it." He kissed the top of her head. "Now, let's go inside so I can take a shower and change clothes before we go out to dinner and the dance."

"Where's the dance being held?" Abby asked as they left the steak house where they'd had dinner.

When they'd arrived, Russ had said something to the hostess, who'd smiled and led them to a cozy, candlelit table in a corner of the crowded restaurant. On their way to the table, they'd passed a couple of Russ's friends with their dates. But other than polite greetings, the couples, as if by unspoken agreement, had stayed to themselves, and Abby decided it was probably because of the romantic holiday they were all celebrating.

"Some of the guys tried to get a private room at one of the restaurants, but everything was already booked up. That's why we're having the dance at the camp-ground activity center," Russ said, helping her into the passenger side of his truck. "The owner is going to fold the divider back and open up the two rooms for us." He chuckled. "Otherwise, we'd be dancing between the pool and Ping-Pong tables."

She grinned. "I'll feel right at home."

He frowned. "You're kidding."

"No."

He shut the door, then rounded the front of the truck to slide in behind the steering wheel. "How big is Crawley?"

"You should be asking how little it is," she said, laughing. "It only has a population of between five and six hundred."

"That's all?" He looked surprised as he drove out of the restaurant parking lot. "I know you said you came from a small town, but I didn't realize you meant *that* small."

"That's all of the people." She grinned. "But the cattle population is a different story. I think the last survey report from the Ag Department listed about five thousand head of cattle on the farms and ranches surrounding Crawley."

"It sounds like it would have to have a lot of wide-open spaces," he said as he drove the short distance to the campground.

"You'll have to visit sometime and I'll show you around," she said, before she could stop herself.

When he parked the truck beside his trailer, Russ turned and gave her a smile that curled her toes inside her Tony Lamas. "One of these days, I'm going to take you up on that offer."

"Do you mean it?"

She knew she sounded pathetically hopeful, but she didn't care. Despite what she'd told Mercedes about not having time for a man in her life or a long-distance relationship, she couldn't bear the idea of never seeing Russ again.

He gave her a quick kiss, then, grinning, reached for the driver's side door handle. "I have a feeling I'm going to be logging a lot of frequent-flyer miles in the near future, honey."

Abby's heart skipped several beats, and she couldn't believe how relieved she felt knowing Russ wanted them to continue seeing each other after she returned home. When he opened the passenger door, she got out of the truck and wrapped her arms around his shoulders. "I'm going to hold you to that, cowboy."

"I'd rather you hold me against *you*," he said, pulling her to him. He kissed her until they both gasped for breath, then, stepping back, took her hand in his. "I think we'd better walk over to the dance before I forget I'm supposed to be a gentleman."

She could tell the toll that all of their recent togetherness was taking on Russ. And, for that matter, the weekend hadn't been all that easy for her, either.

When she'd come to California to see why her uncle Grant had extended his stay, she hadn't counted on finding someone special. But from the moment she met Russ, something inside of her—something she hadn't even known existed—had come to life. In his arms, she felt confident and in control, and with his help, she'd realized that she was nothing like her mother.

Glancing up at his handsome face as they walked toward the building where the dance was being held, she knew beyond a shadow of doubt that her first instincts about him had been right on the money. Russ Gannon was trustworthy and honorable and the only man she'd ever met who came close to having the unwavering integrity she so admired in her uncle Grant.

"Hey, Russ!" A cowboy wearing a black Resistol

with a hawk's feather in the hat band waved to them from a table on the far side of the room.

Russ acknowledged the man with a nod of his head as he guided her toward the table. "There's J. B. Gardner. He said he and his wife, Nina, would save us a couple of seats."

As they walked toward the couple, Abby recognized the petite blonde as one of the women she'd seen sitting in the stands of the arena during the day's events.

"I'd just about given up on you, Russ," J.B. said, standing up when they approached.

Making the introductions, Russ held her chair while Abby seated herself at the table. Then, leaning close, he asked, "What would you like to drink, honey?"

A shiver of need streaked through her at the feel of his warm breath on her sensitive skin. "Cola will be fine."

Watching Russ and J.B. walk toward the makeshift bar someone had set up on the other side of the room, Abby couldn't help but smile. He might make wine for a living, but Russ was a cowboy through and through. His shoulders were wide, his hips narrow. But it was his cowboy swagger that made her heart skip a beat and caused a hitch in her breathing.

"I see you like watching Russ as much as I love watching J.B.," Nina said, smiling.

Abby nodded. "It is a nice view, isn't it?"

Laughing, both women looked at each other for a

moment before Nina spoke again. "Do you know how many women's hearts you've broken here tonight?"

Thoroughly confused by her statement, Abby frowned. "I don't understand."

Nina pointed to several women around the room. "See how they're all watching Russ?"

Looking around the room, Abby noticed several women's gazes following him.

When she nodded, Nina went on. "They've had their sights set on Russ for years, but he never seemed to notice." She smiled. "You're the first woman he's ever brought with him to a rodeo."

"Really?" A warmth she couldn't explain coursed through Abby.

"They'd all love to be in your boots right now," Nina said, nodding. Stopping, she grinned. "Or should I say out of them later tonight?"

Abby felt her cheeks grow warm. Before she could think of something to say, the conversation was cut short when someone cranked up the volume on a CD player and several couples walked out onto the improvised dance floor.

"J.B., you big, handsome stud, they're playing our song," Nina said loudly when Russ and the other man walked back over to the table. "What are you gonna do about it?"

"I'm gonna dance with the prettiest gal in the whole

damned state." They set their drinks down, and J.B. grinned as he took Nina's hand and pulled her to her feet. "Come on, baby. Let's see how many times I step on your toes."

Abby couldn't help but smile as she watched the couple move around the dance floor. It was clear Nina and J.B. adored each other.

"Would you like to dance?" Russ whispered close to her ear. His lips brushed her earlobe, and every cell in her being tingled to life.

Unable to find her voice, she nodded and accepted his hand. As they walked out to join the other couples, Abby was conscious of having several women watching them.

Russ took her into his arms. "Do you know how beautiful you look tonight?"

Startled, she shook her head.

He pulled her close. "All of the single men and half of the married ones are wishing they could be me right now."

Smiling, she shook her head and raised her arms to circle his shoulders. "I was thinking that's the way the women felt about me being with you."

When the song ended and another slow tune began, he asked, "Do you want to sit down or dance some more?"

Abby stared up into his handsome face. She loved the feel of his strong arms around her, his hard body pressed to hers. "I think I'd like to dance."

He drew her even closer, and as they moved in time to the music, she felt as if everyone in the room had disappeared. She no longer noticed the envious female stares following their every move. Nothing else mattered but the man holding her so tenderly against him.

When Russ lowered his head to kiss the hollow below her ear, her heart sped up and a delicious wave of goose bumps shimmered over her. She reveled in the contrast of their bodies and how they fit together so perfectly.

"I could hold you like this all night."

His lips skimming her earlobe caused a searing heat to flow throw her veins. Shivering with a need stronger than anything she'd ever experienced, she tightened her arms around his neck and held on to keep from melting into a puddle at his big, booted feet. But when she felt his strong arousal pressing into her soft lower belly, her knees gave way and she sagged against him.

He caught her to him, and as the lead singer of Alabama crooned about how right it felt to be making love to the woman of his dreams, Abby knew in her heart that's what she wanted with Russ. She wanted to feel the depth of his passion, know the power of his lovemaking.

God help her, but she wanted him in a way that she'd never wanted any other man. She wanted him to make love to her.

Six

Russ reluctantly loosened his arms when he felt Abby start to pull back. Damn! He'd done it again. She had to have felt his rapidly hardening body, and it was no wonder she wanted to get away from him. They couldn't be in the same room without him ending up as horny as a seventeen-year-old boy hiding out in the girls' locker room.

Cursing his lack of control, he took a deep breath and gazed down at the most desirable woman he'd ever known. But instead of the uncertainty he expected to see, passion and hunger darkened her emerald eyes to a beautiful forest green. His heart slammed into his rib cage and his body tightened to an almost painful state.

"Abby?"

Leaning forward, she whispered close to his ear. "Let's go back to your camper, Russ."

"H-honey—" he stopped to clear the rust from his throat "—if we leave here now…"

Her sweet, shy smile robbed him of the ability to breathe as she placed her index finger to his lips. "I know."

"Are you sure?" Was she really telling him she wanted them to make love?

"I've never been more sure of anything in my life," she said, nodding.

The air trapped in his lungs came out in one big *whoosh,* and taking her hand in his, Russ led her back to the table where J.B. and Nina were sitting. "Sorry to cut the evening short, but I think we're going to head back to my trailer."

Grinning, J.B. glanced at Nina, then back at Russ. "We were talking about leaving, too."

Russ nodded as he turned to lead Abby to the door. "I'll see you tomorrow morning."

Outside, he breathed in the crisp February air and hoped that it helped slow the adrenalin pumping through his veins. His recently neglected libido was dictating that he scoop Abby up and run to his trailer as fast as his legs could get them there. But as he put his arm around her shoulders and they silently walked the short distance, he willed himself to slow down and consider what their lovemaking would mean for both of them.

He'd bet every dime he had that this would be her first time. And just knowing that she'd chosen him to be the man she gave her virginity to was enough to send him into complete meltdown. But even though she'd assured him that she knew what she was doing, he had to know that she really wanted to make love with him and hadn't based her decision on the heat of the moment. All things considered, it was completely insane, but he wanted her to need him emotionally as well as physically.

When they reached the door to the living quarters of his horse trailer, Russ stopped to gaze down at her. God, she was the most beautiful creature he'd ever seen, and he couldn't believe what he was about to say. It could very well end what would otherwise be the most exciting and meaningful night of his life. But he had to be certain she knew how much their lovemaking would mean to him.

"Honey, as much as I want this, and as hard as it would be to walk away from you now, I'd rather we didn't make love at all than to have you regret one minute of what we'll be sharing."

The feel of her soft palm as she cupped his cheek sent a flash fire straight to his groin, and to his immense relief, her gaze never wavered. "I know exactly what I want, Russ. And I want you."

Pulling her to him, he buried his face in her herbal-scented hair. "Abby, I want you so damn bad, I can't see straight." Then, kissing her temple, he stepped back and dug his keys from his jeans pocket. "Let's go inside."

His fingers felt clumsy as he hurriedly unlocked the door and turned on the light. But once they were standing inside the living quarters, he took the time to put his hat on the top of the tiny closet, shrug out of his jeans jacket, then help her out of her denim coat. She probably thought he'd lost his mind, but that couldn't be helped. He was doing his damnedest to slow down and get enough blood back into his brain in order to think of what he needed to ask her.

Finally feeling a little more in control, he took her into his arms and held her close. He needed to put to rest, once and for all, the question of her virginity. "I have to ask you something and I want you to be completely honest with me, even if you think it's none of my business."

"Okay," she said, sounding hesitant.

Her warm breath on the exposed skin at his open collar sent a wave of heat straight to his groin, and it took every bit of his concentration to string the words together. "Abby, are you still a virgin?"

He heard her sharp intake of breath a moment before she slowly nodded. "Yes."

His gut twisted. "I was afraid of that."

She leaned back to look up at him. "Does it matter?"

"Oh, yeah. It matters a lot." The vulnerable expres-

sion on her pretty face had him hurrying to reassure her.
"Don't get me wrong. I'm honored that you've chosen
me to be the first man to touch you. But it also means
that to make love to you, I might hurt you." He ran his
index finger along the satiny skin of her jaw. "And I'd
rather die than cause you pain in any way."

Her cheeks turned a pretty shade of pink. "I know
that I might not enjoy our first time together as much as
I will other times," she said, her voice little more than
a whisper. "But why did you want to know?"

"Because now that I know you've never made love
before, I'm going to take things slower and easier than
I might have otherwise." He hugged her close. "I give
you my word, Abby. I'll do everything in my power to
keep your discomfort to a minimum."

A shiver of excitement coursed through Abby at the
heated look in Russ's dark blue eyes as he lowered his
mouth to hers. The contact was so gentle, it brought
tears to her eyes, and she knew he'd make sure their
lovemaking was just as tender and sweet. Any lingering doubts she might have had about her decision to give
herself to him evaporated like mist on the wind.

Her eyes drifted shut when he deepened the kiss, and
as his tongue stroked hers with the promise of a more
intimate union, she felt as if a thousand butterflies had
been released inside of her. His hand sliding from her
back to lift the hem of her T-shirt caused her heart to

skip several beats, and curling her fingers in the fabric of his shirt, she clung to him for dear life.

His calloused hand caressed her skin as he moved it up her ribs to the underside of her breast, and a pulse of need like nothing she'd ever experienced thrummed through her veins. Heaven help her, she wanted to feel his hands on her body, wanted him to touch her in ways no man ever had. But when he released the front clasp of her bra, then pushed the lace aside so he could take the weight of her in his palm, Abby thought she would surely burn to a cinder as waves of heat washed over her.

When her knees failed completely, he caught her to him. "Does that feel good, honey?"

"Mmm."

He grazed her hardened nipple with the pad of his thumb, and she felt as if her soul caught fire. "Why don't we get rid of some of these clothes so I can make you feel even better?" he asked.

When she opened her eyes and met his blue gaze, she realized he wasn't just asking to remove her clothing. He was asking for her trust. Unable to find her voice, she simply nodded and brought her own hands up to the top snap on the front of his shirt.

"Let's do this together," he said, removing his hand from her breast. "I'll take off our boots, then you can remove my shirt."

As he led her over to the couch to remove her boots

and socks, then his, she realized he was setting a slow pace, allowing her to feel comfortable with each step of their lovemaking before they moved on. Emotion filled her at the care he was taking.

When he straightened, he reached for her and pulled her up to stand in front of him. "Your turn," he said, bringing her hands to the lapel of his shirt.

Abby knew Russ was trying to help her feel less vulnerable by having her remove his shirt first. Touched beyond words, she placed a kiss at the top of his exposed collar and delighted in his sharp intake of breath and the darkening of his blue eyes to navy.

Encouraged by his obvious pleasure, she tugged his shirt free from the waistband of his jeans and set to work on the snap closures. She'd never removed a man's shirt before and she found the experience both exciting and empowering.

But when she released the last gripper and pushed the shirt from his wide shoulders, her own breath caught as she reached out to touch the well-defined sinew of his broad chest with trembling fingers. He stood completely still and let her test the thick pads of his pectoral muscles, then outline the ripples covering his flat stomach.

A sprinkling of light brown hair covered his warm skin, then narrowed just below his navel. Unable to stop herself, she traced the thin line until it disappeared beneath the waistband of his low-slung jeans.

Glancing up, she noticed that Russ's eyes were closed, his head thrown back. She was driving him wild, but he was allowing her the freedom to explore his body without interference. Emotion welled up inside of her at his sacrifice.

"Russ?"

"What, honey?" His chest rose and fell with his labored breathing.

Before she lost her nerve, she took his hands and placed them at her waist. "Take off my shirt."

His head snapped forward at the same time he opened his eyes, and, holding her captive with his heated gaze, he did as she requested. Dropping it to the floor where she'd tossed his shirt, he reached up with both hands to slide his fingers under the straps of her bra. Her heart raced, and she wasn't sure that her knees would support her when he slowly slid his palms down her arms, taking the scrap of lace with them.

"You're so beautiful," he said when he cupped her breasts.

He teased the hardened tips with his thumbs, then dipped his head to capture first one nipple, then the other, with his mouth. Abby thought she would surely die from the intense sensations his teasing created, and she had to brace her hands on his biceps for support.

When he lifted his head, he took her into his arms, and the feel of the downy hair covering his chest as it brushed the sensitive tips of her breasts sent ribbons of desire swirling throughout her entire being. Feeling as if warm honey had replaced the blood in her veins, she shivered with a need stronger than she could have imagined possible.

"You feel so damned good, I think I'm going to go off like a Roman candle," Russ said, his voice sounding like a rusty hinge. Setting her away from him, he guided her hands to the button at the top of his jeans. "I don't want to rush you. But if we don't get these off, I'm going to end up hurting something."

Her heart pounded as she pushed the button through the buttonhole, then reached for the metal tab. But when she noticed his arousal pushing insistently against the fly, she shook her head. "I think you'd better do this. I don't want to be responsible for causing you any injury, either."

He glanced down, then, chuckling, he nodded. "You might be right. Zippers and erections can be a dangerous combination."

She watched him carefully ease the metal tab downward, then push his jeans and briefs from his lean hips and down his muscular legs. When he kicked them aside and turned to face her, Abby's heart stopped completely, then took off at a gallop. Russ's body was a work of art—a thoroughly aroused work of art.

The muscles of his wide shoulders, chest and thighs

were well-defined from years of physical labor in the
vineyards. His flanks were lean and sleek. But is was
the sight of his proud, full erection that sent her pulse
racing.

Her gaze flew to his, and his sexy smile caused her
insides to quiver and the butterflies in her stomach to
flap wildly. She said the first thing that came to mind.
"My goodness! That's awfully large."

"Don't be afraid of me." His grin did strange things
to her insides when he stepped forward and ran his finger along the top of her waistband. "I'm just a man like
any other."

Somehow she doubted that was the case, but the feel
of his fingertip brushing the sensitive skin of her belly
robbed her of the ability to speak, breathe or even think.
She tingled where he touched her, and when he silently
asked her with his eyes to take the next step, all she
could do was nod.

Russ's heated gaze held hers captive as he released
the button at the top of her jeans, then slid the zipper all
the way down. Clutching his shoulders for support, she
closed her eyes and held her breath when he slowly
pushed her jeans down her thighs. She felt him kneel in
front of her to lift first one of her legs, then the other, to
remove the jeans completely.

With her eyes still closed, she waited for him to do
the same with her panties. But when he placed his warm

hands on her knees, then slowly skimmed them upward, her body began to tremble with need. His hands stopped at the tops of her thighs, and she felt his fingers trace the elastic around her legs. She forgot all about what she thought he might do next and focused on how he was making her feel.

Caught up in the excitement of his teasing, it took her a moment to realize what he meant to do when he moved his thumbs and they came to rest on the damp fabric between her legs. Her whole body trembled, and she thought she would surely melt when he lightly chafed the most sensitive spot on her body.

Leaning forward, he kissed the skin below her navel. "Do you like that?"

Unable to find her voice, she nodded.

"Do you want me to stop?"

If he stopped now, she was sure she'd die from wanting. "N-no."

"Are you ready for me to take these off?"

The sound of his rich baritone and the light pressure of his thumbs caused a fresh wave of heat to flow through her. "Y-yes."

When he moved his hands to the elastic waistband and removed the sensible cotton panties, she stepped out of them on wobbly legs. She felt an almost uncontrollable urge to cover herself when he straightened and stepped back to look at her. But the appreciation and raw hunger she saw in Russ's eyes stopped her, and she stood proudly before him.

"You're perfect," he said, taking her into his arms.

Her moan mingled with his groan of pleasure as soft, female skin met with hard, male flesh. Sparks of electric current skipped over every nerve in her body at the contact, and caused the threads of desire swirling inside of her to twine together and form a coil of need deep in the very core of her. He kissed her, letting her taste his passion, and when he finally raised his head, they clung to each other as they gasped for breath.

"I—" he cleared his throat "—think we'd better lay down before we collapse."

Abby nodded. "I doubt that my legs are going to support me much longer."

Stepping back, he nodded toward the big bed in the elevated part of the trailer. "Climb in and I'll turn out the light."

She shook her head and bit her lower lip to keep a nervous giggle from erupting. "Not on your life, cowboy. Turn the light off, then I'll get in bed." At his confused expression, she explained, "Can you imagine how undignified and embarrassing crawling into that bed on all fours would be for me? My bare bottom—"

"Don't go there, honey." Groaning, he closed his eyes and she watched his Adam's apple bob up and down as he swallowed hard. "The problem is, I *can* imagine it, and it's about to send me into orbit." He turned off the light. "Now, will you get into bed?"

"Yes," she said, scrambling up onto the wide mattress.

The interior of the trailer was dark, but not so much that she couldn't see his shadowy figure as he bent to pick up his jeans and remove something from the pocket. Her heart raced and she lay perfectly still when he climbed into bed and reached for her. His hair-roughened flesh made her skin tingle and her insides feel as if they'd been turned to warm butter.

"Are you all right?" he asked, kissing her forehead. "Are you still sure you want me to make love to you?"

She knew he was giving her one last opportunity to call a halt to things, in case her nerves had gotten the best of her and she'd changed her mind. His consideration touched her deeply.

"Russ, the only thing I'm certain of is if you don't make love to me, I'll never forgive you," she whispered.

Thanking the good Lord above that she hadn't had a change of heart, Russ cupped her breast with his hand and lowered his head to take her hardened nipple into his mouth. The taste of her was like ambrosia to him, and he didn't think he could ever get enough of her sweetness.

As he circled the tight peak with his tongue, he slid his hand along her side to the flare of her hip, then down to her knees. Her soft, smooth skin was like satin, and as he brought his calloused palm up along the inside of her thigh, she trembled against him.

"Russ?"

He lifted his head from her breast to kiss his way up to her lips, and at the same time, he touched her damp auburn curls. She went perfectly still.

"It's okay, honey. I'm only going to bring you pleasure and make sure you're ready for me."

Lowering his mouth to cover hers, he kissed her deeply as he parted her feminine folds and gently stroked the tiny sensitive nub hidden there. Her nails dug into his shoulders as her passion rose and her lower body moved in time with his hand.

"Does that feel good, Abby?"

"Y-yes."

"Do you want me to do more?" he asked, continuing to coax her body into readiness.

"P-please, do…something," she gasped. "You're making me crazy."

Whispering close to her ear, he let his breath tease her when he asked, "Do you want me inside of you?"

She shivered against him. "Yes! Please…I need—"

"Just a minute," he said, reaching for the foil packet he'd placed beneath his pillow.

Quickly arranging their protection, he nudged her knees apart with his leg, then positioned himself over her. As he gazed down at her passion-flushed face, he didn't think he'd ever seen a more beautiful sight. His chest swelled with an emotion he didn't dare put a name to as he guided himself to her, then slowly, carefully, eased his body forward and into her moist heat. He watched her eyes widen as he continued to move forward. He could tell from the tightness surrounding him that she was tensing in anticipation of the discomfort they both knew was unavoidable.

His body trembled from the need to thrust into her, to completely make her his. But he fought to maintain what little control he had left.

"I feel so…full," she said softly.

He gave her what he hoped was an encouraging smile. "Just a little more and you'll have all of me."

When he felt her become less tense, he once again eased forward until he met the barrier of her virginity. Taking a deep breath, he gathered her to him and lowered his head to hers.

"I'm sorry, Abby," he whispered, covering her mouth with his at the same time he pushed past the thin veil and sank himself completely within her tight heat.

Her startled gasp vibrated against his lips and he hated himself for the pain he'd caused her. But even as he cursed himself, every male instinct he possessed urged him to complete the act of loving her. Clenching his teeth, he forced himself to remain perfectly still and concentrate on the needs of the woman in his arms.

"Take a deep breath and try to relax," he said, brushing her damp hair from her cheek.

The blood pumping through his veins caused his ears to roar, and Russ wasn't sure how much more he could take. With her body holding his captive, her soft warmth surrounding him like a velvet glove, his own body pulsed involuntarily inside of hers and he had to grit his teeth against the red-hot need.

She opened her eyes, and her lips curved up in a shy smile. "That was an intriguing sensation."

Feeling the pressure around him begin to ease, Russ managed a smile. "That's just one of many interesting feelings."

He kissed her forehead and eased his hips back, then forward, as he watched for any sign that he might be causing her more discomfort. When he saw none, he closed his eyes and fought the surge of heat urging him to complete the act of loving her.

"Russ?"

"What?"

"Please make love to me." Her throaty request sent a wave of desire straight to his groin, and he couldn't have stopped himself if his life depended on it.

Slowly rocking against her, he held her soft body to his and fought for restraint. But when Abby began to move with him, to meet him in the sensual dance of love, he thought he'd go up in a blaze of glory.

But all too soon, he felt her body begin to tighten around his, felt her inner muscles cling to him in an effort to hold him even closer. He knew she was close, and quickening the pace, Russ concentrated on bringing her as much pleasure as he possibly could.

Strengthening his thrusts, he felt her inner muscles quiver around him as her passion overtook her and she gave into the storm. Her moist heat pulsing around him, the bite of her nails scoring his skin as she grasped his shoulders and the sound of her crying his name, added to his own rapidly building climax. Groaning her name, he held her to him as he gave in to the fierce need stiffening his body. Then, surging into her one final time, he shuddered as he rode wave after wave of his own release.

When the last of the tremors passed, he buried his face in her soft auburn hair and tried to draw some much-needed oxygen into his lungs. "Are you all right?"

"Oh, Russ."

Her broken whisper caused him to feel sick inside. Raising his head, cold fear snaked up his spine, and he cursed himself as a low-down, sorry excuse for a man when he saw tears streaming from the corners of her eyes.

"Oh, God, Abby. I swear I tried to be gentle. I didn't mean—"

She placed her fingers to his lips to stop him. "I'm fine, Russ."

"Then why are you crying?" he asked, wiping the moisture from her cheeks.

"That was the most beautiful experience of my life." She gave him a watery smile. "Thank you."

Relief flowed through him as he levered himself to her side, then gathered her to him. "No, honey. Thank you for the most meaningful experience of *my* life."

Yawning, she snuggled against him. "Is it always like that, Russ?"

He rested his cheek against her head and enjoyed the feel of her warm breath on his bare chest. "Only when it's the right man and the right woman."

"Mmm." She yawned again. "You're most definitely the right man."

"And you're the right woman," he said, kissing the top of her head. As he listened to her breathing become shallow, his chest tightened at the realization that he'd never find another woman who felt as right in his arms as Abby.

After she drifted off to sleep, Russ lay awake thinking about what they'd shared. Abby had waited a long time to explore her sexuality, and he was honored and humbled that she'd chosen him to be the first man she shared herself with.

But even as grateful as he felt that she'd trusted him to be the man she gifted with her virginity, he knew that nothing could come of their relationship. His life was at The Vines, working for the people who had opened their home to him when he'd had no one to turn to and nowhere else to go.

Besides, Abby deserved the best, and he had very little to offer her. Hell, he didn't even have his own place. What would a well-educated woman like Abby want with a man who had nothing more than a high-school diploma and a secondary degree from the school of hard knocks?

Her life on a Nebraska farm was one that he could only dream of, and although he'd mentioned visiting her, they both knew that wasn't likely to happen. She would return to Crawley, start her veterinary practice and forget he existed. While he would never, as long as he lived, get over holding perfection, then having to let it go.

Russ released a frustrated breath. Abby would be leaving in another week or so, and even though he'd have a hell of a time getting over her, he couldn't bear the thought of being without her. That's why he was going to spend the rest of their time together storing up as many memories as he could until the day came that he had to let her go.

Seven

"**M**ercedes, you look like your mind is a million miles away," Abby said, walking into the woman's office on the second floor of the Louret Winery.

"Actually, it's only a few miles away," she said, motioning for Abby to have a seat. "So, tell me about the rodeo. Did you enjoy yourself?"

Abby felt her cheeks grow warm. "How did you—"

"I overheard Grant interrogating Eli about Russ."

"He didn't."

Mercedes nodded. "Afraid so."

"Oh, good heavens!" Abby's cheeks heated even

more. How many more of the Ashtons knew about her going away with Russ?

It wasn't that she'd tried to hide her relationship with him. But she preferred to keep some things about herself private.

Before she could find something to say, Mercedes smiled. "Don't worry. Your uncle didn't tell Eli about your going away with Russ this weekend. Grant just asked what kind of man Russ is and what Eli knew about him." Mercedes laughed as she leaned back in her desk chair. "Since Eli thinks the world of Russ, he gave Grant a glowing recommendation."

Abby began to relax a bit. "But that doesn't explain how you knew that I'd gone to Wild Horse Flats with Russ."

"I simply did the math," Mercedes said smugly.

"But I don't see how—"

The woman laughed as she ticked off the points on her fingers. "One man leaving town for the weekend. One woman who seemed extremely interested in that man a few days earlier, going missing that same weekend. Add a concerned uncle's questioning of the man's boss and it adds up."

Shaking her head, Abby couldn't help but laugh. "Did anyone ever tell you that you should get your private investigator's license?"

Mercedes shrugged. "I'm not that good, or I'd be able to figure out a way to get into the estate of the esteemed Spencer Ashton."

"Still no progress in meeting with him?" Abby asked sympathetically.

"No. He won't talk to any of us."

"How long has it been since you've seen your father?"

Mercedes looked thoughtful. "I was four when he divorced Mother to marry his secretary, Lilah. And to tell you the truth, I'm not sure I've seen him more than a few times in the twenty-nine years since."

Abby couldn't help but feel sorry for her California relatives. Spencer had walked away from his second family much the same as he'd done Uncle Grant and Grace. The only difference being, he'd stayed in the same area instead of moving over a thousand miles away. It had to have added to the pain and humiliation he'd caused Caroline and her family over the years.

"Have any of you tried going to the estate, knocking on the door and demanding to know why Spencer won't meet with any of you?" Abby asked, wondering if anyone besides Uncle Grant had tried the direct approach.

Mercedes sighed as she shook her head. "I wouldn't be welcome. His wife would probably have a royal fit if any of us stepped foot on the property."

"How rude! You'd think the lady of 'the big house' would be more sociable," Abby said, grinning.

"You'd think," Mercedes said dryly.

When they both stopped laughing, Abby gave the

woman a sly glance. "Didn't I hear someone say they have a lot of charity functions at 'the big house'?"

"They rent the estate grounds and ballroom for special events like weddings and charity fund-raisers," Mercedes said, nodding.

"Do you have any idea when they'll be having the next event?"

"I read an article in the newspaper just this morning about the local equine welfare society holding their annual fund-raiser there tomorrow evening." Mercedes frowned. "Why do you ask?"

"I'm a large-animal veterinarian, not to mention an avid horse enthusiast. And *I'm* very interested in the humane treatment of animals." Abby couldn't believe what she was about to suggest. She'd never crashed a party in her entire life. "How would you like to attend that event tomorrow evening?"

Mercedes sat forward. "Are you serious?"

"Sure." Abby shrugged. "What's the most they can do? Ask us to leave?"

A sly smile curved Mercedes's lips. "If he's not in San Francisco, Spencer might be there. I could try to reason with him, and maybe we'll be able to avoid a more public confrontation."

"That's right," Abby said, grinning. "Actually, when you stop to think about it, you'll be doing him a favor."

"Craig and I were supposed to have dinner tomorrow

evening, but I'm sure I can persuade him to join us." The woman rolled her eyes. "He's always ready to put on a tux and mingle with the society movers and shakers of Napa Valley."

"And I'll see if Russ would like to attend." She didn't think Russ was the type to enjoy something so formal, but she could try.

"Then it's decided," Mercedes said, reaching for the phone. "I'll call Cole and tell him that I'll be out of the office for the rest of the afternoon and all day tomorrow."

Abby frowned. "The event isn't until tomorrow evening. Why would you—"

"Do you have a cocktail dress?" Mercedes asked, smiling as she pressed the phone's keypad.

Laughing, Abby shook her head. "We're going shopping again, aren't we?"

"Yes. And tomorrow we're going to get our hair and nails done." Mercedes suddenly turned her attention to the phone, and Abby listened to her tell her brother she'd be out for the rest of the day. Then, grabbing her purse, Mercedes rounded the end of the desk to take Abby by the arm. "Let's go. I saw a beautiful emerald dress in one of the boutiques in Napa the other day that would be perfect for you."

As she let Mercedes hurry her along, Abby couldn't help but wonder what on earth she'd gotten herself into. She'd never owned a cocktail dress, let alone worn one. There just weren't that many occasions in Crawley that called for anything more formal than boots, jeans and, depending on the weather, a flannel or cotton shirt.

But so far, her trip to California had been filled with firsts. Why not add wearing a formal dress to meet her grandfather?

Now, all she had to do was convince Russ that he should go with her.

As they sat cuddled together on his couch, watching an old John Wayne movie and eating popcorn, Russ wondered what was running through Abby's pretty little head. She'd been giving him strange glances all evening, and a couple of times she'd even acted like she wanted to say something, then changed her mind.

Deciding to find out what was going on, he hugged her close and kissed the top of her head, then asked, "Honey, is there something you want to talk about?"

"Why do you ask?" she murmured, snuggling against his chest.

With her body pressed to his, he had to concentrate on what she'd said. Her answering his question with a question wasn't a confirmation or a denial, but it was enough to raise the hair on the back of his neck and send a shaft of apprehension up his spine. He picked up the remote and paused the movie.

"What's going on?"

He heard her soft sigh a moment before she sat up straight and met his questioning gaze head-on. "Will you go somewhere with me tomorrow evening?"

If she asked him to, he'd probably follow her over a cliff. But the hesitancy in her voice warned him that he'd better ask for a few more details.

"Where are you going?"

"The Ashton estate."

He wasn't sure what he'd expected her to say, but visiting Spencer Ashton's self-made kingdom wasn't it. He'd heard enough about what was going on with her uncle—the Ashtons at The Vines and their quest to confront Spencer—to know that Abby was asking for heartache if she expected a warm welcome from her ruthless grandfather or his gold-digging wife.

"Why would you want to pay them a visit?"

She shook her head. "I still can't believe I suggested it, but Mercedes, her friend Craig and I are going to crash one of their charity functions."

Every one of Russ's protective instincts came to full alert. He didn't like the idea one damned bit. It spelled disaster with a great big capital *D*.

"Are you sure about doing this, Abby? From what I've heard, Ashton's current wife, Lilah, is just short of hostile when it comes to any of Spencer's kids but hers. And as adorable as I know you are, I doubt she'd view his granddaughter any differently."

Abby shrugged. "She won't even know who I am. And from everything that's been said, I'm not sure any of them will recognize Mercedes."

Russ wasn't so sure. "Honey, they may not run with the same crowd as her kids, but you can bet that Lilah Ashton has made it her business to know who Eli, Cole, Mercedes and Jillian are. If nothing else, to keep them away from her kids."

"You really think she's that jealous?" Abby asked doubtfully.

"Oh, yeah." He put his arm around her slender shoulders. "If Lilah Ashton was any other type of woman, she would have encouraged Ashton to stay in touch with his other family."

Looking thoughtful, Abby nodded. "You're probably right. But Mercedes is hoping to see Spencer and convince him that it would be to everyone's advantage for him to meet with Uncle Grant and his other children. I don't think he could argue that airing the family's dirty laundry in the press would be unpleasant for all concerned."

Russ could well understand why no one wanted it to come to that, but the thought of Abby walking into a situation akin to a lamb entering the lion's den didn't sit well, either. Although rubbing elbows with Napa's high society wasn't his idea of a good time, he didn't like, nor did he trust, Craig Bradford to protect Abby and Mercedes from public humiliation. The man was too slick and impressed with himself.

Russ didn't see that he had any other choice. "Do I need a tux?"

"You'll go?" She looked so happy and pleased that Russ decided it would be well worth dressing up in a monkey suit and feeling like a fish out of water just to see her smile the way she was doing now.

He nodded. "There's no way I'm going to let you go by yourself. What time do I need to pick you up?"

"Oh, Russ, thank you," she said, throwing her arms around his neck.

Her obvious delight in his decision to go with her had him deciding that he'd walk through hellfire itself if that's what she wanted him to do. All she had to do was ask.

She leaned back to give him a smile that sent his blood pressure soaring and his heart thudding against his ribs. "You think I'm adorable?"

Smiling back at her, he nodded. "Absolutely. And I intend to show you just how much."

"That sounds interesting."

The heightened color on her porcelain cheeks told him that she knew exactly what he had in mind. The expression on her beautiful face said she completely agreed with his method of choice.

Her soft body pressed to his and the spark of desire he detected in her pretty, green eyes had him forgetting all about charity functions, or that going to the Ashton estate could prove disastrous. All that mattered was the woman in his arms and how much she made him want her.

Rising to his feet, Russ held out his hand and, to his satisfaction, there wasn't a moment's hesitation when Abby took it. Neither spoke as he led her into his bedroom and closed the door. Words were unnecessary. They both wanted the same thing—to once again share the intimacy they'd discovered over the weekend.

He reached up to remove the pink elastic band holding her auburn hair in a ponytail, then threaded his fingers through the silky strands. He loved the cinnamon color, the smell of her herbal shampoo.

"You should wear your hair down more often," he said, lightly kissing her temple. "It's beautiful."

He started to take her into his arms, but to his delight, Abby had other ideas. Placing both hands on the lapels of his shirt, she gave them a quick tug and the snap closures easily popped free. In no time at all, his shirt was lying in a crumpled heap at his feet.

Amused and more than a little curious to see what she intended to do next, he stood perfectly still, watching her. He didn't have long to wait.

She gave him a smile that sent liquid fire coursing through his veins, and it felt as if he'd been branded by her touch when she placed her soft, warm palms on his chest. She lightly moved her fingers over his skin, and Russ sucked in a sharp breath. But when she circled his flat nipples, then skimmed his puckered flesh with her fingertips, it felt as if an electric charge streaked straight to his groin, and it damned near brought him to his knees.

"Do you like that?" she asked, continuing her exploration of his chest and abdomen.

He nodded. "If it felt any better, I'd think I'd died and gone to heaven."

Her hands drifted lower and her sexy little grin warned him there was more to come. "Could you tell me something?"

"What do you want to know?"

She traced the thin line down from his navel to the top of his jeans. "Why do most men have this, even if they don't have hair on their chests?"

Finding enough air to breathe was becoming more difficult with each passing second, and the ability to think, all but impossible. But when her question registered in his oxygen-deprived brain, he couldn't help but chuckle. "You mean the Paradise Trail?"

Her slumberous smile tightened his body further. "That's not really what it's called, is it?"

"Paradise Trail, Treasure Trail, Straight Line to Heaven—it's known by a variety of names," he said, shrugging.

She laughed, and the sound was one of the sweetest he'd ever heard. "You've got to be kidding. I can't believe the way you guys name everything."

"Nope. I'm not kidding." Giving her a meaningful smile, he took her into his arms and leaned down to whisper close to her ear. "As soon as we get into bed, I intend to give you a refresher course on just how that little line got its name."

"I—I'm going to hold you to that, cowboy." She shivered against him, and the feel of her soft, pink T-shirt brushing his chest reminded him that they had several barriers between them before he could do that.

"Let's get undressed so I can show you."

He caught her gaze with his, and together they silently removed each other's clothes. When the last article dropped to the mingled pile of his and her clothing, he drew her to him. The feel of her warm body against his sent a shock wave all the way to his soul and caused him to harden to an almost-painful state.

Her nipples scored his skin, and he didn't think twice about lowering his head to take one of the tight peaks into his mouth. Pleasuring first one coral peak, then the other, he was rewarded by her moan of delight and the way she had to grasp his biceps for support. He loved giving her pleasure.

But when she arched into his embrace, the feel of his erection pressing into her soft lower belly threatened to buckle his knees and had him wondering how much longer he'd be able to keep them both on their feet. Sweeping her up into his arms, he carried her the short distance to place her in the middle of his king-size bed.

Gazing down at the most beautiful woman he'd ever known, he did his best to commit every detail of the moment to memory. Her silky hair spread across his pillow, the passion in her pretty emerald eyes and the contrast of her porcelain skin against the navy-blue sheets was a sight he knew for certain he'd remember for the rest of his life.

When he stretched out beside her, he took her into his arms and, lowering his head, traced her lips with his tongue. She opened for him and he slipped inside, reveling in the way she moaned and pressed herself to him.

Lost in reacquainting himself with her sweetness, in bringing her to new heights of passion with his kiss, Russ was completely unprepared when she moved her delicate hand down his side, then circled him with her soft palm. Her innocent touch sent a surge of red-hot desire racing through him and robbed him of the ability to breathe.

"H-honey, what—" he had to stop and grit his teeth against the wave of intense pleasure streaking through every cell of his being "—do you think you're doing?"

"I hope I'm making you feel good," she whispered.

The husky sound of her voice and her warm breath

feathering over his skin sent a flash of heat straight to his groin. Russ could no more have stopped himself from moving into her innocent touch than he could stop the ocean waves from crashing onto the shore.

But as she stroked his fevered flesh with her soft palms, then explored the heavy softness below, Russ groaned deeply and reached to take her hands in his. Lifting them to his mouth, he kissed her fingertips and shook his head. "Don't get me wrong. I love what you're doing. But much more of this and I can't be held responsible for what happens."

"Really?"

He nodded as he placed her hands on his shoulders, then pulled her more fully against him. "I plan on being inside of you for the grand finale." He kissed the fluttering pulse at the base of her throat. "And when I go, I fully intend to take you over the edge with me."

"Russ, please make love to me." Her throaty plea sent his blood pressure soaring.

Reaching into the nightstand's drawer, he removed one of the small foil packets he'd placed there earlier and tore it open. But to his surprise, when he started to arrange their protection, Abby took it from him.

"Do you mind if I help?"

Swallowing hard, he shook his head. "Do you know how?"

She nibbled her lower lip as she shook her head. "Not really. But it can't be that hard."

Laughing, he guided her hands to him. "That's the problem. I think I'm harder than I've ever been in my life."

Her cheeks colored a pretty pink. "I didn't mean…"

"I know." Grinning, he gave her a quick kiss, then lay back against the pillows. He'd never had a woman take the initiative to arrange their protection. He found Abby's taking charge immensely exciting. "I'm all yours."

Fascinated by what she intended to do, Russ watched her for several moments as she tried to figure out how to put the condom on him. Smiling, he showed her what to do, and in no time, they had the preventive measure in place.

He turned her to her back, then leaned over to kiss her eyes, her nose and the hollow below her ear. "Now, that wasn't too difficult, was it?"

She shook her head. "It wasn't hard at all."

He chuckled as he moved closer and pressed his arousal to her thigh. "Like I told you before, honey, being hard isn't an issue."

"I, uh, think I understand." Her breathless tone heated his blood further and had his heart racing at about a hundred miles an hour.

Without a word, he moved over her. But when he started to make them one, she gently brushed his hand aside and took charge again. Guiding him to her, her emerald eyes sparkled with a hunger that matched his own need, and as he slowly sank himself in her moist heat, Russ was filled with an emotion deeper and more meaningful than anything he'd ever experienced. If he had let himself think about it, it might have scared him spitless. But with her body wrapped around him like a silken sheath, all of his senses were focused on completing the act of loving her.

Their gazes locked, and as Russ set a slow pace, he watched Abby's expression change as her passion began to build. Her cheeks flushed with the rosy blush of desire, and the hungry fire glowing in her eyes made his heart hammer in his chest. She was sharing more than her body with him. She was sharing her heart, her soul.

All too soon, he felt her body begin to tighten around him and he knew she was close to the peak. His own body responded with the need to empty himself inside her, but he held back. He'd made her a promise—that he intended to take her with him when he found release from the storm—and, reaching between them, he touched her intimately.

Her feminine muscles held him to her, as if she was trying to make him a permanent part of her, a moment before they quivered around him as she found the ecstasy they both sought. Unable to restrain himself any longer, Russ let go of the control he'd fought so hard to maintain. His own muscles contracted, then surged, as he gave up his essence and joined her in the mind-shattering release.

Completely exhausted, he used his last ounce of strength to wrap her in his arms and turn them to their sides. Abby was the most responsive, incredible woman he'd ever known, and there wasn't a doubt in his mind that the feelings filling him at that moment went further than the fulfillment of desire, or a man and woman simply coming together out of mutual need.

His heart hammered at his ribs so hard, he was surprised it wasn't deafening. Could he be falling in love with Abby?

When she snuggled against him and dozed off into a peaceful sleep, Russ hugged her close as he stared at the ceiling and tried to come to grips with what he suspected. What happened to his plan of showing her a good time while she was in Napa, then settling back into his old routine once she returned to Nebraska?

But as he lay with her soft, warm body pressed to his, he shook his head at his own foolishness. He had a feeling that he'd never had a chance. Unless he missed his guess, he'd been a goner from the moment their eyes met that first day in the stable.

Eight

With her hand in Russ's, Abby took a deep breath to steady her nerves as they followed Mercedes and Craig across the Ashton estate's east-wing veranda. Not only was she apprehensive about breaking an ankle in the three-inch heels that Mercedes had insisted she buy, now that they were actually ready to enter the home of Spencer Ashton, Abby was having second thoughts.

What had she gotten them all into? Would Mercedes be treated well? Or would Spencer's wife and children descend on her like a flock of vultures?

Abby wasn't worried about what they would say to her. For one thing, they didn't even know who she was.

And for another, she had never had a problem standing up for herself. She barely suppressed a nervous giggle. If there was any doubt about that, they could always get in touch with poor old Harold. He could verify that she was anything but a pushover.

"Are you doing okay?" Russ asked as they approached the entrance.

Nodding, Abby smiled and leaned over to whisper in his ear. "How could I not be feeling fantastic with you as my date? In jeans and chambray shirt you're very handsome. But in a tux you're downright delicious."

"Honey, I was thinking you're the one who looks delicious." He gave her a wicked grin. "But as good as you look in that green dress, I can't wait to help you out of it later tonight."

A shiver of excitement coursed through her. He knew just what to say to get her mind off what they were all about to do. Was it any wonder that she'd fallen head over heels in love with him?

"I'm looking forward to getting you out of that tux, too," she said, feeling extremely breathless all of a sudden.

As they entered the reception hall, Abby couldn't help but marvel at the opulence of her grandfather's estate. The room was very elegant, with its beige fauxstone walls, heavy silk draperies and highly polished marble floors. It reminded her of a palace.

"This is a far cry from Spencer's Nebraska roots," she murmured.

"It's a far cry from the way we grew up at The Vines," Mercedes said, her tone tinged with bitterness. "By all rights, this place should belong to my mother."

Abby couldn't say she blamed Mercedes for feeling the way she did. After Caroline's father left the Lattimer Corporation to Spencer, he'd used his shrewd business sense, and a few illegal moves, to take control of not only John Lattimer's vast holdings and fortune, but also the family estate—a home that had been in the Lattimer family for years. He'd left poor Caroline and their four children with nothing more than the house and small vineyard that had belonged to her mother's family. He had paid a paltry amount of child support for Eli, Cole, Mercedes and Jillian, but beyond that he'd cut them out of his life completely.

Reaching out, Abby gave Mercedes's hand a gentle squeeze. "My great-grandmother Barnett always said that what goes around comes around. One day, Spencer's dirty dealings will catch up with him and he'll end up being the loser."

Mercedes gave her a grateful smile. "I hope I'm around to see it happen."

"Champagne?" a uniformed waiter asked, walking up to them.

Craig took one of the crystal flutes, filled with pink sparkling wine, from the ornate silver tray the waiter held, then looked around the room as he straightened his bow tie. "You don't mind if I mingle a bit, do you?"

"Go," Mercedes said, rolling her eyes.

"Would either of you like champagne?" Russ asked, reaching for two of the remaining glasses.

Abby smiled and shook her head. "None for me, thank you."

Mercedes smiled as she accepted the glass Russ handed her. "Thank you, Russ." To Abby she added, "At least your date is a gentleman."

"Is Craig always this…" Abby's voice trailed off as she tried to think of a diplomatic way to describe how insensitive the man was.

"Callous? Self-absorbed? Shallow?" Mercedes finished for her. When Abby nodded, the woman shrugged. "I always come in second when Craig has the opportunity to circulate with the social elite of Napa Valley. I guess I'm used to it by now."

Before Abby could ask Mercedes why she continued to see the man, a beautiful young woman with long, ash-blond hair and striking green eyes walked up to them. "Welcome to the Napa Valley Equine Society's annual fund-raiser." She smiled and held out her right hand. "I'm Megan Ashton, the hostess and event planner here at the Ashton estate. If there's anything you need, please don't hesitate to let me know."

The moment of truth had arrived, Abby thought as she shook the woman's hand. She noticed that Russ tensed at her side. He was apparently expecting a confrontation, too.

"I'm Abigail and this is Mercedes."

When the woman offered to shake Mercedes' hand, Abby held her breath. "I'm really pleased you could join us this evening."

"Our last name is Ashton," Mercedes said without preamble. "Abby is your niece from Nebraska and I'm your half sister."

Clearly startled by the revelation, Megan's eyes widened and a quiet gasp escaped her lips. "Oh, my. I've always wondered if we'd meet one day."

Before Abby could assure the woman that they weren't there to cause trouble, a tall, red-haired, middle-aged woman hurried over to them. "What are *you* doing here?" she demanded, pointing a perfectly manicured finger at Mercedes.

"Mother, this is—"

The woman's blue eyes sparkled with anger as she cut Megan off. "I know who she is."

"Hello, Lilah," Mercedes said coolly.

"You have a lot of nerve showing your face around here," Lilah retorted. Her voice held a wealth of anger, and Abby suspected that, though the woman might have all the trappings of wealth and position, happiness with Spencer Ashton had definitely escaped her.

Abby watched Mercedes's chin rise a notch as she met the woman's irate gaze head-on. "I have just as much, if not more, right to be here than you do."

Mercedes hadn't raised her voice much above a whisper, but her meaning couldn't have been clearer if she'd shouted it. She was letting Lilah know that she knew her affair with Spencer all those years ago had been a contributing factor to the breakup of Caroline's marriage to him.

"How dare you come into my house and—"

"Whose house?" Mercedes asked quietly. "This estate belonged to my mother's family long before Spencer married her or you became his secretary."

Abby had to give Mercedes credit for keeping her voice low and remaining calm. But Lilah wasn't quite so diplomatic. She looked as if she might pop a blood vessel at her temple, and drew attention to the fact that she'd obviously had plastic surgery. There was no way a woman her age could get away without having a few crow's-feet around her eyes, unless she'd had some kind of cosmetic procedure.

"Get out!" Lilah screeched. "If you don't leave immediately, I'll—"

"You'll do nothing, Mother," Megan said, placing her

hand on Lilah's arm. She nodded at the group of people that had moved in close, no doubt hoping to hear a juicy piece of gossip they could pass along to their friends. "Please. You're creating a scene."

When Lilah looked around at the gathering crowd, she pasted on the most fake smile Abby had ever seen. "Just a little misunderstanding. Nothing to worry about." With a final glare at Mercedes, she turned and strolled from the room like a queen dismissing her court.

"I'm really sorry for Mother's display," Megan apologized. "She can be…difficult at times."

"Is your father going to be here?" Abby asked.

Megan shook her head. "He rarely attends these events." She smiled sadly. "You were hoping to talk to him, weren't you?"

Mercedes nodded. "I thought maybe…" She stopped and shook her head. "Never mind. It's not important."

"I'm sorry," a uniformed maid said, stopping a couple of steps behind Megan. "Ms. Ashton, you're needed in the kitchen."

"I'll be right there." She gave Abby and Mercedes a smile. "I'll only be a few minutes. Please feel free to look around."

"We really should be going." Mercedes smiled sadly. "I'm sorry if we caused you problems."

"Thank you for being so kind," Abby said, meaning it.

"Don't worry about it." Reaching out to take one of

Mercedes' and Abby's hands in hers, Megan smiled. "I'm glad we finally met."

"Megan?" Mercedes nibbled on her lower lip a moment before she reached out and gave the younger woman a quick hug. "Me, too."

Abby thought Megan's eyes looked suspiciously moist when she nodded, then, turning, disappeared into the crowd.

"I'll go find Craig," Russ said, leaving Abby's side for the first time since their arrival at the estate.

"Well, I guess this was a wasted trip," Mercedes said, sounding tired.

Shaking her head, Abby looped her arm with Mercedes'. "I think it turned out to be quite nice. You discovered that Spencer's other Napa Valley offspring aren't all that hostile, even if their mother is."

Mercedes looked thoughtful. "Megan was quite nice, wasn't she?"

"Yes, she was." Wanting to lighten the somber mood, Abby grinned. "Lilah, on the other hand, was a real piece of work. I wonder what she would have done if I'd thrown my arms around her and called her Grandma."

"I can't believe you said that," Mercedes said, laughing so hard, several people turned to see what was so humorous. "You are *so* bad."

"I know. But don't you think it would have been interesting?"

"Right up until the paramedics hauled her away, after she had a stroke." Her laughter fading, Mercedes hugged Abby. "Thanks for being here with me. I wouldn't have had the courage to do this without you."

Abby hugged her back. "I just wish Spencer had been here."

"Maybe another time," Mercedes said, looking resigned.

As she watched Russ and Craig cross the room, Abby hoped for all their sakes that there was a next time, and that Spencer came to his senses. Otherwise, all hell was going to break loose when Uncle Grant went to the press with the story of Spencer's transgressions.

Russ focused on Abby as he and Craig walked over to where she and Mercedes stood by the door of the reception hall. He couldn't believe how well she'd handled the situation with Lilah and Megan Ashton. She hadn't said much, but she'd clearly been the quiet strength that had allowed Mercedes to face the Dragon Lady and come out the winner.

His chest swelled with an emotion he didn't dare put a name to. Abby was amazing in so many ways. She could heal an animal's wound with her gentle touch, dress up and circulate among the social elite like she was born to it, and she had more courage in her little finger than most people had in their whole damned body. Was it any wonder that he was close to falling for her?

But as he thought of how special Abby was, he also thought of how little he had to offer her, and of how one day she'd get tired and move on to some guy who was more her equal. She was as comfortable in an evening dress as she was in jeans and boots, while he felt like a fish out of water when he had to get dressed up and hob-nob with the social set. She'd graduated from veterinary school with honors, and in record time. He, on the other hand, was still enrolled in the school of hard knocks. What kind of a future could they possibly build together with differences like those?

A sinking feeling chilled him all the way to his soul. If he hadn't realized it before, he sure as hell had it fig-ured out now. He had no other choice but to break things off between them before he got in any deeper. Other-wise, he didn't think he'd be able to survive when the time came to let her go.

"I don't know why we have to leave now, Mercedes," Craig complained. "We only arrived a half hour ago. I was in the process of making several useful contacts."

"I just don't feel like staying any longer," Mercedes answered.

As they walked out onto the veranda and Russ handed the ticket for his truck to one of the parking at-tendants, he had an almost uncontrollable urge to plant his fist in Craig's nose. Russ never had cared for the man and now he knew why. Besides his blond surfer-boy good looks and slick charm, there was very little to Craig Bradford. He had all the sensitivity, and about as much of the ambition of a damned garden slug.

"Well, just because you're ready to leave doesn't mean that I am," Craig said petulantly.

Russ watched Mercedes rub her temples as she shook her head. "I'm not really up to arguing about this right now, Craig."

Having heard enough, Russ asked, "Will you excuse me and Craig for a minute?"

Abby shot him a questioning look. "Sure."

"Come on, Craig," Russ said, taking the man by the arm. "We have something we need to talk over."

Craig looked apprehensive. "Wh-what's that, Gannon?"

When he was certain the women couldn't hear what he had to say, Russ lowered his voice to a menacing growl. "Shut the hell up about your damned contacts and think about someone besides yourself for a change. If you'd stuck around instead of going off to rub elbows with people who don't give a rat's ass about you or what you're selling this week, you'd know that Mercedes just had a stressful encounter with Spencer Ashton's wife. She doesn't need to listen to your bitching, pal."

"I don't need you telling me—"

"Save it, Bradford," Russ said tightly. "Just show a little compassion."

Before Craig could protest further, Russ walked back to where the women stood. To his satisfaction, Craig returned to Mercedes' side and, although it wasn't the most sensitive of gestures, reached out to take her hand in his. Maybe there was hope for the man after all.

"What was that all about?" Abby asked quietly.

Russ shrugged. "Nothing. Just some guy talk."

When the attendants pulled his truck and Bradford's Beemer to a stop in front of them, Russ helped Abby into the passenger side, then walked around to slide in behind the steering wheel. He forgot all about the other couple when she gave him a smile that sent his blood pressure soaring.

"Are you ready to get out of that tux, cowboy?" she murmured.

As much as he'd like to consider himself an honorable man, Russ knew that tonight he didn't have a choice. He was going to be selfish and make love to her one last time before he had to let her go.

Forcing a smile, he nodded. "I'm not only ready to get out of this monkey suit, I'm ready to get you out of that sexy little green dress."

"Then what are you waiting for?" she asked, her tone so seductive that his heart went into overdrive and the blood in his veins began to heat.

The ride to The Vines was made in relative silence, and as soon as Russ closed the cottage door behind them, he took Abby into his arms. Resting his forehead against hers, he stared down into her luminous green eyes.

"I've wanted to do something all evening," he said, finding it extremely hard to draw his next breath.

Wrapping her arms around his waist, she smiled. "You mean besides taking off my dress?"

Nodding, he reached up to cup her soft cheeks with his hands as he lowered his head. "I've wanted to do this."

He pressed his lips to hers as he once again explored and tasted the most perfect woman he'd ever known. He was determined to commit every detail of this night to memory, to make their loving something neither of them would ever forget. But when he moved to deepen the kiss, Abby had ideas of her own.

When she slipped her tongue inside to stroke and tease his, the flame igniting in his soul threatened to consume him. She was arousing him in ways he'd never believed possible, and he wasn't even sure she realized it.

As her lips moved over his, her hands busily worked at the stud fasteners of his shirt, and in no time at all she pushed the lapels aside to place her palms on his chest.

She broke the kiss, and the smile she gave him caused his heart to stop completely, then start racing at breakneck speed. Her eyes twinkled with mischief and he wondered what she was planning next.

But he ceased thinking altogether when she began to kiss his collarbone, then nibble her way down to the pads of his pectoral muscles. Every touch of her soft lips on his rapidly heating skin sent a tiny charge of electric current shooting straight through him. But when she touched his flat nipple with her lips, then slowly teased it with her tongue, he felt as if he'd been struck by a bolt of lightning.

"H-honey…" His voice sounded like a rusty hinge, and he had to stop to clear his throat. "I'm pretty sure you're going to cause me to have a heart attack."

The sultry look she gave him when she raised her head sent a shaft of desire coursing through every cell in his body. "Do you want me to stop?"

He swallowed hard in an attempt to moisten the cotton coating his throat. "No."

"Good." Smiling, she took his hand and led him toward his bedroom. "I'm feeling a little experimental tonight. Do you mind?"

The suggestive tone in her velvet voice, the look of hunger in her pretty emerald eyes and the images of what she might have in mind sent a shaft of deep need straight to his groin. What man in his right mind would object to a beautiful woman wanting to have her way with him?

"I don't mind at all," he said, struggling to draw some much-needed oxygen into his deprived lungs. "This is starting to get real interesting."

When they were standing beside his bed, he wondered what she intended to do next. He didn't have long to wait to find out when she slid his tuxedo jacket off his shoulders, then unfastened his cuff links and removed his shirt.

Fascinated by every move she made, he sucked in a sharp breath at the feel of her hands touching his belly as she worked the button free at his waistband. But when she eased the tab of his fly down, her slender fingers brushed against the cotton fabric covering his insistent erection, and he had to grit his teeth against the intense sensations tightening his body.

"I'm not sure how much more of this I can take," he said through gritted teeth. Reaching for the zipper at the back of her dress, he smiled. "As good as you look in this little green number, you're going to look better out of it."

He wasn't prepared for her to step back and shake her head. "Not yet, cowboy. You've been exploring my body for the past few days. Now it's my turn to explore yours."

When she smiled and ran her finger down his chest and belly to the waistband at the top of his briefs, his pulse roared in his ears. "I think I've created a monster."

Her smile just about turned him wrong side out. "That's because you're so good at making love to me."

His heart pounded inside his chest like an out-of-control jackhammer. "I think…there's something…you should know." He felt as if he'd run a long-distance marathon. "If you keep touching me and…talking that way, I'm not going…to be able to take much in the way of exploration."

"Really?" She held his gaze with hers as she slowly pushed his slacks down to his knees.

"Not much at all," he said, sounding strangled. He gritted his teeth and desperately tried to slow the fire building in the pit of his belly.

Straightening, she slid her fingers beneath the elastic band of his briefs, then eased the cotton fabric over his arousal and down his thighs. Her touch just about sent him into orbit. But when she took him into her soft, warm hands, he felt as if his head might shoot off his shoulders like a Roman candle.

Abby used her fingers to trace his length and girth while she cupped the softness below with her other palm. The rush of desire that coursed straight to his groin made him light-headed.

He caught her hands in his and placed them on his chest. "Honey, don't get me wrong. What you're doing feels good. Real good. But if you keep that up, in about two seconds flat, I'm going to disappoint both of us."

"I'm making you feel that good?" she asked, looking pleased.

Russ groaned. "If it felt any better, I'd probably set

the house on fire." He finished shucking his slacks and briefs, then, kicking them aside, he reached for her. "Now it's time for a little retaliation."

Her dimples appeared as a slow grin curved her sensuous lips. "What did you have in mind?"

He held her close as he slid the zipper down the length of her back with one hand. "I've been wanting to take this dress off you all evening," he said, kissing the satiny skin along the column of her neck.

Raising his head, he held her gaze with his, placed his hands on her shoulders and brushed the garment down her arms to let it fall into a pool around her feet. But when he noticed what she had on under the Kelly-green silk, his heart stalled and his knees threatened to fold beneath him.

The scraps of satin and lace barely covered her and couldn't, by any stretch of the imagination, be called underwear. Underwear was sensible and made of cotton. What Abby wore was definitely lingerie. And damned sexy lingerie, at that.

"I'm glad I didn't know you were wearing this under your dress," he said, touching the lace garter belt holding up her nylons.

"Why?" The heightened color on her porcelain cheeks, and her breathless tone, told him that she was as turned on as he was.

He grinned as he unhooked the closure at the valley

of her breasts. "I would have spent the entire evening trying to hide the fact that I was hard as hell." Pulling the straps from her shoulders, he tossed the scrap of lace aside, then filled his hands with her. "You're so beautiful," he said, lowering his head to take one coral nipple into his mouth. Running his tongue over the tight peak, he tasted her, then sucked the tight bud until she moaned with pleasure. "Do you like that?"

"Mmm."

"Want me to stop?"

"I'll never forgive you if you do." She traced her fingers over his own puckered flesh. "Does that feel as good to you as it does when you touch me?"

He closed his eyes as a shudder ran the length of him. "Oh, yeah."

Before she could do anything else that threatened to send him over the edge, he removed the garter belt, nylons and the miniscule triangle at the apex of her thighs. Then, pulling back the colorful quilt, he smiled. "Let's get into bed."

Her smile sent his hormones racing. "Okay. But keep in mind, I'm not finished experimenting."

Groaning, he stretched out on the bed. He was so hot and ready for her, he was sure the sweet torture she was putting him through would send him up in a puff of smoke at any moment.

As he watched, she took a foil packet from the bedside table, arranged their protection, then straddled his hips and guided him to her. His blood pressure spiked, and he gripped the sheets with both hands in an attempt to slow himself down as he watched her body take him in. The feel of her melting around him threatened what little restraint he had left.

Breathing deeply, Russ had to remind himself that this was Abby's night, and he refused to take the control away from her. Even if he was suffering from the need to thrust into her until they both reached a soul-shattering climax.

Her eyes sparkled with heated passion as, without a word, she slowly began to rock against him, and he didn't think he'd ever see a more beautiful sight than the woman holding him so intimately. As she moved, her body caressed him and shredded every good intention he possessed.

The white-hot haze of passion surrounding him blinded him to anything but the need to once again make her his. Unable to stop himself, he grasped her hips and held on as she rode him to the point of no return. Never in his entire life had a woman possessed him so fully. At that moment, she owned him, body and soul.

Her moan of pleasure signaled that she was right there with him, and he felt her inner muscles urging him to completely surrender himself to her. Unable to hold back any longer, Russ thrust into her one final time and, groaning, gave himself up to her demands as they became one body, one heart, one soul.

Nine

As Russ stood at the kitchen window watching the darkness of night fade into the pearl-gray light of dawn, he couldn't stop thinking about the incredible night he'd just spent with Abby. She'd loved him with such unbridled abandon that just the thought of it made him hard.

But instead of rejoining her in his bed this morning, as he'd like to do, he was steeling himself to what he knew in his heart was the best for both of them. Last night, he'd purposely put out of his mind the fact that it was their last time together. He hadn't wanted to think about never again hearing her whisper his name as he brought her pleasure, never seeing the blush of satisfaction on her pretty face when she came apart in his arms.

His chest tightened. He'd never felt as complete, as whole, as he felt when he was with her. From the first time he'd held her, he'd felt as if he'd found the other half of himself.

But their being together was something that would, in the end, spell heartbreak for both of them. He wasn't nearly good enough for her, and he didn't think he'd be able to bear the look of disappointment on her pretty face when she finally figured that out. That's why he had to end things now before either of them got in any deeper.

As he stood at the window, staring blindly at the lake behind the cottage, he sensed her presence a moment before her arms circled his waist from behind. The feel of her soft body plastered to his back sent a flash fire zinging through his veins, and he had to close his eyes against the need to pick her up and carry her back to his bed.

"When I woke up, you weren't there. I wondered where you were." Her warm breath through his shirt felt as if she'd branded him as hers.

Digging deep for the strength to do what he knew was best for both of them, he said, "Abby, we have to talk."

She tightened her hold on him. "This sounds serious."

Taking her hands in his, he removed her arms from around him and turned to face her. He caught his breath.

She had never looked more beautiful than she did now, wearing nothing but his tuxedo shirt.

"Russ?"

"I've been thinking and…" He stopped to clear his throat, then rushed on before he could change his mind, grab her with both arms and hang on for dear life. "I don't think we should see each other anymore, Abby."

The hurt he saw in her expressive green eyes just about ripped his heart right out of his chest, but he admired the way she met his gaze head-on. "Could I ask what brought you to this conclusion?"

He shrugged. "A combination of a lot of things."

"Would you care to enlighten me?" Her voice shook slightly, and it just about tore him apart.

He should have known she'd want an in-depth explanation. "You really haven't figured it out by now?"

"I wouldn't be asking if I had," she said, wrapping her arms around her middle.

His hand was less than steady when he rubbed the tension building at the back of his neck. He hated having to call attention to all the ways he came up lacking. But if that's what it took to make her see reason, then that's what he'd do.

"Think about it, Abby. I don't have a damned thing to offer you, or any other woman." He shook his head. "Hell, I don't even own my own place."

"And you think that matters to me?" she asked incredulously. "If that's all you're basing your opinion on—"

"No, damn it, it's not. Don't you understand? I'm not good enough for you." It looked like he was going to have to spell it out for her. "You're a doctor of veterinary medicine, for God's sake. What could you possibly see in a man with nothing more than a high-school education?"

"I see a man who is kind, considerate and cares deeply about others," she said softly. "And you're an absolute genius when it comes to growing things."

Russ felt like he was getting nowhere fast, and the longer it took to convince her they could never make a go of it together, the bigger the chance his resolve would weaken. He hated himself for what he was about to say. It was a total lie, and he'd rather tear out his own heart than have to say the words that he knew would crush her emotionally. But it looked like he didn't have a choice.

"I thought you knew from the beginning that I was just showing you a good time while you were visiting The Vines. I didn't realize that you thought things were getting serious between us." He took a deep breath in order to force the lie past his tightening throat. "It's been fun, but it's time for both of us to move on."

She recoiled as if he'd struck her, and the horrified look on her face caused the knot twisting his gut to clench painfully. But as he watched, she raised her chin a notch and squared her slender shoulders.

"I'm sorry I misunderstood the situation," she said, her voice flat and emotionless. "I'll be out of your way as soon as I get dressed."

Without another word, she turned, and Russ watched her walk proudly toward his bedroom. Even though she had to be hurting as much as he was, she wasn't about to let him see her break down. It just wasn't her style. She had more courage and class than that.

Feeling like the biggest jerk who ever walked on two legs, he waited until she walked back into the living area. "I'll drive you to the carriage house."

"That won't be necessary," she said, shaking her head. "I know the way."

"Yes, but—"

"I'll be fine, Russ. You said yourself that it's over between us, and that includes you taking me anywhere." The ring of finality in her words just about tore him apart.

When she reached for the doorknob, he had to clench his fists at his sides to keep from reaching for her. "Goodbye, Abby."

He wasn't surprised when she didn't answer him and simply stepped out onto the small porch and closed the door behind her. The quiet click as she pulled it shut sounded like a cannon going off in the ominously silent room. And for the first time since losing his folks in that car accident eleven years ago, Russ found himself fighting back a wave of emotion so strong, it all but knocked him to his knees.

"Why am I not surprised to find you here?"

When Russ looked up to find Lucas and Caroline's son, Mason, walking toward him down the center aisle of the stables, he smiled. "Probably because it's winter and I don't have a whole hell of a lot to do in the vineyard." Seeing each other for the first time in months, the two friends hugged like brothers. "How was France?"

Mason gave him a teasing grin. "The wine is so-so compared to what we make here at Louret, the food is good and the women…well, they're French."

Russ chuckled. "And you've sampled your share of all three."

"Oh, yeah." Mason laughed. "Wouldn't you?"

"Probably," Russ said, noncommittally. Being with any woman other than Abby held about as much appeal to him as having a root canal.

"Whoa! Back up there, buddy." Mason's blue eyes twinkled with mischief. "What's happened while I was gone? Did some woman take you off the market?"

"No."

Mason's easy expression faded into a look of concern. "What's going on, Russ?"

"Nothing." He should have known his best friend would pick up on his pensive mood. Forcing a smile, Russ added, "Things are about the same as always. I'm working in the vineyards during the week and riding bulls on the weekends. In fact, I'm getting ready to leave this afternoon for a rodeo in Pine Creek."

"I'm not buying that it's the same old, same old," Mason said, shaking his head. "You might be able to fool somebody else, but I know you better than that." He placed his hand on Russ's shoulder. "You still keep a beer or two in the refrigerator in the tack room?"

"You know I do." Russ had a sinking feeling that Mason wasn't going to let the matter rest.

"Come on," the man said, motioning for Russ to follow him. "Let's down a cold one while you tell me what's put you into a tailspin."

Seeing no other alternative, Russ walked into the tack room and removed two aluminum cans from the refrigerator. He handed one to Mason, then popped the tab on the other and sat down beside his friend on the wooden bench by the supply cabinet. "There really isn't a lot to tell. I met a woman. We shared a few good times, but now it's over. End of story."

"I don't think so." Mason took a swig of his beer, then shook his blond head. "I know it's none of my business, but you look too damned miserable for that to be all there is to the story."

"It won't matter in another few days, anyway," Russ said, shrugging. He tipped the can and took a swallow of beer. "The lady in question will be leaving Napa soon."

The can he held was halfway to his mouth when Mason stopped to stare at him. "Well, I'll be damned. You're talking about Abigail Ashton, aren't you?" When Russ remained silent, his friend nodded. "I should have known. You've always had a thing for redheads, and she's a real knockout."

"You've met her?"

Mason nodded. "I stopped by the winery before I came down here to the stables. She was in the office and Mercedes introduced us."

Knowing that his friend wasn't going to give up until he had the whole story, Russ blew out a frustrated breath and told him about Abby and how amazing she was. "But I ended things with her yesterday."

"Why?"

"Because she deserves better than what I can give her," Russ answered truthfully.

Mason uttered an expletive that would have had Caroline washing his mouth out with a bar of soap if she'd heard it. "Where the hell is your head, Gannon? Don't you think you should have left that decision up to her?"

"One of us had to be practical." Russ downed the rest

of his beer. "Let's face it, a woman like Abby couldn't be happy for the rest of her life with a guy like me."

"Okay, now I know you're sitting on your brains," Mason said, sounding disgusted.

Russ crushed his beer can with his hand, then tossed it in the trash. "Name me one well-educated woman you know who's found lasting happiness with a blue-collar man with nothing more going for him than the ability to grow a few grapes."

"How about my mother?" Mason looked smug. "She and my dad have been head over heels in love with each other for the past twenty-seven years. I'd say that qualifies as a prime example of lasting happiness." Rising to his feet, Mason tossed his beer can, then picked up one of the saddles. "Chew on that little bit of food for thought as you drive down to Pine Creek. You can let me know I'm right when you get back."

"Did anyone ever tell you that you're a smart-ass, Sheppard?" Russ grumbled.

Mason laughed. "Yeah. You tell me every time you know I'm right about something."

Abby bit her lower lip to keep it from trembling as she hung the green silk dress she'd worn to the Ashton estate in her garment bag, then turned to finish packing her suitcase. She was glad she'd gotten acquainted with her California relatives, but the time had come for her to go back to Nebraska.

Feeling utterly defeated, she sat on the side of the bed and stared at the brochure from the Wild Horse Flats rodeo she'd attended with Russ. She had no idea why she'd kept it. Normally, she wasn't sentimental about those kinds of things. But as she stared at the colorful paper advertising the different events, a fresh wave of emotion swept over her.

Why was he doing this to them?

She hadn't for a second bought into that line of hooey he'd tried to feed her yesterday morning when he'd told her it's been fun, but now it's over. He was too considerate, too caring, to ever take what they'd shared that lightly. In fact, he'd told her before they ever made love that he'd walk away from their relationship before he did anything that would hurt her.

The air suddenly lodged in her lungs and her heart began to thump a wild tattoo. He'd said that he had nothing to offer a woman. He'd told her that he didn't even own a home. And he'd mentioned the differences in their educations. But she'd been so stunned and hurt that she'd only focused on the fact that he was rejecting her, not on what he'd really been trying to tell her. The poor, misguided man couldn't be more wrong.

"My God, he's making us both miserable because he thinks he's doing what's best for me," she said aloud.

She bit her lip as she tried to think of what to do. For years, she'd been afraid of turning out like her mother.

But Grace had never been satisfied and always thought she deserved better than the simple lifestyle a man of the land could provide. And that was all Abby had ever wanted.

But how was she ever going to convince Russ of that?

Before she had the chance to review her options and decide what she could do, there was a light tap on the door frame. Looking up, Abby found Mercedes standing at the open door.

"Are you all right?"

Abby took a deep breath and nodded. "I'm going to be fine. However, one hardheaded vineyard foreman has reason to be extremely worried."

Mercedes frowned as she walked over to sit beside her on the bed. "Did I miss something? I thought you and Russ had parted ways and you were going back to Nebraska."

"I changed my mind." For the first time since she'd left the cottage yesterday morning, Abby smiled. "I'm not going anywhere until he's listened to what I have to say. He might be ready to give up on us, but I'm not."

"Oh, I definitely like the sound of this," Mercedes said, grinning.

Abby nibbled on her lower lip. "Now, if I could just remember where he told me he was competing this weekend."

"Leave that to me," Mercedes said, reaching for the phone. "When do you want to leave?"

"As soon as possible." Having waited twenty-four years to find the man of her dreams, Abby wasn't about to waste a minute longer than she had to.

As Russ stood in line to pay his entry fees and collect his back number for the bull-riding event, J. B. Gardner tapped him on the shoulder. "Is Abby in the stands with Nina?"

"No." A pang of regret that threatened to bend him double ran through Russ as he shook his head. "She didn't come with me this weekend."

"That's a shame," J.B. said, sounding disappointed. "Nina was really looking forward to talking to her."

Russ took a deep breath. "You can tell Nina not to count on that happening again."

"But I thought you two—"

"You thought wrong," Russ said, cutting off his friend. When the cowboy in front of him moved out of the way, he paid his fee to the official seated at the entry table and accepted the back number the man handed him. Turning back to J.B., he felt guilty for having been so curt. "Look, I'm sorry, but it's a sore subject right now."

J.B. nodded sympathetically. "She dump you?"

Shaking his head, Russ took a deep breath as he stepped aside for his friend to pay his entry. "I called a halt to it."

"Have you lost your mind?" J.B. asked. "It was clear as the nose on your face that girl was crazy about you."

"Thanks, J.B. You're really making me feel better," Russ said, unable to keep the sarcasm from his voice.

His friend placed an understanding hand on his shoulder. "Any chance of you two getting things worked out?"

Russ shook his head. "I doubt it."

Without waiting for J.B., Russ picked up his duffel bag and slowly walked to the dressing area where the cowboys stored their gear and got ready for their events. He should be concentrating on what he knew about the bull he'd drawn, stretching his muscles and preparing himself mentally for his upcoming ride. Instead, his mind was about a hundred miles away.

What was Abby doing now? Was she packing to leave The Vines? Or had she already caught a flight to go back home to Nebraska?

As he put on his chaps, he mulled over what Mason had said about a well-educated woman being able to find lasting happiness with a simple man like himself. It was true that Caroline and Lucas Sheppard had made a good life together, and anyone who knew them could verify the fact that they loved each other and were very happy. But could he and Abby do the same?

Buckling the last of the chaps' leather straps, Russ sank down onto one of the benches in the dressing room and thought about how much Abby meant to him. He'd never been in love before, but he knew beyond a shadow of doubt that he loved her with all of his heart and soul.

She'd said that his lack of a college education didn't matter to her, nor did she care that he didn't have much of anything to offer her beyond himself. But could she really be happy with him for the rest of their days? Had he made the biggest mistake of his life when he'd broken things off with her?

"Hey, Gannon, are you going to sit there daydreaming, or are you going to ride your draw?" one of the other bull riders called from the doorway. "You're up next."

Rising to his feet, he walked to the back of the bucking chutes and climbed the steps to the raised platform. He cringed when he noticed his draw. The Shredder had a wicked set of horns, and had earned his name because of the way he used them after he'd bucked off a rider.

When a cowboy tied himself to the back of a bull, he needed every ounce of concentration he possessed to make a successful ride. But The Shredder was bad news, even when a rider had his mind on the business at hand. Unfortunately, Russ wasn't concentrating on the bull he was about to ride. He was too busy thinking about the only woman he'd ever loved.

But taking a turn out wasn't his style, and, stepping over the side of the chute, he settled himself on the dun-colored Brahma's back. J.B. helped him pull his rope tight around the bull's belly, then handed the excess to Russ for him to wrap around his hand.

"You sure you want to do this?" J.B. asked, looking doubtful.

"I might as well," Russ answered, as he jammed his Resistol down tight on his head to keep from losing it during the ride. "In case you hadn't noticed, it's a little late to back out now."

"Then, cowboy, up and ride that son of a gun," J.B. said, grinning.

Russ knew what his friend was trying to do. J.B. was trying to pump him up and get Russ to concentrate on staying with the bull, jump for jump. He appreciated the encouragement, but as he slipped his mouth guard into place and nodded for the gate man to open the chute, he realized it was going to take more than J.B.'s good wishes for him to make a successful ride.

The Shredder came out of the chute as though someone had set off a keg of dynamite under him, and the first bone-jarring jump had Russ shifting his weight to stay in the middle of the big animal's back. But he knew he was in serious trouble when the bull twisted in midair, then settled into a flat spin. Jerked backward and to the side, centrifugal force took over, and Russ found himself flying through the air sideways. His landing on the soft dirt floor of the arena wasn't graceful, but as the bullfighters moved in, he thanked the good Lord above that nothing more than his pride had been damaged.

He started to scramble to his feet and sprint for the safety of the fence, but it suddenly felt as if he'd been hit from behind by a freight train. All of the air left his lungs in one big *whoosh,* and as he fell forward, he felt something hard connect with the side of his head. Pain exploded behind his eyes, and as the peaceful curtain of unconsciousness began to close in around him, his last thought and the last word on his lips was, "Abby."

Ten

By the time she and Nina had made their way from the seats to the training room at the back of the stadium, Abby was shaking all over, and her heart pounded inside her chest. She'd been horrified to see the big, ugly bull ignore the bullfighters and set his sights on running Russ down. But when one of the animal's hooves grazed his head, knocking him unconscious, she'd thought she'd die right then and there. She'd never in her life experienced such abject terror.

"I'm sorry, ladies, but you'll have to return to your seats," a security guard said, stopping them in the hall.

"The only people allowed in the training room are medical personnel."

Thinking fast, Abby nodded. "My name is Dr. Abigail Ashton. I'm Mr. Gannon's doctor."

Technically, she did have a medical degree, just not one for treating people. That's why she'd purposely avoided calling herself Russ's "physician." But the guard didn't know she was a veterinarian, and she wasn't about to enlighten him. All that mattered was her getting to Russ.

The man looked uncertain. "Do you have some kind of identification?"

"Sure, doesn't every doctor carry their degree around with them?" Abby asked sarcastically. But she pulled her wallet from her purse and showed him her driver's license and a credit card issued to Dr. Abigail Ashton. Fortunately, the company that had sent her the card had failed to include the initials *DVM* after her name. "Now, get out of my way or I swear you'll be standing in the unemployment line Monday morning."

"Yes, ma'am," he said, stepping aside.

As they hurried on down the hall, Nina stared at her wide-eyed. "I didn't know you're a doctor."

"I'm not." Abby shrugged. "At least, not a medical doctor. I'm a large-animal vet."

Nina grinned. "Whatever. It worked to get you in to see Russ."

"It was going to take a lot more than one middle-aged

security guard to keep me out," Abby said, meaning it. When she saw J.B. standing outside of a door at the far end of the hall, she asked, "How is he?"

"Out like a light. But don't worry," he hurried to add. "The doc said Russ should be coming around any time."

"Are there any internal injuries?"

J.B. shook his head as he put his arm around Nina. "Russ was wearing his riding vest. It saved him from being hooked by the bull's horns."

"Thanks for the update," Abby said, breathing a sigh of relief as she entered the training room.

A man wearing a black-and-white striped vest, designating him as one of the medical personnel, smiled when she walked up to the side of the gurney where Russ lay. "Are you with Gannon?"

She nodded. "Has he regained consciousness yet?"

"He's in and out," the man said, pulling a chair over beside the stretcher. At her questioning look, he shrugged. "You might want to sit a spell."

As she stood looking down at the man she loved more than life itself, her chest tightened. Russ had a bruise on his left cheek and a lump the size of a goose egg on the side of his head, but otherwise he didn't look bad.

Taking his hand in hers, she felt his fingers move slightly. "Russ, darling, wake up," she said softly.

He murmured her name, and his hand tightened around hers a moment before his eyelids slowly opened and he fixed his blue gaze on her. "A-Abby?"

She brushed his dark blond hair away from his forehead as she looked for any other signs of injury. "I'm right here, Russ."

"You can't be," he said, sounding tired. He closed his eyes, and his jaw muscles clenched as if he were in pain. "You're on your way back to Nebraska."

She placed her hand on his brow and leaned down to lightly kiss his firm lips. "No, darling. I'm right here with you. Where I belong."

His eyes snapped open, and this time she could tell he was fully conscious. "I'm not hallucinating?"

Turning to the emergency medical technician, she asked, "Could you give us a moment alone?"

Nodding, the man silently left the room.

"No, Russ, you're not hallucinating."

"But I—"

"You can't get rid of me that easily." She released his hand and sat down in the chair. "You might be ready to give up on us, but I'm not."

"You're not?"

The look of relief crossing his handsome face was all the encouragement she needed to continue. "Not by a long shot, cowboy. I listened to you yesterday morning, now you're going to hear what I have to say."

"I am?" He gave her a lopsided grin, and she wondered if he might not be too groggy to listen to her.

But taking a deep breath, she met his amused gaze head-on. "I'm not willing to give you up without a fight."

He ran his index finger along her cheek. "I don't think I'm in much shape for a fight, honey."

"Good." His touch felt like heaven and she had to remind herself that she had something more she needed to say. "Before you hear what I drove over two hours to tell you, I have a question."

"What's that?" His deep baritone sent a shiver of need straight to her core.

Abby did her best to ignore the sensation and pressed on. "Where on God's green earth did you get the idea that you weren't good enough for me?"

He frowned, then winced and reached up to rub the side of his head. Apparently, the facial movement had caused the lump just above his temple to hurt.

"I don't have the education——"

"That's a bunch of bull and we both know it." At his startled expression, she smiled. "We all have our place in life, and you have a gift that I've always wanted, but will never have. You can grow just about anything, anywhere your heart desires."

He shrugged one shoulder. "Anyone can do it."

She shook her head. "No, they can't. Do you want to

know the reason I went into veterinary medicine, instead of agriculture?"

"Because you like animals?"

"That's the main reason," she said nodding. "But the other reason is because I kill everything I try to grow. I can't even keep a houseplant alive. Whenever I bring one home, Uncle Grant and Ford make jokes about another innocent plant being doomed to an untimely and torturous end."

"You're probably just trying too hard," he said, chuckling.

"I don't think so." She took hold of his hands. "Don't you see, Russ? Your talent is right here in the calluses you have from making things grow. You may not have a college degree, but that doesn't make you any less of an expert at what you do."

He looked thoughtful and she could tell he was digesting what she'd told him. "I've never looked at it that way," he finally said. "But you might have a point."

"Well, it's about time you came to that conclusion." When he acted as if he was going to get up, she stood up and gently pushed him back down on the stretcher. "I'm not finished talking."

He grinned. "Did anyone ever tell you that you're a bossy little number?"

"I think I've heard that before." She laughed as she remembered what they'd said to each other that first day in the stable. "Did anyone ever tell you that you're slower than molasses in January?"

Chuckling, he reached up to pull her down to him. "Come here, honey."

Abby shook her head. "I told you, I have more to say." When he started to protest, she placed her index finger to his lips. "I love you with all my heart, Russ Gannon."

"You love me?" His sexy grin caused her stomach to flutter.

"Yes, I do. But I have something I need to confess."

He suddenly looked a bit wary. "What's that?"

"Do you know why I remained a virgin while most girls my age have been sexually active for years?"

"You were worried you'd turn out like your mother."

"That's true," she admitted. "But that's not the entire reason."

His smile was understanding when he nodded. "You were afraid most guys would be like old Harold and not take 'no' for an answer."

"Not even close." Smiling at his surprised expression, she cupped his lean cheek with her palm. "Russ, I waited to give myself to the man I wanted to spend the rest of my life with. And whether you like it or not, you're that man."

His grin was back full force. "Is that a marriage proposal?"

"Call it what you will, it's the truth. You're all the man I'll ever want or need," she said softly.

"God, Abby, I love you more than life itself," he said, sitting up to pull her to him. "If you'll have me, I'll spend the rest of my life proving it to you."

"I'm going to hold you to that, cowboy," she said, kissing him until they both gasped for breath. Grinning, she added, "Oh, there's one more thing that you probably need to know."

"What's that, honey?"

"After we get married, there won't be an issue of you not owning your own place." At his questioning look, she smiled. "A third of that big Nebraska farm is mine, and once I'm Mrs. Russ Gannon, it will be yours, too."

He shook his head. "I don't want your land. All I want is you. We'll move to Nebraska and I'll help work the farm, but we'll have a prenuptial agreement drawn up—"

"No, we won't." She kissed him again. "We'll be in this marriage together. Forever. What's mine will be yours and what's yours, will be mine. You got that straight, cowboy?"

He laughed. "Yeah, I think I've finally got it." His expression turned serious. "I love you, Abby."

"And I love you, Russ. With all of my heart."

A week later, Abby glanced at her checklist. The cake would be delivered tomorrow morning and so would the flowers. She and Russ had their marriage license and their rings. But it felt like she was forgetting something.

"Oh, dear God, I forgot to pick Ford up at the airport."

Grabbing the keys to the car she'd rented, she rushed down the carriage house stairs. How could she have forgotten to pick up her brother?

"Where's the fire, sis?" a familiar voice asked as she hurried toward the door.

When she spun around, she saw Ford and Uncle Grant sitting at the kitchen table, looking thoroughly amused. "How did you get here? I mean, when did you get here?" She shook her head. "Oh, I don't care. I'm just glad you're here."

"Uncle Grant. About an hour ago. And I'm glad to see you, too," Ford said, rising to his feet to give her a bear hug. "How's the bride?"

"Scared spitless that I'll forget something," she said, wondering if she should go check her list again. If she hadn't remembered something as important as meeting her brother at the airport, what else had she missed?

"Relax, Sprite," Uncle Grant said, smiling. "Everything will work out."

"Did you pick up your tux?" She thought he'd told her he had, but she decided double-checking wasn't a bad idea, all things considered.

Laughing, her uncle nodded. "And I got the haircut you told me I needed."

With his arm around her shoulders, Ford smiled. "Abby?"

"What?"

"Breathe."

She sighed. "I'm not sure I have time."

Uncle Grant smiled. "Everything is under control, Sprite. Caroline and Mercedes have the ceremony and reception covered, and there really isn't anything left to do but walk down the aisle tomorrow." He rose to his feet and placed his coffee cup in the sink. "Why don't you take a break from all this wedding stuff and introduce Ford to his brother-in-law-to-be?"

Ford nodded. "Yeah. I have a few things I want to discuss with this guy."

"Oh, stop the overprotective-big-brother act," Abby said, grinning. "You're going to love Russ."

"I doubt that." Ford shook his head emphatically. "I don't love guys."

Happy for the excuse to see Russ before the wedding rehearsal that night, she removed her jacket from the coat tree beside the door, then took Ford by the arm to pull him along. "Stop your macho act and come on. I can't wait for you to meet Russ."

As they walked toward the stable, Ford asked, "What's going on with Uncle Grant?"

Abby had expected Ford to question her on what their uncle had been doing in Napa Valley. When she'd called to ask him to come to California for her wedding, Ford had expressed his concern about their uncle's obsession with meeting Spencer Ashton.

"He says he's going to stay as long as it takes to see Spencer," she answered.

"On the ride from the airport he said he's going to the media with the story about Spencer's illegal marriage to Caroline," Ford said. "He's hoping that gets the bastard's attention."

"Nothing else has worked." Her heart ached for Uncle Grant. He was such a good man. He deserved answers to his questions about why his father walked away all those years ago. "I don't think Uncle Grant wanted it to come to this, but Spencer didn't give him any other choice."

Ford nodded. "At least one good thing has come from this mess."

"And that would be?" she asked as they entered the stable.

"We're getting you married off."

Abby laughed. "Yes, but I'm not leaving home. Russ and I are going to live on the farm."

"Did I hear my name mentioned?" Russ asked, stepping out of the tack room. He walked up to her, wrapped his arms around her and kissed her until she felt lightheaded. "How's my best girl?"

"She'd better be your only girl," Ford said firmly.

Russ nodded. "The one and only. Unless, of course, we have a daughter."

Ford's eyes narrowed. "Abby are you—"

"No."

Russ figured he'd be talking to Abby's brother at some point before the wedding. He'd already received a fatherly speech from her uncle.

"Honey, as much as I'd like to spend the rest of the day holding you, I think Mercedes was looking for you earlier. Why don't you go up to the winery and see if she needs your help with something?" He gave Ford a meaningful look. "I'll keep your brother company while you're gone."

"That sounds like a good idea," Ford said, nodding.

"You're not fooling me." She rolled her eyes and shook her head. "Ford is going to give you the brotherly warning. And you're going to tell him that he has nothing to worry about." She gave him a quick kiss. "Just remember, I don't want any black eyes or split lips in my wedding photos."

Both Russ and Ford remained silent while they watched her walk out of the stable and down the path toward the winery.

"You're going to have your hands full," Ford warned. "There isn't a whole lot that gets past her."

Grinning, Russ nodded. "I wouldn't want her to be any other way." He motioned for Ford to follow him. "How would you like to give me the brotherly lecture over a beer?"

"Gannon, I have a feeling you and I are going to get along just fine," Ford said, grinning.

The next afternoon, in the upstairs bedroom Mercedes said had been hers when she still lived at The Vines, Abby stared at herself in the full-length mirror. The dress she and Mercedes had picked out truly was gorgeous. With a scoop neckline and tiny seed pearls adorning the white lace and satin, it made her feel like a princess.

"You look beautiful, Abby," Caroline said, adjusting her veil.

"Is Russ here?"

"Yes, dear." Caroline gave her an indulgent smile. "In fact, I think he arrived an hour earlier than the time Mercedes told him to be here."

Turning to face her, Abby smiled at the woman who had been kind enough to offer her home for the wedding. Caroline had even insisted on helping pull the wedding together on short notice in order for Abby to return home and start her clinic in time for the calving season. "Thank you, Caroline. I truly appreciate everything you've done for my family."

"Lucas and I have been happy to have you here at The Vines," Caroline said, her smile genuine. "You, Grant and Ford are part of our family now."

Tears blurring her vision, Abby hugged the older woman. "You're the best."

Caroline embraced her, then, stepping back, dabbed at her eyes with a lace handkerchief. "Russ is like a son to us, and I couldn't be happier for both of you."

A tap on the door drew their attention a moment before Uncle Grant stepped into the room. Tall, with just a touch of gray at his temples, he looked very distinguished and handsome in his black tuxedo.

"My God, Sprite, you're beautiful."

"You're not so bad yourself," she said, walking into his open arms.

"I can't believe you're old enough to be getting married," he said gruffly as he held her close. "It seems like just yesterday I was bandaging your scraped knees and helping you with your homework."

"It's time," Mercedes said, entering the room in a rush. "And it's a good thing, too." She laughed. "Mason and Ford have already threatened to tie Russ down if he doesn't stop pacing."

"I'll see you downstairs, dear," Caroline said, lightly kissing Abby's cheek.

Mercedes sniffed back tears as she handed Abby a bouquet of pink roses and white baby's breath, then, giving her a quick hug, followed Caroline from the room.

"Are you ready to give me away?" Abby asked when she and her uncle stood at the top of the stairs.

"I'll walk you downstairs and I'll place your hand in Russ's." He shook his head as he offered her his arm.

"But I'm not giving you away. You'll always be my little Sprite. I want you to remember that, Abby."

Tears filled her eyes. "I love you, Uncle Grant. Thank you for taking care of me and Ford all these years."

"I wouldn't have had it any other way, Sprite," he said, placing his hand over hers where it rested in the crook of his arm.

As much as she loved her uncle, when they descended the circular staircase and she caught sight of Russ standing by the fireplace in the living room, Abby forgot everything else and focused on the man she loved. He looked so handsome that her heart skipped several beats.

Stopping in front of him, Uncle Grant placed her hand in Russ's. "Love her and take care of her."

"For the rest of my life," Russ said, his gaze never leaving hers.

"I love you, Russ."

"And I love you, honey."

Uncle Grant gave them both a fatherly smile, then, kissing her cheek, stepped aside. And Abby pledged herself to the only man she knew she'd ever love.

* * * * *

SOCIETY-PAGE SEDUCTION

BY
MAUREEN CHILD

Maureen Child is a California native who loves to travel. Every chance they get, she and her husband are taking off on another research trip. The author of more than sixty books, Maureen loves a happy ending and still swears that she has the best job in the world. She lives in Southern California with her husband, two children and a golden retriever with delusions of grandeur.

Visit her website at www.maureenchild.com

Look for Maureen Child's exciting new Nocturne™ novel, *Vanished*, available in March 2010. Her next Desire™, *Seduced Into a Paper Marriage*, will be an April 2010 publication.

To my mom, Sallye Carberry, for more reasons
than I could possibly list here! I love you, Mom.

Prologue

1968

Spencer Ashton leaned back in his dark brown leather desk chair and allowed himself a smile. He'd come a long way from Nebraska in a very short time.

But not far enough.

His smile faded even as he turned in the chair to stare out the window at the palm trees waving in the wind. Palm trees—a symbol of California and a reminder of just how different his life was now in comparison to his old world. He caught the glimmer of his reflection in the sparkling glass and studied it. He knew his own attributes as well as he knew his bank balance. Paid to be honest—at least with yourself.

He was young, reasonably good-looking and ambitious. All traits that had served him well so far. Only three years with Lattimer Investment Banking and here he sat. In a corner office. He'd earned it. He'd toadied to John Lattimer, said all the right things, been all the right places and he'd *learned*. Learned enough to know that he'd never be satisfied working for someone else.

He wanted it all.

Wanted to put light-years between the man he was now and the man he'd been. If a brief flicker of guilt raced through his mind at the thought of the young wife and family he'd abandoned, he wiped it out fast. He hardly ever thought of Sally these days. Who had the time? He was a man on the fast track to success and wouldn't waste his energies by looking back.

Nodding slowly, thoughtfully, he decided then and there to *never* look back again. As of now, this moment, he had no past. He was starting over. A fresh slate. Nowhere to go but up.

The Lattimer Investment Banking business was a good step, he told himself. "But one day, it'll be Ashton Investments."

He could see it all so clearly. Himself, feared and admired by other lesser men. Employees jockeying for his good favor. Business rivals praying he wouldn't pull the rug out from beneath them. He would have a house twice as big as Lattimer's and he for damn sure wouldn't keep an employee as ambitious as himself around.

"Power," he murmured, smiling again as a late afternoon breeze tossed the long, lacy fronds of the trees right outside his office. "It all comes down to power. And what a man's willing to do to get it."

"Spencer?"

He stood up instantly at the sound of his boss's voice. Lattimer never knocked, damn it. Irritation scrambled through Spencer's system, but he quashed it with ruthless determination. He couldn't afford to piss off the old man. Not yet, anyway.

"John," Spencer said, smiling as though he wasn't imagining Lattimer out on a street corner with a tin cup and a handful of pencils. "Good to see you." Then he shifted his gaze to the young woman clinging to Lattimer's right arm.

Steering the petite blond woman farther into the office, John said, "I wanted you to meet Caroline, my daughter." He winked down at her. "My only child and the apple of my eye."

Daughter?

Why hadn't he known the old pirate had a kid?

Spencer's agile mind quickstepped. Pretty, in a nondescript, quiet way, Caroline Lattimer had green eyes, a nice figure and the polish and confidence of a woman raised with money. Obviously, her dear daddy doted on her, and Spencer, being a man who never failed to recognize opportunity when it stepped up and slugged him, gave her a slow smile.

She ducked her head, then looked up at him with, he was pleased to see, *interest*.

"Miss Lattimer," he said, taking her hand in both of his and feeling a quick jolt of pleasure at her nervous, indrawn breath, "I'm *very* pleased to meet you."

"Daddy's told me so much about you," she said, her voice quiet, cultured.

Shy, he thought and inwardly smiled. Though she was pretty enough and the daughter of a wealthy man, her own innate shyness had probably kept her from having too much experience with men.

Which only worked to his advantage.

Spencer kept her hand in his and stroked her skin with his thumb. And while she smiled up at him, he planned her seduction. His mind worked like a calculator as he figured out just how much time it would take to convince Lattimer's only child to fall in love with him.

Not long at all, if he played his cards right. And after that? Well, marrying into the boss's family was not exactly a *bad* idea.

After all, there was more than one way to get power.

And once he had it, he'd never let it go.

One

Present

"What do you *mean* the bride's missing?" Megan Ashton stifled the instinct to lunge for her sister Paige's throat. No point in killing the messenger.

"I mean we can't find her," Paige said in a whispered rush, her hazel eyes darting from side to side. *"Anywhere."*

"Perfect." Megan plastered an unconcerned smile on her face and nodded absently at the handful of guests littering the small parlor. She couldn't afford to look worried.

Grabbing her sister's elbow, she steered Paige

across the room and out the right-side French doors leading to a wide stone veranda. When they were out of earshot, Megan reached up, took her headset off and clutched it in one tight fist. "Did you check the garden?"

Paige inhaled sharply, then blew the air out in a rush. "*Duh*. We checked everywhere. I even poked into every bathroom on the ground floor. She's nowhere, Megan. And I'm guessing she's not coming back."

"What do you mean?"

Paige sighed. "She left her wedding gown in the bride's room."

"Oh, God." Megan felt the first swirls of panic and fought them off as she would any other would-be attacker. As the event planner at Ashton Estates and Winery, she'd *never* had an event fail—and this would *not* be the first. All she had to do was think. Okay, think *fast*.

She glanced at her younger sister. Paige's light-brown layered hair ruffled in the breeze and worry glittered in her eyes. The Ashton family "genius," Paige had graduated college at nineteen, then she'd jumped right into business school at the University of Southern California, before leaving to come home and help out on the estate. Megan didn't know what she'd do without her.

Paige bit at her bottom lip and clenched her hands together at the waist of her simple black skirt. She shot an anxious glance toward the hall where wedding guests were still expecting the ceremony to take place in the next few minutes. "What're we supposed to do now?"

"What we *don't* do, is panic."

"Right. How do we do that?"

"Beats me," Megan muttered and lifted one hand to smooth back an errant lock of blond hair that had escaped the tidy ponytail at the back of her neck. Voices murmured behind her and a squawk came from the headset she was still clutching.

This was a nightmare.

Well, a potential nightmare.

Thoughts, ideas, plans raced through her mind, presented themselves and then were dismissed. None of them were good enough to pull this mess out of the fire. Blast it, what kind of woman ran away from her own wedding fifteen minutes before the ceremony?

And what in heaven's name was she supposed to tell the groom?

As if reading her mind, Paige shook her head. "I'm so not going to be the one to tell that groom his bride vamoosed."

Megan winced.

Simon Pearce, would-be groom and gazillionaire, was not going to take this news lightly. The man had arranged this wedding with all the care and diligence of an invasion. Having his plans quashed at the last minute was going to go over like a case of measles.

Megan reached up and rubbed a spot between her

eyes, but all she managed to do was massage a budding headache into a full-blown migraine.

She'd been dealing with Simon Pearce for more than a month now. He was gorgeous, irritating and rude. He snapped off orders and expected people to jump. In fact, until this morning, Megan had never once *seen* the blushing bride. Pearce had taken care of everything. He'd made all of the decisions concerning the wedding that wasn't going to be happening and right at the moment, Megan could almost understand why the bride scampered. She wasn't exactly looking forward to telling Mr. I-Know-Everything-Don't-Bother-Me-with-Details that he'd just been jilted.

"Oh ye gods," she murmured and lifted her face into the wind sweeping in from across the vineyard. The scent of the nearby ocean surrounded her and the chill of the March breeze cooled her heated cheeks. Unfortunately, it didn't do a thing for the knot in her stomach.

"That about covers it," Paige said and leaned back against the gray stone balustrade. Crossing her arms over her chest, she tipped her head to one side and asked, "So. What do you want me to do, boss?"

Megan nearly laughed. *Boss* indeed. Nobody told Paige what to do. Of course, that was probably an Ashton family trait, since Megan didn't take orders any better than her sister did.

And at that thought, memories of a conversation

she'd had with her father just two nights ago filled her mind briefly before she shut them off. Another man used to giving orders and expecting them to be obeyed. But, she didn't have time right now to worry about what Spencer Ashton was going to say when she refused to go along with his latest plan.

At the moment, she had her own predicament to pull out of the fire.

"This cannot be happening," she muttered and started pacing, the sound of her heels clicking furiously against the polished river stones. "The food's hot, the cake is gorgeous, the musicians have been tuning up for a half hour." She threw her hands wide, then let them slap down against her thighs. "There are *reporters,* for heaven's sake, stationed right outside the hall. The minister's inside tapping his foot and the groom is probably chewing on rocks. Why would the stupid bride do this to me?"

"Um," Paige pointed out, "my guess is she wasn't thinking about *you.*"

"Right." Megan inhaled slowly and exhaled the same way. She tried a quick chant, but didn't have the patience for that, so she jumped right back at her problem. "Okay, fine. We just have to do the best we can."

"And that is…?"

Megan pulled in another deep breath and held it for a moment or two, just to steady herself. "You go into the hall and mingle. Chat up the guests and keep smiling, for pity's sake."

"Uh-huh," Paige said, pushing away from the stone railing. "Then what?"

"Then," Megan said, settling her phone's headset back into place, "*wait.* I'll talk to the groom, tell him what's going on and let him decide how he wants to handle it."

"Better you than me," Paige said.

Megan snorted. "Yeah. This must be why I make the big bucks, huh?"

Simon Pearce checked his gold wristwatch for the dozenth time in the last ten minutes. According to schedule, he should have entered the hall five minutes ago and even now be just about hitting the *I do* phase of the ceremony.

He tapped one finger against the glass face of the watch and tried to quell the licks of anger lapping at his insides. This delay would only foster more delays in the remainder of the day's schedule—and that was unacceptable.

"Want me to find out what's going on?"

Simon shook his head at his friend and assistant, Dave Healy. "No. Give it one more minute, then *I'll* ask some questions."

Dave shrugged and leaned one shoulder against the far wall. "It's your funeral."

"Wedding, you mean?"

Dave smiled. "All in the way you look at it."

"Right." Simon paced the confines of the small

antechamber off the main hall. Dave had never been in favor of Simon marrying Stephanie. Since Dave himself was happily married to his college sweet-heart, he was under the impression that *love* should have something to do with a wedding. Well, Simon knew differently. Love only got in the way. Muddied the waters. Better to deal with a marriage as you would with any business merger.

He stalked to the wide bank of leaded windows overlooking the pool and gardens, and stared blankly out at the early spring day. Most of the trees were still bare-limbed and the rosebushes were just beginning to pop with buds. But there were a few splashes of deep rose and burnt orange from an assortment of fall and winter flowers lining the walkway leading to the pool house. He concentrated on those as his brain worked.

He thought of Stephanie Moreland, the woman he should have been marrying at that moment. They'd known each other for several months and when Simon had proposed only six weeks ago, she'd ac-cepted with calm dignity. Exactly as he would have expected her to react.

She was just what he was looking for in a wife. Elegant, intelligent and wealthy enough in her own right that he needn't be worried she was after him for his money. Though there were no starry bursts of ex-citement when they were together, Simon was con-tent enough. He needed a wife—specifically to help him in business. There were quite a few firms out there who were old-fashioned enough to think that an unmarried man was too unsettled to be trusted.

With Stephanie by his side, he could continue to grow Pearce Industries as planned.

"Which is *why*," he muttered, checking his watch yet again, "we need to get this wedding completed."

When the wide oak double doors behind him opened, Simon turned. The wedding planner stepped into the room, and his gaze pinned her in place.

Megan was a tall blond with cool green eyes and a limited store of patience. On more than one occasion over the last month or so of dealing with her, he'd seen her bite her lip to keep from arguing with one of his decisions. She seemed to be efficient, though, which was no doubt why the Ashtons kept her employed at their estate.

At the moment, however, she looked as though she'd prefer being anywhere but where she was.

One of his strengths in the world of business was reading the opposition's expressions. One look at the woman's troubled eyes and pinched mouth told him that he wasn't going to like whatever she had to say.

"Mr. Pearce."

He spoke up instantly and went right to the heart of the matter. "What seems to be the problem?"

She stepped into the room, closed the doors behind her and shot his assistant a quick look.

Simon did the same. Dave Healy shrugged and

slid his gaze back to the woman crossing the tiled floor with measured steps. Reading her hesitation correctly, Simon said, "You can speak freely in front of Mr. Healy."

"All right then," she said, swallowing hard and squaring her shoulders, "I'm sorry, Mr. Pearce, but your bride seems to have disappeared."

"Excuse me?" He bit the two words off.

But the cool blond wasn't affected by the simmering anger in his voice. She simply stared him down. "Ms. Moreland has left the estate."

"That's impossible."

"Apparently not."

Anger jittered inside him, but Simon put a lid on it, fast. Temper wasn't going to solve this problem. "Have you called her cell phone?"

"Yes," Megan said and once again shot an uneasy look at Dave. "She's not answering and her voice mail says that she'll be out of the country for the next few months."

Out of the country.

Quickly, Simon's brain raced back to his last conversation with his fiancée. He seemed to remember her saying something about moving to London for a while. But of course, he'd dismissed it out of hand, since he had too many business deals working at the moment to be that far away. It seemed though that Stephanie had decided to go without him.

Pushing the edges of his navy-blue jacket back, he

slid his hands into his slacks pockets and tried to think past the cold fury raging within. He'd selected his bride with care. He'd thought they were on the same wavelength. Marriage without messy emotions. A tidy merger of two families to the betterment of each of them.

Now he'd been jilted.

An old word, but appropriate.

Deep inside him, anger fluttered into life again.

Stephanie's leaving was a personal slap, certainly, but Simon wasn't hurt. Even now, he could admit that his bride's disappearance was more infuriating than devastating. He wasn't foolish enough to pretend, even to himself, that theirs had been a love match. Now, Simon considered the repercussions once word of this got out and didn't like the images his mind produced.

The scandal this would cause would set his merger with the Derry Foundation back weeks, if not months. The elder Derry was old school. He was only willing to deal with solid family men— and Simon didn't have the time to find another suitable wife.

Damn it.

This simply did *not* happen to Simon Pearce.

He never lost.

And he wasn't about to start now.

"I am sorry, Mr. Pearce," Megan was saying, and he shifted his gaze back to her. "If you'll tell me what you'd like me to say to your guests, I'll handle the announcements."

He studied her—not for the first time in the last month—and noticed just how lovely she was. Her blond hair was neatly drawn back from a heart-shaped face. Her wide green eyes were solemn now, but he'd seen them sparkling with laughter and dancing with indignation. She was intelligent, educated and coolly sophisticated. Over the last month, he'd noticed that she worked hard and had the ability to get things done. A trait he admired. She was even approximately the same size as Stephanie.

In short, she was perfect.

And frankly, the situation was just a little on the desperate side.

Studying her, he said, "Actually, Megan, I'd like to ask you a different sort of favor."

Puzzled, she glanced from him to Dave and back again.

Sensing her unease, Simon turned to his best friend and said, "Dave, give us a few minutes, will you?"

"Sure." The other man strode across the room, opened the doors, slipped through and then closed them again.

"What kind of favor did you have in mind?" Megan asked.

"It's one only *you* can help me with," Simon said, watching her eyes to more accurately gauge her response. "I'd like you to marry me."

Two

At twenty-five, Megan had been in charge of event planning at her family's estate for three years. And in that time, she'd thought she'd seen it all. She'd held garden parties, Victorian teas, a baby shower for a senator's daughter, even a celebration for the oldest member of the local DAR chapter.

But this was the first time she'd been proposed to by a jilted groom.

Megan blinked, shook her head, then thunked the heel of her hand against her skull right above her left ear, as if trying to clear up a sudden case of deafness. "Are you crazy?"

"Not usually."

"Somehow, that's not really comforting."

He smiled, and she told herself to pay absolutely no attention to the sudden shift inside her. Weird reaction, and totally not the point. But she would dare any woman standing within three feet of the man to *not* feel the almost magnetic attraction he put out there.

Well over six feet, he had thick, wavy black hair that was stylishly cut to look as if it hadn't been styled. His eyes were the color of summer fog and his features looked as if they'd been carved from old oak by a loving sculptor. The man was a walking hormone-call to women.

"I'd like you to marry me," he said again as he checked his watch, then shifted his smoke gray eyes to her. "As quickly as possible."

She laughed shortly. *Marriage?* "You've got to be kidding."

That smoky gaze darkened as he fixed it on her and she felt the power of it right down to her bones.

"I never joke."

"Too bad," Megan muttered, thinking this had to be some sort of prank. "You'd be good at it."

This just wasn't happening, she thought, suddenly wishing his assistant would come back into the room. Because if Simon Pearce was actually serious, then he was a nut job.

"Look, Mr. Pearce—"

"Call me Simon."

"I don't think so. Mr. Pearce—"

"Megan," he interrupted her quickly. "I need a wife. I need to be married this afternoon."

"Why?"

"Why what?"

"Why the big rush to be married?"

"That's not really important."

"It is if you're asking me to be the bride."

He sighed, checked his watch again, then buttoned up his suit jacket. "Very well. Let's just say that a married man looks more 'settled' to some of the people I do business with."

"Are they Neanderthals?"

One corner of his mouth lifted and Megan caught herself hoping he'd smile again. Not a good sign. In the last month, she'd seen him impatient, harried and bored, but until a few minutes ago, she'd never seen him smile. Maybe he saved the most potent weapons for desperate situations.

"They're...*conservative*," he explained.

"That's unfortunate—and weird, but I guess you know that and—"

"Megan," he interrupted again.

She had to bite down on a rush of temper. Seriously, did people let him get away with this all the time? "It's rude to interrupt."

"So it is," he acknowledged with a nod. "But I am in a hurry and I'd like you to hear my proposition before refusing out of hand."

Wouldn't hurt to let him talk, she told herself. Besides, he was taking this whole *the bride has left the building* news way better than she'd thought he would. "Okay, go ahead."

"Good. I need a wife," he said, "and you seem to fit the bill."

"By being female?"

"Certainly a step in the right direction."

She saw a flash in his eyes and felt the reaction hit her low and hard. "This is ridiculous," she pointed out.

From beyond the closed oak doors came the silky sounds of the string quartet hired to play for the guests. Outside, sunshine poured down on the Ashton family estate and slanted through the wide windows to lay in golden shadows on the tiled floor. And here in this room, a crazy man was making his pitch.

"Not really," he argued. "Arranged marriages have been around for centuries."

"Yes, and didn't they work out nicely? How many women, I wonder, ended up locked in towers or chained in dungeons…." Megan wished to heaven the man's assistant—or keeper—or whatever the heck he was, would come back inside.

He blew out an impatient breath. Ooh. Getting frustrated, was he?

"There's no dungeon at my house, I swear."

"Uh-huh."

"I'll give you whatever you want if you'll do me this favor."

"It's a little more than a favor," she pointed out. "Favors usually consist of walking your dog or feeding your fish or—"

"Money?" he coaxed. "How much would it take?"

"I'll ask my pimp," she snapped back, insulted.

He seemed to realize his mistake instantly and lifted both hands in apology. "Sorry. Sorry. What can I tempt you with, then?"

"Mr. Pearce…"

"I need to be married, Megan. There are reporters outside, television cameras. I can't avoid them, and the gossip surrounding a jilted bridegroom is something that would hurt my business." He scrubbed one hand across his face and suddenly looked a lot more…human than he had before. "The scandal would probably put my mother in a hospital."

Megan winced at the thought. Okay, it wasn't just business he was concerned about. That made her feel better—and worse. She couldn't marry a stranger to keep his mother out of the hospital, for heaven's sake.

Although, a small voice in the back of her mind taunted, her father wanted her to marry a veritable stranger for a lot more mercenary a reason.

Instantly, she snapped back to a scene in her father's study two nights before.

"You're twenty-five now, Megan," he said, studying her as he would a horse he was considering buying.

Megan half expected him to inspect her teeth, but

*kept her thoughts to herself, since Spencer Ashton
was never interested in anyone's opinion but his own.*

"And it's time you married."

*She scrambled for something to say, but couldn't
come up with anything.* Married? *She'd hardly dated
in over a year—not since her last boyfriend had accepted a tidy buyout from her father.*

"And," *Spencer went on and she listened, knowing that forewarned was forearmed,* "since your taste
in men is abysmal, I've taken the liberty of finding
you a suitable husband."

"Excuse me?"

"Husband, Megan. I'm sure you know the word."

"Yes, and I appreciate it, Father, but—"

"William Jackson," *Spencer said and leaned back
in his oversize, dark maroon leather chair. He braced
his elbows on the armrests and studied her over his
steepled fingers.* "Son of Senator Jackson."

"Willie?" *Horrified, she took a step toward the
desk, amazed that her knees were still holding her upright.* "You want me to marry Willie Jackson?"

"Senator Jackson has agreed," *he said quietly,*
"that once our children are married, he will speed
up the passage of a certain bill that will go a long
way toward solidifying my enterprises here on the
Coast."

*Ah… There it was. This wasn't about Megan, not
that she'd really considered it was. This was about
helping Spencer's business. And really? Didn't every*

conversation eventually wander back to the most important thing in his life? Ashton Industries?

"So basically," Megan said before she could think better of it, "you get Willie a wife and the senator gives you California."

Spencer frowned tightly and Megan felt the very familiar sensation of a cold stone dropping to the pit of her stomach. She'd done it again. It never failed. She'd been trying most of her life to win her father's approval, but no matter what, she always seemed to come up short.

But Willie Jackson?

"You could do worse. William is a fine young man from a good family."

Keep quiet, *her brain insisted, but her tongue just didn't get the message in time.*

"He's an idiot," Megan blurted. "A sweetheart, but an idiot."

"That'll be enough," *Spencer muttered and sat up straight, resting his forearms atop his meticulously neat desk.* "William Jackson is the man for you."

"Father," Megan argued, "the man goes to sci-fi conventions with his dog."

Spencer winced.

"In matching costumes," *she added.*

"You'll help him to mature."

"I won't do it." *Good heavens, had she really said that? Even as the words rushed from her mouth, Megan actually saw* them, *dancing in the air before her eyes. Like colorful splashes on a blackboard, they stood out in the room, refusing to be overlooked.*

Her stomach spasmed and she felt the way she had as a child, when she was waiting for a punishment she knew was coming. She clenched her hands at her sides and lifted her chin in spite of the dread swamping her. She had to draw a line somewhere, didn't she? She had to be a grown-up at some point. Had to stand up to the man who'd been both hero and dragon in her life. She had to speak up for herself or end up married to Willie and sewing sequins onto his dog's cape.

"I don't believe I heard you correctly."

"Yes you did, Father. I'm not going to marry Willie."

His features darkened, color rising up from his throat like an incoming tide. His eyes flashed and his mouth thinned into a grim slash of disapproval.

And still, Megan stood her ground.

Her knees were wobbly, but she stood it.

"We'll discuss this when you're more rational."

"I'm perfectly rational."

"No, you are not. What you are," he said, "is dismissed." He didn't look at her again. Instead, he opened a drawer, pulled out a manila folder, picked up a fountain pen and began to work—as if she were already gone. As if everything were settled. As if she'd already agreed to the marriage.

Which was, of course, exactly the way he saw it.

And Megan thought now, as she resurfaced from the memory, her father was just relentless enough to eventually wear her down. Spencer Ashton would never give up. Unless she was already married…

"Look at this like a business proposition," Simon was saying.

"Business."

He perked up, his gray eyes sparkling with anticipation as he realized she was beginning to waver. "I'll give you anything you want," he said.

Was craziness contagious? she wondered. Was she seriously considering agreeing to marry Simon Pearce? Okay, yes. Because here, she could call the shots. And, it would give her the added benefit of being able to face her father and explain that it was impossible for her to marry Willie.

Besides, how bad could it be?

Simon was gorgeous, rich and—okay, crazy. But mental stability wasn't that big a deal, right? Of course, there was crazy and then there was *Willie* crazy.

"Do you have a dog?" she blurted.

"Huh?" His brows drew together. "No."

"Okay," she said on a sigh of relief, "that's good."

"If you say so," he murmured, giving her a look that said plainly he had a few concerns about *her* stability.

"I have a few conditions," Megan said.

He nodded. "I'm listening."

Oh God, she was really going to do this. Her stomach swirled and her hands went damp. But she started speaking quickly, not giving herself a chance to second-guess this nutso decision. "We have to stay married for one full year."

"A year?"

"Yes." That way, she'd have enough time to find a woman for Willie. Impossible though that seemed at the moment, she firmly believed in the old adage that there was *someone for everyone.*

He thought about it for a long moment, then nodded. "Agreed."

Okay, that was easy. *"And,"* she added, "no one can know that I'm just a last-minute replacement bride." She started pacing, feeding the nervous energy pounding through her system. "I don't care how you explain it—say we were swept away or that it was love at first sight—whatever." She stopped, turned around and stared at him, her gaze locking with his. "I won't have your friends and family thinking I'm just the emergency wife."

"Love at first sight?" he mused, that half smile tugging at his lips again.

"It could happen."

"If you say so." Folding his arms over his chest, he tipped his head to one side and asked, "Is that it? No more conditions?"

"One more." If she was going to do this, then she was going to do it right. She wouldn't have people whispering or feeling sorry for her or being embarrassed by a "husband" who was still dating. "I expect you to be faithful for the duration. No cheating whatsoever."

His eyes narrowed to match hers. "I don't cheat," he said tightly. "And I'll expect the same from you."

Megan stared into his eyes for a long minute and was reassured by his steady gaze. She nodded, relieved on that score anyway. "Agreed."

"Good. Any more conditions?"

"No, I think that does it."

Simon was stunned. He'd expected her to ask for money. *Lots* of it. And frankly, he'd have been more than happy to pay. But she'd surprised him and that didn't happen often. Intrigued, he studied the woman he was about to marry and wondered how many other surprises she had in store for him.

"So it's a deal?" she asked, walking closer and holding out her right hand.

He looked down at her slim white palm, then lifted his gaze to hers. "Not quite yet. I've a condition of my own."

"Which is?"

"If we're going to stay married for a year," he said, "and neither one of us will be... 'dating' anyone else, then it will be a *real* marriage."

"Meaning?" She swallowed. Hard.

"I think you know what I mean," he said, then reached out and took her hand in both of his. Her skin was smooth, soft and icy with nerves. "When I make a deal, I don't cheat—"

"Neither do I," she said quickly.

"Good. But I'm not going to live a year without sex, either."

"Um…" She tried to slip her hand from his, but he only held on tighter. Megan had lived the last year without sex and she hadn't exactly withered up and died—but she had a feeling a man like Simon Pearce wasn't used to going without female company for longer than a few days at a stretch. And, if she were going to be honest here, at least inwardly, she could admit that being celibate wasn't all it was cracked up to be.

Scowling then, she tipped her chin up and met his gaze squarely. "I guess that's reasonable. Okay then, shall we say, once a month?"

He laughed. "Twice a day."

Her eyebrows shot straight up. "What're you, a rabbit?"

He smiled and told himself that a year with this woman was going to be way more interesting than marriage to Stephanie would have been. Never once in the several months he'd known her had Stephanie surprised him. Or made him want to laugh. Megan, though, was a different story altogether. Certainly he'd known she'd never go for sex twice a day. But a smart negotiator started high.

"You have a problem with twice a day, then?"

She nodded. "You could say so. How about once every three weeks?"

He shook his head and rubbed his thumb across the back of her hand. "Once a day."

She blew out a breath and a stray lock of blond hair ruffled slightly, then drooped down to lie alongside her cheek. Narrowing her eyes at him, she offered, "Once every two weeks."

"Every other day."

She scowled at him. "You know, I could probably think better if you'd let go of my hand."

"I like your hand."

"You're an interesting man, Mr. Pearce."

"Thank you. And it's *Simon*."

"Fine. Simon. Once a week."

He hadn't enjoyed a negotiation so much in years. He could see the wheels in her brain working and told himself that this emergency marriage might be more entertaining than he had a right to expect. "Three times a week."

"Two."

"Done."

"Oh, boy." She cleared her throat, nodded jerkily, then snatched her hand free of his grasp.

He didn't want to think about why his fingertips suddenly itched to touch her again. About why his hand felt *empty* without hers in it.

"One more thing," she said and had his attention again.

"Which is…?"

She reached up and tucked that stray lock of hair behind her right ear, and for the first time, Simon noticed the flash of small diamond-stud earrings.

"The, uh, *wedding night,*" she said, her voice starting out soft and picking up strength as she continued. "You're not expecting it to start tonight, right?"

The purely male part of him wanted exactly that. He wanted to feel her skin beneath his hands. He wanted to peel her out of her very attractive but sensible black skirt and white silk blouse. Desire boiled within, sudden and nearly overwhelming and it was that realization more than anything that had him reassuring her. He wasn't a man to be led by his hormones.

"Why don't we take a little time to get to know each other?"

She smiled and he read mischief in her eyes as she asked, "Say, six months?"

"Is this going to be another negotiation?" he asked. "Because if it is, you're starting high."

"I learn fast."

He nodded, amused in spite of himself. "How about a week?"

She hesitated.

"*One* week," he repeated.

She tipped her head up to meet his gaze directly. She thought about it for a long minute, then slowly nodded. "One week."

Her grass-green eyes glittered and the pulse at the base of her throat pounded. When she licked dry lips and swallowed hard, Simon drew in a long, deep breath to steady himself. Why hadn't he paid closer attention to her over the last month? How had he *not* noticed those eyes? That mouth?

To disguise the unexpected thoughts racing through his mind, Simon checked his watch one more time. "You should go put your wedding gown on. I'll tell the minister we'll be ready in five minutes."

She shook her head sadly. "You seriously have a clock fixation, don't you?"

"Just one of my many attributes."

"Or curses."

He smiled. He could afford to now. He'd turned a near disaster into a triumph. "Megan, you'll be able to spend the next year learning my every quirk. But right now…"

"Right. Get dressed. Get married." She turned for the door, her heels clicking noisily against the tiles. When she reached the door, she grabbed the knob and looked back over her shoulder at him. "Sure hope you know what you're getting us into."

Then she was gone and Simon could only tell himself that *of course* he knew what he was doing.

He *always* knew.

Three

Late-morning sunlight darted through the floor-to-ceiling windows lining the great hall. The dark crimson silk draperies were open wide and the spotless window glass sparkled like diamonds in the light.

Only a handful of guests were seated in the deeply cushioned white chairs staggered on both sides of a narrow aisle. At the head of that aisle, a minister stood, bible open on his palms. Beside him, Simon waited, tall and gorgeous, his gaze locked on Megan.

As she moved slowly down the aisle, following her sister Paige, still wearing her pale-yellow blouse and simple black skirt, Megan had the opportunity to question her own sanity. She was wearing another

woman's wedding dress, and though it was beautiful, it wasn't one she'd have chosen for herself. Ivory
lace covered her arms and chest, and the silk beneath
if felt cool against her skin. The skirt of the dress was
wide, brushing against the rungs of the chairs as she
passed and the sound it made was like anxious whispers. She was about to marry another woman's fiancé, in front of witnesses she didn't know. And in
about a week, she'd be sharing her bed with a man
who would be both a stranger and her husband.

Her head was spinning, so she stopped thinking.

Paige, only a step or two ahead of her on the aisle,
was the only member of Megan's family present—
not exactly how she'd imagined her wedding day, by
any means. She could still hear Paige's arguments
and every one of them had been logical and rational.

Yet none of them had been strong enough to dis-
suade her. If there was one thing Megan could admit
about herself, it was that once her mind was made up,
that decision was set in concrete. Besides, if she had
a choice between Simon Pearce and Willie the Weird,
she'd pick Simon anytime.

Paige paused at the head of the aisle and Megan
knew without actually having to see it that her
younger sister was giving Simon a *hurt-my-sister-
and-die* look. And she smiled to herself, grateful as
always to know that Paige was on her side. No matter what.

The former bride's family and attendants had left.

Simon had spoken to the minister and now everyone here—with the exception of the bride—was relaxed and ready. Heck, by pulling a few strings, Simon had even managed to procure an emergency marriage license. In his own way, Simon was every bit as powerful as Spencer Ashton.

Megan shivered at the thought.

Then she stepped up beside Simon, took a deep breath and felt his fingers close around her right hand. Warm, she thought. Warm and strong and somehow…comforting.

The minister started talking and, truth to tell, she wasn't listening. She was having what felt like an out-of-body experience. She couldn't be sure of course, since it had never happened before, but what else could explain the light-headedness? The ringing in her ears? The blurry swim to her vision?

"I do," Simon said, his deep voice reverberating through the room before dancing along her spine, sending her nerve endings into a frantic skip.

Oh, boy.

Her turn.

Megan focused her gaze on the minister and noted the beads of sweat on his forehead and idly wondered if he was as nervous as she was. He seemed nice enough. She'd spoken to him about last-minute details only an hour ago. Of course then, neither one of them had known *she* would be the bride.

"I, Megan Ashton," she said, repeating the ancient words as the reverend led her carefully through her vows.

Beside her, Simon stiffened. *Ashton?* As in Ashton Estates? Ashton Winery? Ashton, dozens of other enterprises?

He wondered why she hadn't told him. Then reminded himself that he'd been working with the woman for the last month or more and had never inquired of her last name. Hadn't seemed important. She'd simply been Megan, the event planner.

He stared down at the woman swearing to be faithful to him and only to him and he at least understood why he hadn't been able to coax her into this wedding with the promise of *money*.

And while his thoughts raced, he realized that this emergency marriage was going to be complicated. He'd long been a favorite of the paparazzi that made their living stalking celebrities. But Simon Pearce marrying one of the Ashton heirs would have those notorious photographers—not to mention reporters—slavering like wild dogs. The Ashton family was as well-known as his own and the media would have a field day if they got wind that this marriage was anything but the real deal.

"You may kiss the bride."

Simon's thoughts dissolved at the words and he turned to face Megan. All around them, people watched but all he could see were her eyes. Brilliant, grass-green eyes. Sparkling with humor, wariness and just a touch of regret.

"Second thoughts?" he whispered, lifting one hand to smooth another stray lock of hair behind her ear.

One corner of her mouth quirked. When she spoke, her voice was as hushed as his. "Oh, yeah. Second thoughts and thirds and fourths and—"

He silenced her the best way he knew how. Bending his head, he covered her mouth with his, cutting her off mid-sentence. A flash of something unexpected leaped through him and caught Simon completely off guard.

Lifting his head again, he stared at her as if seeing her for the first time. She looked as surprised as he felt. There was heat here. Something he hadn't felt in—well, ever. And he wasn't entirely sure that was a good thing.

This was a marriage of convenience—in the most literal terms. Thinking it was anything else would only cause more problems.

And yet…

Unable to deny himself, Simon bent to kiss her again and instantly felt that jolt of lightning-like sensation shoot through him. Her mouth surrendered to his.

She leaned into him, tipping her head back farther as she lifted onto her toes to meet his kiss.

Desire pulsed through him with the rattle and roar of thunder. Reaction shuddered through Megan, too, and her response fed his own.

He forgot where they were.

Forgot they were strangers.

And lost himself in the taste of her.

Pressing her close to his body, he held her tightly, firmly, until he could feel her every curve. The delicate lace of her gown scraped against his fingertips. Her scent, a faint floral blend, filled his head. His tongue swept into her mouth as he fed the urge within him clamoring for more. She was warm and sweet and open and he dived into her, groaning, giving himself up to the sensations coursing through him.

She clung to him, giving as much as she took. Her breath brushed his cheek, her hands slid up his back and when she sighed into his mouth, Simon felt the slam of it as he would have a punch to the middle.

Applause.

Laughter.

These sounds and more finally worked their way past the fog of passion clouding Simon's mind. Slowly, reluctantly, he ended the kiss and looked down at her. Her pale skin was suffused with color, her mouth looked full and puffy, her eyes dazzling in the sunlight. He wanted her more than he'd ever wanted anything in his life.

And because the urge to take her had him by the throat, Simon gritted his teeth and took a deliberate step back from her—distancing himself not only from his new bride, but from the very real threat of losing his self-control. Something he'd never done before.

Something he *never* allowed to happen.

Forcing a smile, he took her hand and turned to face the guests already crowding up the aisle to congratulate them.

"Everything's running smoothly, so stop worrying—at least about the reception," Paige said.

"It just feels strange to not be running around checking on everyone," Megan told her and smoothed one hand down the front of her secondhand wedding gown.

"Uh-huh." Paige looked at her with wide eyes and shook her head. "It's strange to you to not be running the show, but *not* strange to be married to a man you don't know?"

"Okay," Megan admitted, letting her gaze slide over the small crowd until it landed on *her husband*. "That's strange, too."

"I can't believe you did this."

"Yes, well, me neither," Megan said and told herself she was imagining the heat of Simon's gaze. "But better him than poor Willie."

"Father never would have made you go through with that," Paige insisted.

Megan shifted her younger sister a sharp look. "Have you *met* our father?"

"Okay, maybe he would." Paige pushed her hair back out of her eyes, covered the mouthpiece of the headset she wore with one hand and whispered, "But what do you think he's going to say when he finds out what you did?"

Oh, Megan didn't want to think about that. She really didn't. Already, her stomach was churning in anticipation of the showdown that was looming in her near future. Her father would be furious. But, even he couldn't make her marry someone else when she was already married.

Laying one hand flat against her stomach, Megan breathed deeply, an old trick she'd been practicing for years. Deep, slow, even breaths were usually enough to curb the roiling nausea that confrontations with her father were sure to cause.

"Yes," Paige said, speaking now into the headset. "I'll be right there."

"What is it?" Megan asked. "What's wrong?"

"Nothing I can't handle," Paige murmured and gave her sister's hand a pat. "Just a minor crisis in the kitchen."

"If it's Jean complaining about the caterer again, tell him I said that he has to—"

"You're the bride today, remember?" Paige asked, already stalking toward the back of the hall and the kitchens beyond. "I'll handle it."

Megan nodded and fought the urge to run and take care of the problems herself. Since being put in charge of the events planning at the estate, she'd made a real name for herself. She worked hard, took care of every detail and had never had an event fail.

"Thinking of skipping out on me?" Simon's deep voice came from right behind her. Startled, Megan jumped and turned to face him.

"Sneak up on people often?"

"Didn't sneak. Walked."

"Well, walk louder," she suggested and tried to look past him at his guests, on the other side of the hall.

"Time for some pictures," he said and took her elbow in a firm grip.

"Oh, Simon, I don't think we—"

"A *real* marriage," he whispered, dipping his head so that his breath dusted her ear. "Remember?"

"Right."

First, the happy couple stepped out into the sunlight for the benefit of the media gathered outside the reception hall. Cameras clicked, reporters shouted questions and through it all, Simon kept a proud smile on his face and one arm around Megan's shoulders—just in case she got cold feet and made a run for it.

But she didn't. To give her her due, she stood her ground, lifted her chin and smiled beautifully for the media. He doubted Stephanie could have handled the situation as smoothly.

Once the news frenzy was over, they stepped back inside to be surrounded by the small cluster of guests. More cameras flashed while people smiled and offered congratulations. Simon kept his arm around her shoulders and held her close, playing the part of a doting groom to perfection. Megan chatted, smiled and posed for pictures until her cheeks hurt from smiling. She accepted champagne from a server and took a long gulp, hoping it would soothe her dry throat and scattered emotions.

Simon's mother, a small, elegant-looking woman with short, stylishly cut silver hair, wearing a pale-blue designer suit, dabbed at teary eyes and gave Megan a warm hug. "My dear," she muttered, "you look lovely."

"Thank you, Mrs. Pearce."

"Please," the woman said, "call me Phoebe. I just know that you and I are going to be good friends."

Oh, Megan felt awful. Phoebe was being so nice and Megan was lying. To her. To everyone there.

Desperately, she tried to think of *something* to say even while wondering why Simon hadn't explained any of this to his own mother, at least.

"Phoebe, I'm so sorry I didn't get to meet you before, but this was all very sudden and—"

"Never mind, honey," Phoebe interrupted as smoothly as her son made a habit of doing and Megan knew immediately where he'd picked up the trait. "I never cared for Stephanie, you know. Cold eyes. But you—" she stopped, reached up and cupped Megan's cheek. "You have good eyes. And a lovely smile. I know you'll make my son very happy."

Oh man.

Could guilt actually *kill* a person?

The next couple of hours passed in a blur. Dinner and cake were served, and never once did anyone mention the fact that the bride had been exchanged at the last minute. The handful of people attending the ceremony were there for Simon and apparently, Megan thought, Simon Pearce wielded even more power than her father. Enough so that a change of bride didn't merit the flicker of an eyelash.

By the time the party was over and Megan was back in the bride's room changing into her own clothes, she felt as though it had all been a strange sort of stage play. And now that the play was over, the lead actress could go back to her everyday job.

Until Simon opened the door.

"Hey!" She snatched up the wedding dress she'd just peeled off and held it to her chest like a Victorian maiden. "Do you mind?"

"Not at all," he said, one corner of his mouth lifting as he stepped into the small antechamber and closed the door behind him.

Megan blew out a breath and glared at him.

It didn't faze him.

"I'd like a little privacy," she said when it became clear he wasn't going anywhere.

"We're married now, Megan," he retorted and sat down on an armchair near the door.

"We don't even know each other," she reminded

him and sidestepped to the adjoining bathroom, still clutching the dress in front of her.

"We have to start somewhere."

"Not while I'm undressed."

"Fine. I'll close my eyes."

She opened the bathroom door, stepped behind it and peeked around the corner at him. "I don't trust you."

"Hardly the start of a happy marriage," he said, head tipped back, eyes closed.

Working quickly, Megan dropped the wedding gown and reached around behind her for her skirt and blouse. Pulling her clothes on, she talked while she moved. "This isn't your ordinary marriage though, is it?"

"It could be," he said.

She sneaked another peek at him. Eyes still closed. That was something, she supposed, and hurriedly buttoned up her blouse, then tucked the hem beneath the waistband of her skirt.

"Your mother *likes* me," she said.

"You say that like it's a bad thing."

"It is. We're lying to her. And I don't like it."

"I'll explain everything to my mother."

"Good. She seems nice." Megan bent down, grabbed up one of her black three-inch heels and slipped it on, then did the same with the other.

Finally dressed and feeling just a little more in control of the situation, she stepped out from behind the open bathroom door and said, "It's okay, you can open your eyes now."

He did, then stood up and walked across the room to stand in front of her. "Why didn't you tell me you were an Ashton?"

She cocked her head to one side and stared up at him. "I worked with you for a month, Simon. It wasn't a secret."

"But you never said."

"You never asked."

"True," he admitted, then unbuttoned his suit jacket, brushed the edges of the jacket back and jammed his hands into his pockets. "I should have. As it is, you being an Ashton is going to make this more…complicated."

"How?"

Late-afternoon sunlight shone through the windows overlooking the gardens and the pool beyond. The scent of roses filled the air, riding on a soft breeze that swept through the partially opened window.

"The newspapers will be more interested than ever in our marriage. You must see that."

She hadn't thought of it, but she supposed he was right. Heaven knew the media was always hounding her father about one thing or another. But growing up in the public eye, she tended to forget about it. Now though, she was beginning to see that being the daughter of a powerful man and the wife of another could make her more interesting to photographers and reporters.

"It's just for a year," she reminded him.

"Yes, but now it's more important than ever that we present the facade of a *real* marriage." He took two steps away, stared out the window, then shifted her a look. "The honeymoon in Fiji is a good start of course." He checked his watch and nodded to himself as if making a mental note. "We'll just have time for you to pack—don't worry about bringing a lot, we'll make a quick stop in Paris so you can shop."

An offer that would have had most women quivering in anticipation. But Megan was not most women.

"Fiji?" She shook her head. "Sorry, I can't."

"What do you mean, you can't?" he snapped and turned to face her. "You agreed to play this part, Megan."

"The part of a marriage, yes. The honeymoon thing? No thanks. I have a job."

He laughed shortly. "A job? You work for your family."

Megan stiffened. Happened every time someone assumed that she was a spoiled little rich girl just amusing herself by throwing parties.

"My job's important to me. And I'm good at it," she said tightly. "And in the next two weeks, I have two weddings and a sixteenth-birthday party here on the estate. I can't leave. And I wouldn't even if I could."

"Really?" he asked, his eyes narrowing. "And why's that?"

"Because, Simon," she said, walking toward him and not stopping until she was close enough to jab him in the chest with her index finger, "I may be the surprise exchange bride, and I may get married wearing someone else's idea of a gown and I even may be forced to wear a ring—" she waved her hand in his face for emphasis "—chosen for someone else, but I'll be damned if I'm going on another woman's honeymoon."

Simon frowned at her. "What's wrong with the ring?"

He'd missed the whole point. Not surprising though, Megan thought as she drew her head back and looked at him in stunned stupefaction. "It's not *mine*," she said flatly and looked down at the gaudy, wide gold band, boasting a too-big diamond surrounded by emeralds.

She'd never have chosen anything like it and the fact that she was stuck with it was only going to be a constant reminder that her marriage *wasn't* real. That she'd married a stranger. That she'd picked up another woman's castoff and had made it hers.

"You don't like diamonds?"

He sounded so surprised, she almost laughed. "Every woman likes diamonds," she replied. "But I don't like yellow gold and I don't like gigantic rings that will get caught on everything and I don't like emeralds."

He frowned thoughtfully. "I could—"

"Never mind," she said and felt good interrupting him for a change. "It doesn't matter. I said I'd do this and I will. But I'm not going to pretend to go on a honeymoon to Fiji, of all places, with a man I don't know."

Silence thundered around them for a long minute when she stopped speaking, until finally Simon said, "It's been a long time since anyone's had the nerve to argue with me like that."

Megan laughed shortly and headed for the door. "Welcome to your new world."

"Where are you going?" he demanded.

"Back to work," she said tightly. "I've got preparations to finalize for next week's wedding."

When she walked out, Simon was left alone, the only sound to be heard, the steady click of her heels as she left him.

Four

"**Y**ou're really certifiable, aren't you?" Paige leaned against the wall in Megan's office, feet crossed at the ankles, arms folded over her chest. "Not only do you marry strangers, but now, you're refusing a honeymoon in Fiji?"

Megan spared her sister a quick glance, then looked back at her computer screen. Two hours since the wedding and none of it felt real. She still couldn't believe she'd actually done it. But the gaudy ring on her left hand was proof enough to remind her.

She'd tried not to think about what she'd signed up for. Maybe Simon had caught her in a weak moment. Maybe if she'd taken her time and thought about it, she wouldn't have agreed. But, if she hadn't, then she'd still be dealing with the problem of her father and Willie-the-would-be-groom.

Which was enough to make her shudder.

"I've got work here, Paige. I can't just take off for two weeks."

"Right. Because no one else but you is qualified to make some phone calls and keep caterers in line."

Megan sighed and leaned back in her chair. Her office was just behind the main reception hall on the first floor of the estate. Here in this room, she'd created her own little world. The walls were a soft rose, complementing the rough brick of the fireplace on one wall. Muted impressionist paintings lined the other walls and the furniture was feminine without being overdone. The room was warm, welcoming, and as unlike the rest of the Ashton family showplace as she could make it.

Through a connecting door that led into the catering kitchen, she could hear the low rumble of voices and the occasional rattle of dishes. Through the bay windows overlooking the broad expanse of lawn at the front of the house, she had a view of the wide circular driveway with the oversize reflecting pool dead center.

And at the moment, her new husband was standing beside that pool, cell phone clapped to one ear.

Paige strolled toward the front windows, then glanced back at her sister. Wiggling her eyebrows, she urged, "*Look* at him, Megan. The man's gorgeous. Who *wouldn't* want to get him off onto an island and out of that oh-so-elegantly tailored suit?"

"Me, that's who." Megan blew out a breath then stood up and walked around her desk. Crossing the soft oriental carpet stretched out across a cold marble floor, she stopped alongside her sister and watched the man she'd married. "Okay, fine. He's easy to look at."

"Easy? Oh, he's better than that."

"Yeah. He really is." And that kiss, Megan thought, remembering the first touch of his mouth on hers. She hadn't expected to feel so much *everything*. It had been like standing in the middle of a power plant when there was a system overload. Sparks, lights, electrical charges jumping through her body. "But it doesn't matter."

Paige reached out and touched her hand to Megan's forehead. "Nope. No fever."

"Funny." Megan pushed her sister's hand aside. Watching as Simon reached up and pushed one hand through his wind-tousled hair, she swallowed hard and then told herself to get a grip. She didn't have anything to worry about. They'd already agreed that there wouldn't be any sex for a week.

And why, she thought, was she suddenly regretting that little agreement? Because Paige was right, she told herself. She *was* certifiable.

"Well," Paige said with a shake of her head, "I still say you should have gone to Fiji."

"I can't."

"Okay, I get it," her sister said. "But you should at least leave *here* before Father gets home. Unless you want your wedding day and the day of your death to be remembered with one fond anniversary."

"Oh man…" There'd been so much going on, so much to think about, she'd completely forgotten about Spencer Ashton. She hadn't wanted to consider her father at all. Because once she did, she'd have to face up to the task of telling him that she'd shattered his dreams regarding Senator Jackson.

And that scene wouldn't be a pretty one.

Megan's stomach twisted at the thought. All her life, she'd tried to please Spencer. She'd tried to be the kind of daughter he wanted. The kind of Ashton heir he expected. As a girl, she used to dream of having him *really* look at her one day and say, *I'm proud of you, Megan.*

Though she hated to admit it, even to herself, there was still a piece of that little girl inside her. Still waiting for Daddy's approval. It didn't seem to matter that she'd grown up. That she'd accepted long ago that Spencer Ashton would never be the kind of father she'd once dreamed of.

"And that's not even taking Mother into account," Paige muttered.

"Oh, this just gets better and better," Megan said. Why hadn't she thought this through? Now she was stuck having to tell both her parents that she was married and to try to explain why neither of them had been present. Good times.

"So what're you going to do?"

Megan shot her sister a quick look, then headed back toward her desk. Snatching her purse out of the bottom drawer, she slammed the drawer shut again and stood up. "I'm going to take your advice and get out of here. Fast."

Simon Pearce was not a man to be brushed off.

So he for damn sure wasn't going to be ignored by his new wife.

Wife.

He was married to one of the Ashtons. And he wondered if that meant he'd have to be civil to Spencer. That went against the grain. Spencer Ashton had the reputation of a hungry barracuda, and the scruples of a con man bilking a church lady out of her life savings.

Late-afternoon sunlight sparkled on the surface of the reflecting pool and Simon squinted against the glare. A warm breeze ruffled the still water and brushed past him, carrying the nearly cloying scent of roses from the well-manicured garden.

He tightened his grip on the cell phone in his hand and tried to concentrate on what Dave Healy was saying. But it wasn't easy.

"Simon, if you're not headed to Fiji as planned, then why can't you take the meeting with the Franklin company?"

Damn it, he'd worked for the last four weeks to clear his schedule long enough to allow a honeymoon. And now that he had the time, he wasn't at all sure he wanted to give it up. "Because whether or not we leave town together, Megan and I have to at least give the *impression* of being happy newlyweds."

"You really think this is a good idea?"

Actually, Simon had been wondering that himself, from the moment Megan announced her full name to the minister. An Ashton, for God's sake. What were the odds of his *accidentally* marrying a woman whose family was more well-known than his own?

He reached up and scraped one hand across his face. The media were going to be all over them for at least the next few weeks. Hell, there'd probably be paparazzi hiding in his oak trees, with telephoto lenses aimed at his house.

Simon had already seen the avaricious glitter in the eyes of the reporters. He'd smoothly explained away the fact that Megan's parents hadn't attended her wedding by saying that it had been a spur of the moment thing—then tried to gloss over the fact that his *own* mother had been there. This was going to get complicated. The very least he needed was a few days to talk to Megan. To make their plans. To learn how to face the world as a united front. Or the jig would be up almost before it began.

"It's the *only* idea," Simon said. "Besides, it's done and over with now. Megan and I are married and we'll handle whatever comes next."

Dave gave a long-suffering sigh and Simon almost smiled. "Fine. I'll handle Franklin. Good luck with the little woman."

"Right." Simon snapped the cell phone closed and half turned to look at the ostentatious facade of the Ashton estate.

Cream-colored stone seemed to glow in the late afternoon light. The mansion squatted at the top of a hill, giving its residents a beautiful view of the vineyards below. Window glass winked at him as the sun slanted across the front of the house and Simon scowled at the place. It looked like one of those mansions built in the last century by robber barons with more money than taste.

He'd heard people say that, when the house was owned by the Lattimer family, it had been smaller, yet elegant. But once Spencer Ashton took over, he'd "improved" it. He'd added two massive wings, tacked on conical towers at the end of each wing and, in general, taken a nice little country house and transformed it into a palace.

And it felt as warm as its cool marble floors.

Slipping his cell phone into his jacket pocket, Simon started across the crushed gravel drive, headed for the front doors. Past time to retrieve his wife and get started on their faux marriage.

* * *

"What're you supposed to pack for your marriage?" Megan muttered, throwing the doors to her walk-in closet wide. Okay, fine, she'd be sending for *all* of her things if she was going to be married for a year. But for right now, she needed to throw a few things together.

The question was, what?

Blindly, she stalked into the closet, swept an armful of clothing off the rack and walked back to the queen-size bed where her suitcase lay open and waiting. She'd been packing for herself for years, despite her mother always insisting that it was the maid's job to do those little chores. Megan liked knowing what she'd have and what she wouldn't. No point in being surprised.

So as she worked quickly, efficiently, her mind was already racing ahead to the other things she'd need. Makeup, hairbrushes, did her new husband have a blow dryer? She'd better take hers.

In fact, she was so busy with the task at hand, she didn't hear her mother enter the room.

"Would you care to explain?"

Megan's hands stilled and she winced a little before looking up to see Lilah Jensen Ashton standing at the foot of the bed.

At forty-nine, Megan's mother was still a beauty. Her chin-length red hair, kept looking natural by frequent trips to her favorite salon, was elegantly casual as always. Her cream-colored designer pants set was jazzed up by the dark-crimson silk blouse she wore beneath her jacket. Gold gleamed dully at her ears and her wrists. Thanks to a diet of coffee and salads, Lilah's figure was as trim as it had been when she'd first gone to work as Spencer Ashton's secretary. Her blue eyes were sharp and rarely missed much.

"Hello, Mother." Megan straightened up and prepared herself. Confrontations with her mother had been few and far between over the years. Though Megan loved her mother, she also knew that Lilah would have been just as happy to never have had children. Not that she didn't love her kids, but Lilah's "maternal side" was narrow and not very deep. She'd always been more interested in her clubs and charities than she had in raising kids, leaving Megan, Paige and their brother Trace to be more or less raised by a succession of nannies. "I didn't see you come in."

"Not surprising," Lilah said, waving one elegant hand toward the open suitcase. "You have other things on your mind, don't you?"

Well-aimed thorns of guilt jabbed at her. "Yes, well, I would have told you about it, but you were at the fund-raiser this afternoon and—"

"Do you realize what sort of position this puts me in?"

Megan took a deep breath. "I know Father will be upset about my not marrying Willie, but—"

"Don't imagine for a moment that I'm concerned with your father's reaction to this," Lilah said, cutting her daughter off neatly.

People interrupted her all the time, Megan thought irritably. Why had she never noticed before? And of course her mother didn't care about Spencer's reaction. The two of them had been living separate lives under the same roof for years.

Taking a deep breath and blowing it out again slowly, Megan said again, "I am sorry, Mother."

Actually, she was sorry for a lot of things. Not least among them, the fact that she and her mother had never been close. But that ship had sailed years ago. No point in mourning it now.

"Please, Megan." Lilah's voice was cool. "If you had wanted me to know about your 'wedding,' you would have said something. What I want to know is, how long have you been planning it?"

"Uh…" Damn. She and Simon hadn't discussed this. Should she tell her family the truth? Admit that she was just his emergency wife? Sure, and then live with their knowing glances for the next year? No, she didn't think so. Besides, if she were to survive her father's fury over this, she'd have to convince *him* at least that this had been in the planning stages for at least a few weeks.

And to convince Spencer, she'd need Lilah to believe her, too. She wasn't an idiot. She knew her parents' marriage had stopped being about anything but convenience years ago. Growing up in a house, a child learned fast if his or her parents loved each other. And there'd never been that feeling in this house.

But if her mother believed her, then Lilah would stand up to Spencer, if only because she loved to see the man's plans thwarted.

"It was pretty sudden actually," Megan said and told herself that at least she wasn't lying. "He pretty much swept me off my feet."

One of Lilah's eyebrows lifted. "I find that hard to believe, Megan. You've never been one for spontaneity." She stood up, smoothed the front of her slacks, then stepped around the edge of the four-poster bed and stopped within a foot of her daughter. Staring at her, she said slowly, "But the damage is done, in any case. Have you given any thought at all to how this situation of yours will make me look to my friends?"

"What?" Megan watched her mother and noted the color suddenly rushing into her normally milk-pale cheeks.

"It will look as though you didn't want your own mother at your wedding, Megan," Lilah explained just in case her daughter had missed the point. "How am I to explain that to my friends?"

"I didn't mean to upset you, Mother." Megan curled her fingers into her palms and felt the impression of each of her nails digging into her skin.

The fact that she'd married a man her mother hadn't even met didn't seem to bother the woman. The real problem was how to stave off embarrassment in front of the ladies of the Napa League. For heaven's sake. Megan wasn't even sure why she was disappointed. Or angry.

She'd learned long ago that Lilah wasn't exactly the milk-and-cookies type of mother. She'd given birth to three kids and then calmly handed them off to be raised by people she *paid* to give them attention.

And yet, there was still a small corner of Megan's heart that ached to be loved. To be wanted. To have the sort of relationship with her parents that other people took for granted.

"You didn't think of me at all, you mean." Lilah spared her daughter a slight frown—and really, given her propensity for cosmetic injections, a slight frown was probably all she could manage. "I should think I deserved at least a little consideration."

"You're right." Megan heard herself saying the same words she always said when faced with a family confrontation. She always gave in. Always tried to smooth troubled waters. At least here at home.

Funny, but she never had any trouble taking on crabby caterers or furious florists. She could stand up for herself with her brother and sister. She'd had no trouble at all laying down the law to Simon Pearce.

But when it came to speaking her own mind to her

parents, she retreated into little-girl-Megan mode, trying and failing to please.

"Too little too late." Reaching up with one hand to unnecessarily smooth her still perfectly coiffed hair, Lilah stared at her for a long minute, then said, "I hope you know what you're doing, Megan."

"I do," she said, the repetition of her wedding vow echoing inside her head.

"Do you?" Lilah shook her head and, briefly, there was a glimmer of something in her eyes. Sympathy? Understanding? Whatever it was though, it was gone in a heartbeat. "I wonder. You do realize that you're leaving the home of one powerful man only to go to another man much like him."

Was Simon so much like her father? In the last few weeks, she'd worked closely with the man. Had come to know him—at least a bit. Yes, he was rich and powerful. But she hadn't noticed any of the coldness her father carried around inside him.

Megan had made her decision to marry Simon on instinct. And now she had to wonder if she'd jumped from the fire into the inferno.

"I wish you luck, Megan." With those few words, Lilah was finished. She turned and swept from the room, her head held regally high, her steps long and swift, showing her exasperation and displeasure all at once.

"That went well." Megan sighed, dropped onto the bed and let the silence seep into her bones. Her stomach churned and her head ached. Oh yes. This was just as she'd always imagined her wedding day. Fighting with her mother, avoiding her father and packing in solitude for a quick escape from the estate.

"Good God, Megan," she whispered. "What were you thinking?"

A short, sharp laugh shot from her throat and she pulled in a deep breath in a futile attempt to quiet the thousands of butterflies surging in her stomach. And, when that didn't work, she looked around her, trying to find comfort in familiar surroundings.

Her room hadn't changed much over the years. Well, except for getting rid of the shelves of dolls and replacing them with miles of books. Books she'd read and lived in. Books she'd pretended to be a part of when the reality of life as a poor little rich girl had become too much.

The walls were a pale green—a departure from the beige her mother insisted on throughout the house. The French doors opening onto her private balcony were open, and the soft March wind blew in, lifting the white sheers into a slow dance.

This one room in the Ashton estate was comfort. Home. Safety. She'd come here to hide as a girl when her parents' arguments became loud enough to travel up the wide staircase from the first floor. Years later, she'd come here to cry the night her father had told her that he'd bought off her last boyfriend.

And she'd dreamed here about having someone of her own. A husband. A family.

Now she had the husband, but it was nothing like she'd dreamed it would be. Was her mother right? Had she blindly walked into a marriage that was going to be the mirror image of her parents'?

And if so, how would she ever make it through the year they'd agreed on? Straightening her shoulders, Megan told herself that she didn't have to. She could back out now. What did it matter to her if the media clamored around Simon Pearce and hassled him about his 24-hour marriage?

Even as she considered it though, she remembered her father's threat to marry her off to Willie. Besides, she'd made a deal. Megan had never gone back on her word. Not to anyone. And she wasn't about to start now.

No matter how much she wanted to.

"Rough day?"

Her head snapped up and her gaze locked on Simon, standing in the open doorway of her bedroom. And suddenly, however her marriage had begun, now it looked like a lifeboat dropped into a stormy sea.

Five

Simon's house wasn't as big as the estate.

But then, whose was?

From outside, the structure was a series of sharp angles made from weathered gray wood and glass. It looked forbidding and modern and completely out of touch with the gentle rolling green hillsides. But inside, Megan thought as her gaze slid across the foyer, was a whole different story.

Here, Simon's home looked warm, welcoming. Acres of gleaming wood floors led off in all directions and she peeked in at the rooms she passed on her way to the stairs. Overstuffed sofas and chairs, muted throw rugs, well-polished wood furniture, Tiffany lamps, their stained-glass shades shining jewel-colored splashes of light on their surroundings. Everything about the place whispered comfort. A far cry from the estate—where the first rule she and her siblings had learned was *don't touch.*

She shifted her gaze to Simon, carrying her suitcase, as he led the way upstairs. The stair balustrade was deeply carved, with pine boughs and flowers twining the railing as if they were springing to life right out of the wood. Framed paintings lined the pale yellow walls and the stair runner picked up the yellow in narrow stripes of faded cream.

The ticking of a grandfather clock at the foot of the stairs followed after them, like a heartbeat sounding out each step.

"It's pretty," she said lamely, more to combat the silence of the big house than for any other reason.

"Thanks." He turned right at the head of the stairs and stalked along a wide, well-lit hallway, with Megan hot on his heels.

When he stepped into the master suite, Megan stopped in the doorway to simply stare. Very male, the room was dominated by a four-poster bed big enough to play softball on. Megan swallowed hard and told herself she should be glad of the bed's size. She could hug one edge and hope Simon stayed on the other. At least for the week she had coming to her.

And when that week was up? A tingle of anticipation zapped her and Megan tried not to shiver.

Good heavens, what had she gotten herself into? *Stop thinking about the bed.*

The rest of the room was furnished simply, but tastefully. A wide bank of windows made up one wall and the view was amazing—she could see practically the whole valley stretched out below her. Cushioned window seats with plump pillows beckoned daydreamers, and a cozy love seat rested in front of a brick fireplace, its hearth cold at the moment.

She moved into the room as Simon tossed her suitcase onto the bed and she caught a glimpse of the master bath—miles of sky-blue tiles and a tub big enough to host the softball team when they finished their game on the giant bed. Oh boy.

"Feeling better?"

She shook herself out of her thoughts and slanted a look at the man watching her. "As opposed to what?"

One corner of his mouth lifted then flattened out again. "You weren't looking so hot when we left your house."

"Gee, thanks. What every bride longs to hear."

"Look," he said, stuffing his hands into his pockets as he walked toward her. "I know this hasn't been an easy day—"

"It's been an *interesting* day."

He kept walking, one long stride at a time until he was standing just inches from her. His cologne reached her, some musky scent that seemed to dive right for the pit of her stomach and beyond. Whoa. Okay, she needed to get a grip.

His eyes, the color of coastal fog, stared at her and she felt herself nearly being hypnotized by them. She couldn't look away. Didn't want to. And what did that mean for heaven's sake?

Several long moments ticked past and she was struck again by the silence in the big house. At home, there was always something going on. People talking, shouting, music drifting from either her room or Paige's. Trace had his television on, with those annoying sports-announcer voices dribbling into the hallways.

But here, she was pretty sure if she opened the window, she'd be able to hear grass growing.

It gave her the heebie-jeebies.

"Is it always this quiet?" she asked suddenly.

He paused, cocked his head as if listening, then shrugged. "Yeah, I guess so. Why?"

"Don't you think it's a little…eerie?"

He laughed. Shortly, harshly, as if he wasn't used to laughing and Megan wouldn't have been surprised if that were true. A shame, she thought, because laughter did great things for his eyes. And his mouth. And—never mind.

"Worried about ghosts?" he asked.

"No," she snapped back, just a little irritated. "I'm just not used to all this quiet."

"You'll get used to it," he assured her.

"Or I'll find a way to fix it," she told him.

One eyebrow lifted as he studied her. "This is going to be a long year, isn't it?"

Now Megan smiled for the first time since that morning. "You betcha."

Simon watched his new wife move around the kitchen and was amazed at how much at home she seemed. She'd changed into a pale green T-shirt and white shorts that displayed her long, tanned legs to an incredible advantage. Not that he was noticing or anything. "I would have thought an Ashton wouldn't know one end of a toaster from the other."

She shot him a quick look over her shoulder as she rummaged in the stainless steel refrigerator. "My brother and sister and I all learned our way around the kitchen early." She straightened up again, her arms full of bacon, eggs and bags of vegetables. Slamming the fridge door shut with her hip, she carried her booty to the granite island in the middle of the room.

Standing on the opposite side of the counter from him, she unloaded her things and grinned. Simon's breath caught in his chest and he had to remind himself to breathe. Why hadn't he noticed her smile before? During the last few weeks they'd worked together more than a dozen times and yet, that smile had never hit him quite so hard before.

Then it dawned on him.

Working with him rarely induced people to smile.

"I'm not saying we're great chefs or anything," Megan was saying as she broke several eggs into a cobalt-blue mixing bowl. "But if left to our own devices in a kitchen, we wouldn't starve."

"Your mother taught you then?" he asked, remembering his own mother insisting that he learn to cook—saying she wouldn't have his future wife blaming her for raising a helpless man.

Megan laughed again. "Oops. Sorry." She shrugged as she grated cheese and then added it to the mixture of eggs she'd already whipped into a froth. "But the thought of my mother willingly walking into a kitchen just struck me as funny." She shrugged. "Our cook taught the three of us. We used to spend a lot of time in the kitchen. You know, after school or in the summer…"

"You enjoyed it." It wasn't a question. He could see it in her eyes.

"Sure. What kid wouldn't? Being able to make a mess and play with fire?" She grinned again and Simon felt the same punch of awareness slam into him. And even as he savored the sensation, he reminded himself that this was not a *real* marriage. That they'd both come into this unusual arrangement knowing that it would end in a year.

Still, he reasoned, that didn't mean he couldn't enjoy the year while it was here, did it?

Rummaging around in the drawers of the island,

she found the knife she was looking for, then went to work on the vegetables. Broccoli, bell peppers and mushrooms fell beneath the quickly moving blade until she was satisfied. Then she reached up to the wrought-iron cage above the island and pulled at a copper-bottomed pot.

As she did, the hem of her tight T-shirt lifted, baring her belly button and enough smooth, tanned skin to make Simon curl his hands into fists to keep from reaching for her. Instead, he got up abruptly, went to the fridge and opened it. "Want a beer?"

Megan finally freed the skillet she'd been working on and dropped back down. Slanting him a look, she said, "You're asking an Ashton…of Ashton Estates and Winery if she wants a *beer?*"

"Yeah."

She nodded. "Just checking. And yes, I would."

He smiled to himself as she walked to the eight-burner stove built into a wall of honey oak cabinets. Slapping the skillet onto a burner, she dropped a slice of butter into the pan and melted it before adding the eggs, cheese and vegetables.

"Now," she said, pausing for a sip of the beer, "I don't want you getting used to this kind of treatment." Glancing at him, she continued. "I make a great omelet, but that's not to say I'm going to cook one every night."

He cradled his beer between his palms and looked at her. Her wide green eyes sparkled in the overhead light and her hair fell in a long, thick ponytail to just below her shoulders. She smelled like summer and smiled like a devil. She was going to torture him, he could feel it coming. He told himself he never should have agreed to that whole one-week getting-to-know-each-other-thing. Who said you had to know a person before having great sex?

And just looking at her told him the sex would be incredible.

His body went hard and tight and he had to fight for control. Something that hadn't happened to him since he was a kid. Simon Pearce wasn't a man to be led around by his hormones for God's sake.

When he finally spoke, his voice was harder than he'd planned—but hell, it was her own fault. Why'd she have to look so damn good?

"I've got a cook, Megan. I didn't marry you for your culinary talents."

The smile faded from her face and she took another drink of beer before setting the bottle down on the blue-tile counter. Picking up a wooden spoon, she stirred the egg mixture until the vegetables were evenly distributed, then turned the fire down and faced him.

"If you've got a cook, why am I doing this?"

He scowled and took another drink of beer, hoping the cold, frothy liquid would wash away the knot in his throat. "Because I gave her and the housekeeper two weeks off. I was supposed to be in Fiji, remember?"

"Oh. Right." She glanced at the pan on the stove and, apparently satisfied, left it and walked toward him. "So for the next two weeks, it's just you and I in this house?"

"Yep."

"Alone."

"Yep."

She sighed. "Well, I hope you know how to call out for pizza."

Simon smiled. "I think I can handle that."

Megan nodded. "Then we should survive."

Megan lay in the dark and watched moonlight play on the ceiling.

Weird.

She tugged the hem of her short silk nightgown down over her thighs, turned her head on the pillow and stared into the shadows, trying to make out Simon's profile in the gloom. But since he was clear on the other side of a bed the size of the European continent, it wasn't easy.

She wondered if he was still awake.

Wondered if he was wearing pajamas or—gulp—sleeping nude?

She wondered why she was wondering.

She wondered if you could go crazy just from thinking too much.

"You're awake, aren't you?"

His deep voice shattered the quiet and startled

Megan enough that she gasped in a breath. "Sorry. You scared me."

"How?" he asked, and she heard the amusement in his voice. "You knew I was here."

"Yeah, but the bed's so big, it sounded like your voice was coming from the next county."

"I like plenty of room," he said.

She kept her gaze fixed on the moonlit ceiling and told herself she really shouldn't think about why he liked all that room. Had he had teams of cheerleaders in here? All at once?

As if he could hear her thoughts, he said wryly, "I move around a lot in my sleep."

"Uh-huh." She wasn't convinced.

The silk sheets rustled and she felt a tug, so she clamped her arms at her sides to hold the slippery sheets in place.

"Worried?" he asked.

There was that amusement again, Megan thought and scowled to herself.

"Should I be?" she countered, shifting her gaze from the ceiling to the bank of windows and the star-filled sky beyond. "I mean, you did promise to give me a week."

"I did."

"Is your word any good?"

"It is," he insisted, despite the fact that the silk sheets moved and pulled again.

He was coming closer.

She knew it.

Even though, with a bed this size, it might take him all night to edge his way over to her side, Megan sucked in a deep gulp of air and held it.

"So you're not sneaking over here in the dark, then?"

"Sneaking?" he repeated, and didn't his voice sound a lot closer now? "No. Moving, yes."

"Well, cut it out." She inched a little bit more toward the edge of the bed. Much farther though and her whole right side would be hanging off the mattress, and wouldn't that make a pretty picture?

"Nervous?"

Oh yeah. He was definitely closer.

She could smell his cologne again.

And his musky scent that was somehow comforting and mysterious all at once was doing something very strange to her insides. Because it's dark, she told herself. Everything is different at night. Sights. Smells. Instincts.

She knew this because her instincts were, at the moment, screaming at her to turn *toward* him, not away. She'd been getting those little spirally feelings about him ever since dinner. Sitting across from each other at a granite counter and sharing beer and omelet had somehow been…cozy. And every time he smiled, she felt the same punch of something dizzying sweep through her.

And now that they were alone. In a bed the size of an ocean. Well, instincts were hard to fight.

Still, she tried.

"Why would I be nervous?" she countered and hoped that her voice really hadn't creaked on that last word.

"We *are* married, you know," he said, and this time, his voice was just an arm's reach away.

She did *not* reach.

"Yes," she agreed, trying to hold on to the slippery silk sheets despite his attempts to pull at them. "But we agreed to no sex for a week."

"Who said anything about sex?" he asked.

Megan closed her eyes and gulped. His voice was a whisper of temptation in the shadows. The night closed in tight around them and she swore she could hear her own heartbeat crashing like a bass drum.

"Then what are you talking about?"

"Just," he said as he slid up next to her, stopping just short of touching her, "being close."

Megan laughed and her nervousness disappeared in a flash. "Oh, boy, I haven't heard that one since junior high."

He stopped moving closer and she could almost hear the insult in his voice. "Excuse me?"

Ridiculous, but the affront in his tone had her relaxing. Loosening her grip on the silky sheets, she turned onto her side and finally looked at him. She was only mildly surprised that they were nearly nose to nose.

"Close?" she repeated, smiling. "You just want to

be close? Is that along the lines of 'we don't have to do anything, I just want to hold you'? Or is it more like 'I won't do anything you don't *want* me to do'?"

He frowned at her. "I only meant that we don't have to sleep on the edges of a very big bed to avoid having sex."

"True," Megan said, studying his face as well as she could in the moonlight. But his gray eyes were more shadowed now, almost unreadable and his expression was closed. "I think I can restrain myself—and *you.*"

His jaw worked as he studied her and she wondered what it was he was trying so hard not to say. But she'd probably never know, since he took a deep breath, blew it out in a rush and said, "You don't have to worry. I don't force myself on women."

Okay, she'd insulted him and she really hadn't meant to. But jeez, he was really encroaching on her personal space and the fact that she didn't really mind was especially irritating.

"I didn't mean that."

"What did you mean?"

"Just—oh for heaven's sake, I didn't mean anything, okay?"

"Good." He jammed his pillow up beneath his neck, sighed and then closed his eyes.

Megan watched him for several seconds before whispering, "What are you doing?"

He opened one eye. "Going to sleep."

"Um…don't you think you should move back to your own side of the continent?"

His mouth curved. "No. I'm comfortable."

She just stared at him for a long minute, but he didn't open his eyes again and in seconds, his breathing was deep, even, telling her he was sleeping.

"Well," she murmured, "at least *one* of us is comfy."

Six

The next couple of days slipped past in a rush.

Megan managed to avoid any confrontations with her father simply because he was nowhere to be seen. He left the estate before Megan arrived for work and returned long after she left.

Which should have calmed her down a little.

Instead, it had the opposite effect.

She felt like a turkey the day before Thanksgiving—on edge and waiting for the ax to fall.

And Simon was being no help at all.

She couldn't relax at work because she was just too busy—not to mention keeping a wary eye out for her father. And she couldn't relax at "home," because Simon was *everywhere*.

At least that's how it felt.

If she took a swim in the pool, she climbed out to find him standing there holding a towel for her. If she took a walk in the garden, he was right behind her. If she tried to sleep in that gigantic bed, he slipped across the mattress to lie right beside her, *guaranteeing* she wouldn't be nodding off.

But tonight, for the first time since her all-too-hasty marriage, Megan had the big wood-and-glass house to herself. Simon was working late—he'd left a message for her on the answering machine saying he didn't know when he'd be home. And if she felt a small stir of disappointment, she told herself it was only because she was now used to having him dog her every footstep.

So to prove to herself that she was indeed enjoying the solitude, Megan cranked up the CD player and let a little classic rock and roll vibrate through the empty house. Then she went into the master bath, dumped a gallon of bubble bath into the massive tub and turned on the faucets. While jasmine-scented bubbles stirred the surface and steam lifted to fog the mirrors, Megan stripped out of her work clothes and dropped everything onto the cool sky-blue tiles. Then she picked up the bottle of brute cuvée sparkling wine, which she'd liberated from the tasting room on the estate, and poured herself a glass. With the first sip, she smiled and breathed a relaxed sigh.

Setting the glass down on the countertop, she looked into the mirror and watched herself scoop her hair onto the top of her head and pin it into place. Then, grinning, she picked up her glass of wine and stepped into a tub made for a queen.

Hot water still rushed into the tub, and as she settled herself, Megan felt the strain of the last couple of days drain away. Cool wine, hot water and the soothing scent of jasmine. Everything a girl could need.

"Okay," she murmured, having another sip, "not *everything*." And just like that, her thoughts returned to the man who was her husband. Her brain had been doing that a lot lately, she realized. While talking on the phone to suppliers or caterers, she caught herself doodling Simon's name on a pad of paper. While talking a nervous bride through her first visit to the reception hall, she remembered her own walk down that aisle and the look on Simon's face just before he'd kissed her.

Her body stirred uncomfortably and she shifted, sliding down deeper into the frothy water. Scowling now, she said, "It doesn't mean anything. Of course you're a little itchy. You're sleeping beside a naked man every night."

She groaned tightly and remembered the morning after their wedding when Simon had tossed back the covers and walked across the room stark naked. It had taken every ounce of her willpower not to call him back and demand he do incredible things to her body.

"Oh man." Megan gulped at the wine to ease her suddenly dry throat. It didn't help.

As the water sluiced over her skin, she sat up, leaned forward and shut off the taps. Now there was just the slosh of the water around her and the music surging from the other room. She tipped her head back and stared out the bay window beside her at the night. The first time she'd showered in here, she'd worried about giving a peep show to whoever might have a handy telescope.

But Simon had reassured her, saying that they were on top of a hill in the middle of thirty acres—so her privacy was ensured in the second-story bathroom. And now that she could relax about it, Megan had to admit that it felt a little decadent to be naked in front of an uncurtained window.

"Okay, either too much wine or not enough," she muttered and looked over at the bottle sitting where she'd left it on the counter. "Damn it."

"Thirsty?"

"Whoops!" Megan shouted and slid beneath the veil of bubbles, all the while glaring at the doorway. Simon grinned and leaned one shoulder against the doorjamb. "You scared me to death."

He straightened and shrugged off his suit jacket, tossing it behind him into the bedroom. "You would have heard me if you didn't have the music on so loud."

She stretched out one hand and gathered in a few more bubbles, arranging them strategically over her still-submerged body. "You could have said something."

"I did."

"Oh. Right."

He smiled and held up the bottle. "More wine?"

"Yeah, please." Carefully, she held up her glass, keeping a wary eye on the bubble front.

"I'll join you if you don't mind."

"Sure," she said, thinking there was plenty of wine to go around.

He refilled her glass, then left the room and came back with another for himself. After filling it to the rim, he took a sip, smiled his approval. "Not bad."

"We, of Ashton Estates and Winery, thank you," she said, lifting her glass in salute. "This is our most popular wine, you know," she continued, hoping to fill the silence even if she was only talking about wine. "People buy it by the vat load and—what're you doing?"

Setting his glass down on the counter, Simon unbuttoned his shirt and yanked the hem of it out of his trousers.

"Simon?" Megan kept one eye on him and the other on her quickly dissipating blanket of bubbles.

"Joining you," he said and undid his belt, then the button and zipper of his slacks. "You said you didn't mind."

"Joining me in the wine," she said quickly, holding up her glass and pointing at it for emphasis. "The *wine*."

He picked up his glass, took a sip, then studied it, frowning. "Not enough room for both of us in there."

"Very funny."

"But there's plenty of room in there," he said, nodding at the tub.

Her body sizzled.

Whoa.

Megan gulped in air and when that didn't help, gulped down more wine. Good heavens. She hadn't meant—didn't think he'd—but now he—*help me*.

He undressed quickly, dropping his clothes onto the floor to join her own discarded heap of clothing. Megan closed her eyes, telling herself it was way safer that way.

But she peeked anyway.

Couldn't help herself.

And she was willing to challenge *any* woman to be able to look away from a body like Simon's.

He was tall and lean, yet well muscled. His abdomen was a sharply defined six-pack and his chest was broad, tanned and only lightly dusted with black hair. His hips were narrow, his legs long and his—she swallowed another mouthful of wine. *Oh, boy.*

Simon picked up his wineglass and stepped over the edge of the tub. He winced and hissed in a breath. "I didn't know you were trying to boil yourself alive."

She shrugged, then scooped more bubbles up to

her neck in a futile attempt to hide the body he'd already gotten plenty glimpses of. "I like hot water."

"There's hot, and then there's simmering," he muttered, sliding carefully into the water on the opposite side of the tub from her. As he quickly became accustomed to the heat though, he had to admit it felt great. Ordinarily, he wasn't the kind of guy to go for jasmine-scented bubbles—or baths, for that matter—but he was up for something new. Something...*interesting.*

"I thought you were going to work late," she said, gulping at her wine.

"I was," he admitted, then frowned to himself. He'd had every intention of staying at the office most of the night. But thoughts of Megan had haunted him, making concentration impossible. How was a man supposed to think about bottom lines when he couldn't get a certain woman's *bottom* out of his mind?

This had never happened to him before.

He thrived on control.

Simon Pearce ruled his universe.

He took another slug of the cold wine and let it slide down his throat. Then his gaze shifted to his wife. The woman who had moved into his house and upset his routine. The woman he wanted under him, over him, around him. The woman he fantasized about making love to.

The woman who was making him nuts.

"So how's work?" she asked.

"Great." One word, ground out of a suddenly tight throat.

"Yeah, me, too."

He frowned thoughtfully. "Have you heard from your father yet?"

"No," she said and tried to shrug the thought aside, but he saw the glitter in her eyes that told him she was worried. "I don't know what he's waiting for either."

"Maybe he's not as upset as you thought he'd be."

She laughed shortly, but there was no humor in it. Only more worry. "Trust me, that's not it."

"So why would he wait?"

"To up the tension," she muttered reluctantly. "That's how Spencer Ashton maneuvers." She frowned and sipped at her wine again. "'Keep your opponent off guard,' that's his number one rule. And he uses it even with his family. Heck," she corrected herself, "*especially* with his family. He's always been like this and I fall for it every time." She slapped the bathwater and sloshed a mini wave over the edge of the dark blue tub. "Instead of putting it out of my mind, I fret about it and think about it and in general drive myself nuts long before Father can lower his boom."

Simon's brain whipped through memories of his own childhood and mentally compared his parents to hers. Or at least, their fathers. Simon's father had been a great guy. Good father, honest businessman and devoted husband. All in all, a hard act to follow—which was probably why he'd taken so long to decide to get married. And why, when he did make the decision, he'd chosen a woman who didn't have high expectations of love. Because damn it, he didn't like the idea of divorce. Even though he'd walked right into marriage with Megan with a divorce all neatly laid out for them at the end of a year.

But, he thought now, that year-end was a long way away and for the moment, he was in a bathtub, with his wife. Maybe he couldn't help her with the worries clogging her mind, but with very little effort, he should be able to take her mind off of it for a while. He stretched out his legs and his foot brushed her hip.

She jerked upright, giving him a brief but tantalizing glimpse of her peaked pink nipples. Then she was underwater again, glaring at him. "Hey! Personal space!"

"It's a tub, Megan," he drawled slowly. "There's not enough room for personal space."

"It's a big tub," she countered, narrowing her eyes at him.

"Big enough," he allowed.

Her eyes went to slits. "Big enough for what?"

"All kinds of things."

"Okay, bath time over," she announced, then added, "close your eyes."

He grinned, laid one arm on the rim of the tub and lifted his glass for another sip. "I don't think so."

"What?"

"I said, if you want to get out of the tub right now, you'll have to do it with an audience."

She inhaled sharply, deeply, and Simon thought, if looks could kill, he'd be dead, buried and his grave danced over.

"Not much of a gentleman, are you?"

"Nope." But damn, he was enjoying himself.

She grumbled something he was probably better off not hearing, then glanced to where her robe hung on the back of the door, more than six feet away. Apparently, she was trying to figure out just how good a look he'd get at her if she made a run for it.

"Why don't we just sit here and relax together?" he suggested, shifting his legs and moving along the circumference of the tub, inching closer to her.

"You're inching," she accused.

"Who, me?" Yep. Really enjoying himself. And he couldn't remember the last time he'd smiled this much.

Megan blew out a breath and drained the last of her wine. Holding her glass out, she said simply, "More."

Simon nodded, reached over the edge of the tub for the bottle and topped both glasses off. Then he set the bottle back down and moved in closer—as he'd been planning to do all along.

The woman tormented him without even trying.

She was acting like a reluctant virgin and had him behaving like a cartoon villain.

He really liked it.

She watched him. "You're inching again."

"No, now I'm actually sliding."

"Why?" she asked.

"Are you serious?"

She blew out a breath. "Okay, fine. I *know* why. But we agreed to a week to get to know each other."

He smiled slowly and watched her teeth tug at her bottom lip. Amazingly enough, he felt that tug all the way to the tips of his toes. "What better way to get to know each other than by sharing a bath?"

"Oh I don't know...*bowling?*"

He chuckled and slid up beside her, pulling her close. The hot water rushed around them, slapping at them, caressing them. "We're not dressed for bowling."

"Seriously Simon..."

"Why be serious now?" he asked, dipping his head closer, closer. He tasted her. One quick nip of her mouth that left his senses reeling and sent his heartbeat into overdrive. His body went rock hard and needy, and the pulse point at the base of her throat jittered as if she knew exactly what she was doing to him.

"Because," she said, leaning her head back against his arm and staring up into his eyes. "We made a deal and—"

"The deal was, no *sex.*"

"You've really got to stop interrupting me."

He grinned. "Sorry. What were you going to say?"

"Uh..." She stared up into his eyes. "About what?"

He set his wineglass on the wide edge of the tub

and dropped his free hand into the water. He just wanted to touch her. *Had* to feel the soft silk of her skin. He needed it more than his next breath. Wanted it more than anything he'd ever wanted in his life.

And couldn't have stopped if there'd been a gun to his head.

He cupped her breast, thumbing her nipple and Megan sighed, arching into him and tipping the rest of her wine into the water.

"Simon…"

"This isn't sex," he reminded her, his voice a soft hush, barely heard over the slosh of the water as she moved. "This is just touching."

"Yeah," she said on a sigh, "but…"

"Let me touch you," he whispered, dipping his head to where her nipple just crested the surface of the water. He took the small pink bud into his mouth, tasting her, teasing her. But it backfired on him.

Not only was he tormenting her.

He was driving himself over the edge.

One taste would never be enough.

"Simon, oh, don't stop…."

Her voice, in breathy little gasps, fired his body and punched his emotions. As he suckled her, he trailed his free hand through the water, down the length of her body, skimming across her skin with the lightest of touches, while she moved and groaned beneath him. Every instinct clamored at him to grab her, hold her tight, bury himself inside her and push them both toward an explosion of pleasure.

Instead though, he corralled his own needs and focused on the soft slide of her skin against his. On the delicious curves and valleys of her body. On the hush of her sighs in the jasmine-scented air.

He drew on her nipple and felt her hand sweep up to cup the back of his head, holding him to her as if she were afraid he'd stop. But he wouldn't. Couldn't. He wanted more. He wanted *all*.

Her hips lifted in the water as his hand found her center. He covered her with his palm and felt her heat rise up to meet him. He groaned and ran the edges of his teeth across her nipple. She moved again, twisting slightly, the cooling water sloshing high and over the edge of the tub.

Then he slipped one finger into her warmth and she moaned softly, gently. So he pushed another finger inside her and as he plunged her depths, his thumb caressed the small, sensitive core of her until she trembled in his grasp.

Her hands tightened on him. Short, neat nails scraped his back even while she held his head to her breast. She groaned, arching high into his touch, rocking her hips, climbing a peak he'd taken her to.

He felt the wracking shudders that rippled through her and held her close as she soared over the edge of want and shouted his name as she fell.

* * *

Megan's skin was all pruny, she had a bruise on her knee from slamming it into the side of the tub and she'd pulled a muscle in her neck.

And she'd never felt better.

She practically skipped down the staircase, wrapped up in her plush forest-green robe. She felt warm and loose and should have been completely ashamed of herself for how she'd spent the last hour.

But she wasn't.

She hit the bottom of the stairs and did a quick little two-step toward the hall that would take her to the kitchen. After all, she was *married,* right? If she wanted to let her husband take her to the stars and back again, while sitting in a bathtub the size of an Olympic pool—God, she wanted to go back upstairs and do it all again.

"Megan," she muttered, "you're shameless. Aren't you lucky?"

While Simon was upstairs, showering off the jasmine bubbles, she was headed for the kitchen to take out plates and more wine. Her thoughtful, very talented husband had already called for pizza, and right now, Megan thought she could probably eat the delivery guy's car.

She was halfway down the hall, still enjoying the shivery leftovers still humming through her body, when the doorbell sounded out and she slid to a stop. "Wow," she said, turning for the door and doubling back. "When they say under thirty minutes, those pizza guys aren't kidding."

She ran down the hall and would have tried sliding, but her bare feet wouldn't have slid on the wood floor anyway. The doorbell pealed again, so she hurried, wondering why the pizza man was in a bigger rush than his customers.

Making a mental note to try sliding down that long hall with socks on one day soon, Megan yelled up the stairs to Simon, "Pizza guy's here, bring your wallet, my prince!"

Then she threw open the door and came face-to-face with her father.

Seven

Simon headed downstairs, wearing only the slacks he'd hurriedly dragged on when he heard Megan shout. Already pulling a twenty from his wallet to pay for the pizza, he stopped halfway down the staircase and watched Spencer Ashton step into the house.

Soft light from the overhead chandelier danced over the man and his daughter, and the breeze slipping through the still-open door lifted Megan's hair from the collar of her robe. She looked pale and uneasy, her fingers nervously smoothing the edges of her robe, fiddling with the cloth belt around her narrow waist.

"What do you think you're doing?" Spencer demanded and Simon moved one step farther down the staircase. The older man either didn't notice him or didn't care. He didn't even give Megan a chance to speak before he answered his own question. "Do you really think I'll allow you to defy me this way?"

"I wasn't trying to defy you." Megan took one long step back from her father and Simon went on red alert. Every protective instinct he had clicked in and only revved up as Spencer stared his daughter down and continued talking.

"I waited for you to come to your senses," the man growled and his deep voice reverberated through the house like a dank, thick fog. "Two days. Two days, Megan, and you didn't come to apologize."

"Apologize?" she echoed.

"Finally, it became apparent that that wasn't going to happen."

"I'm glad you understand, Father—" Megan stiffened her shoulders and lifted her chin. She swung her hair back from her face and Simon felt a stab of pride. She looked like a damn queen, even in a dark green bathrobe.

"On the contrary. There is nothing about this I *understand*." Spencer's eyes narrowed and his features went grim. "Your sudden marriage is nothing more than the act of a rebellious child."

"*Child?*"

Simon heard the outrage in Megan's voice and wondered why in the hell her father couldn't.

"You listen to me, Megan." The older man shook one finger at her as if it were a pointer in the hands of a surly teacher. "I want you to pack your things. I'll take you home, start the annulment procedures tomorrow and by the end of the week, this marriage will be forgotten. Senator Jackson owes me a favor or two. He can expedite things."

"So I can marry his son?" Megan's hands clenched and dropped to her sides.

"Of course. As we'd planned." Spencer checked his watch as if he'd already wasted enough of his time on this.

Simon gritted his teeth. Neither of the Ashtons had noticed he was there, listening. And though he wanted to rush downstairs and ride to the rescue, he also wanted to hear what Megan had to say. Would she cave in to her father's demands, or would she honor the agreement they'd made?

"I can't do that," she said and her voice got firmer with every word. "No, I *won't* do that."

The man looked as surprised as he would have been if a dog had suddenly told him to go fetch his own stick. "I beg your pardon?"

"I said I won't leave my husband."

"Your *husband.*" Spencer snorted. "You don't even know the man."

"I've known him for six weeks, Father," Megan retorted and instead of backing up again, she actually moved in a little closer to her father. "I met him at the estate while I was planning..." Her voice trailed off.

Simon smiled to himself. She wasn't about to admit that they'd *met* while she was planning his wedding to someone else. And it was only then he realized that she was right. They *had* known each other for six weeks. He'd watched her do her job, balancing her skills with organization and her ability to soothe people in already tense situations.

Hell. She'd stood up to *him*. And not many people were able to say that. He liked her. More than that, he respected her. Still, he wanted to shout encouragement, but he also didn't want to distract her.

"I'm married, Father," she said. "You're just going to have to deal with it. Simon's my husband and he's going to stay that way."

That was all he needed to hear. Simon cleared his throat and when the two people in the foyer turned to look at him, he started down the stairs again and gave Spencer a stiff smile. "Good of you to drop by," he said, as he moved to stand beside Megan.

Spencer breathed deeply, quickly and the color in his face darkened furiously. "This is no social call."

"Then why don't you explain to me exactly why you're here, in *our* house, shouting at *my* wife?" Simon dropped one arm around Megan's shoulders and pulled her close. She leaned into him as if grateful for the support.

"Your wife." Spencer nearly snorted the words.

"I'm here," he said, dismissing his daughter and focusing his fury on Simon, "to end this charade. Megan is engaged to the son of an old friend of mine and I intend to see to it that that marriage takes place."

Simon laughed. He knew it was the one thing that could either deflate or enrage an opponent and at the moment, he didn't care which effect it had on the man. He didn't like Spencer Ashton. He'd heard enough rumors and innuendos over the years to make it a point to steer clear of him. And the last few minutes had convinced him that had been a good decision. "Since Megan's already married, I don't see the point of this visit. You're wasting your time and ours."

"You forget who the hell you're dealing with, Pearce," Spencer said, his already florid face ruddy with temper. A vein throbbed in his temple as he shot a glance at his daughter. "Megan is my daughter. She'll do as she's told. This situation will be taken care of."

"Just a darn minute, Father." Megan wrapped one arm around Simon's waist as if holding onto a talisman. "I'll do what I please. I'm not a child anymore and you don't run my life."

"I beg your pardon?"

If Ashton's voice had been any colder, Simon thought, he would have been spitting ice cubes.

Megan sailed right on—only the tight grip of her fingers against his bare skin letting him know how much she hated doing this in front of him. "I told you I wouldn't marry Willie. Now, I'm married to Simon. And there's nothing you can do about it."

Simon squeezed her shoulders in solidarity, then shifted his gaze from his wife's stony profile to the man still glaring at him. "You have your answer. And that should take care of any business you had here," he said. "So I think you should be leaving."

Spencer's eyebrows shot up and his eyes widened in shock. "You're asking me to leave?"

"No," Simon corrected and silently congratulated himself on keeping a rein on his temper. "I'm *telling* you to leave."

"You son of a bitch, if you think you can—"

Exasperated, Megan blew out a breath. "Father—"

Simon pushed her behind him and hoped she'd stay there. He wasn't looking forward to planting his fist in his wife's father's face, but if he had to, he wanted her out of the line of fire.

Just then, another car pulled up in the long circular driveway and parked, motor running. An electric pizza sign on its roof blinked red and white and its horn tooted a greeting.

"Our dinner's arrived," Simon said, and taking advantage of Spencer's surprise, stepped forward and took the man by the elbow to steer him toward the doorway. The older man didn't let him get away with that for long, though.

He yanked his arm free, sent his daughter a look

of frustrated fury, then glared at Simon again. "This isn't over."

"It's long past over." Simon had had enough.

He dealt with powerful men every day. He was used to the egos, the confidence and the arrogance. Had even been accused of being fairly arrogant himself. He'd built Pearce Industries into a conglomerate worth millions by knowing how to defuse a situation and how to bend when necessary. But never once in all of his negotiations had he ever entertained the notion of plowing his fist into another man's face.

Until today.

Watching emotions churn in his wife's eyes, hearing her father talk to her as though she were a low-level employee made Simon want to throw the man out on his ear. And even while he was forced to choke down the urges, a part of him was stunned with the force of the need to protect that was choking him.

"I suggest you go home, Mr. Ashton," Simon murmured through gritted teeth. He kept his voice low, so that only Spencer heard him. "And don't you *ever* come into *our* home and bully my wife again."

The older man met his gaze for a long moment and Simon found himself hoping the bastard would try to throw a punch. But that wasn't Spencer Ashton's way. Even furious, the man retained complete control of whatever emotions he allowed himself.

"Yo!" Behind Spencer, the pizza delivery kid

bounded up the narrow brick walkway and rocked on his heels. "Somebody in this place call for pizza?"

"We did," Simon said, sparing the kid a look before turning his stare back on Spencer. "Are we clear?"

The older man's jaw worked as if he were grinding to bits the angry words he wanted to spit out. "We're clear, Pearce."

Simon smiled tightly. "Thanks for stopping by."

"Cool car, dude." The kid was eyeing Spencer's low-slung European sports car with envy etched into his face.

"Get out of my way." Spencer nearly bowled the boy over in his fury.

"Jeez, chill why don'cha?" The boy with long blond hair and dimples shrugged off Spencer, handed the pizza to Simon and said, "Eighteen ninety-five— not including tip."

"Right." Simon gave him twenty-five dollars and closed the door on the kid's burbled thanks. Turning to face Megan, he looked into her eyes, and not knowing exactly what else to say after the set-to with her father, said only, "Pizza smells good."

She inhaled sharply, blew the air out again in a rush, and stared at him for a long moment before grinning. "My hero."

His heart swelled. He should have laughed it off. She probably hadn't meant it as any more than a joke. But instead, those two simple words ricocheted around inside Simon's chest until they pinged into his heart and heated him clear through. He'd never been anyone's hero before and damned if he didn't like it. "Your father'll get over it, Megan."

She shook her head, but she was still smiling. "No he won't. But it doesn't matter. Not anymore. I'm just glad the confrontation's done. I do want you to know though, that I could have handled him. I've been doing it on my own for years."

"I know," he said and shifted his grip on the pizza box. He'd seen her gearing up for the argument. Had witnessed her putting up defenses she'd no doubt spent a lifetime designing. And he couldn't really explain what had driven him to step in. Couldn't even explain it to himself. All he knew for sure was that the driving urge inside him that had demanded he defend his wife had been the most overpowering sensation he'd ever known. "I just couldn't stand there and let you take the hit for a marriage that was all my idea in the first place."

She laughed shortly. "You didn't exactly drag me to the altar by the hair, you know. Like I just told my father. I make my own choices, Simon. If I hadn't wanted to marry you, I wouldn't have."

He inhaled sharply as she moved in closer. The scent of Italian spices and tomato sauce was thick, yet he managed to catch a whiff of the jasmine-scented bubble bath still clinging to her skin. Instantly, his body hardened at the reminders of what they'd been doing upstairs just a few short minutes ago. And the images of what he'd like to be doing right now.

"I just wanted to help," he said, forcing the words past a knot the size of a football lodged in his throat.

"I know," Megan said and moved even closer to him, looking up at him through wide green eyes that looked as clear and sharp as the first grasses of summer. "That's why I'm saying thank you. I've never had anyone stand beside me like that before. I liked it."

She smiled again and his heart turned over. He wondered how in the hell a simple smile could pack such a punch.

Simon's throat was tight. "I won't let him—or anyone else—talk to you like that."

"I know that, too," she said and reached up to cup his cheek in her palm. "And it feels really…*good,* to have someone with me. To not be on my own. I mean, I didn't actually *need* the cavalry, but I was really glad when it—you—arrived."

"Yeah?"

"Yeah." Then she went up on her toes, slanted her mouth against his and kissed him hard enough and long enough to make his knees shake and his blood boil. When she was finished, she stepped back, grinned up at him and grabbed the pizza box. "C'mon hero, let's eat."

He watched her walk down the hall toward the kitchen. His gaze dropped to the curve of her behind and everything in him tightened to the point of pain. But if she wanted a hero, then he'd be one. Even if it meant eating pizza when he'd rather be devouring *her.*

The next few days rushed past and the end of their first week together was looming. Megan's nerves were already stretched to their breaking point. She was hardly sleeping anymore. She worked all day at the estate, then came home at night to an empty house.

Since that night when they'd shared the bubble bath, the night he'd faced down Spencer at her side, Simon had kept himself at a distance. It was as if he was suddenly regretting their standing together as a team. Regretting making himself into her momentary hero.

He worked late every night and when he did come home and slip into their bed, he kept to his side of the vast mattress—driving her crazier than when he'd been sneaking up on her. He was up with the dawn and out of the house before she'd had her shower.

Megan threw a quick, anxious look at the closed front door, then turned and stalked down the long hallway, her heels clacking on the shining wooden floor.

"And now *this.*" Her stomach jittered and her mind raced. She'd been thinking all day. Thinking about what she'd seen, what she'd heard and what she'd done. Now, she had to think about how she was going to tell Simon.

"Darn it, he married me to *avoid* a scandal. Now, he's going to be dragged through one." Oh, she didn't doubt it for a minute. There was no way the Ashton family would be able to bury this one. Sooner or later, the news would leak and then the papers would be all over all of them.

Despite what her mother had tried to do.

"Oh, God." Megan stopped, rubbed her temples in a pitiful attempt to erase the headache that had been pounding behind her eyes all afternoon. But it wouldn't go away. Just as the memory of her own mother's callous cruelty wouldn't fade.

"Megan?"

She whirled around at the sound of Simon's voice. While she watched him, he stepped into the house, dropped his leather briefcase and walked toward her. "What's wrong?"

"Well," she muttered thickly, "guess I don't have much of a poker face, do I?"

"Not so much," he said, one corner of his mouth lifting, then falling again before it could become a real smile. "Tell me."

Here it was. She'd been waiting for him for what felt like forever and now that the time to talk to him was here, Megan felt her throat close up. She fought past it. "I don't even know where to start."

Taking her hand, he pulled her into the living room, off the foyer. The big room was dark and as he entered, he hit the light switch and puddles of golden lamplight spread across the room, chasing the shadows. Big overstuffed couches sat across from each other, with a wide oak coffee table between them. A cobalt-blue vase held a double bunch of white carnations and daisies that Megan had brought home only the day before. And somehow, looking at the simple cheerfulness of that bouquet made Megan feel even worse.

She pulled her hand free of Simon's and started pacing again. Somehow, she had to keep moving. As if trying to keep up with her racing mind—which, she told herself, was simply impossible.

"What the hell's going on, Megan?"

"Scandal for one," she blurted, unable to think of a gentle way of putting it.

"What—"

"I'm getting to it," she said and realized that now *she* was interrupting *him*. They'd come a long way. Shaking her head, she continued in a rush, "A woman came to the estate today. Her name's Anna Sheridan."

"And…?"

"And," Megan repeated, still stalling. Stupid. Just say it. "She came to talk to my mother. About her nephew."

Simon frowned. "Your mother's nephew?"

"No, Anna's."

"Anna has a nephew."

"I just said that," she snapped, then held up one hand. "Sorry. Sorry. It's just that I've been thinking about this all afternoon and dreading telling you and at the same time *wanting* to tell you to, you know, get it out of the way, and now that you're here, I'm talking all around it and not saying a damn thing, which is really stupid, but I can't seem to stop and oh God, I need to draw a breath." She stopped, slapped one hand to her chest and felt the furious beating of her heart. Dragging one breath after another into her lungs, she locked her gaze with his as he came closer.

"Megan, what the hell is wrong?" Simon grabbed her shoulders the minute he was close enough and she felt the warmth of his hands right down to the bottom of what felt like a very cold soul.

She drew on that heat and held it close as she nodded. "I'm getting to it. Just not very efficiently. Okay, Anna Sheridan's nephew. Jack. A baby, really. Not even two yet. She had a picture. Cute little guy. Red hair. Green eyes. Great smile."

His lips twitched. "And you hate kids? The picture brought out a long-buried childhood trauma?"

He was joking. He was being nice. Damn it.

"No. No, it's nothing like that." She looked up at him so she could watch his eyes. "Little Jack is my half brother."

"What?"

"My *father*—" and she said the word with a bitterness that had been filling her mouth all afternoon "—had an affair. Probably should say *another* affair to be accurate. Though to be absolutely accurate," she muttered, "you'd probably need a scorecard. Anyway, he had an affair with Anna's sister Alyssa. Alyssa died after giving birth and Anna's been raising Jack—my father's son."

"Whoa."

"That about sums it up." Megan stepped away from him and swept one hand through her hair as she turned to stare out the front windows at the darkness beyond the glass. Instead, she saw her own reflection—and Simon's, standing right behind her. God. Was he wishing he'd married anyone but her? Probably. And who could blame him? "Anyway, Anna came to the estate looking for—I don't know. Money? Help? Recognition?"

"What happened?"

"About what you'd expect." She sighed and felt the cold, damp fingers of shame reach out for her again as she remembered. "Father wasn't home. But my mother was."

"And?"

She watched his face in the glass. Somehow it was easier talking to his reflection than to turn and face him. "And my mother practically threw her out. God." She closed her eyes, suddenly unable to face even the mirror image of Simon's face. But as soon as her eyes were closed, she saw her mother again. Saw the hard expression on her tight features and heard the withering tone of her voice.

Megan had long known that her mother wasn't a tower of warmth. But seeing her like that… "Her

voice was like ice. She dismissed Anna Sheridan and
the—and here I quote—'bastard' child. She told
Anna that if she tried to come to the estate again,
she'd bring charges of extortion against her."

"I don't even know what to say."

"That's okay," she said, finally opening her eyes.
"Neither did I." She wrapped her arms around her
own middle and finally forced herself to turn around
and face her husband. "At first, all I could think was,
oh boy, another scandal. Won't Simon be pleased.
You married me to avoid scandal touching your family, your business."

"Life happens, Megan. Scandals blow over."

She cocked her head to one side and stared at him.
"That's not what you said a week ago."

He shrugged. "I'm growing as a person?"

She laughed shortly and shook her head. "Fine.
Maybe my father's scandals won't rub off on you.
That's something to hope for, I guess."

"There's something else, Megan. Something
that's bothering you more than worrying about tab-
loid reporters."

"Yeah," she said and met his smoky-gray eyes.
"There is." And it had been torturing her all day. She
could hardly say the words, but she had to. "Simon,
I watched my mother turn that woman away and I
couldn't take it. Just couldn't. Mother's never been
what you'd call a really *warm* person. But somehow
I never thought of her as completely cold, either. But

today…" She shook her head and swallowed hard. "There was a part of me that was absolutely terrified that I could be like her. That one day I'd wake up and my voice would be just like hers. That I'd get swallowed up by the cold. That because she's my mother, I'm capable of that kind of callousness."

"You're not."

She choked out a laugh. "You said that too fast. You didn't think about it."

"Didn't have to."

Oh God, she wanted to believe him. But if a person could inherit the color of her parents' eyes or hair, couldn't she also inherit a cold heart? Or an empty soul? And why was she being so damned poetic?

She smiled wistfully. "I hope you're right. But because of my own fears, I caught up with Anna outside. I told her to go to Caroline Sheppard for help." She laughed shortly, harshly. "If ever there was a woman to help another with my father's cruelty, it would be Caroline."

"I'm not following."

"Not surprising. Caroline used to be married to my father. The estate originally belonged to her family. Then my father divorced her to marry my mother and—" She threw both hands up and let them slap against her sides again. "Now Caroline's married to Lucas Sheppard—"

"And they run Louret Vineyards," Simon put in, obviously catching on.

"Right," Megan said, "Ashton Estates and Winery's archenemy." Megan sighed, shook her head and said, "Listen to me. It sounds like a soap opera, doesn't it?"

He stepped up to her and settled both hands on her shoulders again, then slowly, he rubbed her upper arms as if trying to drive away a chill. "Families are complicated."

"Some more than others."

"What you did for Anna?" He dipped his head until he could look into her eyes. "That was kind, Megan."

"Maybe," she said and shook her head. "I hope Caroline can help her. But the bottom line is, I'm not even sure if I did it because it was the right thing to do or if I was trying to convince myself that I'm nicer than my mother. Sad, huh?" She looked away from his eyes, unable to meet that steady gray stare. "I just don't know. The only thing I do know is, what I did wasn't enough. That little boy is my father's son, damn it."

"You gave her more than your mother did."

"Yes, and now for my reward, I get to feel as though I've betrayed the family." Oh, and she didn't even want to think about how Spencer would take the news of her stepping in to help his mistress's sister and his illegitimate child. Oh yeah. That should be a fun scene.

On the other hand, she thought, since her father

still wasn't speaking to her, maybe she wouldn't hear anything from him at all.

"God, I'm a mess," she whispered and leaned her forehead on his chest.

Simon wrapped his arms around her and held her close, pressing her up against him. He'd stayed away from her these last few days, knowing that he was walking a razor's edge of control. And now tonight, he was holding her, and all he wanted to do was comfort. Thoughts of having her, sliding his body into hers, kissing her, tasting every square inch of her skin were fading, becoming more tender, more caring.

His heart ached for her, knowing how it felt to be torn between what you saw as your duty and what you knew to be right. He'd been doing his duty by his family ever since his father had died when Simon was seventeen. He'd been lucky enough to actually enjoy what he did for a living, but even if he'd hated it, he would have done it. He understood family loyalty. And knew what it had to have cost her to take a chance on ostracizing herself from those she loved by doing what she thought was right.

But damn he was proud of her.

"So," he said, enjoying the feel of her pressed up against him. "You pretty much had a crappy day."

She didn't even lift her head, but she did sigh heavily. "You could say that."

"You did good, Megan."

"I hope so," she admitted, then paused for a long

moment before asking, "What if I'm like my mother, Simon?" Her voice was a whisper and he almost missed the words because of the roar of his own heartbeat. "What if I'm that cold inside? That unfeeling?"

"You're not," he said, and willed her to believe. Grabbing her shoulders, he set her away from him enough that he could look into her eyes. "You're the warmest woman I've ever known. Stubborn, sometimes irritating," he added with a half smile, "but warm."

One eyebrow lifted. "Irritating?"

He grinned. "Figures that's the word you latched on to." Then his smile faded as he watched her worried gaze. "You did the right thing, Megan. You always do the right thing. You should trust your own instincts more."

She stared up at him and he felt the power of her green eyes slamming into him. He read the hope shining in their depths—and something else, too. A flash of heat, of desire, and his body jump-started into life.

"Trust my instincts?" she asked.

"They're good instincts," he said, and smoothed her hair back from her face with a tender touch. Her hair was soft and thick, and her skin as smooth and warm as sunlit glass.

He wanted her more than he'd ever wanted anything else in his life.

"Then I'll trust them. Starting right now." She

moved into him, went up on her toes and, wrapping
her arms around his neck, she kissed him so long and
hard and deep, Simon could have sworn his hair
caught fire.

Eight

The week wasn't officially over.

And Megan couldn't have cared less.

She wrapped her arms around Simon's neck and hung on while she kissed him hungrily, desperately. She poured everything she had into that kiss. Heart and soul, hunger and need, she let him know without words just how much she wanted him. Just how frantically she *needed* him.

A full minute later, she realized that he wasn't responding. He hadn't grabbed hold of her. Hadn't kissed her back. In fact, he was standing stiff and still, looking—and feeling—pretty much like a wax representation of Simon Pearce.

When that knowledge finally clicked into her brain, Megan broke the kiss and pulled her head back to look up at him. In the golden lamplight spilling throughout the living room, his smoke-gray eyes looked dark and dangerous. And her stomach jumped in reaction.

Her breath staggered in and out of her lungs. Her own heartbeat was deafening. Her blood pumped and parts of her body that had been sorely neglected over the last year were alert and ready to party.

But Simon was staring over her head at the wall behind her, tension etched into his features.

"Hello?" she said, her voice just a little ragged. "Anybody home?"

He swallowed hard and slowly lowered his gaze to hers. His pale, smoky-gray eyes were the color of thunderheads just before a huge summer storm. He didn't speak. He made no move to touch her. She just hung off his shoulders like a human cape.

"You know," Megan said, never taking her gaze from his, "that was a pretty good kiss you just missed."

"Didn't miss it. Trust me."

She tilted her head to one side and tightened her arms around his neck. "Uh-huh. So, why didn't you join me? Kissing's always more fun if two people do it."

He inhaled sharply, deeply, and through his starched white shirt, Megan felt the hard slam of his heart.

"The week's not up," he pointed out, through clenched teeth.

"What?" She'd heard him. She just couldn't believe it.

"I said, the week's not up till tomorrow." Simon's jaw muscle ticked. "We had a deal."

"So you're not going to do anything until the official end of the week."

"That was the deal."

He didn't sound happy about it, but he did sound determined. A part of Megan appreciated that. Nice to know that the man kept his word. However...

She combed her fingers through his hair, dragging her nails across his scalp and smiled to herself when he closed his eyes and gritted his teeth harder. "The thing is," she whispered, dropping small, nibbling kisses along his jawline between words, "I—don't—want—to—wait—"

He growled.

Actually *growled,* and something inside Megan turned over, then sat up and begged. She'd never wanted anyone as much as she did Simon Pearce right at that moment. Tall and strong and sure of himself. He wasn't the easiest man in the world to know, but she knew what she needed to know. He was honorable. Old-fashioned word, but a good sentiment. He wasn't afraid of her father. Also a good thing. He treated her like she had a brain—very sexy.

And he could do things to her body with the touch of a single finger that no other man had ever been able to do.

"Megan," he said, his voice just as stiff as the rest of him, "you had a crappy day. You're upset, you're vulnerable—"

"Simon…" She sighed and her breath brushed the base of his throat. The pulse point there jumped in response and she smiled to herself. "Stop being so damn *reasonable*."

She looked up at him.

He met her gaze and fires flared in the depths of his eyes. Fires that reached out for her and inflamed every square inch of her body.

Wow.

"Be sure," he ground out.

Megan smiled and shook her head. "If I get any more sure, I will officially be attacking you."

"Good point." He bent his head, took her mouth with his and gave her everything she'd given him only moments before.

Megan held on for dear life and jumped headfirst into a raging river of passion like she'd never known before. His mouth ravaged hers. His tongue tangled with hers, his arms came around her, pulling her so tightly to him, she was afraid she wouldn't be able to breathe—though a part of her wouldn't have cared, so long as he kept on kissing her.

Nothing mattered beyond Simon's mouth on hers, Simon's body pressed against her, the hunger stampeding through her system.

A week ago, she wouldn't have believed that she'd

feel like this. A week ago, she'd looked at Simon as a virtual stranger—and perhaps the solution to the problem of Willie Jackson.

Now, tonight, he was so much more.

He'd stood alongside her, making them a team. He'd comforted her, laughed with her, and annoyed her. He was in her mind all the time and in her dreams every night.

His hands swept up and down her back, holding, touching, exploring and all Megan could think was, she wanted his hands on her skin. She wanted to feel the heat of him, feel the imprint of each of his fingertips as he stroked her and drove her body higher and higher.

Simon tore his mouth from hers and dropped his head to the curve of her neck. His mouth, his teeth, his lips worked against her throat and chills raced up and down her spine. "Simon…"

"No more talking," he muttered against her neck. "Just feeling."

"Right," she said, agreeing with a sharp nod. "Feel. Want to feel more."

"Good. Very good." His mouth dipped a bit lower, nestling on the pulse point at the base of her throat and she tipped her head to one side, hoping he'd stay there for a minute or two—or forever.

His mouth was a wonder.

"Want you," he murmured, his words coming in an agonized whisper, strangling with need.

"Me too, want you, too," she agreed, scraping her hands up and down his back, wishing she could just blink and have his suit coat and shirt gone.

"Now."

"Oh yeah," Megan said, mind whirling into oblivion. She couldn't think. Didn't want to think. Just wanted him. "Now."

His hands came around to her front, swept up between their bodies and as he continued to nibble on her neck, his fingers made quick work of the buttons lining the front of her pale-green silk blouse.

"Faster," she said, amazed at the fire burning within her.

To please them both, he grabbed the edges of her blouse and gave them a yank, shooting the remaining buttons into every corner of the room. He tugged the fabric off her shoulders and down her arms and then all that stood between Megan and Simon's hands on her body was her bra. He made quick work of that, too, and in an instant, his hands were cupping her. His thumbs and forefingers tweaked and teased her nipples, setting off a chain reaction inside her that had Megan gasping for air and choking out encouragement.

"Your mouth," she whispered. "I want your mouth on me."

"Yes." One word, ground out through a tight throat and Simon fought through the cloudy haze of passion obscuring every thought but need. Had to have her. Had been thinking of nothing but this for days, what seemed like years.

Every night, she lay within an arm's reach and was still untouchable. Every day, he tried to fill his thoughts with work, with the very thing that had been his focus most of his life. Instead, Megan was there with him, every moment, every hour. Thoughts of her plagued him, infuriated him, tortured him.

He'd told himself only that morning that it would all be over tomorrow. That once they'd slept together, once he'd buried himself inside her, tasted all she was and all she promised, then he would be satisfied. Then his world would slip back onto the tracks and all would be as it should be.

Now though, with her in his grasp, her warm sighs and eager hands only served to feed the need, not satisfy it.

Dropping to his knees in front of her, he dragged his hands down the length of her body. When he hit the waistband of her skirt, he unzipped the fabric and pushed it down her legs, dragging her panties, a fragile scrap of black lace, along with it. And then she was there, in front of him, naked and willing and just as hungry as he.

Her knees wobbled and he caught her, hands on her bottom, steadying her, even while drawing her legs apart gently, carefully, despite the urgent need inside him.

"Simon, I want—"

"I want, too," he whispered brokenly. "I want *you.*"

Then he leaned toward her and covered her center with his mouth. He tasted her as she gasped and swayed in his grasp. His tongue teased her center, flicking gently over the sensitive nub of flesh at her core.

"Simon!" Her hands fisted in his hair and she locked her knees even as she leaned into him, holding him to her as if half-afraid he would stop.

He couldn't stop.

Wouldn't stop.

Not until he felt her body dissolve. Not until he'd tasted her pleasure and experienced her surrender. Again and again, he swiped her warm flesh with his tongue, driving her higher and faster with every stroke. His grip on her behind tightened, her sobbing gasps urging him on until she cried his name and swayed violently in his grasp.

As the last of the tremors rocked her, he eased her onto the floor, the soft fabric of the oriental rug cushioning them both. She lay, spent, staring up at him as he quickly tore off his own clothes and then leaned over her.

"Simon, that was…" She smiled and lifted both hands weakly, as if unable to come up with just the right word.

He did it for her.

"…just the beginning." Then he parted her

thighs with his knee, positioned himself between her legs and slid into her slick heat with a groan of satisfaction.

Her body closed around him, holding him tightly and Simon's vision blurred.

She reached up for him, taking his face between her palms and pulling him down for a kiss. Her lips parted and her tongue touched his, tangling, dancing intimately in an imitation of his body moving in and out of hers.

Over and over, he felt the rush of desire take him by the throat and squeeze. He felt the wild fulfillment of being inside her. Of touching her so deeply.

He broke their kiss and looked down into her summer-green eyes and lost himself in the clear, soft depths of them. Her hands slid up and down his back. She lifted her legs and rocked her hips, moving with him in a rhythm that was as old as time and as new as a breath.

And when her tremors began again, Simon dipped his head for another kiss and kept them joined completely as they chased each other into the light.

Megan's back hurt.

She was pretty sure she had rug burn on her behind.

Her legs were cramping.

And if he tried to move, she'd have to kill him.

Suddenly, he did move, trying to pull free of her

body, but she held him still after releasing one soft gasp. "Don't," she warned, clamping her arms tightly around him and holding him to her. "Don't move."

He chuckled shortly and his warm breath dusted the curve of her neck. "If I don't, I'll smash you."

"I'm sturdier than I look," she assured him, closing her eyes to better enjoy the sensation of his body moving within hers again.

He propped himself up on his elbows and stared down into her face. "Wouldn't you rather move upstairs?" he asked, a half smile curving his mouth. "You know? To an actual bed?"

"Mmm…" She rocked her hips and nearly smiled herself when he hissed in a breath. Good to know she wasn't the only one going up in flames around here. "Later."

"Right," he said, punctuating the single word with a long, slow kiss that ended with him nibbling on her bottom lip.

"That was really amazing, Simon," she said when her mouth was free again. "I mean, *amazing*."

"Yeah," he admitted, "that about covers it."

Megan felt loose and limber and, okay, a little achy, but in a good way. Her body was humming, her mind was in neutral and for now, that's just how she wanted it.

"Think we could do that again?"

He grinned. "Is that a direct challenge?"

"Does it have to be?" She rocked her hips again,

and reached down with one hand to stroke the curve of his backside.

He sucked in a gulp of air and pushed his body hard against hers. "Nope."

"Oh, boy." She held on as he rolled over onto his back, somehow keeping their bodies locked together despite the quick move. And then she was straddling him, and his hands, his wonderful, clever hands with their long, sensitive fingers, were on her breasts, tugging, teasing, cupping and stroking.

Megan sat up straight and arched her back, moving into his touch even as she took his body deeper within her own. She felt the hard, solid strength of him, pushing higher, higher until she would have sworn he'd actually touched her soul.

He groaned and she opened her eyes to watch him as she took him. Power filled her and it was a delicious and heady drug. She moved on him, rocking back and forth, then swiveling her hips in a slow, tight circle that set off incredible sensations deep inside her. In reaction, he lifted his hips, arching higher into her body, as if he couldn't be deep enough, close enough.

"Megan—" His hands tightened on her breasts, fingers delicately squeezing her nipples, and she reached to cover his hands with her own.

His eyes glazed over and his mouth worked as he fought for control. Then his gaze shifted to their joined hands and he groaned tightly. Megan watched his inner battle and smiled to know that she could push such a strong man to the brink of powerlessness.

"Enough," he muttered and tried to move, to shift her to the carpet so he could roll atop her and set their pace.

"Not even close," she whispered, lifting her arms high above her head as she rocked atop him. "Let me, Simon, let me take you this time."

"You're killing me, Megan," he managed to say, though every word sounded as though it had cost him dearly.

She shook her head and smiled as she rode him, lifting her body, then lowering it again, taking him deeply, then releasing him in a slow, languorous dance that drove them both to the edge of desperation. Her body tensed, a sense of anticipation climbing within, marking each second with breathless wonder. Sensation after sensation coiled within and every time she moved on him, she soared a little higher.

She leaned back then, arching her spine and tipping her head back, shifting his body's position inside her until he was pressing on exactly the right spot to send her hurtling into space.

"Simon," she whispered, never breaking pace, never slowing as she continued her erotic dance atop his body. "Simon, I feel—"

"I feel it, too," he murmured, and his voice was a sigh in the roar of her own blood.

As she moved on him, he dropped one hand to the

joining of their bodies and stroked her with a single fingertip. Again and again, he caressed her until she was trembling, aching for the release she knew was hanging just out of her reach.

She gasped, she fought for air, fought to hang on to the rising climb of her body's tension. She wanted that climax and at the same time, didn't want this moment to end. She wanted to trap them somehow in time—right here, right now. To hold this position for eternity—this one exquisite moment just before the tremendous release she felt getting nearer.

Simon's body bucked beneath her as he exploded, she heard him shout her name and still, he touched her, never stopping, never easing until all at once, she saw stars erupt behind her closed eyelids and felt the world rise up and then dissolve around her.

And she wondered...who had taken *whom?*

Two hours later, they were sprawled across the continent of their bed. The remains of a hastily grabbed snack lay scattered across the sheets and a half-empty bottle of wine was being passed back and forth between them.

Megan put her mouth on the bottle and tipped it back, taking a long drink of the smooth, tart wine. Then grinning, she said, in the stuffiest voice she could manage, "An impudent wine, with the grace of maturity and just the slightest touch of adolescence."

Simon's mouth twitched as he took the bottle from

her and had a long drink himself. "Tart, yet sweet. Bold, but not too sassy."

"Not bad," Megan said, nodding. "You've been to wine tastings before."

"A few," he admitted, leaning against the pillows stacked against the carved headboard. He lifted one knee and rested his forearm atop it. "None as casual as this one, though."

"Casual?" Megan asked and crawled across the mattress until she was right next to him. She couldn't stand to stay on the opposite side of the wide mattress. She needed to touch him, to trail her fingertips across his skin, to smooth her hands over his whole body, to feel him get hard for her again.

Oh boy.

She collapsed in a heap over his broad and really exceptionally well muscled chest. Every bone in her body felt like an overcooked noodle. She'd never been so limp with satisfaction—and so hungry for more. "I think we're dressed very appropriately."

He ran his palm over her behind, squeezing, stroking, and Megan damn near purred as she moved beneath his touch. Honestly, who would have guessed that stiff and stern Simon Pearce had so many hidden talents? The man was a wizard. He'd done things to her body tonight that she hadn't even dreamed of. He'd taken her higher and faster than she'd ever been before.

And, she wanted him again.

Her heart rolled over in her chest.

More, she wanted *him* to want *her.*

"If we keep this up, we'll kill each other," Simon mused, his hand still caressing her bottom with long, lazy strokes.

Megan didn't want to move. Didn't want to risk him stopping touching her. But she chanced a look over her shoulder at him. "There are worse ways to go."

"True." His eyes darkened. Even in the pale, soft light thrown from the lamp on the nightstand, she could see his features tighten. She watched hunger flash in his eyes and she swallowed hard.

Megan's stomach pitched and swirled.

Her mouth went dry and certain other parts of her body dampened in anticipation. Oh, she'd had absolutely no idea what she was getting herself into when she'd agreed to a temporary marriage to Simon Pearce.

And if she *had* known?

"I have to have you again," Simon whispered, his voice a soft growl in the shadows. As he spoke, his hand slipped down between her legs, his fingers delving into her heat.

Megan parted her thighs for him then slid her eyes closed and concentrated on the incredible sensations building within her again.

If she'd known?

She wouldn't have waited a week.

Nine

"**I** don't care if the Peabody Corporation withdraws from the deal." Simon leaned back in his desk chair and stared at his assistant.

Dave Healy shook his head, blinked, then tipped his left ear toward his boss. "Excuse me? Would you mind repeating that?"

"Funny." Wryly, Simon smiled. "I mean it, Dave. If the old man wants to pull out of this deal, that's his business. Let him find someone else willing to put up with his antiquated ideas about building a company."

Morning sunlight slanted through the bank of windows behind Simon's desk and sketched out tall panels of light on the steel-gray carpet. Dave Healy stood in one of those slashes of gold, clutching a manila file folder.

"Never thought I'd hear you say that."

"To tell you the truth, neither did I." Simon straightened up again, planting both elbows on the gleaming black surface of his desk. Even while Dave talked, Simon's brain wandered. Something he'd noticed happening more and more often lately—since Megan had entered his life.

The last few days had been hard on her. The papers were full of the latest Ashton scandal and Megan fretted over every headline. Her father's illegitimate child was news and every reporter in the state was constantly looking for a fresh angle from which to attack.

He knew she was more worried for him and for his business than she was about herself, and though he appreciated it, he kept trying to tell her she didn't have to be.

True, scandals were bad for business, especially when dealing with people like Manfred Peabody—an old coot who would have been much more comfortable living out his life in Victorian England. But it wasn't as if this scandal actually touched his family. Pearce Industries was safe. Spencer Ashton was an ass, but it wasn't going to affect Simon. Except, of course, for the effect the old goat was having on Megan.

And even as that thought slid through his mind, he realized that just a couple of weeks ago, he

couldn't have imagined feeling that way. But things
had changed now. Megan was his wife and he wasn't
going to let old man Peabody—or anyone else for
that matter—insinuate that she'd done anything
wrong just by being born an Ashton.

Megan.

Lately, everything came down to Megan. He
hadn't expected this "temporary" marriage to be anything more than a convenience. But it was quickly becoming so much more than that.

She was creeping into every corner of his life.
And that was something he hadn't counted on.

"Simon!"

"Huh?" He blinked and looked up at Dave. The
man was shaking his head and grinning.

"Where the hell is the steely focus and single-
minded concentration that makes Simon Pearce a
man to be feared across the mortal globe?"

A short, sharp laugh shot from his throat as he
stood up and shoved his hands into his pants pockets. Shrugging his shoulders, he looked at Dave and
admitted, "Hell if I know."

His old friend nodded thoughtfully. "It's about time."

"What's that supposed to mean?"

"It means," Dave said, stuffing the file folder
under his left arm, "that you've been living for this
company for too long."

Simon frowned, but didn't argue. Hard to when
the man was absolutely right.

"You've always been eat-sleep-breathe work," Dave went on. "That's not healthy."

He snorted and walked around the edge of his desk. On the far wall, a sterling-silver clock ticked off the hours until he could go home again. Until he could be with Megan. Damn it, he *had* lost his focus. He eased himself down and perched on the edge of his desk. "Healthy," he said. "This from a man who thinks of French fries as vegetables."

Dave grinned. "My point is," he said, ignoring that last little jab, "you're allowed a life, Simon, and you haven't been getting one."

He frowned. "I have a life."

"The company doesn't count."

"It's all that ever has counted," Simon said softly.

"Until now," Dave pointed out. He took a step closer and slapped Simon's shoulder. "Megan's good for you, Simon," he said. "I'm glad you've got her."

"Temporarily. Our deal was for a temporary marriage."

Dave laughed and turned for the door leading into his own office. He opened the door, then paused to look back at his boss. "Aren't you the man who's always believed that deals were born to be renegotiated?"

Even after Dave left, his words hung in the air, like a…what? Challenge? Suggestion?

Simon's fingers curled around the edge of the cold black desk and he stared hard at the clock on the wall while his mind raced. Did his marriage really have to remain temporary? Did he *want* more from Megan?

He didn't know.

All he could really be sure of was that he wanted Megan now.

Tomorrow was too far away to be worried about.

And yesterday was too empty to remember.

"Charlotte, I think I'm going nuts."

Megan stalked across the living room of the small guest cottage where her cousin Charlotte lived. The rooms were tiny, but beautifully kept with warm, polished wood floors and beamed ceilings. A tiny one-story structure, it was built of stone and wood, and when she was a girl, Megan had believed it to be a storybook cottage, complete with fairies and pixies and everything else a little girl dreamed of.

Now, it was simply her cousin's home. Charlotte Ashton had never cared for living at the main house, preferring her own company in this cozy place. Besides, the greenhouses were just behind the cottage, keeping things easy for the woman who created beautiful floral arrangements for the events held on the estate.

"You're wearing a hole in the floor," Charlotte said quietly.

"Sorry, it's just—" Megan stopped and threw her hands wide.

"You have to pace when you're anxious. I know."

Charlotte sat curled up on a dark-rose sofa, a velvet throw pillow clutched to her chest. Her long, straight black hair hung down well past her shoulders and looked like a silk cape she'd tossed on for effect. She was tiny and patient and soft-spoken—all the things Megan wasn't.

Perhaps that's why they got along so well.

Megan took a deep breath, blew it out, then dropped onto a dark green side chair. The overstuffed cushion rose up around her like a comforting hug. "The newspapers are full of Father and his latest—I don't even know what to call it."

"Episode?" Charlotte offered.

"As good a word as any." Megan shook her head, then reached up and pushed one stray lock of blond hair behind her ear. "Reporters are hovering outside the gates, attacking every car that leaves, phoning the estate, pestering customers who are just here for a wine tasting." She paused for breath. "And yesterday, one of the TV crews actually made a sixteen-year-old cry at her own birthday party." She cringed, remembering how the young girl and her friends were chased down the drive by an overeager reporter and his cameraman. "Mother won't talk about it, Trace keeps his head buried in work, Paige pretends everything is normal, Father refuses to say anything—even told me himself this morning that since I had chosen to turn on him, taking my husband's side over his, that he owed me nothing. No explanations, nothing."

She cringed inwardly, remembering that scene in her father's estate office only that morning and wondered how she could ever have imagined that Spencer might want her opinion. Then she shook it all off and said, "And Simon…"

"What about Simon?"

"I don't know," Megan admitted and added silently that that was what she was most worried about. Simon hadn't said anything about this latest disaster of her father's. Not since that first night when she'd broken it to him and then they'd… Her body went hot for one gloriously amazing moment, and then that feeling drained away completely. "God, Charlotte, I don't know what to do. What *can* I do? This is all just a mess."

Charlotte's features hardened. "You know I'm no fan of your father's, Megan."

"I know and maybe that's why I came to see you. Everyone at the main house is walking on tiptoe around the place as if leery of stepping out of line. But how can we?" she demanded of no one. "When Father's the one who keeps moving that line?"

"You act as though you're surprised by all of this," Charlotte said and leaned forward to pick up her cup of tea off the small round coffee table.

"And I shouldn't be, you mean."

Charlotte shrugged and took a sip of her tea. "I can't blame you for not wanting to see the truth about your own father. But Megan, I've known the truth for years. The man cannot be trusted. At all."

Megan told herself she should be insulted. She should feel the urge to leap up and defend her father. She always had before. She'd spent so many years trying to explain away Spencer's behavior, his attitude, his treatment of others, that it was almost second nature to her now.

But the sad fact was, she couldn't do it anymore. She couldn't even manage to convince *herself* that Spencer was the kind of father she'd always wished him to be. In the last two weeks, it was as if blinders had suddenly been ripped off her eyes and she saw him not as she'd wanted him to be, but as he really was.

A man who had sneaked around on every wife he'd ever had. A man who made babies and then walked away. A man who hadn't spoken to her in anything but monosyllables since the night he'd accused her of defying him. No, there was no defense for Spencer.

Not from her.

Not anymore.

"God," she whispered. "You're right." An admission she'd never have said out loud before now. She might have thought it, but she never would have allowed herself to be disloyal enough to say it.

The last two weeks had apparently changed more than her love life. Megan smiled to herself as she realized that, somehow, she'd stopped looking for her father's approval. Maybe it was just that she'd finally acknowledged that it would never happen.

But maybe it was something more.

Maybe it was that she'd finally discovered that having her father approve of her wasn't as important as approving of *herself*. She straightened slightly in the chair and thought about that for a moment. A small ribbon of satisfaction snaked through her system and Megan smiled.

Charlotte looked at her over the rim of her teacup and her dark-brown eyes glimmered in the late afternoon sunshine spearing through the wide window. "You're going to be all right, aren't you?"

"You know?" Megan said slowly, "I think I am."

"I'm glad."

"Thanks."

"Glad for me, too, because now that you've finally accepted some of the truths about your father, I can tell you something."

Her voice was so serious, her features suddenly drawn into lines of tension, Megan instinctively leaned toward her. "What is it? Is something wrong?"

"That's just it. I don't know."

"Charlotte…"

She took a deep breath, then another swallow of her tea, as if to gather the strength to say what she had to say. "You know how your father's always insisted that my mother died?"

"Yeah." Charlotte's parents were David, Spencer's younger brother, and Mary Little Dove Ashton, a Sioux. When David and Mary died, Spencer brought their children, Walker and Charlotte, to live at the estate.

"I don't believe it," Charlotte said softly.

"You think your mother's still alive?"

"I have to find out," she said. "I have to know one way or the other. Walker thinks I'm crazy, but Megan, something inside me is telling me not to believe your father's version of the story."

Would her father really have lied about Mary Little Dove's death? Megan wondered. And a moment later, she admitted that yes, if it had served his purposes at the time, he would have.

Reaching one hand across the table, Megan waited until her cousin took it in a firm grip. Then, their hands joined in solidarity, Megan said, "Find out, Charlotte. And if you need any help, just call."

Phoebe Pearce smiled at her daughter-in-law and stood up in welcome as Megan made her way through the crowded restaurant.

Her nerves were skittering badly, but Ashtons learned at an early age how to hide anxiety. Megan plastered a broad smile on her face and leaned down to give the tiny woman a quick kiss on the cheek. "It was so nice of you to invite me to dinner."

"Nonsense." Phoebe waved one hand as she took her seat again, then deftly flicked her pearl-gray napkin across the lap of her stunning forest-green silk suit. "When I learned that Simon would be working late tonight, I just knew it would be a good chance for the two of us to get in a little girl talk."

Girl talk.

How bad could it be?

Phoebe seemed very nice, but Megan was still feeling the pangs of guilt for marrying the woman's son under false pretenses. At least though, she knew that Simon had kept his word and explained the real situation to his mother.

"Would you like a drink, dear?"

"Wine would be nice," Megan said.

"Of course." Phoebe smiled again and motioned to a waiter hovering nearby. "I should have known an Ashton would prefer wine." She spoke quickly to the waiter and then turned back to Megan. "I've ordered a lovely chardonnay I think you'll enjoy."

"Thank you." Megan wished it were sitting in front of her right now, since her throat was dry and those nerves were doing a mambo up and down her spine. When those nerves hit her throat, she started talking, as if to assure herself that she was just dandy. "I do prefer chardonnay and you know, everyone thinks the grapes will be wonderful this season."

"I didn't realize that your family bottled chardonnay."

"Oh, we don't," Megan said quickly, falling into talk of grapes with gratitude. "But we do grow the grapes and then use them in our cuvée."

"Of course. It must be fascinating, the making of wine."

"Well, to be honest, I'm not much involved with the actual winery." Her brother Trace was the estate manager and could probably have told Phoebe everything she'd ever wanted to know about wine and more. But Megan and Paige, beyond helping with the harvests as children, had nothing at all to do with the actual winery. "I run the events at the estate and—"

"Oh I know, dear, but still. You're there. A part of it all. The vineyards, being at the mercy of the weather, all very earthy and exciting."

Megan smiled, despite the interruption. "Not very exciting when you're a child and expected to help out at harvest time. Then you just get muscle cramps and blisters on your fingers."

While Megan talked about everything and nothing, the waiter arrived and poured their wine. Then, after giving them a moment to study the menu, he took their orders and disappeared again.

Megan sucked in a great gulp of air and told herself to stop babbling. In an attempt to get her runaway mouth under control, she let her gaze sweep around the crowded restaurant. Each of the dozen or more tables were covered with crisp white linens and boasted a small, round vase bursting with spring flowers. The soft, silky sounds of classical music drifted from the snow-white piano in the corner of the room as a young woman in a pale pink gown delicately stroked the keys.

Everything was beautiful.

Phoebe was very nice.

So why did Megan feel so on edge?

"I wanted to talk to you privately, Megan," the older woman said.

This is why, Megan thought, wondering what her mother-in-law had in mind. "Yes?"

"About Simon." The older woman smiled and her pale-gray eyes shone with good humor. "As his mother, I simply have to congratulate you and tell you how happy I am about your marriage."

"Really?"

"The change in him these past couple of weeks is nothing short of extraordinary."

"I'm sorry?" Megan hadn't expected this at all. In fact, given all the gossip surrounding her father at the moment, she wouldn't have been surprised if Phoebe had demanded that this temporary attachment to her son end immediately. And she couldn't have blamed the woman for it, either.

Phoebe reached out and covered Megan's hand with one of hers. "My dear, you've done wonders for him."

Confused, Megan simply stared at her.

"I had lunch with him only yesterday and he was…relaxed in a way I've never known him to be. He smiled. He enjoyed himself." She smiled again and winked. "He didn't rush me through lunch so that he could return to work."

Megan shook her head. "I don't think that's because of anything I—"

"Nonsense." Phoebe smiled at the waiter as he set their dishes in front of them. When he was gone, she spoke up again. "A man who's happy at home becomes happy in every area of his life."

"Phoebe," Megan said quickly, before she could be interrupted again, "I know Simon told you the truth about our marriage."

"Certainly."

"Then you know that we're not—"

"In love?" Phoebe finished for her and Megan gritted her teeth at yet another interruption. "I wouldn't be so sure, my dear."

She tried to argue the point, but didn't get far. "Really, Phoebe…"

"Megan," the woman said, "I've known my son a lot longer than you have. And I can tell you that I have never seen him like this before. It's as if he's found something he hadn't known he was missing. And that something, my dear, is *you*."

Megan's heart lurched a little, but she didn't allow herself to actually believe Phoebe. The woman may think she could see love when she looked at Megan and Simon. But all she was really seeing was good chemistry.

Right?

A marriage that had begun with a business deal couldn't really turn into something more, could it? Neither of them had been looking for love when they'd stumbled into this marriage of convenience. Neither of them had so much as mentioned the word.

Now that Phoebe had though, it was as if all bets were off. *Love.* Was it possible? Was it something she should even be considering? Her insides dipped and spun and her heartbeat stuttered irregularly. Megan's brain whirled as she tried to think about a year from now and saying goodbye to Simon.

Pain, sharp and swift, jabbed at her and she swallowed hard. If, after two weeks, the thought of leaving Simon was painful, how much worse would it be after a whole year?

Oh, God.

Phoebe was probably wrong about Simon's feelings—after all, he'd shown no signs of wanting anything more from Megan than he had when he'd proposed.

But, the older woman had been dead on target about one thing.

Somehow, over the last two weeks, Megan Ashton Pearce had fallen in love with her husband.

Ten

The third week of Megan's marriage was radically different from the first two.

Those first couple of weeks, she and Simon had had his big house all to themselves. They'd had a little time to get used to each other. To get used to the idea of being married—and then they'd had time for other things. *Lots* of other things.

That first night of lovemaking had opened the door to more amazing nights than Megan would have thought possible. They'd made love in practically every room—even once on the stairs. They'd taken long showers together and shared cozy, intimate meals together in the kitchen. Just the two of them in that big house, they'd never worried about privacy or having someone overhear their conversations.

But that was all different now.

Now, their full-time cook was ensconced in the kitchen, so there were no midnight refrigerator raids. There were maids in and out of every room in the place, so there were no make-out sessions on the sofas. There was a full-time gardener, so there was no more lovemaking under the trees in the backyard.

"Not that there was much chance of that now anyway," Megan muttered. After all, Simon was spending more and more time at work and less and less time with *her.* He left home early in the morning and often wasn't home until ten or later. It was as if he were trying to avoid being at the house—or rather, being with *her.*

Megan wrapped her arms around her middle and stalked around the confines of her bedroom. The house, despite being full of people now, felt empty when Simon wasn't there.

Despite what his mother Phoebe had had to say at the restaurant the week before, Megan was sure that her new husband was regretting this temporary marriage. Her heart ached just a little, but she put a stop to that really fast. She had no right to be hurt—or disappointed.

This marriage was just what it had started out to be. A convenience. A pretense, with good sex. No one had said anything about happily ever after. No one had mentioned the word "love." No one, including her, had anticipated their feelings changing.

She stopped at the wide windows overlooking the backyard and the hill that rolled on down through the valley. Plopping down onto the wide cushioned window seat, she stared out through the glass at the darkness beyond. She hadn't bothered to turn any lights on in the bedroom. But there was a low fire burning in the hearth, more for atmosphere than warmth, and the flames were reflected in the glass. The sky overhead shone with pinpricks of light and the moon slanted a spotlight down onto the manicured gardens below.

Resting her head against the wall, she let her gaze wander the darkness while her mind raced over too many thoughts at once. The newspapers were still hounding the Ashton family—apparently there were no fresh scandals anywhere else to knock them off the front pages yet. Spencer had closed himself off from everyone, refusing to talk about Alyssa Sheridan or the boy. Simon kept assuring Megan that her father's troubles didn't bother him—but how could she believe that?

"It's your own fault," she murmured, tracing one finger across the cool glass. "Who the hell told you to fall in love with your husband?"

Stupid.

Simon wasn't interested in love. He'd made that clear the day they'd been so hastily married. All he'd been looking for was a way to keep his family and his company free of scandal. A one-year marriage. Strictly business.

But now scandal had found them anyway and Simon…damn it, she could tell. He was distancing himself from her. She felt it. Even when they were in the same bed, even when he was holding her or sliding his body into hers, she felt him pull away. And she didn't know how to stop it—or even if she should try.

So she couldn't very well add to the wonderful blend of misery by admitting she'd gone and fallen in love with him.

"Oh yeah," Megan said, turning around to slide off the cushioned bench, "my life's a party."

"Am I invited?"

Her head snapped up and her gaze shot to the open doorway of the bedroom. Simon stood there, jacket hooked on an index finger and flung over one shoulder, his tie opened and the top button of his dress shirt undone. He looked tired, a little harassed and too damn good.

She swallowed hard and wondered if she'd ever get used to the simple joy of just looking at him. God, he could turn her insides to a gooey puddle with one glance out of those fog-gray eyes. No point in letting him know that, though.

She cleared her throat. "What?"

"You said your life's a party." Simon echoed her words as he stepped into the room and closed the door behind him. "I was just wondering if I was invited or not."

How could he not know that *he* was the party?

And how was she going to be able to live with him for a whole year and *not* eventually blurt out the truth about how she felt? Oh, she wished she were a better liar. Or even a better actress.

She sucked in a gulp of air, told her nerves to shut the hell up and forced a smile. She'd just have to find a way to keep the fact that she loved him her own little secret.

Now that he was home though, thoughts and worries rushed out of her mind, leaving her body hungry and her heart trembling. He might not love her, but even as he mentally distanced himself from her, she knew he still *wanted* her. So for the moment, she'd let go of tomorrow and concentrate on tonight.

"Sure you're invited," she said and walked toward him, her bare feet silent on the thick, plush carpet. Slipping out of her robe, she let it slide down her arms to hit the floor, leaving her wearing only a silk pale-green camisole and matching panties. The cool night air brushed her skin, but she didn't feel it. How could she ever feel cold when Simon's heated gaze was on her?

One dark eyebrow lifted as he watched her approach. "Just what kind of party is this?"

Even his voice was rich and dark and sexy. The deep rumbles of it rolled through her, setting her nerve endings on fire. Firelight cast dancing shadows across his features and flickered in his eyes.

"It's a 'you're late and I missed you' party."

He frowned slightly, tossed his jacket to the foot of the bed. "Didn't mean to be this late, but—"

Megan shook her head, reached up and covered his mouth with her fingertips. "Doesn't matter. You're here now."

One corner of his mouth lifted and something flashed in his eyes. "Just in time for the party?"

"You're the guest of honor, actually."

"Yeah?" he asked, allowing her to pull him over to the wide continent of their bed. "What do I win?"

"Me." Megan unbuttoned his shirt, dragged the end of his tie free and tugged it off of him. Then scraping her hands along his arms, she pushed his shirt down and off, then slid the palms of her hands across his chest. He hissed a breath of air through gritted teeth and she smiled to herself, loving the knowledge that in this, at least, she could touch him.

She couldn't tell him she loved him.

But she could show him.

Dipping her head, she pressed her mouth to the base of his throat and sighed against him as his hands came up to stroke her skin beneath the silk of her camisole.

"You feel so good," he whispered, his breath brushing the top of her head, ruffling her hair. "You always feel so damn good."

"I'm glad," she said, her words muffled as she continued to kiss him, moving, shifting, until she tasted first one of his hard, flat nipples and then the other.

He groaned, clutched her to him and fell back onto the bed.

She lifted her head and looked down at him. His features tight and drawn, his eyes were now the color of night smoke, dark with need, glittering with desire. If she couldn't have his love, she would at least claim his need.

For now.

For this one moment, Simon Pearce needed her. Wanted her.

And that was all that mattered.

"I don't know what you're doing to me," he admitted, reaching up to stroke her hair back from her face, over her shoulder. His voice was rough, as if he were forcing the words out past a tight throat. "But I think about you all the damn time."

That was something, wasn't it? He thought about her. He wanted her. It wasn't love, but it was something.

"I'm glad of that, too."

"I have to have you, Megan."

"I'm right here." She dropped a kiss onto his mouth, tugging at his bottom lip with her teeth.

"Not close enough," he groaned and flipped her over until she lay beneath him. "Not nearly close enough." In seconds, he had her naked and writhing beneath him. His hands, his fingers, his mouth, were everywhere. He touched her and flames erupted. He kissed her and the inferno started. He tasted her and explosions shattered through her body.

Megan twisted on the sheets, hungry. Hungrier for him now than she'd been that first time. She couldn't seem to have enough of him. Every time only made her want him more. Was this love? she wondered. This crashing, thundering need to be with him, under him, a part of him?

And if it was, how would she ever live without it?

Then her thoughts shuddered to a halt as he moved away from her long enough to strip out of his own clothes. She watched him in the firelight, and fed her own hunger. She'd never expected to feel so much. To feel so deeply. And now that she did, she was sure she'd never be able to survive living with him and knowing that he didn't feel it, too.

Then he was back, covering her body with his, kissing her, sighing into her mouth, wiping every thought from her mind. The brush of his skin against hers was magic. His hands slid over her body and she lifted into his touch, needing more, wanting more. Wanting all of him.

Everything but Simon fell away.

Everything but this moment disappeared.

"This is crazy," he murmured against her throat as he positioned himself between her thighs. "Your scent stays with me always. Your sighs are in my dreams. Your face is in front of me all the time. I hear your voice when you're not even there."

She smiled and clutched his words to her, holding them as close as she held him. Closer even, since she tucked them away into her heart, to warm her later, when reality crashed back down on her. When he was gone and she was alone and trying to remind herself that love had not been a part of this bargain.

"Take me, Simon," she whispered. "Take all of me."

She arched into him, lifting her hips in silent plea.

He caught her hands with his and planted them on the mattress on either side of her head. And leaning in for a kiss, he pushed himself into her depths while claiming her mouth. Their tongues mated, danced, as their bodies moved in a rhythm older than time. As the first tremors rocked her body, Megan heard him whisper her name before he took the leap and fell with her.

Later, as she lay beside him in the firelit darkness, she watched him sleep, and wondered how she would survive losing him.

"The new contracts are being messengered over." Dave stood in front of Simon's desk, waiting for a reply.

"Fine. Let me know when they arrive."

"Hey," Dave said, "curb the enthusiasm. Not safe for your heart."

Simon sighed and leaned back in his chair. Forcing a grim smile, he asked, "Better?"

"God no."

"It's the best I can do."

"What the hell's going on, Simon?"

Good question, he thought. But what was the answer? He spent his days trying to stay busy enough to keep thoughts of Megan at bay—then he spent his nights trying to climb inside her body. Where was the logic in that? Where was the control? He used to be in charge, damn it.

"I don't know. Miserable mood, that's all." He sat up again, grabbed his silver pen and dragged a sheaf of papers toward him. "Your best bet is to stay far away."

Naturally, Dave plopped down into the closest chair, stretched out his legs in front of him and said, "Talk."

Simon snorted. "About what?"

"Megan, of course."

"This has nothing to do with Megan."

"Right." Dave actually laughed as he shook his head. "Who're you? Mr. Advice to the lovelorn?"

"Hell no, but I'm as close as you've got."

"Sad but true." Simon leaned back in his chair again, tossed his pen to the desk top and then shoved one hand through his hair with enough strength to snatch himself bald. "Fine. She's making me nuts."

"This is a good thing."

"For you maybe, not for me."

"Why?"

"Because I don't *do* love, damn it."

"Who said anything about love?" Dave's grin was huge and his damn eyes were practically twinkling.

"Swear to God, if you laugh, I'll clean your clock."

"No laughing. Just enjoying."

"Good for a man to have friends who can relish his pain."

Dave spread his arms wide. "I do what I can."

"Trust me, you've done enough." Simon pushed back from the desk, stood up and started pacing. Hell, he felt as though if he didn't move, he just might start unspooling. Was that even a word? "This is all your fault," he muttered.

"Okay, how did I get into this?"

"You're the one who said I should have a life. That Megan was good for me."

"Guilty as charged."

Shaking his head, Simon walked faster, as though he were trying to escape the thoughts plaguing him, but there was just no way he could run fast enough—or far enough. "I started thinking and damn it, that wasn't a good thing either. Because the more I thought about it, the more I realized that I'm in love with her."

"That's great!" Dave jumped up to congratulate him, but Simon just sneered.

"It wasn't in my plan."

"Screw the plan, Simon," Dave said. "You finally found somebody and I think it's great."

"Oh yeah, *great*." Simon stopped dead and glared at his best friend. "I don't want to be in love. Love is chaos. And I don't like chaos."

"Well, welcome to the world, Simon." Dave

leaned back against the desk. "Nobody's in control all the damn time."

"*I* am," he argued, then scowled again. "At least I used to be."

Dave chuckled.

Simon's gaze narrowed on him. "And I will be again."

"Oh, this I gotta hear."

"Fine. Listen up." Crossing the room toward his oldest friend, he talked while he walked. "I figured it out this morning. All I have to do is make Megan admit she loves me first. *Then* I regain control."

"You're nuts."

"It makes sense." Warming to the whole idea now that he'd said it out loud, Simon went on. "Think about it. First one to speak loses power—if it's true in business, then why shouldn't it be true in love?"

"Because love isn't supposed to be about one-upmanship."

"Right. Remember why you surprised Peggy with the week's stay in Hawaii last summer?"

Dave stiffened. "That's different."

"You said it was so that *you'd* be the one making the romantic move. So you'd get the brownie points."

Rubbing the back of his neck, Dave said, "There's a flaw in there somewhere."

"No there's not," Simon said, walking back around his desk to sit down again. "I've pulled off way more hostile takeovers than this. You'll see. I love Megan. I know she loves me, too." He stopped, thought about it, then nodded. "Yeah. She really does. All I have to do is somehow get her to admit it before I do. How hard can it be?"

Dave scowled at him. "Why does that have the ring of 'famous last words'?"

"He's our father, Megan," Paige said, striding across the reception hall floor. "Of course I'm going to support him. You should be, too."

"I tried that. You know I did." Megan shook her head and followed her younger sister, heels clicking noisily on the glossy marble floor. She knew Paige wasn't listening to her. Didn't *want* to hear her. And Megan was sorry for it. She and her sister had always been close. And now that the scandal over baby Jack had stirred things up in the family, it was as if everyone were taking sides—and she and her sister were on opposite sides of the fence.

"Honestly," Paige muttered darkly. "To listen to you and Trace, anyone would think Father was some kind of monster."

Megan's headache pounded in time with her steps. Trace. Her older brother. At least she had the satisfaction of knowing that he felt the same way she did.

As she walked, Megan's careful gaze swept the hall, absently checking that everything was ready for the wedding reception to be held there the following day. Round tables, each sitting ten people, dotted the floor. Pale peach linen tablecloths were spread over them and the matching slipcovered chairs were pulled up close. Vases atop every table waited for the peach roses that would arrive in the morning. Along the far wall, several smaller round tables marched in a long line, seating for the bridal party. And on the opposite end of the hall, a wide area was set apart for dancing.

A soft breeze drifted through the open veranda doors on either side of the hall and carried the scent of roses with it.

Everything was as it should be. Whatever else might be going on around Megan, she'd managed to at least keep her work on track. As she acknowledged that thought, she told herself it wasn't hard to work, when that's all you really did anymore.

Paige stopped at the wide double doors and turned to face her as she approached. Megan looked at her sister's stubborn features and wanted to sigh. She might have finally accepted that their father was not the man she wished he was, but clearly Paige still had hopes. And she wasn't alone, either.

Their mother, Lilah, refused to even discuss the matter of Spencer's illegitimate son. More than that though, she refused to believe that anything at all was wrong. She blindly insisted that her life was as perfect as she'd always claimed it to be.

Cousin Charlotte, of course, had never liked or trusted Megan's father, but Charlotte's brother

Walker was Spencer's right-hand man. Together, Walker and Paige kept trying to insist that everything would work out. That the man they were so busy defending didn't really *need* defending at all.

And Megan was tired of arguing the point.

"Okay," she said as she came up close to her sister. "I'm sorry. We won't talk about Father anymore, all right?"

Paige blew out a breath, then smiled and laid one hand on Megan's forearm. "Thanks. And you'll see. Father will explain everything and the rumors will fade away as soon as the newspapers find someone new to pick on."

"I hope you're right," Megan said, though she didn't hold out much hope. She had a feeling that as far as her father was concerned, things were going to get worse—not better. She only hoped that Paige wouldn't be too crushed when she was finally forced to see her father for what he really was.

Eleven

Over the next few days, Megan felt…jumpy. It was as if she were waiting for the other shoe to drop.

The sun warm on her back, she continued on her walk through the vineyard. She loved the smell of the vines and the freshly turned earth. She loved walking the long, orderly rows of just-budding vines because it gave her a sense of connection—of continuity. And yet, even being out here wasn't enough to dispel a vague sensation of impending doom.

"Okay," she murmured to herself, after checking to make sure no one was standing around watching the crazy woman talk to no one, "you're getting a little dramatic, Megan. Dial it down a notch or two."

But how could she?

Even avoiding reading the newspapers and watching television, she was aware of the trouble her family was going through. And she was more than aware of just who was responsible for this mess.

Her father.

"Hey, talking to yourself is not a good sign."

Megan turned around so quickly, her low-heeled black pumps caught on a grapevine root and she rocked unsteadily until her big brother grabbed her elbow and held on. "Thanks," she said, "but next time, if you're going to scare me, wait until I'm barefoot at least."

Trace grinned and Megan couldn't help smiling back. The man was just gorgeous. Six feet tall with an athletic build, eyes as green as her own and light brown hair, when he smiled, women lined up in front of him just to melt.

"Wasn't worried about you," he quipped. "But take it easy on the grapes, huh?" That said, he went down on one knee to inspect the knobby, gnarled vine as if checking to make sure Megan hadn't done any damage.

"Nice to know I come in second to a vine."

"Hey, if we could make cuvée by squeezing your pretty head, it might be a different story." He stood up, reached out and touched the tip of her nose with his index finger.

Megan felt a rush of love for the big brother she'd

always adored—even when he was stealing her toys and hiding them just for the heck of it. He'd always been there for her. Always ready to listen, or to give advice—even if she didn't want it.

Which today, she suddenly realized, she really did. Maybe that's why she'd walked down to the vineyard in the first place. Maybe her subconscious had steered her in Trace's direction because she'd known deep in her heart that she just had to talk to someone who would understand.

"Why so serious all of a sudden?" he asked, then stopped and nodded. "Ah. You saw the morning paper."

"I stopped reading the paper almost two weeks ago."

He winced. "Then you don't know."

"Oh, God." For the first time in her life, Megan knew absolutely what the phrase about experiencing *a sinking sensation* actually meant. "What?"

Draping one arm around her shoulder, Trace started walking and Megan fell into step beside him.

"One of those eager-beaver reporters got tired of rehashing the same old story about our new little half brother—"

"And..." Oh man, she didn't want to ask. Didn't want to know. But how could she *not* know?

"And," Trace said on a long sigh of either frustration or disgust, it was hard to tell which, "it seems there are more skeletons dancing in Father's closet than anyone guessed at."

Megan stopped short and looked up at him. "Tell me."

Frowning, he shifted his gaze from her to the wide sweep of the vineyard. And slowly, just like always, his features relaxed, despite whatever he was thinking. Being out in the field was like that for Trace. "You won't like it."

"Goes without saying."

He nodded. "Seems our father was married *before* he married Caroline Lattimer Sheppard. To a woman named Sally Barnett."

Megan blinked. "Okay, surprising maybe, but how does that compare to his having a child and trying to hide it?"

"Because, little sister," Trace said, letting his gaze slide back to hers, "Father never bothered to get a divorce from his first wife."

It was a good thing Trace still had a grip on her shoulders because Megan swayed with the impact of his words as surely as she would have if someone had punched her in the stomach. *Never got a divorce?* "How is that possible? What kind of person does that?"

A muscle in Trace's hard jaw twitched. "I think you already know the answer to that one, Megan."

"Oh my God," she whispered, then leaned into her brother, drawing on his stalwart, dependable strength. "If he didn't divorce his first wife, then his marriage to Caroline wasn't legal, so his divorce and marriage to *our* mother wasn't legal either and—"

"Right," Trace muttered thickly, giving her a brief hard squeeze. "Which means," he continued, "this vineyard might be going back to the Sheppard family—through Caroline."

"It'll be turned over to Louret Vineyards?" she whispered, suddenly understanding the magnitude of what she'd just learned. "You're right. Father got this vineyard in the divorce settlement. But if he and Caroline were never actually married…"

"…Then there would be no divorce—or settlement."

"God, Trace, we could lose the estate? The vineyard? The winery?"

"That about covers it." He started walking again and Megan kept pace, despite her wobbly knees.

"I'm an idiot."

"Interesting segue," Trace said and there was a touch of humor in his voice now.

Megan dropped her head to his shoulder. "I came out here, looking for you, I guess. I wanted to ask your advice."

"Always happy to tell other people what to do."

"I know," she said and sighed softly. "Now though…"

"What's wrong?"

"It's—Trace, I don't know what to do about Simon."

"Your husband? What're you talking about?"

She stopped and he looked down at her, all concern. "I was worried about the scandal surrounding baby

Jack and how it would affect Simon and his business. Now there's *this*. I just don't know what to do. I don't want to drag Simon down with the rest of us."

"He's your husband, Megan."

"I know." This wouldn't work. She couldn't ask Trace if he thought she should stay with Simon or leave him unless she explained the whole weird story of their marriage. And she wasn't prepared to do that. So quickly, she changed the subject. "There's more. I'm worried about Paige, too. She still trusts Father and now with this…it's really going to hit her hard."

Trace's features tightened and old pain shimmered in his eyes. "She'll have to find out, Megan. She'll have to see it for herself, just like we did. Like I did."

"Trace?"

He shook his head. "Let's just say that I learned five years ago just how treacherous our father can be."

"What happened?" Five years? She'd still been in college. What could have happened that she didn't know about?

"I'm not going into it, Megan. It's over." He blew out a breath. "But I will tell you that Spencer Ashton screwed me over. Cost me the only woman I've ever loved."

"Oh, Trace," she said softly, reaching up to cup her brother's cheek in her palm. An ache settled in her heart and she wished there was something she could do, or say, that would help. But judging by the stark, raw pain in his eyes, there was nothing.

He sighed again and gave her a half smile. "I don't know what's going on with you and your husband, Meg. But I will tell you to trust yourself. And if you have to make a choice between family and your heart, choose your heart."

Sounded simple. Now all she had to do was figure out what her choice would be. Megan wanted to scream. Her father's greed and blind ambition had brought them all to this point—and now it would probably cost her the future she might have had with Simon.

"Mrs. Pearce—a comment for our readers?"

"Over here, honey, smile for the camera!"

"Hey, how's it feel to know your father made you a bastard?"

Megan gritted her teeth and kept her gaze focused straight ahead. She'd thought that once she left the Ashton estate behind, she'd be free of the reporters. But no. There were at least a dozen of them, complete with news vans and cameras, staked out at the foot of the driveway leading to Simon's house.

They were going to ruin him. Ruin a man who'd made the mistake of marrying an Ashton. *Don't look,* she warned herself. Don't give them the satisfaction of seeing her cry. Of seeing her pound the steering wheel in frustration.

"Hey, what's your new hubby think of dear old dad?" another reporter shouted as he skittered sideways, bending down to look into the driver's side window. "Bet he's sorry he ever hooked up with you, huh?"

She slammed on the brake, jerking the car to a stop. Whipping her head to the left, she glared at the big-mouthed, rude, obnoxious reporter and snapped, "You leave my husband out of this."

The reporter, a short bald man with eager eyes and a smarmy grin shook his head. "No can do, honey. Simon Pearce is big news, too. And when he's linked to the Ashton family high jinks, well, that sells papers."

Cameras flashed, microphones were jammed at her, reporters and TV crews jostled for position and Megan could have sworn she felt the earth beneath her shudder and shake.

Simon.

Big news.

Linked to the Ashtons.

God.

"So," the reporter asked, taking her stunned silence for a decision to talk to the press, "what about it? What's Simon 'Squeaky Clean' Pearce have to say about the family embarrassment?"

She inhaled sharply, thought about telling them all to go to hell, then pictured *that* little confrontation on the front page and the six o'clock news and changed her mind. "No comment," she snapped and stepped on the gas.

It did her heart good to see the reporters skip back

out of the way of her tires. But that flush of pleasure only lasted a second or two, then the lead weight of reality settled in the pit of her stomach and she knew it wasn't going anywhere.

It was time to make that choice she and Trace had talked about.

By the time Simon got home, it was after ten and he felt as though he'd done ten rounds with a heavyweight champion. Dropping his briefcase to the floor, he leaned back against the closed front door and closed his eyes. Damn, it had been a nightmare day.

Reporters had buzzed around his offices, futilely hoping for an exclusive interview. The phones had rung off the hook and Dave had spent most of the day soothing Pearce Industries' clients and snarling at people demanding comments on Spencer Ashton's latest mess. Plus, there was an encampment of reporters parked at the edge of his driveway.

Simon should have been furious.

His company was under fire. He personally was being stalked by reporters. His family was being drawn into what promised to be an ugly situation played out on the front pages of every newspaper in the country.

And yet...

All he'd been able to think about all day was how this was affecting Megan. At the thought of her, he pushed away from the wall. "Megan?"

His shout seemed to echo in the stillness. There was no sign of anyone in the big house. It was as if Megan and his employees had all disappeared.

Scowling at that mental image, he stalked across the hall toward the staircase and the bedrooms above. Damn, she was probably alone and crying. He wanted to go and tell Spencer Ashton just what an ass he was for hurting his daughter. He wanted to find Megan's dragons and slay them. He wanted to—damn it, he wanted to love her. Wanted her to love him.

He should never have come up with that stupid plan to wait her out. To make her confess her love first. He should have told her as soon as he'd recognized just what a lucky bastard he was. Should have told her that he wanted this marriage to be real.

His footsteps sounded overly loud in the quiet and he tried to shrug off the sensation of abandonment that clung to the house. Taking the stairs two at a time, he hit the landing at a dead run and raced down the carpeted hallway toward the master bedroom. He pushed the door open, and felt his heart drop to his toes when he didn't see her. Then he rushed to the bathroom. No sign of Megan. Anywhere.

His gaze dropped to the gleaming blue-green tiles and noticed that her wide array of creams and lotions, her hairbrush, even her toothbrush, were missing. His heart stopped momentarily. "Doesn't mean anything," he muttered. "Not a thing." She wouldn't leave. Not without a word.

Not without telling him, damn it.

But anxiety chewed on him, nibbling at the corners of his heart, tearing at his soul with dread as he turned and headed back out into the hallway. It was a big house, he told himself. She could be anywhere. "Megan?"

He swallowed hard as he took the stairs going down, just as quickly as he had going up. By the time he hit the foyer again, Simon's insides were churning and his brain was racing.

Then he saw her. Standing beside the open front door, looking at him with a world of pain in her eyes and a steely determination on her face.

"Megan." He started toward her, but she backed up, shaking her head.

"Don't, Simon. Don't make this harder. On either of us."

Harder? What could be harder than that feeling of mindless despair when he couldn't find her?

"What're you talking about?" His blood rushed through his veins, clouding his vision, thundering inside his head.

"I'm going."

"Going where?" Two words. All he could manage.

"Doesn't matter," she said and swallowed hard. Her summer-green eyes filled with tears she frantically blinked away. "I'm sorry. Sorry about all of this. The mess with my father—you being involved. I'm sorry."

Damn it. He took a step closer, but she kept pace, backing up until she was now on the porch, with the night behind her. He was too wary to try to get closer. "You don't have anything to be sorry about."

She laughed, but there was no humor in it, only regret. "I'm an Ashton," she reminded him wryly. "Apparently, that's more than enough reason to be sorry."

"This isn't about you, Megan," Simon said and wished to hell she'd come back into the house. So they could talk.

She shook her head again and lifted her chin in a defiant tilt he recognized. "I'm packed."

Panic rushed through him again, this time making his knees weak. "Packed? Why?"

"I'm leaving, Simon. I have to. You saw the reporters out there." When he opened his mouth to argue, she cut him off. "They're not going to be leaving anytime soon. This thing with my father is only going to get worse and I'm not going to bring your family down with mine. I won't do it, Simon."

"Don't you think you should let me decide that?"

"No. Decision's made. We had an agreement when we got married. No scandals, remember?" She gave him another smile and a wrenching pain slammed through him as he read goodbye in her eyes.

"Megan, don't."

"I'll sign the divorce papers as soon as they're ready." She turned away and started walking. "Goodbye Simon."

He couldn't move. He wanted to chase her down and drag her back. Hold her tightly enough that she couldn't walk away from him again. But he suddenly felt as though he were made of stone. He couldn't force life into his limbs. He stood there like a man who'd been cut in two and didn't know enough to fall down.

The night swallowed her while he stood alone in the big house that had her memory stamped all over it.

His plan had failed. She hadn't said she loved him first, so she'd left, never knowing how much *he* loved *her*.

Not knowing that by leaving, she was killing him.

Twelve

Hiding out on the estate wasn't exactly the brainiest idea Megan had ever had. After all, it was like trying to hide from sharks by diving off the Great Barrier Reef.

The Ashton estate was like a medieval castle under siege. No one but family was allowed in, all tours and events had been canceled. Reporters still clustered outside the gates. Freshly hired security guards kept them at bay, but that didn't mean they'd stop trying to get an interview or a picture or a comment from anyone going in or out of the main gate.

She'd come home after leaving Simon two days before because she couldn't think of anywhere else to go. Pitiful. But the only place she wanted to be was with Simon. And since she couldn't do that, what did it matter where she went?

At least here, on the estate, she was protected enough that she didn't have to deal with the media. Charlotte had welcomed her into the cottage, since Megan couldn't bear the thought of moving back into her old rooms in the family home—just the idea of having to deal with her parents right now gave her cold chills. Charlotte though, busy with her plants and flowers in the greenhouse, gave Megan plenty of space and time to herself.

Now, all she had to do was try to find a way to keep herself busy until thoughts of Simon faded away. Shouldn't be more than twenty or thirty years. How hard could it be?

She flopped back into one of the comfy, squishy chairs in the cottage living room. "Oh, God…"

"Why don't you come and help me in the greenhouse?" Charlotte walked into the room and stopped beside her. "Take your mind off of things."

Megan sighed and patted her cousin's hand. "Thanks, but we both know I suck at the whole Mother Nature thing. In ten minutes, you'd be able to *hear* your plants screaming for help. I'd just be getting in your way."

Charlotte smiled. "I don't mind."

"And I appreciate it," Megan said, looking up at her cousin. Her features were serene, but her dark eyes shone with worry and Megan appreciated her cousin's unspoken concern. "But I'm just lousy company, Charlotte. I think I'll take a walk or something."

The other woman shrugged and gave her a half smile. "Or, you could take a drive. Back to your own house. To your husband."

Megan's heart twisted and the rippling pain of it shot throughout her body with lightning-like precision. "I can't. I can't drag him through this mess."

Charlotte cocked her head to one side and studied her for a long moment before asking, "What makes you think you would have to drag him? Maybe you should give him the option of deciding for himself."

"Say I did," Megan countered, "say he decided to stay with me and because of that decision, he lost clients and his family was hurt by what's going on with *our* family. Then what? How long before he resented me? How long before he couldn't stand the sight of me?" She shook her head. "No thanks. My way's better. Quicker."

"Megan…"

She lifted one hand and rubbed at the ache in the dead center of her chest, but it didn't help. Nothing would help. Ever. She'd be walking through the rest of her life like this. In pain. Might as well get used to it. Megan stood up, reached out and gave her cousin a brief, hard hug, then pulled back. "I appreciate what you're trying to do, really."

"But butt out?" Charlotte asked, smiling.

Megan managed to briefly return the smile. "Gently put, but yeah."

"Okay," her cousin said and started for the back door that would lead her across a tidy garden to the greenhouse, "but remember, if you change your mind, I'm here if you want to talk."

Alone, Megan headed for the front door of the cottage and stepped out into a splash of sunshine that dappled the stone pathway with light spearing through the sheltering leaves of the nearby trees. She wandered along the path, then stepped off into the lush green grass and let her gaze sweep wide across the manicured lawn. Rolling hills of rich green stretched out in front of her like swatches of velvet. Well tended flower beds were a riot of color—purple, yellow, deep red—and their combined scents filled the air.

Yet for all the beauty surrounding her, Megan felt as though she were locked in a dark room. Worse, deep inside, she knew there was no way out. This was a lose-lose situation all the way around.

Simon had spent the last forty-eight hours trying to find a way into the Ashton estate. But it was like trying to sneak into Fort Knox. The security guards out front weren't letting anyone through, damn it. Every time he tried to phone, he was told politely, but firmly, that the Ashton family was not accepting calls at the moment.

"Not even from husbands," he muttered grimly and stared down the burliest of the guards, who'd planted himself in front of Simon's car like a cement pylon with sunglasses. His fists squeezed tightly around the steering wheel and he forced himself to fight for calm. Not easy, when all he wanted to do was push his way past the guards, stomp onto the estate and turn the place upside down if he had to, to find Megan.

Megan.

God.

He scrubbed one hand across his face and felt the scrape of whiskers against his palm. Hell, he hadn't even shaved. Hadn't been able to think about anything or anyone but his wife, since the moment she'd walked out of the house two days ago.

He should have chased her down. But by the time he'd been able to coax his nearly paralyzed body to move, she'd driven off into the night and he'd missed his chance. Missed the chance to tell her he loved her. Needed her. Would not live without her and she'd just have to learn to live with it.

"Great. Good plan," he told himself, disgusted. "Sure to win the heart of any woman. Start telling her what to do."

He was in bad shape. But he'd have been much worse off if he hadn't gotten a telephone call just an hour ago. Charlotte, Megan's cousin, had phoned him and asked just one question. "Do you love her?"

As soon as he'd convinced her, Charlotte had invited him to the estate and assured him that she'd get him past the guards. All he had to do now was be patient. It wasn't easy though. Not when he was so close.

Finally, one of the guards nodded at him, opened the gate and allowed Simon's car to pass through. Anticipation rattled around inside him as he followed the drive, headed for the small stone cottage Charlotte had described. *What if Megan wouldn't listen?*

He pushed that thought aside.

She *had* to listen.

Had to believe.

With her back against the gnarled surface of a tree trunk, Megan stared at the vineyards, stretching far into the distance. Plucking a blade of grass from the blanket beneath her, she shredded it methodically and let her mind race where it would. Naturally, it went straight to Simon. His image rose up in front of her. His scent wafted around her, competing with the strong earthy scent of the garden. And everything inside her yearned to go to him. To throw herself into his arms and feel him holding her close.

How would she ever bear to be without him?

"You're not an easy woman to talk to."

Her eyes flew open and she shifted a quick, disbelieving look over her shoulder. Simon. Here. And not looking very pleased about it. His features were grim and shadowed by at least a day's growth of whiskers. He wore jeans, a wrinkled white pullover and black sneakers. As he came closer, she could see the spark of something dark and dangerous in his eyes. She pushed herself to her feet, determined to have this confrontation on equal footing.

"We don't have anything to talk about," she said softly, letting her gaze feast on him. Had it really only been two days? It felt like weeks, months, since she'd last seen him, touched him.

"That's what you think."

"Simon—"

"You had your say, Megan." He stopped a foot away from her.

So close and yet still so very far away. Her heart ached, and her fingers itched to smooth his rough jaw. He looked as frustrated and exhausted as she felt. "Simon…"

"Uh-uh. My turn." He kept a tight grip on a folded newspaper in his right fist. "Two nights ago, you didn't give me a chance to talk. You just laid down your rules and walked out."

"It had to be that way," she argued and felt the first sting of tears fill her eyes. But she refused to let them fall. She'd cried enough over the last couple of days and wouldn't do it again now. In front of him. At least, she thought, maintain a *little* dignity.

"According to you."

"According to our *deal*," she reminded him. "Remember? The no-scandal thing?" She choked out a harsh laugh that scraped her throat and hurt her heart. "Well look around, Simon. Scandal Central."

"You think I care?" Simon stepped in closer, until she was no more than a breath away. Damn it, he'd been wanting nothing more than to talk to her for two long days. Now that he was here, with her right in front of him, talking about doing the right thing and scandals, he just wanted to grab her and shake her. And then kiss her senseless. "Do you really think I give a good damn what's happening to your family right now?"

She sucked in a breath and drew her head back.

He shook his head in frustration. "That came out wrong. Of course I care. But only to the extent of what it's doing to you. I don't want to see you hurt, Megan."

"Then you'd better leave now," she whispered.

He heard the crack in her voice and everything in him tightened protectively. He didn't want to see her hurt, but he was doing a damn fine job of it himself at the moment.

Sucking in a long, deep gulp of air, he blew it out again in a rush and admitted, "I'm just a little nuts today."

"I'm getting that."

His lips quirked. "Megan, when you left—"

"I had to—"

"—it almost killed me."

"Oh, Simon."

"I can't lose you, Megan." He rubbed the back of his neck viciously. "*Won't* lose you." Then he handed her the newspaper. "Here. Read this."

"What're you…?"

"Just read it. Then we'll talk."

As her gaze dropped to the front page of the *Times,* Simon kept his own gaze fixed on her face. He saw every emotion as it flashed across her features. Read wonder and then surprise and then pleasure in her eyes and he hoped it would be enough.

"I don't understand," she whispered, never lifting her gaze to him.

"Then read it out loud. Maybe it'll help."

She nodded tightly.

"Pearce Speaks Out. Simon Pearce, in an exclusive interview, stated that his wife, Megan Ashton Pearce, is the most important person in the world to him. He assured this reporter that he and his wife will continue to support her family in this difficult time."

"Clear enough?" he asked, and this time, his voice was gentle, as if he were trying to coax a wild deer close.

She took a shuddering breath and looked up at him. Her beautiful green eyes awash with tears, he took hope from the tremulous smile curving her mouth. "Oh Simon, I don't know what to say."

Frustrated and just a little worried, Simon blurted, "Don't you get it, Megan? I *love* you. I should have told you before. But I was an idiot. I wanted to make *you* say it first, so I wouldn't lose control of the situation." He laughed sharply, shortly. "That was so stupid, because the minute I said 'I do' to you Megan, I lost control. And I don't even want it anymore. All I want is you."

"Simon, I love you, too. But I didn't want to tell you because we'd agreed to a temporary marriage."

"Nothing temporary about us, Megan. Not a damn thing. If I had another hundred years to love you, it still wouldn't be enough."

She lifted one hand to cup his cheek. "I only left because I didn't want you to be hurt by what was happening with my family."

He caught her hand with his, then turned his face and planted a kiss in the center of her palm. "The only way I can be hurt is if you leave me."

"Then you're destined for a lifetime of happiness, Simon," she said as she stepped into the circle of his arms and held on tight. "Because I'm not going anywhere."

His arms wrapped around her like a vise, pressing her close. "Damn right you're not."

She laughed and the music of it filled his soul, and Simon sent a quick, heartfelt thanks to whichever Fate had granted him a second chance. How had he ever lived without her? Still smiling, he lifted his head and looked down at her. "You know, it's a good thing you're coming home with me."

"Really?" She tipped her head to one side and teased, "Why's that?"

"Because, Mrs. Pearce, have you stopped to think at all that you could be pregnant?"

Megan's smile faded, her eyes went wide and her mouth dropped open. "Oh for heaven's sake." She went limp in his grasp. "With everything that's gone on in the last few weeks, can you believe I never even thought about it?"

He hadn't either. Not until the night she'd left him alone in that too-big house with nothing to keep him company but thoughts of what might have been. And in those first lonely hours, he'd been forced to acknowledge that when he'd lost Megan, he'd lost all hope for a future. For a family. With the only woman he'd ever loved.

Now though, he had her back in his life, in his heart. And he swore silently that he'd never do anything to risk what they'd found together. A swell of love for her rushed through him with the force of a tidal wave that surged to every corner of his soul. Staring down into her summer-green eyes, he felt himself hoping they'd have a house full of children and that each of them would have her eyes.

"Yeah well," he said, pausing to drop a kiss onto the tip of her nose, "I've been thinking about it for the last couple of days—"

"And…?" She watched him, those fabulous eyes of hers bright with happiness.

"And," he repeated, still dumbstruck with the force of his love for her, "I'm hoping you are."

"Really?"

"Really," Simon confessed. "But if you're not, we'll just have to try harder."

"Sounds like a lot of work," she said, shaking her head solemnly, despite the smile tugging at the corners of her mouth.

"Lady," he said, lifting her off her feet, "ask anybody. Simon Pearce *loves* hard work."

And he swung her in circles until they collapsed with laughter, tangling together in the shade of the oak tree, lying in the cool, damp grass and sharing a promise of the future with a kiss.

* * * * *